Tor Books by Poul Anderson

Alight in the Void
All One Universe
The Armies of Elfland
The Boat of a Million Years
The Dancer from Atlantis
The Day of Their Return
Explorations
The Fleet of Stars
Harvest of Stars
Harvest the Fire
Hoka! (with Gordon R. Dickson)
Kinship with the Stars
A Knight of Ghosts and Shadows
The Long Night
The Longest Voyage
Maurai and Kith
A Midsummer Tempest
No Truce with Kings
Past Times
The Saturn Game
The Shield of Time
The Stars Are Also Fire
Tales of the Flying Mountains
The Time Patrol
There Will Be Time
War of the Gods

WAR
OF THE
GODS

POUL ANDERSON

TOR®
fantasy

A TOM DOHERTY ASSOCIATES BOOK
NEW YORK

This is a work of fiction. All the characters and events portrayed in this book are either products of the author's imagination or are used fictitiously.

WAR OF THE GODS

A Tor Book
Published by Tom Doherty Associates, Inc.
175 Fifth Avenue
New York, NY 10010

Tor Books on the World Wide Web:
http://www.tor.com

Tor® is a registered trademark of Tom Doherty Associates, Inc.

ISBN: 0-812-53925-7
Library of Congress Catalog Card Number: 97-19383

First edition: October 1997
First mass market edition: February 1999

Printed in the United States of America

0 9 8 7 6 5 4 3 2 1

To
Diana Paxson
farer in lands afar

WAR
OF THE
GODS

I

The gods themselves fought the first war that ever was. Odin and his Aesir held Asgard, loftiest of the nine worlds in the Tree. Theirs was lordship over the sky, wind and weather, sun and moon, the stars and the Winterway across heaven and the flames that dance cold in the north. The hunters among them roved the wildwoods with bow and spear, while others bred fleet horses and broad-browed kine. Their wives blessed their homes and brought forth strong children. Odin himself sought ever for knowledge, wandering widely, searching deeply.

West of Asgard lay Vanaheim, where dwelt the Vanir. They were gods of earth and sea, harvest and fishery, plow and ship, of love and birth but also of much that was dark and lawless. They knew not wedlock, but bedded whomever they liked. Their women were often witches. Yet these were a folk gifted and high-hearted, maybe more kindly than the stern Aesir.

Below the worlds of the gods lay the worlds of men, elves,

dwarves, and jotuns. These last, sometimes called thursir, were the oldest of the races, being sprung from Ymir. Many were giants like him, if not so huge. Others were trolls or monsters. Still others were more humanlike, even comely. Not all stayed in Jotunheim, north beyond the sea that rings mankind's Midgard. Nor were they all uncouth or unfriendly. Some had been the mothers of gods. Some were wise, with a lore that went back to the beginning of time. Always, though, jotuns remembered how Odin and his brothers slew Ymir their forebear.

The gods raised their halls and halidoms. They played at draughts with pieces made of gold. At a well beneath that root of the Tree which is nearest Asgard sat the three great Norns, who cut the runes that say what every life shall come to. There each morning the Aesir foregathered to think on what works they would do. Peace made its home among them and beneath the roofs of men.

But, slowly, ill will bred. Men in Midgard were offering to whatever gods they saw fit. Most turned to the Vanir for the kind of welfare that that race could best bestow. The Aesir began to feel aggrieved.

Heimdall left Asgard and fared about on earth, naming himself Rig. Wherever he was an overnight guest, he begot a son. From them sprang the stocks of thrall, yeoman, and highborn. When Kon, youngest offspring of Jarl, was grown, Rig came back to teach him the skills whereby he made himself the first king. In this wise did Heimdall lure to the Aesir a following that outnumbered the worshippers of the Vanir.

Forth from Vanaheim went Gullveig. So blindingly fair was she to behold that she became known as Heid, the Shining One. But she was the worst of witches. Madness she sowed in the minds of men, and to evil women she gave delight. Wickedness awakened anger, which led to woe. Having brought bane on Midgard, she dared cross the rainbow bridge to Asgard.

Before she could wreak further harm, Odin bade the gods slay her. There in his hall they smote her with spears. She laughed at them. They burned her and she stepped from the ashes aglow like molten gold. Thrice did they thus fail of her death. Thereafter she left them, to seek Vanaheim again and tell what had befallen her.

Outraged, the Vanir moved on Asgard. From his high seat, which overlooks every world, Odin saw them coming, weapons aflash, footfalls and hoofbeats athunder. He led the Aesir out to meet them. When they drew nigh, he cast his spear over their host. So began the first war that ever was.

It reached earth, too. Men fought each other, as they do to this day. They called on the Aesir, and Odin granted victory to his chosen. But his own war he could not win. Helped by their black arts, the Vanir at first kept the field in most battles. They thrust up to the very walls of Asgard and broke them down.

The Aesir rallied and drove them back. To and fro the strife surged, year after year, laying both lands waste. Ill tended by its gods, earth suffered as grievously. Men hungered, struggled for scraps, and could seldom spare a beast to slaughter for the high ones. In their mountain fastnesses the giants muttered of Ymir and whetted their iron.

At weary length, Odin wished for keener sight, to see how the ruinous quarrel might be ended. In Jotunheim, under the second root of the Tree, flowed from a spring the waters of wisdom. There dwelt Mimir, its keeper since the beginning. Odin made the long and dangerous trek thither to ask a drink from it. Mimir answered that that could only be if he paid, and the price was an eye out of his head. This Odin gave. So did he become Mimir's oath-brother. The jotun fared back with him to Asgard and gave him many good redes.

One was that he seek out the lore of runes. Odin did, though now he must go beyond death itself.

When he returned, the insights he had won showed him ways to calm down his warriors and get word to his foes. The two holy tribes laid their arms aside and met. They spoke of how venom had come into the air, who bore the blame, and who should yield to whom. In the end they agreed to share offerings, wealth, and lordship.

To keep the pact, they exchanged hostages. The Aesir gave two to the Vanir. One was Hoenir, who with Odin and Lodur had made the first man and the first woman from ashwood and elmwood and breathed life into them. The other was Mimir. The Vanir thought well of tall, handsome Hoenir and took him into their highest councils.

Likewise did the Aesir welcome Njord, the Van who held sway over the sea, and his two grown children, Freyr and Freyja. They liked it not that he had had them by his sister Ingrun. Their own law forbade the mating of close kin. Still, Freyr was the foremost god of earth, the soil, and its riches. Freyja was the foremost goddess of love, begetting, and birth, the most beautiful being who ever walked in Asgard. She was also a mighty witch, who taught the Aesir the spellcraft of her folk. Odin shunned it, holding it to be unmanly and untrustworthy. However, it was well to have knowledge of its workings.

For a while, then, the gods were once more at peace. But men were now always making war, the giants were restless, and the dragon Nidhogg gnawed at the deepest roots of the Tree. The Aesir felt need to raise anew the walls around Asgard, stronger than before.

To them came a man who said he could do this in a year and a half. The wage he wanted was the sun, the moon, and Freyja for his wife. At first the gods would hear naught of it. But Loki urged them to bargain him down, making the time no more than half a year. He could never meet that. Whatever he did build, they would have for nothing.

In their war against the Vanir, the Aesir had learned about trickery. They overcame any qualms and heeded Loki. Nevertheless they were astonished when the man agreed, as long as he could use his stallion, Svadilfari. They swore oaths with him, promising him safety while he was in their midst. He set forthwith to work.

Dismayed, the gods saw how fast it went. The man split off stones that looked too big for anything to move, but Svadilfari easily dragged them off and shrugged them into place for his master. Day by day the wall rose, high and unbreakable. As the half year neared its end, only the gateway was left to mortar together.

The gods met in Odin's hall. Freyja took the lead in cursing Loki. They cried that if the mason got his earnings, Loki would pay with his life. The sly one told them to have no fear.

The next morning, as Svadilfari hauled yet another load toward Asgard, a mare trotted out of the woods. She whinnied, pranced, and raised her tail at him. Off he went after her. He heeded not his owner's shouts and ravings, but passed from sight among the trees.

And so the work was not fully done in time, and Odin told the mason he should have nothing. Rage overcame him. He burst out of the seeming he had laid on himself. A giant stood and roared at the half-finished gate. His threats and foul words became too much for Thor. The storm god smote him, and a crushed skull was the wage that he got.

Some months later Loki returned, leading a colt with eight legs. He had been the mare, and this was his offspring. He gave the colt to Odin. It grew up as Sleipnir, swift as the wind and tireless as death.

Thenceforward the jotuns reckoned the gods for oathbreakers, and few stayed friendly to them.

Meanwhile the Vanir had been looking askance at the hostages whom they kept. True, Hoenir gave sage judgments. Yet that was always after he had whispered together with Mimir. If Mimir was not there and some hard question was put to Hoenir, he said merely, "Others must decide this."

When they heard how Freyja had been set at risk, the anger that smoldered in the Vanir flared wild. They seized Mimir, cut off his head, and sent it back to Asgard.

There Njord and his children had already spoken so bitterly that swords barely stayed in sheaths. Now Loki egged on the sons of Odin until they heeded him and bound these three for vengeance.

A giant named Hymir dwelt by the sea. Raw and harsh, he nonetheless had some tie to the Aesir. Odin had fathered warlike Tyr on a goddess who later wed Hymir. At Loki's behest, the captives were brought to him for warding. When they were alone, Loki told Hymir he should give the Vanir shame because of what their folk had done. Ever was Loki a brewer of mischief.

Hymir swallowed the tale. He set Freyr and Freyja on a skerry in the cold midsea, among trolls, drows, and bewildering magics. Njord he kept fettered in his hall. When first the god came there, cast down helpless onto the floor, the daughters of Hymir mocked him and even pissed in his mouth.

Odin had had nothing to do with this. He was too taken up elsewhere to know of it. After the head of Mimir was in his hands, he bore it off and treated it with herbs so that it would never rot. Thereupon he cut runes and sang spells to awaken it. The eyes opened and the lips spoke. Dead, Mimir had learned what none among the living knew.

Odin left the head at the well beneath the Tree. There daily it slaked its thirst with the water of wisdom in which lay his eye. Often afterward did he seek the head out and take counsel from it.

When he returned to Asgard and found what had become of the hostages, he was frightful in his wrath. Too much trouble was afoot already, without sundering the bonds between the gods. As grimly as on the battlefield he shouted his orders for the freeing of Njord, Freyr, and Freyja. That was not easy. The witchcraft clung to them and could only be lifted slowly, after terrible strivings. But at length they were hale again. The sons of Odin led them home to him, begged their forgiveness, and offered them a huge redress.

Freyr and Freyja were willing to take it, among other treasures a wonderful sword for him and a car drawn by cats for her. It pleased them to dwell in Asgard and work unhindered in Midgard. They acknowledged that their kin had also done wrong.

Njord, though, was in no soft mood after what he had suffered. He spurned the holding called Ship-haven that was offered him, along with everything else. He forswore the friendship he had plighted and readied himself to go back to Vanaheim.

Odin foresaw a new war among the gods that would bring doom on them all. He must try to fend it off. Calling upon his utmost powers, he reached forward in time—which is not the same for gods as it is for men—and brought that to pass which had never happened before and never would again.

II

Up into the hills that rise north of the Scanian lowlands came a small troop riding. At their head fared Braki Halldorsson, chieftain in Yvangar and thane of the Dane-king Gram. He was a burly, weather-beaten man, his

beard gray below shaggy brows and blunt nose. A byrnie hung
rustling and darkly gleaming from his shoulders. Behind him
went a youth of fourteen winters, more lightly clad, the king's
older son, Gudorm. Unhelmeted, his hair shone in the woodland shadows like another spot of sunlight. Rearward of him
rode a young thrall-woman who clutched a suckling babe to
her breast. Her eyes were wide with fear.

A half score of men wound after them. Few had other
armor than a helmet, a wooden shield hung at the horse's
rump, maybe a leather coat with iron rings sewn on it. Most
bore axes or spears, not swords. They were sons of yeomen,
called by the chief of their neighborhood to follow him.
Withal, they were tall and strong; their legs reached down
around their shaggy little steeds almost to the ground. No robbers or roving Norsemen would have attacked this band.

Yet uneasiness was upon them. It grew with every step forward. None let himself seem daunted, but glances flickered to
and fro. Often somebody ran tongue over lips or swallowed
hard. The only sounds were from hoofs on earth and wind in
boughs. When suddenly a raven croaked, men started and
knuckles whitened over spearshafts.

They had reached wilderness. The path was hardly more
than a game trail, writhing upward. Brush hemmed it in beneath trees, gray-barked beech, gnarly oak, gloom of fir, gran-
ite boulders strewn among them. Where for a short span the
wood thinned out, sight swept across slopes, ridges, and dells
murky with growth. Wind shrilled cold. It harried clouds over
a wan sky, making the sunlight blink. It soughed through leaves
going yellow with fall. Most wanderbirds had already flocked
south; a hawk wheeled alone aloft.

The wood again crowded thick where a great branch
stretched high above the path. Nailed to it, bleached by many
years, the skull of a bear grinned downward. Braki drew rein,
lifted a hand, twisted about in the saddle, and said through the

wind noise, "I know this mark. We near the giant's house. Hold still when we get there and make no sudden moves. You're too few to withstand him. Let me talk." He clucked to his horse and trotted on.

His men set their teeth together and followed. Regardless of the words, Gudorm could not keep hand off sword hilt. The thrall wench whimpered. When the babe cried out, she bared a breast and held him tightly to the nipple as if it were she who drew warmth and strength from him.

The path bent past an outcrop of rock. Braki rounded it. His horse reared and neighed. There stood two hounds, wolflike but coal black, well nigh as big as it was. Their eyes smoldered, their fangs glistened. A man yelped. "Hold still, I told you!" Braki flung back. He fought his mount to a standstill while the hounds bristled and growled. "Vagnhöfdi!" he shouted. "Call off your dogs! Braki is here. We have sworn peace, you and I."

Someone ahead winded a horn. The deep sound of it echoed from hillsides and shuddered in men's bones. The hounds lowered their ears, turned, and trotted back. Braki made his horse follow them. His men could do no less.

They came out on a hillcrest. Cleared, it overlooked the highland wilds from ridge to ridge. The house that stood there was roughly built of stone below and logs above, chinked with clay and moss, roofed with turf. But few kings owned a hall so huge. Smoke from a hole overhead blew off across the treetops like storm clouds. Through an open door passed glimmers of fire, with heat and rank smells.

The giant waited outside. Thrice the height of a big man he loomed, and more than broad enough to match. Unkempt black hair fell around a shelf of brow, craggy nose, and cave of a mouth. Beard spilled halfway down to a belt studded with spikes. His coat, breeks, and boots were of hide. A nine-foot club was in his grasp and a scramasax of matching size at his hip.

Thunder might have been speaking: "Hail, Braki. I bade you always to come by yourself, when come you must. Why have you brought this pack along? Am I to kill them for you?"

The thrall wailed. Men stiffened in their seats. Gudorm flushed angrily. Braki waved them to stay quiet.

Looking straight up at the thurs, the chieftain said, "It's not for my own sake I'm here this time, Vagnhöfdi. I needed guards along the way lest harm befall the sons of my king."

"What are they to me?"

"This. Their father is fallen in war. His foeman, the Norse King Svipdag, now holds Denmark and means to seek lordship in Svithjod and Geatland as well. Let him gain his wish, and he will rule on either side of you. Likewise will his son after him. Folk are breeding children who grow up landhungry. Svipdag and his kindred have sworn no oaths with you."

"Hunh," rumbled the jotun. "This I knew not." After a bit: "Well, I will guest you overnight, at least, and we will talk."

Braki's followers loosened their grip on their weapons. Things were going as he had promised them.

Once this giant had murderously raided farms newly founded along the edge of the wilderness. When warriors from the whole shire drove him back, he sent blights on the crops and murrains on the livestock. But Braki's grandfather had also known somewhat of magic. He broke those spells. Then he sought out the giant by himself.

The two of them came to agreement. Vagnhöfdi would let men be if they did not fell trees, hunt, or otherwise make trouble in these high woodlands off which he lived. Since then, the chiefs in Yvangar had seen to it that the pact was kept. Now and then one of them had had reason to seek him out—such

as Halldor, to settle what should be done about beasts wild or
tame that strayed off their rightful grounds, or Halldor's son
Braki swapping iron tools for furs.

Nonetheless Vagnhöfdi understood that there were
bounds upon him. He was a terrible foe who might well put
a host to flight, but if too many men came at him for too long,
he would die. It would happen very fast if they offered to Thor
and the god chose to help them.

Thus Braki and his following led their horses into that end
of the house where other kine were, saw to them, and sat
down, feeling bolder than before. They found themselves in a
single vast room. Dim eventide light straggled in through
scraped skins stretched across the windows. More came from
the fire leaping in a trench dug in the earthen floor. Heat billowed, sparks glittered, smoke curled blue and bitter. By the
restless glow eyes made out rough-hewn pillars and, barely, the
crossbeams and rafters above. Night already lurked in every
corner, slipping closer as the sun outside went low. There were
neither high seat nor benches; one sat on the ground, drank
ale from bucket-big wooden cups passed hand to hand,
gnawed coarse bread and roasted meat.

Only two others dwelt here, Vagnhöfdi's mate, Haflidi,
and their daughter, Hardgreip. The mother was withdrawn, a
half-seen bulk busy at cooking. Hardgreip served, then squatted nearby, eagerly listening. The guests thought she would be
sightly, in an unkempt way, if she were of human size.

Cross-legged before Vagnhöfdi, who hulked over him like
a cliff, Braki said: "You may have heard that kings and other
highborn men commonly give children of theirs to lesser folk
to raise. It is a mark of honor, and helps make fast the bond
between the families. Well, I have been foster father to Gudorm here, and did my best for him till he was ready to return
to King Gram.

"Now, as I told you, Gram is gone, slain in battle against

King Svipdag. Before leaving for that war, he sent Gudorm back to me for safekeeping. He felt the lad was too young to go along with him. Svipdag's a ruthless one who'd most likely have him killed lest later he seek revenge. Gram had a second wife who bore him this second son, the bairn Hadding. When she got the news, she also sent her child to me, with a trusty man and a wet nurse.

"Gram and I were good friends, who'd fought side by side in the past. But I'm no more than the leading yeoman in an outlying shire of the Danish kingdom. If Svipdag's men come ransack my steading and neighborhood, I can do nothing. It seems me best that I hide the boys away with you. You'll find that the Skjoldungs are not an unthankful breed."

"Hm, hm," growled Vagnhöfdi, tugging his beard. "We here are strangers to humans, ill fitted to rear the sons of a king." He was not being lowly, which was not in him. His hundreds of years had made him canny.

"Gudorm is close to manhood," Braki said. "As for Hadding, belike from time to time I can smuggle in whatever he may need, or come myself to help teach him. I'll leave his nurse, too."

"No," said Vagnhöfdi. "My daughter has lately borne a child, which died. The milk still aches in her."

He did not, then or ever, say who the father had been. Maybe he did not know. Maybe she did not. She had met someone in the woods who kindled her—another giant? A god, with something in mind that went beyond lust?

The thrall wench gasped, then broke into sobs of gladness, off on the rim of the men's ring.

"I must think on this," the jotun added. "Stay the night and we will talk again tomorrow."

The sun went down. He and his woman sought the high-piled skins on which they rested, and drew other pelts over them. Braki and his troop laid whatever each of them had brought along on the floor.

"Ugh," muttered Gudorm in his ear. "Must I truly den in this filth and loneliness?"

"Take what you can get," answered Braki curtly.

Little Hadding was silent. Hardgreip had clasped him to her dugs. His eyes at those white hillocks, watching the fire die down, were blue and bleak.

III

G udorm had been well taught about his father's world. He knew that the Saxons lived south of Jutland, a folk not unlike his. East of them, along the southern shores of the Baltic Sea and inland, were tribes whom the Danes lumped together as Wends and looked on as uncouth and backward, speakers of outlandish tongues. Beyond these, Gardariki reached on into endlessness. Its dwellers were akin to the Wends, and likewise split among chiefdoms and tiny kingdoms that could never muster much strength. However, they were more skilled and well off. Some of this they owed to Northerners, who oftener traded with them than raided, and had begun to settle among them, building towns on the great rivers.

Northward from Saxland ran the hills, heaths, woods, and farms of the Jutish peninsula. The Anglians in its southern half marked themselves off from the Jutes elsewhere, but these folk were both of the same stock as other Northerners, with the same speech and ways of life, and no one king had brought either of them together under his sway. Thus the Danes were moving in on them. Already the far end of Jutland, where the Skaw thrusts out into the Skagerrak, was Danish, as all the islands eastward had long been.

The nearest of those islands, across the waters of the Little Belt, was Funen. East of this, across the Great Belt, lay the biggest, Zealand. Many lesser islands were scattered about. Beyond Zealand was the Sound, and beyond this strait, on the mainland, was Scania, likewise Danish.

North of the Scanian shires were the Geats, and north of them the Swedes. However stalwart man for man, the Geats were rather few, and most times acknowledged the overlordship of the Swedish king. His kingdom, Svithjod, widespread, wealthy, and old, was said to have been founded by Odin.

Westward over the mountains was Norway, a clutch of quarrelsome and changeable small realms. Some few were strong enough that they must be reckoned with.

North of all this and back down around the gulf that met the Baltic Sea were the Finns, wild tribesmen with a tongue and gods all their own, not warlike but breeding many wizards.

The Danes believed they had their name from Dan, who long ago hammered them into oneness. However, the kingly house that among them became the rightful one, theirs by the will of the gods, stemmed from Skjold. Tales tell how he came ashore from none knew where, a babe in an oarless boat, his head resting on a sheaf of wheat. He grew up to be so strong and deep-minded that men thought his father must be Odin, who had sent him to them. They hailed him their lord, and well did he do by them, victorious in battle, openhanded in hospitality and gift-giving, just in his judgments, and wise in the laws he laid down.

Still, those were unrestful years, and most of his sons died young, in war, feud, storm at sea, hunting bear or boar, even of sickness. Rather late in life he sought the hand of Alfhild, daughter of the foremost Anglian king. The Saxon Skati wooed her too. He was a jarl at home, second in rank only to his own king. He dared Skjold to settle things by the sword. Skjold killed him in fair fight and wedded the woman.

She bore Gram, who came to be as mighty as his father. However, he was headstrong and reckless. Nor was he overly kind to women. First he took to wife the daughter of his foster father, then after a while gave her away to a friend of his whose deeds in battle he wanted to reward.

Then he heard that Gro, daughter of the Swedish king Sigtryg, had been betrothed to a thurs. More to win renown than for her sake, he went there with no one along but his friend. Dressed in hides of goat and wild beast, a club in his hand, he met her in a woodland as she rode with her serving maids to a pool where she would bathe. Horror smitten, she thought he must be a jotun himself. Still, when his man spoke to her on his behalf, she boldly defied him, until at length Gram cast off his hairy dress and roared with laughter at his trick. Her heart, suddenly lightened, turned to him and he soon had his will of her.

This meant war with King Sigtryg. Wizards said that only gold could fell him. Gram bound a lump of gold to a shaft, sought out the other man, and smashed his head open. Afterward he met Sigtryg's brothers on the field and slew them.

Gro bore him Gudorm, as well as girl children, but she was no longer a happy woman.

Somewhat later Gram's mother Alfhild died. Old King Skjold soon followed her. His grieving folk loaded a ship with treasure, laid him therein, and set her asail over the sea, back into the unknown whence he had come.

Thereupon they hailed Gram their king. By war and wiles he set about bringing the Swedes, who now had no firm leadership, under himself.

Svipdag was king in Ranriki, where southern Norway faces out on the Skagerrak. He too was a hard-driving warrior, who overcame his neighbors and took lordship throughout those parts around the great bay. But he was an Yngling, of the house that had always ruled in Svithjod. A forebear of his, a younger son, had gone to Norway and taken sword-land for lack of anything better. Svipdag felt he had more right to Svithjod and its wealth than any Skjoldung. He raged to see Gram forestalling him.

His time came after years. Gram was making slow headway, for not only the Swedes but the Geats fought him stubbornly. So one summer he set off instead against Sumbli, a Norseman who had seized mastery over a goodly number of Finns. Gram wanted that scot of furs, hides, thralls, and other wares, to help him in his Swedish war.

When he got to Finland, Sumbli asked if they could bargain instead of fighting. Gram went to his hall. There he saw his daughter Signy and fell head over heels. He offered peace if he could have her.

But then a stiffly rowed ship brought news from home. While Gram was gone, Svipdag had taken a fleet across the Skagerrak and down the Kattegat. He was harrying throughout Denmark. Gram must needs hasten back. As he sailed near, the Norsemen withdrew, leaving slain folk, burnt homes, and looted burghs. They had also carried off his sister and a daughter he had by Gro.

Yet rather than seek revenge at once, he left as soon as he could for Finland and Signy. Awaiting no trouble, he told most of his earlier following to stay behind, look after their kin and ward the land. With three ships bearing warriors and gifts he beat his way slowly back up the gulf against foul winds and heavy seas.

When at last he reached his goal, he found more bad tidings. Sumbli had no liking for him nor faith in him. Already before he first came, word had gone back and forth across the water about giving Signy to the Saxon king Henrik. When Gram had hurried off, Sumbli sent after this man, who was swift to heed. The wedding feast was now ready.

Gram's icy stillness was more frightening than even his outspoken wrath. He had too few spears with him to make a straightforward onslaught. Instead he donned shabby clothes, put on a hooded cloak that shadowed his face, and went on foot to Sumbli's hall. At such a merry time, strangers were welcome. One or two guards did ask him if he brought anything. He answered that he was skilled in the healing arts. While the hall filled with guests and the mead horns came forth, he hunkered down among other lowly folk. As everybody grew drunk, he worked his way toward the high seat where Henrik sat with Sumbli, the bride across from them among her women. Once in reach, he whipped a sword from beneath his cloak and slew Henrik in one blow.

No other man had gone in armed at this hallowed time. Gram hewed a path over the hall, snatched Signy up in his left arm, and cut his way onward to a door. Off into the gathering dusk he ran, got to his ships, and put to sea.

Next year after harvest he raised a host and steered for Norway to avenge his daughter, sister, and kingdom. He found more foemen than he had looked for. With anger in their own hearts, the Saxons had listened to what Svipdag's messengers asked of them and sent warriors to stand at his side. Gram fell in a battle where the Danes suffered sore loss. Svipdag busked himself to go win kingship over them.

Signy had not been glad when Gram reaved her away. She yearned back to Finland. Yet she had lately borne a son, Hadding, and did not wish the bairn slain in his crib. Wherever she went with him, she feared Svipdag's killers would fol-

low. Therefore she sent him secretly off to Braki, as his half
brother had openly been sent, in hopes that the chieftain could
somehow save him.

All this and more did Gudorm know. He might have
passed it on to Hadding when the younger boy came to speech.
But by then Gudorm was no longer there.

IV

A wind out of the north bore tidings of oncoming winter. Rain slanted before it, mingled with sleet. Bare
boughs tossed and creaked above sere meadows.
Stubblefields were becoming mires. Now and then the eye
caught sight of a farmstead, huddled into itself, but it was soon
lost again in the gray.

A log road stayed passable. Four horses drew a wain along
it. Their breath smoked white. The wain was big, decked over,
richly carved and painted. Gripping beasts entwined with each
other along the sides; faces gaped and scowled on the hubs, as
if the bumps and groans of their wheels were threats they uttered; iron rang against free-swinging iron—all to frighten off
drows and other uncanny beings. Queen Gro sat there, together with four serving women. They were well clad against
the cold, in furs and heavy cloth. Likewise were the score of
guardsmen who rode ahead and behind, but water tumbled off
their helmets and ran down their spearshafts.

Shadowy at first, then high and dark, a stockade showed
forth before them. Crows had long since picked clean the
heads of illdoers which King Gram had staked on top, though
hair still clung to a few. Warriors at the gate took hold of
weapons and bade the newcomers halt. When they heard who

it was, they let the troop through and a man sped to bring word of these guests.

Here wheels and hoofs banged over cobblestones. Buildings crowded close around. Most were small, wattle-and-daub with turf roofs from which smoke drifted low along the peaks. They were stables, workshops, storehouses, homes for lesser folk. Noise rang: speech, footfalls, hammering, lowing, cackling, bleating. Smells of fire, cookery, beasts, dung, and wet woolen coats hung heavy. Pigs, dogs, barnyard fowl wandered free. Men, women, and children peered from doorways as the queen passed. Some fingers drew signs in the air.

Highest in the thorp stood a hall. Timbered and shingled, two back-stepped stories rose with dragon figures at every gable end. Around the upper floor ran a covered gallery. At the back were a cookhouse and a bower where women could spin and weave. Here, not far from the fisher and trader town Haven on the Sound, was one of the best of the dwellings Skjold had built for himself around Denmark.

Gro's wain stopped at the front door. Grooms took over the horses while she and her men stepped down and went inside past more guardsmen. None of those were Danes.

Beyond the entry, where they left their weapons and cloaks, the main room reached a hundred feet. On this murky day shadows shifted everywhere about in it. The air lay blue and sharp with smoke, which was not rising well. However, many lighted lamps were set forth, not only of clay but polished stone and finely wrought bronze. Light also flickered from the fires on hearthstones along the floor. It touched on wainscots and hangings behind the platform benches that lined the walls and were also chests for storage. Graven with the shapes of gods, heroes, and beasts, the pillars upholding the crossbeams seemed half-alive.

Rushes rustled under Queen Gro's feet as she strode to the high seat where King Svipdag sat, at the middle of the east

wall. She went fearless, her face stiff, a tall woman still handsome to behold. Above her pleated linen undergown, silver
brooches at the shoulders linked the loops of embroidered
front-and-back apron panels. Embroidered likewise was the
kerchief covering the brown coils of her hair. The right brooch
also clasped a loop of fine chain from which dangled the keys
of her own household. Amber beads glowed around her neck
and gold rings gleamed on her wrists.

"Greeting and welcome," said the king, carefully rather
than heartily. "Come sit beside me. Let your followers take
their ease. There is mead for all, and a feast under way."

Gro watched him for a span before she answered, "Well,
since you asked me to come here, I should think you would
make ready for me."

He was a big man of some forty winters, his dark hair and
pointed beard beginning to grizzle. Two scars seamed a thick-
boned, hook-nosed face. He too was well garbed, in fur-
trimmed kirtle, blue breeks, and elkhide shoes. She could
easily enough understand his Norse burr.

He stiffened at her haughtiness, curbed himself, and said,
"I mean to show you more honor than I hear has been yours
lately. But if you will not talk with me, you can go home tomorrow."

"Oh, I have given thought to this since your messenger
came," she told him. "We shall talk."

She stepped up to the high seat and settled herself. He
beckoned her guards to take places nearby and shouted for the
serving folk, as loudly as if he were aboard ship. Soon everyone had a brimful horn but her, who got a goblet of Southland glass. Svipdag signed his with the Hammer. "Let us drink
to peace between us," he said.

"Peace for now, at least," said Gro.

"May it be for always."

"We shall see about that, shall we not?"

Nonetheless, tautness slackened off a little. Over the years she had gotten men into her hire, one by one, who felt more beholden to her than to King Gram. Some were Swedes or Geats. These she had brought with her. They were not unwilling to drink, eat, swap tales, and make merry with Svipdag's Norse. Meanwhile she and he spoke together in undertones.

Next day they met alone in a loft room of the hall. Long were they there. Sundown was close, unseen through a fog that swirled and dripped outside, when he said, "We seem to be coming to an understanding. If you will wed me, you shall have queenly honors here in Denmark."

She knew well that he had a wife at home in Ranriki, and two more in the neighboring lands that he had made his. This she did not care much about. He would seldom be with her either. Gram had left her side before his death, not briefly for a leman but altogether for Signy. She, Gro, was the daughter of a king, whom Gram had slain.

"For this, I am to give you my help and counsel," she said.

He nodded. "The Danes are not glad of me. But I want no more from them than what belongs to a king, landholdings, scot, honor, and defense against raiders. I will not often be here, nor will I take Danish levies abroad. My mark is Svithjod, which welters leaderless. I cannot overmaster it unless Denmark stays quiet at my back. Aid me to that, Gro, and you shall be queen also among the Swedes and Geats—your folk."

"To that end," she said slowly, "you must bring the great men among the Danes to agreement, jarls, sheriffs, chieftains."

"Even so." Svipdag spoke harshly. He would have liked better to overwhelm anybody who gainsaid him.

"It begins with Gram's close kin, his cousins, his daughters by different women, their fosterers and husbands," she went on. "You must give them not only surety, but weregild according to how near in blood they are."

"With you beside me in rede and deed, I hope this may be done."

"Some will say no. They can be set on and killed, unless they flee the land first. It will bring others to a kindlier mood."

"Yon Signy could have her throat cut out of hand," said Svipdag with a grin.

Gro shook her head. "No. That would only enrage her friends and her father. You can ill afford the trouble he could make for you. Let the Finn-woman go back to him." She spat it out. In truth, though, Signy's blood was Norse.

Svipdag barked a laugh. "Already you begin earning the morrow I will give you."

She stared straight into his eyes. "You shall have no more from me, but only ill will and whatever harm I can do, unless I get one thing above all others."

"I think I know what that is," Svipdag growled.

She nodded. "You must recall my son, Gudorm, swear peace with him, and give him a high standing. For this I came here when you asked, and I will take no less."

"Well, I will try," Svipdag said, "but what if he will not?"

"We shall see how that goes," Gro answered. "Bring my son to me and let me speak with him."

The upshot was that Signy sold what she had to buy a ship and hire a crew. In spring, when weather allowed, she sailed off to Finland. Meanwhile men of Svipdag's crossed the Sound and rode through Scania to Yvangar.

Braki and his wife gave them a grudging welcome. His was no kingly dwelling. A well-built house and its outbuildings stood around a stone-paved yard. Kine grazed widely about, fields awaited the plow, and leaf buds laid green mist over a woodlot. Many other steadings were in sight. Beyond lay the wilds, where men logged, hunted, fished, and trapped. The uplands that were forbidden them lifted hazy blue in the north.

All these farms had bred sturdy young men and looked to Braki for leadership. Svipdag's riders spoke softly as they asked for Gudorm and told what they had for him. Braki said that he was not here and it would take days to reach him. The chieftain would go, but with only a few close-mouthed followers. The Norsemen could cool their heels in his home.

So he came back to Vagnhöfdi's house. The giant took him in with gruff good cheer and they all sat about the fire, in a rank gloom, while wind hooted outside and from afar sounded the howling of wolves.

Braki gave Gudorm the word given him. "You may return to Denmark for peace and power, if you will swear yourself to King Svipdag."

"But this is wonderful!" cried the youth.

"Your father fell at his hands," Braki said.

Gudorm flushed, looked away, and mumbled, "Here I can't even see to the well-being of my mother. And how could I ever hope for vengeance? Instead of skulking in the woods till I die like an outlaw, why can't I—win back honor—if I take a weregild worthy of my father, and, and keep his blood alive?"

"Bide your time," rumbled Vagnhöfdi. "Who knows what may happen? Bide your time."

"You never say anything else!" Gudorm screamed. "I'm sick of it!" He leaped up and ran out. Nor did he come back until after dark, when the rest were asleep.

In the morning Braki took him off alone. Gudorm told his foster father how he hated this rough and lonely life and was bound that he would take Svipdag's offer. Braki put it a little more mildly to the thursir.

They made Gudorm swear that he would utter no word to anyone about Hadding. Hardgreip said he must not leave yet. She seethed strange things in a kettle, cut runes in an ash stave, daubed them with blood from a nick she made in his thumb, and sang eerily beneath a crooked moon. "If you betray us, a doom will come on you that is not good," she told him.

"We had no need of your nasty witchcraft," he said, white-faced, "and I will be well rid of you."

Thereafter he rode off with Braki, and from Braki's home back to Zealand. Svipdag met him without much warmth but with full honor, while Gro watched. The king paid him for his father's death and, Gram's jarls being all dead or fled, made Gudorm, young though he was, jarl over the whole of Denmark. Men said to each other that belike this lad would more trustworthily keep the peace and gather in the scot than someone might who was full grown.

Now Svipdag led a fleet over the Sound and up the Baltic shore to the Skerrygarth. Rowing through that many-islanded water, deep into Svithjod, he landed, struck swiftly, and took Uppsala. There he held a great slaughter to the gods, and began overrunning the whole kingdom. Houses burned, men fell slain, women were made booty, until one by one the shires yielded to him.

His thoughts about Gram's child by Signy were few and short. It was not with its mother. Nobody could tell him where it might be, nor felt that it mattered. What danger was in a mewling babe? Belike she had left it at some poor croft, where neighbors would hardly mark it among the other bantlings. If it lived to grow up, it would know nothing more than how to grub a meager living out of the ground. Svipdag soon forgot about it.

V

Nursed at the breasts of a giantess, Hadding grew swiftly and strongly. Before long he was eating the same fare as the rest: meat from the hunt, fish from the waters, milk and cheese and butter from the cows, bread from grain that mother Haflidi grew in a clearing and ground on a quern as big as a man. Roots, leaves, sedges, mushrooms, and grubs were food to pick up along the trail. In their seasons came also nuts, berries, and the honey of wild bees. Vagnhöfdi brewed ale and mead, but Hardgreip taught Hadding that every spring and every stream had its own taste, its own magic.

Much else did he learn from the thursir. Going by himself rather than with the hounds, he became a keen hunter, wily trapper, patient fisherman. He could flay a quarry, cut it up, cook its meat, tan its skin, find uses for guts and bones. He could make and wield a fire drill, weave branches together for a shelter, read clouds and winds to foreknow weather, find his way by the heavens both day and night, bind up a wound or set a broken limb. He shaped stone and iron into tools for which he whittled the hafts. The iron itself Vagnhöfdi found in bogs and brought back to wrest from its ore with his overhuman strength.

The wilderness was Hadding's home, which he came to know through every depth and every change. He wandered through the quick rains and quickening leaves of spring while returning birds darkened the sky with wings and filled it with clamor. He was out in the long days and light nights of summer, green growth and sun-speckled shade, warmth and thunderstorm and the manifold smells of life. He ghosted under trees gone red and yellow in fall, his feet rustling nothing, and from hilltops looked into hazy farnesses or down at drifting mists. He ranged through winter on skis and skates, unheeding of cold, not only beneath the low sun but after dark if it was clear and the stars gleamed in their hosts above the snow.

Yet always the waters drew him most, above all the biggest lake thereabouts. As often as ever he could, he sought its banks and gazed over its shining reaches. When a wind ruffled it, something thrilled in him and the lap-lap of wavelets was a song. He would strip off his clothes, wade out through the reeds, and swim for hour after hour like an otter. In a dugout boat he kept there he could spend a whole day dreaming more than fishing. Besides a paddle, he used a mast and sail he had made, awkward though the rig was. He wondered mightily about the sea of which he had heard. Someday he would go seek it. The longing waxed as his body lengthened.

Otherwise his childhood with the thursir passed happily enough. It did not trouble him that they overtopped him so hugely. He took that for given. They were kind to him in their rough way, though when they got a little heedless he might be knocked three or four yards aside and blossom for a while in bruises. They shared much of their lore, tales and verses going back to the beginning of the worlds, their speech deep and hoarse and slow. Thus he picked up something of the Old Tongue from Jotunheim. Mostly, however, they spoke the speech of his folk when with him. It was better fitted to the things of Midgard.

They had their feast times during the year, which were not the feasts of men but remembered such happenings as the shaping and slaying of Ymir, the binding of Garm and Fenris, and, more merrily, Utgard-Loki's fooling of Thor. Mirth came easily to them, for they were of simple heart.

Yet they could be terrible. When Vagnhöfdi was angry, he would bellow, fling boulders about that splintered the trees they hit, launch a landslide, or seek a bear to kill with his naked hands. Hardgreip, who had fondled and sung to and cared for Hadding in his babyhood, liked to run down a deer or an elk, slash it open, and wallow like a wolverine on its bloody carcass, ripping the raw meat with her teeth.

Hadding did not take to these ways. Braki had told him, aside, that they were not seemly for a man. Still, Hadding did not hold them against his fosterers. Mostly Hardgreip was more brash than mad. Seen from afar, so that she dwindled in sight, she was like a good-looking young woman, full bodied, heavy bosomed, her hair long and raven black, her face high in the cheekbones, curved in the nose, broad in the lips, with slant green eyes under thick brows. After Hadding turned from boy to youth, he often found himself a post from which he could watch her thus. It was best when she sought a pool to bathe in. He did not feel ashamed, for he knew she knew what she did, and she flashed him a grin.

Once, out alone on a winter night, he spied a band of light elves riding by. Starlight glittered on their helms and byrnies as it did on the snow; northlights danced on high like the banners that streamed from their spears. White too were their horses, slim and wind-swift, bounding from worldedge to worldedge in a few heartbeats. Above them flew a great owl. They sped past in utter stillness, but as they left Hadding's ken their leader sounded his horn. Those notes haunted him for years.

When he told this in the house, Vagnhöfdi scowled and rumbled that that had been no lucky sign. The light elves were too friendly with the gods. The swart elves sometimes did jotuns' bidding, but one must beware of them too. They were as safe to deal with as wolves.

He also disliked the dwarves. Miners and craftsmen who had wrought many wondrous things, they were greedy, short-tempered, and apt to lay curses that worked through lifetime after lifetime. Vagnhöfdi called it good that none dwelt underground hereabouts.

Monsters formerly laired in these wilds, nicors lurking under meres in wait for beasts or men, trolls that liked human flesh best, hagbirds, a dragon. During his hundreds of years he had killed most of them after they made trouble for him, but it was still wise to shun some hills and lakes.

Other beings he could not fight. He and his steered clear of them: night-gangers, land-wights, the unrestful dead. Yet this was not altogether so. Hadding learned that when he went with Hardgreip on a trek of three days that ended in the dark.

Haflidi had been plowing her field. For this she needed no horse or ox, but pushed the ard herself. She turned up a slab of rock into which runes had been chiseled. When she brought it home to her mate and daughter, who had knowledge of such things, they were disquieted and muttered to one another. Already they had seen forebodings elsewhere. A cow gave birth to a calf without a head. One day the earth shuddered and boomed underfoot. One night the full moon was the hue of clotting blood. "Seek word from the drow," Vagnhöfdi told Hardgreip. "You are better at a graveside than I am."

She hung back for a heartbeat or two, then her mouth stiffened and she agreed. Having packed food to take along, she set forth at dawn. Hadding had boasted he would go too, and she said low that she would be glad of any fellowship.

On open ground he could not keep up with her strides unless he ran, but later they went through trackless, tangled brush, thorn and withe and twisty boughs knitted together like ringmail, with fallen logs and scummy green pools in among them. Even more than he must she push, squirm, fight her way step by step. Fog swirled and dripped. Snakes slithered, frogs croaked, carrion crows jeered in the offing. Where shadows lay thickest, Hadding saw rotten wood glow blue. At night he lay close against the warm, breathing bulk of the giantess. They were too weary to speak much.

Toward sunset of the third day they came to a knoll on which stood a dolmen raised by folk unknown and long gone. The earth had fallen away from its great stones. Spotted with moss and lichen, they reared stark out of crowding willow scrub. "Keep well back of me," Hardgreip warned Hadding. "Whatever happens, do not get close."

Thus he followed little of what she did in the twilight and heard merely snatches of what she sang. When full night had fallen, starless, moonless, and sightless, high flames shot up. He saw her black against their icy white. The dolmen groaned. Something trod out of it to stand before her. She cried her wish aloud. Hadding could barely make out that a horrible whisper answered.

The thing went back into its mold, the fire died away, and Hardgreip returned to him. "Let us be off," she said in a thin voice. They pushed blind through thickets that lashed and tore at them, until they found a stream and a cleanly rushing waterfall. There they stopped, toppling into a sleep full of nightmares.

Afterward, on the way home, Hardgreip told him only, "I never awaited a good word from the drow, nor did I get any. I do not well understand what he did say, and do not think my father will either. But he spoke of dooms to come upon us." She gave him a long look. "And he said you are not what you seem, Hadding, and your lot is still more strange. I know not what that means."

Shaken, he kept silent.

Later, though, as they regained their own woods, the darkness lifted from their breasts. "Well, I knew already that no one, man or thurs or god, lives forever, nor the worlds themselves," she said, "and whatever our weird may be, we shall not

meet it this year." For his part, when they reached his beloved
lake he drew strength and cheer from the beholding, and wondered more keenly than ever when he could go find the sea.

These jotuns were, indeed, wonted to magic. They were not
deeply learned in it, but they could cast spells of some power
for help, harm, or the searching out of what was hidden. They
tried to teach Hadding. He showed no gift for it, and what
must be done was too often loathsome to him.

"As you wish." Vagnhöfdi sighed, like a wind through tall
pines. "The craft is tricky enough for those who have skill, so
best if you leave it be. I will show you a bit, however. In time
you'll go from us, and we know now you'll fare on wild ways.
Let me give you the words that will bring me to your side,
though you be halfway across Midgard. Use them in your
direst need, for only once can I come to you thus."

Aside from that, Hadding picked up no more than loose-
floating scraps of witchy knowledge. He might cast runes for
guidance or carve them for luck, he might take warning from
a happenstance that struck others merely as odd, but he never
became a warlock.

Maybe this was Braki's doing. Faithful to the son of his
dead king, the chieftain and a few yeomen went two or three
times each year to the giants' dwelling to spend days with
Hadding. From him the boy heard about men and their ways,
their whole world beyond these wilds, what had gone on in it
aforetime and what was going on now. Braki told him about
the gods and the uneasiness between them and the jotuns;
Vagnhöfdi liked not to hear such talk. Braki said that the high
runic magic was one thing but the seething of witch-brews and
calling on the underworld was an ugly other.

First and foremost did Braki make clear to Hadding who
he was, how he came to be here, what he had lost that was his
by right of blood and what burden of revenge that blood laid

upon him. The chieftain brought weapons along, gave them to Hadding, and drilled him ruthlessly in their use and in war-craft.

He knew no humans but these. Their guestings were seldom and short. Yet ever more as he neared manhood he yearned for the life that was theirs and his, home fires, farings, friendship, women, offspring, towns, riches, ships, and lands new to him lying across the sea, the sea.

He was the son of Gram. His father lay unavenged while he, who should be king of the Danes, hunkered in the house of a backwoods thurs, set snares for beaver, and raided birds' nests for eggs. More and more he brooded on it, alone afar in the wilderness or under stormy skies on bare hillcrests. More and more of his time went to work with sword and shield, hewing at foes he raised up in his mind.

Then Braki brought woeful news. Gudorm, Hadding's half brother whom he did not remember, was slain.

Men thought that belike Gudorm's mother, Gro, had always secretly egged him on against her husband, Svipdag. Lately the tale went among them that after she died her ghost came and told him to take arms. Be that as it may, he did. Riding around Denmark from Thing to Thing, he got himself hailed king at those meetings and called warriors to follow him. But Svipdag was too quick. He brought a mighty host down from Svithjod, and Gudorm fell on the battlefield.

Hadding raged. Braki told him he could do nothing yet and must abide a while longer. When the chieftain had gone home, Hadding grew curt and sullen. Vagnhöfdi and Haflidi bore with it. Hardgreip tried to draw him out, failed, and watched him with a sorrow that slowly became something else.

In spring, after a hard winter, men rode again to the house. They did not linger and Braki was not among them. The chieftain had fallen sick during the bitter weather, had tossed abed

fevered and coughing, and then gone down hell-road. They had
laid him out with his weapons and heaped a barrow over him.

Hadding left the house. He was away for three days and
nights. The bond that had held him there was broken.

VI

He came back toward evening, halted in the open doorway, and stood while his sight wonted itself to the
gloom within.

The three thursir sat eating. Even cross-legged on the floor,
they loomed higher than he, shadowy bulks, fleeting glitter off
eyes and teeth. Smoke from a low fire drifted about them. Its
sharpness mingled with smells from the cowstalls at the rear.
After the woodland, that was a thick air to breathe.

"Welcome back," rumbled Vagnhöfdi, and "Are you hungry?" asked Halflidi. Hardgreip sighed.

"No, I have fed today on my kill," Hadding said, "but I will
drink farewell with you, for tomorrow I go home."

"What?" cried Hardgreip. "Here is your home!"

He shook his head. "Denmark is mine. Too long have I
been away. Too long has my father's foeman been alive."

"If you go against him alone," said Vagnhöfdi, "it's not he
who'll fall. Are you a berserker, to howl and slash at a throng
of men till they cut you down?"

"You promised you'd fight at my side."

Now it was the giant's shaggy head that shook. "Once do
I dare do that, but no more. If they knew a jotun was warring
in their world, they'd call on the gods, and Thor would soon
be there. I have no shield to stop his hammer."

"I am a Skjoldung," said Hadding, "kin to the gods."

"And a tricky lot they are," Vagnhöfdi growled. "Stay, lad, at least a few more days, and I'll try to help you think."

"Oh, stay," Hardgreip breathed. "Would you so coldly forsake those who love you?"

Her look clung to him. Tall and broad-shouldered he stood, lithe and strong, in a huntsman's green wadmal kirtle and breeks, knife at belt, spear in hand, bow and quiver slung on his back. The light streamed in to make molten gold of the hair that fell from a headband to his collarbones. As yet he had no real beard, but down of the same hue glowed on cheeks and chin and above the firm-set lips. His nose was straight, his eyes glacier blue, his voice rolling full out of the deep chest.

She saw a slight wavering on his face and said gladly, "I know you're not heartless and thankless."

Hadding sighed. "Well, if you want it so much, I will stay those few days, but no longer. I will not. I cannot."

"Yes, I feel that," Vagnhöfdi said heavily. "You are whatever it is you are, and no man may flee his weird."

"But come in, do," Haflidi bade, "and we'll be merry together this evening as of old."

That did not happen. They drank, they talked of small things and their former days, but Hadding grew fiery and Vagnhöfdi more glum. Hardgreip alone kept trying for lightness.

But when Hadding and Haflidi had lain down to rest, he made out through the darkness that Hardgreip drew her father aside and whispered with him.

In the morning after they had broken their fast she smiled down at Hadding and said, "Shall we take this day free, you and I? Let's seek out places we like and enjoy them anew." He thought she hoped it would lessen his eagerness to be off. Nothing could do that, but meanwhile he was willing to take some ease. There would soon be little of it for him.

They walked off together, she matching her stride to his,

from the house on the hilltop into the woodland beneath. The day was mild and bright, a few clouds catching the sunshine aloft, a breeze sweet with young grass, new-budded leaves, and the earliest flowers. Trees made a rustling roof over the game trail they took, through which light fell in shafts and flecks amidst the shade. A squirrel ran up a bole, a ruddy streak quickly gone in the green and gold above. Birdsong trilled.

"Yes, this land is fair, and I will ever remember it," Hadding said.

"Is that all you will do, remember?" Hardgreip asked. Looking up, he saw a glint of tears on the great face. Their eyes met, turning at once away, and both of them flushed.

After a while they came to an opening. Here rocks heaved up, thickly mossed, to hold off the beeches that ringed them in. A spring gurgled and glittered among them. It made a shallow pool from which a streamlet purled off. One bank of the pool was free of boulders, blanketed with the same moss, soft and springy.

The day was growing warm. It baked rich smells out of the ground, smells of the life everywhere swelling and begetting, drunk with lustiness.

"Ah, I know this spot," Hadding mumbled into the silence.

"Well you might," Hardgreip said, "as often as you've watched me here."

Suddenly she grasped his arm. Her hand was huge and hot, he felt the blood throb in it, but the grip was tender. Astonished, he looked again into her eyes. They shone upon him like the sun.

"Hadding," she gasped, "don't go away. Stay. Take me, have me. Now!"

"What?" he blurted, staggered.

"Make me your first woman, take me in your arms, me

who took you in mine when you were new-born, me at whose breasts you drank, who kept you alive. Give back what I gave you!"

He stared, bewildered. She let go of him and withdrew by one of her long paces. Still he saw her towering, clad merely in a shift, her bare feet catching at the earth and her arms raised high above the tousled black hair. She broke into a chant.

> *Why and for what have you whiled away*
> *Your life all alone, this length of years?*
> *Your wish is for war, you want naught else.*
> *No loveliness lures; you've left it aside,*
> *Willful and wanton and wild as you are.*
> *You've hardened your heart against happiness,*
> *You seek but to slake your sword in blood,*
> *Never to know a night at peace,*
> *Bedding a bride who brings you joy.*
> *Grim are you grown, and gruesome your ways.*
> *Wrong have you wrought in your recklessness,*
> *Scathefully scorning and scoffing at love.*
> *Empty this anger out of your soul,*
> *Give now to goodwill and gladness a home,*
> *Be moody no more, but make me your bride!*
> *For I bore you, a bairn, at my breast one time.*
> *Remember my mothering, the milk I gave you,*
> *And how I held you and helped you thrive,*
> *Awake to keep watch on your welfare always.*

And he wanted her. With his whole being he did. Of late, when he woke at night to the growls and grunts, the thuds and thumps that meant the giants were coupling, it had been well-nigh more than he could bear. His daydreams about Hardgreip flogged him into running for miles, plunging into icy waters, wolfishly hunting and slaying. Yet he had known they were hopeless, and today he could only stammer, "It cannot be. You, you are a jotun. I am a man. You are too big for me."

She threw back her head. Her laughter bellowed like the call of a cow elk in heat. "You are big enough, my love. Yes, I am a jotun, but I'm also a witch, and can be whatever I want and you want."

A new stave rang out.

Be fearless, youth, and follow in friendly wise to bed.
Soon shall you see me shifting my shape to what you wish.
Lengthening my limbs, or lessening my tallness,
Ever do I alter in every way myself,
My height as I would have it, to heaven raising me
Up through the clouds where Thor goes on thunder-booming
  wheels.
But next, if it be needful, back near to earth I draw
My head that loomed on high, and humanlike I am.
Featly I reforge me from form to form at once,
Manifold the makings. It may be that I go
To littleness and lowness ere leaping forth anew
In scope until I scan the sky around my brows.
Now am I short and shrunken, then shoot aloft once more.
Moonlike waxing, waning, I wear no sameness ever.
If word you've had of werebears, you'll wonder not at this.
I dwindle in my dwelling to dwarf, who was a giant,
Not firm, not fixed in sight, but fleeting hastily.
I broaden the embrace I brought so close before.
My girlish arms reach outward, but inward draw when huge.
My being twines between the twain of great and small.
To meet the strong I stand in stalwart mightiness,
But slight I am and slender when sleeping with a man.

As he gasped, she blurred to his sight. For a score of heart-beats he saw smokiness spinning and heard it whistle, like a whirlwind. Then Hardgreip stood again before him, tangle-haired, hard-breathing, but a woman, half a head less in height than he was. She laughed afresh, her voice now not deep but only low and husky. She pulled off her gown and spread her arms wide. Sweat gleamed on her breasts and belly. The smell of it overwhelmed him. He came to her and they enfolded one another. Her lips and tongue thrust at his. Her hands groped at his clothes. He scrambled out of them. She pulled him to the ground and bestrode him.

VII

Yet after a sennight Hadding said that now he would go.

"From us, who raised you to manhood?" Vagnhöfdi asked.

"From me, who made a man of you?" Hardgreip laid to that.

Hadding's back stiffened. "I would be less than a man did I abide when my father and brother lie unavenged and he who slew them sits in the high seat of the Skjoldungs."

"My hope for aught else was faint," Vagnhöfdi said, "and I cannot foretell what will come of it, but this I know, that something beyond the world of men is at work here."

Nor was Hardgreip truly surprised. She and Hadding had talked in between tumblings. "You shall not go alone," she told him.

Vagnhöfdi looked at her. The blood beat high in her face. "This is not unawaited either," he said, "but for you, such a trek can have no good ending."

"Would you rather I stayed behind?" she answered shamelessly. "My longing would set the woodland afire."

Hadding reddened too and his eyes flickered elsewhere, but he said nothing against it. He could use such a waymate, both for pleasure and for the jotun might she could wield at need.

"Then this evening we will drink farewell," Vagnhöfdi said, while Haflidi wept like a melting glacier. Hardgreip frowned at her mother and thereafter gave all her heed to her lover. As the mead cups passed around, they two became the merry ones.

At dawn the four of them woke and the twain made ready. Hardgreip dressed like a man, in some of the clothes Braki had brought for Hadding over the years. She also took a sword and spear from among the chieftain's gifts, now that she was going about in human size. She bore the food and the other gear, for besides weapons such as hers, Hadding slung on his back a shield, helmet, byrnie, and underpadding, as well as bow and arrows. Vagnhöfdi gave him a purse of gold and silver to hang beside his knife.

"I shall not see my daughter again," the giant said, "but this is her own will and doom. You and I may meet once more, fosterling."

The thursir stood outside their house and watched as the wanderers strode off down the hill. A last time Hadding and Hardgreip looked back and saw them huge against the sky. Then they were lost to sight behind the trees.

The days of walking through wilderness went peacefully. At length the woods opened up on the rolling lowland of Scania and the path met a rutted road. A bit farther on this led to Yvangar. There Braki's eldest son gave hospitality, together with news of the outside world.

"Svipdag holds most of Svithjod and has laid the Geats under scot," he said, "though his grip is as yet uneasy and he must fight every year to quell uprisings. Thus he's not much in Denmark, which has been quiet since Gudorm's fall. But they're restless there too. Harvests have been meager and folk mutter that this is for lack of the rightful king."

"I am he!" cried Hadding.

"By birth, yes, or so my father always held. Still, you'd better go slowly and warily till you've gathered a strong following. How you may do that, I can't guess, and I must say between us that your friend does not strike me as a lucky sort."

"We will go on anyhow and spy things out for ourselves," Hadding said.

First he made his host send word around the neighborhood of a feast he would give. He bought kine and pigs for it, but foremost a horse, which he slaughtered at Braki's howe. Hardgreip dipped twigs in the blood and sprinkled it on the folk, then scattered the twigs and read the runes on them where they lay. "I see only a strangeness," she said, "naught that I can understand." Even so, after the holy meat was cooked men ate heartily of it and spoke well of the dead man and his deeds. Hadding took that for a good enough sign, though mostly this had been his way of thanking the chieftain.

Braki's son gave him and Hardgreip horses, on which they rode away southward. Farmsteads yonder often lay far apart, with stretches of marsh or wildwood between. That night the wanderers must camp in the open. It was welcome. While Hardgreip was passing herself off as a youth, they could not bed together. "Foolishness," she grumbled after their first bout, as they rested under the moon. "Why should anyone care what we do with ourselves?"

"Braki taught me that such is the law of the Aesir," Hadding answered. "Men must heed it lest those gods forsake them."

Her fist smote the earth. "Their law is not mine!"

But he saw by the wan, shadowful light how she grew troubled. She shivered as if the chill of the dew that gleamed around them had seeped into her. "What's wrong?" he asked.

"There have been too many warnings and forebodings," she mumbled. She turned to him and caught him tightly against her. "Make me forget it for this night."

Next day brought clouds, a wrack like smoke flying low. Rain-showers slashed. They made mud of a road that had become a mere track. It wound among fields gone back to weeds. Wind skirled through scattered hursts, tossing their leaves like beggars' rags. Twice the wayfarers spied burnt-out farmsteads in the offing. War, a feud, or robbers from the hinterland had passed through here. Hadding and Hardgreip clutched their spears and spurred their horses onward.

They were glad when, late in the day, they came on an un-touched dwelling. It was poor: a small house and barn huddled under their turf roofs with no other home in sight. Plowland still lay bare. Meadow slanted rank down to the reeds along a mere. Behind that water gloomed more wildwood. Lifetime by lifetime, men had been gnawing farms out of such wastes, felling and draining, but it was hard, slow work and they lived in fear of revengeful land-wights.

Two hounds bounded forth, barking and growling. Hadding swung his spearshaft to drive them off. He gave Hardgreip the bow and quiver. "String this and nock an arrow, then stay mounted at my back," he bade her. Braki had taught him that strangers were not always to be trusted. They rode to the door. He got down and knocked.

A half-grown boy opened it. The ax in his hand would not help him much. Hadding smiled. "Greeting," he said. "We are passersby who'd be happy if we got shelter for the night." He leaned his spear against the wall to show he meant nothing worse.

Oftenest folk at a garth made guests welcome. In return for food, drink, a place to sleep, maybe the loan of a woman if the householder felt so minded, they saw new faces, heard new voices, and got word of happenings elsewhere. Besides, it was a luck-bringing thing to do.

This lad, however, only stood there in his shabby wadmal with drooping head. Streaks on the sooty skin showed where he had wiped his eyes. "Come in if you like," he said dully, "but know that my father lies dead."

"Sad tidings," Hadding answered. "We'll not trouble you in your grief. Belike we can make do in your barn."

"No," Hardgreip said from the saddle. Her voice shuddered. "Let us into the house." Hadding looked over his shoulder and saw her sitting, taut as her bowstring, against the windy gray sky.

The boy saw too. The sight overawed him. "Come under our roof," he quavered. "I'll take care of your horses."

Hardgreip close behind, Hadding trod into the single low room. A peat fire burning blue on the hearthstone gave a little warmth. More came from a few kine stalled at the far end, along with smells of them and their dung. He heard them stir, champ their feed, and breathe, but they were shadows to behold. A clay lamp and four rushlights sent flickerings through smoke and the murk that already hung thick. A roughly made bedstead stood at either wall. Otherwise there were only three stools, a wooden chest, and household tools. Food hung from the crossbeams, a haunch of meat above the fire. Withal, this was a well-kempt home, rushes on the floor, a stone-weighted loom in one corner.

A woman met the newcomers. The braids of her hair shone yellow in the dimness, but toil had gnarled her hands and most of her teeth were gone. A toddler clung to her skirts. Two older children hung back, their eyeballs white in the gloom. "We cannot give you good guesting, but a bite to eat

and a place to lie down you may have," she said, as wearily as
her son. "I am Gerd, the housewife here. This day my man
Skuli Svertingsson died. Tomorrow we'll bury him as best
we can."

Hadding named himself only, not his father nor his fellow,
and asked, "What did he die of?"

"I know not. He felt ill, and suddenly was gone. Yesterday
he went into the woods looking for a strayed cow. Maybe a
swart elf shot him."

He lay washed and cleanly clad, his eyes closed for him and
the jaw bound up. Hardgreip went over and peered narrowly.
He had been long and lean. His nose thrust like a crag from
the ashen face and gray-shot beard.

Hadding told the wife he was sorry and promised whatever
help he could give. "I can hew a coffin from a log, we can both
dig, and we'll leave a piece of silver in his grave," he said. She
struggled not to weep.

Hardgreip plucked his sleeve. "Come outside with me,"
she murmured. Hadding followed her.

Rain had stopped for a while. Mists eddied over the sodden ground. Westward the clouds had parted enough to let
through a nearly level sunbeam. It turned the mere blood red.
Water dripped off roof and trees.

Hadding looked down into his leman's eyes. They burned
like the pool, though her fingers where she caught at his wrist
were cold. "Here I can work a spell," she hissed. "We've had
too many bad foretokenings. If we know what lies ahead, we
can make ready for it and belike win free."

"I have always heard that the will of the Norns stands not
to be changed," he said misgivingly.

Her voice sharpened. "Would you go blind toward your
foemen if you could scout them out first? I've lived far longer
than you, and learned somewhat about the underworlds."

"What do you think to do?"

"This man is newly dead. His soul has not yet fared far. It will be easy to call back. But he has been beyond time. I will make him foretell for us."

Hadding's skin crawled. "That's an ill repayment for the widow's kindness."

"Ha, shall a dirt-grubber and her brood hold back the last of the Skjoldungs from what is his? Hadding, I, who made a drow speak with me, am going to do this. Best will be if you help, but will you or nil you, it shall happen."

Her keenness overwhelmed his youthfulness. Besides, if she turned herself into a giantess again, he could not stand against her. He watched unhappily while she cut a shoot off a blackthorn, trimmed it to a short stick, and carved runes in it. When she was done, night was falling fast and rain gusted anew. They went back inside.

"There is something we must do," Hardgreip told Gerd. "Keep off, you and your children, and you'll come to no hurt. Otherwise dreadfulness can befall you."

The woman gaped and cringed. Loath though Hadding seemed, he did not gainsay his friend. His sword could easily put an end to her family. Gerd moaned. She herded her youngsters back in among the kine.

Hardgreip stoked up the hearthfire. From a household jug she poured water into the household kettle and set it above. From her pack she took things Hadding had not known she had brought along, leaves of nightshade, a dried toad, a bat's wings, the withered navel string of a stillborn, and uglier stuff. She cast them into the water and cast the garb off herself. Naked she stood in the shifting flamelight and thronging shadows, holding the runestave above the kettle and chanting while that which was within came to seethe.

Hadding stood as if frozen. It was worse than at the dolmen. Never, in all his years with the giants, had he seen this side of her.

Steam swirled white over Hardgreip's hand and the stick. The dark wood glistened. She gave it to Hadding. "Now," she said, "put this beneath his tongue."

He had thought himself fearless, but as far as he had already gone, he dared not now do anything but obey. Step by stiff step he went over to the deathling. The flesh was dank to touch as he unbound the jaw. He must pry it open. Hastily he shoved the runestave crosswise into the dry mouth between the teeth. At once he stepped back.

Hardgreip took his place by the bed. She raised her arms. "Waken, Skuli," she shrilled. "By the might that was Ymir's, I call you to come, I bid you read the morrow for me. No rest in the grave shall you elsewise have, but the fires of Surt shall burn you, the snakes of Hel shall nest where your heart was, and the eagle at the end of the world shall tear you until the ending of all the worlds. Rise and speak."

The body stirred. Widow and children wailed in the cowstall. It heard them not. Wrenching itself along inch by inch, bones grinding together, it sat up. The eyes opened. They were filmed and empty, but a red smoldering moved in them. The head jerked to and fro until it found Hardgreip. A voice grated around the runestave.

> You drew me from the dead. Now doom shall fall on you
> Who haled me out of hell. Ill hap and woe be yours.
> From the mold that was mine has your magic most foul
> And cruel now called me to come from the shades
> That I answer your asking with all that I know
> Of what shall fare whence and go whither for you.
> My word is of woe that awaits you, and death.
> Unwilling I wended here, witch, and must speak,
> My tongue bearing tidings of terrible things.
> Soon hence from my house you will hasten your steps
> Away to a wilderness, wandering lost

Till horror shall have you, a hideous end.
You will wretchedly rue the wrong that you did
In dragging the dead from the darkness up
By trollcraft to travel the troublous road,
Bound to your bidding. Abide now the time
When fearsome foes take fell revenge.
You drew me from the dead. Now doom shall fall on you
Who haled me out of hell. Ill hap and woe be yours.

The head creaked around until the unblinking, tearless eyes caught Hadding. He stood his ground, helpless though he was, and heard:

Yet know that as the net of night pulls close about her,
The fishers thereon flensing her flesh down to the heart,
Clutching with their claws and cutting with their teeth,
Ripping, tearing, rending the reddened stumps and rags,
Unshaken shall your luck still shield you from them, Hadding,
Not hurling you to hell but holding you alive
To walk and do your work within this world a span.
The witch must pay the weregild for wickedness she did.
She raised me from my rest, she robbed me of my peace,
She dared make mock of death. To dust she shall go down.

Again the eyes laid hold of Hardgreip.

You drew me from the dead. Now doom shall fall on you
Who haled me out of hell. Ill hap and woe be yours.

The body fell back and was still, glaring into the night below the roof. Wind howled, rain dashed.

Hardgreip stared elsewhere. After a long time she whispered, "I think we had better go."

Hardihood roused in Hadding. "No," he said. "We will

spend the night here and tomorrow do what I plighted: bury
this man we wronged and leave him what grave goods we
may." To the back of the house he called, "Gerd, come out.
It is done. You've nothing more to fear."

Nevertheless nobody slept.

VIII

T he day was well along before Hadding and Hardgreip
were done and could leave. Hardly a word had been
spoken throughout. Gerd gave no thanks for the coffin Hadding made, the spadework they both did, what they left
in the grave, or even the gold coil he set on her arm, much
though she could buy with it. He awaited nothing else and was
only glad to get away.

He and the thurs woman likewise kept still as they rode.
The weather had cleared, but held scant warmth. Brush
hemmed in the muddy path, too narrow to fare on abreast,
overhung by leaves from which water dripped cold. Those
branches hid the sky, dusked the ground, filled the deeper
reaches among the boles with blindness. Mist sneaked low, in
wan streamers. The only sounds were plop and squelch of
hoofs, creak and rattle of harness, clinking of drops where
they struck. As the gloom thickened toward evening, an owl
began to hoot.

"We'd better stop soon and make ready for the dark,"
Hadding said at last. His voice was flat with weariness. "The
first open spot we find, so these orc-loving trees can't piss
on us."

"Hereabouts that will likeliest be a fen," she answered as
grayly.

They learned otherwise. The path swung around a clump of willows, and there lay a meadow. True, its grass was wet, but someone had made a brushwood shelter. That could not have been long ago, for it stood tightly woven yet. Indeed, it was big enough to be called a hut. The juniper boughs that floored it were dry on top, thick and springy for sleeping on.

"Why, our luck has turned," Hadding said. "With the time this will save us, we can coddle ourselves."

"Praise not the night until dawn," Hardgreip mumbled. The spark of heartiness died in him.

Still, here they would stay. He saw to the horses while she gathered wood that was not soaked. She started a fire while he banked dirt behind to send heat in through the opening of the shelter. They cooked some dried meat and ate it with flatbread though without much hunger. Drink was rainwater sucked from the moss on fallen logs. By the last twilight they stowed their things inside and settled down.

The boughs rustled as they fumbled out of their clothes and drew the saddle blankets over them. Hardgreip pressed close against Hadding in the dark. "Hold me," she begged. "Love me. I am so alone."

It was as if the grisliness he had witnessed clung to her. "I'm worn out," he said, not altogether untruthfully. He did make himself put his arms around her. She smelled not of woman but of fear.

After a while, though, he fell into unrestful sleep. Dreams gibbered at him. Now and then he woke. A full moon had cleared the treetops. The drenched grass outside shimmered like ice. Hardgreip's eyeballs glistened in the shadows. She was lying awake. He said nothing, and soon the dreams overran him again.

Her scream roused him. Sounds of ripping and tearing followed. He sprang up. The top was torn off the hut. Moonlight

streamed through a mangled wall. It dappled a hand coming
in from above.

The hand was as broad as he was tall. Black hair bristled
over it. The moon-glow sheened on fingernails like claws. It
groped after Hardgreip. She cowered away. Her mouth
stretched wide. Her arms flailed air.

"Grow big!" he yelled. "Grapple it!"

Her wits returned. As the fingers found her, she became
whirling, whistling smoke. It curdled back into flesh. Her bulk
broke open another wall. She caught hold of the hand and
wrestled with it.

A wild gladness flared in Hadding. Here was a real thing to
fight. By the fitful moonlight he found his sword, drew it, and
hewed.

"Ya-ah!" he shouted. "God-foe, die!" The blade flew. Each
time it struck, he felt the shock in his shoulders. The iron bit
deep. Blood sprang forth. It stank like a rotting lich. Wherever
a drop splashed on him, it seared.

To and fro the struggle swayed. The hut gave way. Its knitted branches fell over his head. He could not see what loomed
beyond the hand. But he swung his sword.

So did he cut through flesh, sinew, bone at the wrist joint.
The poison blood spouted. Hardgreip lurched and fell. She
gripped a hand with no more arm behind it. A howl blasted
Hadding's ears. Earth trembled and thundered to hasty footfalls.

They passed from hearing. He stood panting in the wreckage. Hardgreip threw the hand off her. She climbed to her feet
and loomed gigantic under the moon. Its beams made glisten
her sweat and tears. Her breath sobbed like a stormwind.

"We live," said Hadding wonderingly.

"We cannot—bide—here," rasped Hardgreip.

"No." As the battle rage ebbed, he too began to shudder.

His welts burned. The stench sickened him until he threw up. And what else might come out of the night?

He clenched his teeth and got to work. First he rolled in the grass to wipe the venom off him. Damp softness and smell of soil were like a friendly, stroking palm. Thereafter he searched about. Mad with fear, the horses had broken their tethers and bolted into the woods. Nicked and blunted, his sword was nearly useless. He took Hardgreip's instead, for she had no great skill with it. Their garb and gear were strewn everywhere around. He gathered what he could and cleaned vileness from it as best he was able. When he found a stream he would wash everything fully.

Hardgreip had been hugging herself and shivering. "Grow small," he called aloft. "Else you'll make too much noise and show too clearly, plowing through the brush."

She dwindled and stood before him, hands clasped above her loins, tangled locks falling past bowed head to hide her face. "What shall we do?" she asked meekly.

"Anything can find us if we keep to the path," he said. "We'll get far off it and trust the wilderness can hide us. Tomorrow we'll strike south, going by the sun, and ought to come on lands of men sometime."

"That should be wise for you." He could barely hear her.

"No, now, you are not foredoomed," he said with more cheer than he felt. "We overcame this troll. Let the rest beware."

"Maybe I can have you by me for a few days yet," she sighed.

They donned their clothes, loaded up their outfits, and set forth. The way was slow and hard. Though the moon shone bright enough to drown out most stars, its light seeped between the leaves in patches, spatters, and dim edgings. Hadding made his way well-nigh inch by inch. For all his woodcraft, he stumbled against logs and boulders. Undergrowth snared his feet, branches whipped his face. As he pushed awkwardly through unseen brakes, he thought how everything swished and crackled, and what a trail he must be leaving. Formerly Hardgreip would have taken the lead, deft as a wolf. The will seemed to have bled out of her and she dumbly followed him.

"Come morning, we can rest as long as we like," he said once. The words rang so empty that he spoke no more. His breath went in and out, hot and harsh.

Suddenly he felt the ground slope downward. He knew not whether it was into a dale or merely a hollow. By day he could have chosen whether or not to go around. In this murk he deemed that to keep straight ahead was belike less bad. At least he should find water somewhere below. Thirst smoldered in his mouth and throat.

Down he went. Black shapes became hazy. As steep as the ground was, he misunderstood why. He believed he was only in a thicket where the leaves overhead blocked off even more light than before.

The wood opened. He burst out into heavy fog. It billowed soundless around him, moonful but blotting up sight. A few trees and bushes stood blurred, everything else was a wan nothingness.

"Hoy," he muttered, "we'd better turn back." He looked after Hardgreip. He saw her not. The fog swirled and dripped.

Dismay smote him. She must have blundered from him in their blindness. But she could not be far off. "Hardgreip!" he howled. "Stay where you are. Call and I'll seek you. Hardgreip!"

A shriek went saw-toothed.

Something snarled. Wings beat on high. Feet bounded. Brush foamed and snapped. There went noises of ripping and breaking. The woman screamed. Over and over she screamed.

Hadding drew his sword. "Stand fast, Hardgreip!" he called. "Fight! I'm coming!"

He plunged about, high and low, right and left. The fog smoked thicker. The wildwood scratched and snagged. The racket seemed to be from everywhere and nowhere. After a while it lessened. He heard growls and thought he heard bones crunch between jaws. Then he was alone in utter stillness.

Not until after sunrise did he find the blood-soaked earth, the blood-smeared leaves, and the blood-red scraps. He buried what he could.

IX

Now Hadding wandered friendless through days and nights that he lost track of. Sometimes he slept in a yeoman's house, saying little about himself and taking leave early in the morning. Oftener he laired in the wilds and lived off what he could catch. Mostly he bore south, though he knew it brought him ever nearer his foes and he with not one man to stand beside him. This was the way he had said he would take, and he cared naught what might lie at the end of it.

Yet he was young. Slowly the horror and grief went from him and hope awakened. He became altogether healed when he reached the shore and for the first time beheld the sea.

Woods decked the downward-rolling land almost to the water's edge. Close by they thinned out until only scattered evergreens, dwarfed and wind-gnarled, grew amidst harsh grass. The strand was shingle, round gray rocks where kelp lay strewn in ropes and yellow-brown heaps. The day was bright and windy. No great surf arises along the Baltic Sea, but waves ran high, scud blowing off white manes, green and gray out to a blue worldrim. They rushed and crashed and shouted in their strength. Gulls flew like snow. Their mewing called him outward. The air tasted and smelled of salt. He drank deep of its keenness and laughed aloud.

Shedding his clothes, he ran out and plunged. This was no quiet lake. Here he wrestled and frolicked with the water. When he ducked below, he could keep his eyes open in its brininess and see how weed swayed and fish flickered through amber depths. Head up again, he spied two seals not far off, sporting like himself. When he waded back ashore, even the chill of the wind on his wet skin and the itch of salt afterward welcomed him to the home for which he had always longed.

After a while hunger and thirst nudged his thoughts earthward. He must find water he could drink. Hunting could not be good here, and he only knew how to fish inland. There he must soon withdraw, unless men dwelt somewhere nearby. He would try for that. To keep the sun glare behind him, he walked east.

The sun went ever lower. Its beams strewed shivery gold across the waves. His shadow lengthened before him. The strand narrowed as the land slowly rose. Near sunset he spied a high bluff overlooking the sea and bent his steps toward it. From the top he might find a mark to make for.

Climbing the gorse-begrown slope, he saw a man on the height. Hadding's heart jumped. Though the stranger seemed also alone, he loosened the sword that had been Hardgreip's in its sheath and took a firmer grasp on his spear before going on.

"Hail!" he cried, waving his free arm. "I come in peace."

The other looked his way but stayed on the edge of the bluff. Nearing, Hadding made out that he was very tall, lean but wide-shouldered. Under a long blue cloak that flapped in the wind were goodly clothes. A wide-brimmed hat shadowed his face. From beneath it streamed long hair and beard, wolf gray. His only weapon that Hadding could see was a spear, of length befitting his height, the head blindingly agleam in the level sunlight.

"Hail," he called back through the shrilling air. His voice was as deep as the voice of the sea. "I have been awaiting you."

Astonished, Hadding came nigh. When he halted, he looked upward into a gaunt face where the left eyelids were closed above a hollowness. The right eye glared ice blue and winter cold. Hadding could barely meet it. Awe came upon him and his own spear sank in his hand.

He felt somehow that it would be unwise to hide any of the truth from this man. "I am Hadding Gramsson, faring by myself," he said low.

"That name belonged to a son of the former Dane-king," said the other.

Hadding straightened. "I am he. I seek what is rightfully mine and revenge for the wrongs done my kin." Surely he did best to go boldly forward. "May I ask who you are?"

"I now bear the name Gangleri. At times I have been a ferryman." More the old one did not say about himself. The name might well not be what his father gave him; it meant Wanderer.

"You tread wild ways, Hadding," he went on. "How shall you, single-handed, win your kingdom?"

"I must find that out," said the young man.

The gray head nodded. "The heart of your forebears is in you. I will give help."

The sun was almost down. Its light blazed over the sea. The wind blew louder and colder. No more gulls were about, but two ravens flew from the woods and wheeled past before winging off again.

Eeriness chilled Hadding. "Why would you do this?" he asked.

"I like brave men," said Gangleri. "And while I often fare alone, I am never forlorn, for I know more than most. You will do well to follow my redes."

This must be a wizard, Hadding thought. His life with the giants had somewhat wonted him to magic. After what happened of late, he misliked it. His thews tightened.

Gangleri read it on him and said, "There is the low lore and there is the high. Shun the first, honor the other. But it does not behoove a warrior to be afraid of either."

At that, pride lifted in Hadding and he answered, "I will hear you out."

A bleak smile stirred beneath the shadowing hat. "It begins in worldly enough wise, my friend. To win what is yours, you need followers. This means a renown that will make men rally around you and the wealth whereby to reward them. Well, not far hence a band makes ready to fare overseas in viking." Gangleri pointed east. Hadding saw what he had not heeded earlier, smoke blowing raggedly from beyond a tree-grown ridge. "I have come among them these past few days and made myself known as a soothsayer and healer. They will take you in on my word. Thereafter it is for you to show what stuff is in you."

Overwhelmed, Hadding stammered, "I have nothing to give you for this but my thanks. When I come into my own, you shall not lack for gifts."

"I hope for another repayment than gold," said Gangleri. "Let us be off, to get there before dark."

He set forth with such long strides that Hadding could barely keep up and had no breath to spare for talk. The sun sank behind them but the sky was still light when they topped the ridge and saw the viking camp.

Hadding forgot all doubt and dread. The ships before him were too beautiful.

They lay grounded along an inlet, clinker-built galleys, narrow of beam, sweetly curving upward fore and aft. Some had decks at the ends, others were wholly open. Sternposts were finely shaped and graven. A stempost might also be, or it might be left short and straight for the mounting of a figurehead. A steering oar was set at every starboard flank. Rowing oars were racked on trestles together with mast and yard. Paint livened the hulls, red, yellow, blue, green black with trim of white or gold. Greater and lesser together, they numbered nearly a score. To Hadding it was as if already they strained to be off.

Men swarmed over the grass, among leather tents and campfires. Banners on poles flew above flashing metal and loud merriment. "You come none too soon," Gangleri told Hadding. "The last crew they were waiting for has arrived this day."

He led the way down to them and through their midst. All who saw him fell quiet as he passed. Hadding could understand why. Uncanniness enwrapped Gangleri like his cloak and shone like sea fire in his one eye.

They halted before a big man who stood outside a tent beneath a banner on which galloped an embroidered red horse. He was roughly clad in wadmal and short leather coat. His ruddy hair was getting thin on top and a scar puckered his mouth. Yet the warriors around him listened closely when he spoke and said nothing against his words. A side of beef roasted on a shaft above their fire. The smell of it made Hadding's belly growl.

"Be welcome back, Gangleri," the lordling greeted. "Who is this you bring along?"

"A man for you," the old one told him. "Hadding, meet

Lysir Eyvindsson, chieftain in Bralund, who has gathered this
fleet and leads it."

Lysir frowned. "We've crew enough, without an untried
youth," he said.

"Your name will outlive you if you take him," Gangleri answered. "Men will never forget that it was you with whom he
first sailed. Here is Hadding, son of the Dane-king Gram."

Amazed oaths crashed from lips. "Mighty tidings, if true,"
Lysir blurted. Gangleri gave him a look and he went on hastily,
"Of course it's so when you've said it. But I thought the child
must have died long ago. How many even remember he ever
lived?"

Hadding overcame what shyness he had felt and stepped
forward. "Mine is a strange tale, yes," he owned. "But I've been
told I'm much like my father in both soul and skin. Who
among you knew him?"

"I fared with him to war, year after year," said an aging man
shakily. "I was there when he fell before Svipdag's Norse and
Saxons. Yes, now it's as though he stood again before me,
young."

"I saw Queen Signy on a trading voyage I made," said another man. "She had wedded the king of Dynaborg in Gardariki. A kinsman of his later overthrew him, and I hear she
killed herself rather than give up her standing as she had done
aforetime or go in the bed of her husband's slayer as Queen
Gro did. It seems me that something of her shows in you."

"Be welcome, then!" roared Lysir. "Ale! We'll drink to the
Skjoldung!"

Men heard and came over. Soon the whole viking host was
aseethe. A great feasting began, horns hoisted freely. By leaping firelight, which touched smoke with a hue of blood,
Hadding stood forth against the dark and told what had befallen him. Waves rushed and beat under his words.

"This is no small thing," said Lysir at the end. "King Svipdag will not be glad when he hears of it."

Gangleri's eye gleamed from below his hat as the old one stood offside among shadows, leaning on his spear. "Do you fear his anger?" he asked.

Lysir shook his head fiercely. "Thor thunder me if I do! Too long has he laid too heavy a scot on us Danes, and meanwhile our farms and fisheries give niggard yields—maybe worst here in Scania, where we're closer to him in his Uppsala."

"More folk than Danes bear him ill will," said a skipper. Swedes and Geats had come to this meeting place too. "But he's a mighty lord, as Jarl Gudorm learned."

"Either you crawl before him and cast Hadding out," Gangleri told them sternly, "or you plight yourselves to the son of Gram."

Lysir nodded. "We'll talk about that in the morning," he said. "First, let's drink once more to the gods. May they send us wisdom—and luck, which is better."

Men woke late and agreed they should let their heads clear before they decided. Thus the fleet stayed aground through that day and night. In the afternoon the vikings gathered. Not all were eager to risk King Svipdag's wrath. However, none wanted to go home at once. Nor need they swear any oath, except that they would take Hadding as one of themselves while on this voyage.

Lysir went further. Not only did he give the young man a full outfit of clothes and gear, he swore brotherhood with him. They two gashed their arms and each let his blood fall into the footprints of the other.

This laid a bond on the men from the chieftain's household. No few of the vikings then cried that they too would take up weapons for Hadding, should he ever call on them. If he won, great honor and riches would be theirs. If he lost, belike they would die, but so everybody must. All that lasts is the fame a man leaves behind him.

Gangleri stood tall and watchful. Only afterward did it come to them that when he promised Lysir a name that would outlive him, he had not said that the chieftain himself would be much longer on earth.

At eventide Lysir told Hadding what they were after. Eastward over sea were the low shores of Kurland. It was a land of woods, fens, and deep river dales, broken by the farms and thorps of its Wendish dwellers. Man for man the Kurs were tough, but they had less skill in smithcraft and warcraft than did speakers of the Northern tongue. Hence vikings were wont to raid them for thralls, or else wring from them a scot of the furs that were their only other wealth.

Lately, though, a king had arisen among them, hight Loker, who by war and wiles brought many of their clans under his sway. Thus he could raise a host to reckon with. He had also hired a band of warriors from across the water. These Danes, Swedes, and Geats were not merely his bodyguard, they led and stiffened the Kurland levies in battle. More than one viking crew had since come to grief.

"My brother died there three years ago," Lysir said. "To avenge him I've gone widely about, getting men to join me here in a bigger fleet than erstwhile." He grinned. "When we've broken Loker we'll sack his burgh. I hear he has stored up a hoard of gold like a dragon's."

Hadding thought that with his share of the loot he could begin gathering men for his own revenge.

At dawn the sailors busked themselves to go. While, wading and shouting, they launched their ships, Hadding bade Gangleri farewell and thanked him for his help. "We will meet again before long," said the old one. "By then you will have learned something." As they left, he stood watching them till he was lost to their sight. The last they saw of him was the gleam of his spearhead. Two ravens flew high above.

Sweeps creaked in row-holes, driving the ships outward. Aboard his, Lysir unwrapped a carved and painted dragon head. He left it off near friendly shores, lest it anger the landwights, but now he set it up to snarl at the prow. Thereafter he put Hadding at the helm and showed him how to steer.

Likewise did Hadding take his turns bending his back and tautening his thews to the oar stroke. He won to knowledge of knots and rigging, the care of a craft, the ways of doing things, the signs by which to set a course. There was time for this and more, because the crossing was not as short and easy as hoped. Clouds boiled up from the worldrim and over the sky; wind drove a lash of rain and spindrift; waves ran huge, gray and green and thunderous, beneath a storm-howl so loud that men could barely hear each other bellow and a cold that smote to the bone. Those who did not bail were at the oars, striving to keep the bow headed into the seas. Drenched, their hands blistered where calluses had worn away, skin cracked and stinging from salt, numb with weariness, they fought on.

Well northward were they driven, to claw off the lee shore of Gotland, before the storm waned. After that a fog rolled in. That dripping, silent blindness was in its way still more fearsome. When at last it lifted, the fleet was scattered.

Dauntless, Lysir spent days cruising to and fro in search. By ones and twos and threes he found the other ships. Mild weather cheered the crews. They raised masts to let the wind work for them. When it was not fair, they poled out the sails and tacked across it.

All these skills did Hadding gain, wonderfully fast. "It's as though you recall what you were born knowing but had forgotten," Lysir murmured, "and as if our woes came on us for you to do so the sooner."

Hadding reddened with pride. The swing and throb under

his feet, the reach of sight across restless mightiness, tang of salt and pitch and sunlight, whistling wind and rushing water, the ship like a living thing, like a woman clasping him, they were his; here he belonged.

The vikings had suffered no wreck, which seemed to them to bode well, but some hulls needed work and everyone needed quiet, uncrowded sleep. They sought back to Gotland and went ashore. Folk who saw them coming fled inland. Lysir's men did not give chase, nor sack the steadings thereabouts. This island paid scot to the Swede-king, and though he was now Svipdag, that might change someday. Best not to make bitter foes needlessly. They contented themselves with rounding up what kine they found and holding a strand-hewing. The meat tasted good after nothing but stockfish and sodden flatbread. They filled their water casks, fixed their ships, dried themselves out, and put to sea anew.

And thus they came to Kurland. They made landfall south of the gulf that Lysir sought and bore along the coast until they found it. Far across the land, the smoke of watchfires lifted. "That is as well," said Lysir. "To do more than strike and run, we must meet Loker. The earlier the better. We're late as is—not much time for plundering after the fight, if we're to be home for harvest."

They dragged their keels onto a sandy beach well within the gulf. On their left, farmland stretched green, a stockaded hamlet in the offing. All dwellers had gone inside with their livestock. Doubtless a man or two had galloped away to tell the king. On the right, thick with undergrowth, a wildwood loomed, farther than eye could follow. "I chose this landing because of that," Lysir told Hadding. "If we stand in front of it, the foe can't outflank us." The young man took the fore-thoughtfulness to heart.

Lysir likewise held his crews back from trying to take the stronghold. "We'd spend lives for scant gain," he said. "Once we've beaten Loker, we'll grab it off readily enough, and everything else we want."

Still, they grumbled, and quarrels flared in the three dreary days afterward. "This too is part of warcraft," Lysir taught Hadding: "how to wait."

Then at last iron blinked, horns dunted, feet and hoofs thudded, shouts rang raw, as the Wendish host arrived. It stopped a ways off, hundreds of men. A few leaders went on horseback, banners afloat overhead, and at the middle were ranked a few score in helmets and byrnies like the riders, the king's Northern troopers. Otherwise the newcomers were tribesmen. Some of them had kettle hats and might wear a leather coat besewn with iron rings, but most owned merely cap, breastplate, and leggings of boiled hide, and maybe a shield. Their weapons were axes, spears, knives, and clubs that might or might not have stone heads. Such short bows as the vikings saw among them were better fitted for hunting than battle, and none of them was a slinger. Though outnumbered, Lysir's folk bragged that what lay ahead would be more a reaping than a fight.

First, while men growled and glared across the ground between and shifted bristling from foot to foot, he sent one forward bearing a white shield and his word. The vikings would go peacefully home on payment of ten marks of gold to each and a hundred to himself, or the value in furs and thralls.

Loker spat and ordered the man back. As he left, the king flung a spear after him, soaring over his head.

"He learned that from his Northmen," Lysir muttered. "It means he'll slaughter us all for the gods."

Hadding gulped. "It'll go the other way," he answered. He heard his voice waver. Anger at that burned unsureness out of him.

"We'll try for it," said Lysir, "though no man shuns his weird."

He raised the horn slung at his shoulder and blew the battle call. A yell tore from both sides. In a ragged wave, the Kurlanders sped against the vikings.

A guardsman came at Hadding, armed and armored like him. Hadding's left hand tightened on the grip of his shield while he swung at his foe's. The sword bit into the wood. The guardsman leered and twisted it. Almost, he wrenched Hadding's blade loose. Too late, the youth remembered how Braki had warned him about that trick. His strength surged. Somehow he kept hold of his weapon, pulled it free, and clashed it against the other blade. For heartbeats the two men strained. For the first time Hadding looked into the eyes of someone he meant to kill and who meant to kill him. It was an eerie closeness, well-nigh like love.

The swords slipped free and smote afresh. Hadding felt a blow on his shoulder as if from afar. Ringmail and the padding beneath stopped it. More swift than the older man, he saw an opening and struck for the leg. He felt steel bite into flesh and break bone. The warrior groaned and fell. His blood spouted wildly red. He writhed halfway up and chopped. Hadding knocked his blow aside and cut at his neck. More blood geysered. The man crumpled. He jerked once or twice and lay still, like a heap of rags. Through the reek of his own sweat Hadding caught a sharp stench as the deathling soiled himself.

Another was in on him, and another. He gave blows, he took them, seldom knowing what came of it, for the maelstrom of strife bore him away. He pushed, tried to stand fast, slipped and barely recovered, hewed and blocked and hewed again. The breath gusted in and out of him through a throat gone dry as a stone in a fire. There was no time for rage; he was too busy staying alive. Yet always a part of him kept aside, aware, glad of each stroke he dealt or thwarted. He grinned as he fought.

The tide swept him in among the Wends. Two he killed.

Then a big, yellow-bearded man swung an ax at him. It batted
his sword aside and split his shield. He would have lost that
hand had the blow not torn the grip from him before the edge
went deep. The axman roared. His hands slid apart along the
helve of his weapon, to hold it at either end. Thus its hard,
leather-wrapped wood turned Hadding's blade. As the ax
lifted, the wielder brought both hands toward the lower end.
The head whirred down with his full might behind. It could
have cloven helm or byrnie. Hadding sprang aside quickly
enough. Before the man could raise his ax anew, Hadding
leaped in and caught him across the brow. He reeled back,
screaming, blinded with his blood and the skin hanging down.
Hadding slew him.

The Skjoldung stared about. He had come to the edge of
battle, hard by the wildwood. Only dead men and writhing,
moaning wounded were near. Beyond them, the fight had broken into clumps of struggle across the reddened grass. But
Loker's Northmen were still a single troop with their king at
the forefront, thrusting on like an iceberg. Even as he watched,
Hadding saw Lysir's banner go down before them. He saw the
chieftain fall, a spear in him through the riven ringmail. The
guardsmen trampled over him on their way forward.

The vikings broke. They turned and ran for their ships.
There some took a stand, shield by shield. Loker's men had
been winnowed too; the hale among them were also hurt and
weary. Moreover, it took time to fell what vikings were left
elsewhere on the field and bring the Kurlanders together for
a last push. Meanwhile a rearguard of seamen kept the strand
clear for their shipmates to launch the craft.

Foemen in between cut Hadding off from them. Half a
score of wounds on him soaked his undercoat and breeks. His
breath sobbed in and out. The hand that clutched his blunted
sword shook as badly as his knees. He could never win
through to the shore.

Three Kurlanders spied him, whooped in glee, and started
his way. He could not withstand them. He slipped into the
brush below the trees. With his wilderness skills he could
shake them off. After that he could only keep going for as long
as his strength lasted.

X

D usk was becoming night when he stumbled from a
brake out onto an open patch somewhere in the wilds.
Trees stood as giant blacknesses around it. Above them
glimmered the first two or three stars. What light there was
turned the bog grass leaden and sheened sullenly off puddles.
Ground squelched underfoot. It still smelled miry and the air
still hung warm, but mists had begun to rise as earth cooled
and a ghostly white haze drifted low. Silence brooded.

A man stood at the middle of the lea, armed with a spear.
A broad hat shaded his face. His beard fell iron gray down the
front of his cloak. Behind him waited a stallion of the same
hue, tall enough for his great height.

Words rolled slow: "We meet again, as I foretold."

Hadding was too numb for amazement. He hardly felt pain
any longer, hunger or thirst, will or woe. Blood loss and weariness had gutted him. Were it not for this sudden sight he
would have dropped here, slobbered the foul water, and toppled into sleep. Barely could he stand, swaying, and mumble,
"What now will come of it?"

"I said you would have learned something," the old one
answered, "and a man must know not only how to overcome
foes, but defeat itself. Tonight you shall have what is better."

"Well met, then, Gangleri, if you are more than a dream."

"Come." The Wanderer beckoned. Hadding lurched toward him, stubbed a foot on a root, and fell. Gangleri caught him. Held against the cloak, half swooning, the Skjoldung felt himself lifted in one arm. Gangleri bore him easily over to the stallion. It seemed to him that that steed had too many legs, but he could not tell through the querning in his head. Gangleri set foot in stirrup and swung up to the saddle. Hadding lay at his breast. Gangleri spread the cloak over him and whistled. The horse burst into gallop.

They should at once have crashed through brush. Instead, Hadding felt as if they sped uphill a while before they found an uneasy road. Down that they went so fast that the air was a gale around them. He nestled unwonderingly into the muffling darkness.

After a time that had no meaning for his stunned soul, the ride ended in a thunder of hoofs on stone. With a racketing neigh the stallion reared and halted. Gangleri dismounted, Hadding in his clasp as if the warrior were a bairn. The young man heard iron ring, a door clashed shut behind; Gangleri carried him onward.

At last the old one lowered him to a bench. He sat slumped, striving weakly to stay awake.

"Here," said the deep voice. "Drink."

Hadding opened heavy eyes. Gangleri loomed over him, holding a horn of gold. It was so long and broad that Hadding needed both hands to take it and bring it to his mouth. What was within smelled like honey and summer meadows and the hot pitch that caulks ships. When he tasted, it was a kiss on his tongue and a fire throughout his flesh.

"Drink well," Gangleri bade him. "This has mended worse hurts than yours."

Hadding obeyed with a waxing greed. As he drained the

draught, strength flowed into him. It washed away pain. His sight cleared, his hearing sharpened. He saw first the figures molded on the horn. They showed it raised by a woman in welcome to a man who came riding with two ravens aflight above him. Elsewhere they showed other men feasting and fighting. He glanced at himself. Though his mail was battered, sword dulled, clothes torn and blood-clotted, every gash had scarlessly knitted together. He was healed and hale.

He rose and looked about, bewildered. He seemed to be in a hall, alone with Gangleri. He could not be sure. The bench was cunningly made and inlaid with gold. Behind it was a wainscot of the finest oak, carved in strange shapes. A bearskin covered the floor under his feet. But he could not see to the end of the building, nor to the crossbeams overhead. It was too huge, and full of a blue twilight. He thought the nearer pillars had the forms of men. Blurs here and there might be hangings, dim moons might be shields, and fires might be burning far off. But he could not tell.

His look sought Gangleri. The one eye caught his two. A chill went through the renewed warmth in Hadding. "Who are you?" he whispered. "Where is this?"

"I have said what I have said and brought you where I have brought you," answered the old one.

His honor came back to Hadding. "You have saved my life. How may I thank you?"

"The night is not yet done," Gangleri warned, "and it is not yet well for you to linger here."

"Where then should I go?"

The Wanderer spoke gravely:

> *When back you fare, foes will grip you,*
> *Bind you for beasts to tear,*
> *Booty of wolves; but keep those men*
> *Lulled by the telling of tales*

> *Until from drink they drowse to sleep,*
> *Letting you burst your bonds.*
> *Leave them behind.*—

He went on. Hadding listened dazed, grasping after understanding. It slipped from his fingers. He dared not ask.

"Now come," Gangleri said at the end, and strode off.
Hadding followed.

They walked a long way through the gloaming. A door
sheered iron banded, so high that its top was unseeable. Gangleri laid hold of a golden ring on the bolt and swung it wide.
They trod forth into cold stillness under a blaze of crowding,
unwinking stars. The stallion waited.

"Ride before me," Gangleri bade. He helped his guest up.
When they were on the saddle he again wrapped his cloak
around Hadding, over his head. He whistled. The horse galloped off.

Now, though, Hadding was himself. More and more he
thought it unmanly thus to cower hooded on another man's
breast, in the crook of his arm. Anger kindled. He fumbled
at the cloak, drew a fold aside, and stuck his head out.

Night lay everywhere hollow around him. Stars gleamed,
fewer and smaller than erstwhile, the stars as they shine above
the world of men. Far below, their light shimmered on the sea.

Wind shrilled and cut.

"Look not on what is forbidden," he heard.

He drew his head back under the cloak and shuddered.

After a time beyond time the way bent down. The steed
halted. Gangleri opened the cloak. His spear slanted earthward. The warrior heeded and slid off, onto the ground. He
stared up. The rider sat tall against a murky tanglewood.

"Go seek your weird," Gangleri told Hadding. He wheeled
his horse and trotted into the wild. Soon he was gone among
its trees and shadows.

Hadding shook off the frozenness in him. He stood on the battlefield, at daybreak. The east had grown white, setting waters and dew agleam. By that glow he made out a few beached longships; the rest had gotten away, with sorely dwindled crews. Dead men lay strewn, stiffened, ugly hued, emptily gaping and glaring. Carrion birds had been at them, though at this hour only sleepy twitters sounded from the wood. Yestereven the Wends had cut the throats of viking wounded and taken their own into the stronghold hamlet yonder. Bands of them were searching in this dawn for their fallen.

Somehow they had not been aware of the newcomers until Gangleri left. Now they spied Hadding. They took him for a raider who had slipped into the wild, lost his way, and blundered back. Yelling, they pelted toward him.

He was alone, shield gone, sword all but useless. Yet he awaited them calmly. He knew they would not kill him out of hand. Whatever else the old one might be—and it seemed unwise to wonder much about that—he was surely a wizard whose spaedom would come true.

XI

King Loker was riding about the hinterland. When he came back, Hadding was brought before him. The stronghold was wattle-and-daub hovels crowded together between the upright, sharpened logs of the stockade. Livestock herded in for safekeeping had been taken out again but left their dung and its stench everywhere within. The king and his men would be glad to go home on the morrow. He had stayed this long only to see how things stood with the folk hereabouts. This captive could well be the last matter he need deal with.

Rain was falling. Most of the Kurlanders must squat outside. Their leaders had no better shelter than these foul huts. It did not milden Loker's mood. He sat on a chest among some of the warriors, a big, dark man, and glowered. Hadding stood bound in front of him, two Northmen guarding.

"Well," said the king, "at least we have one of you alive." He had learned the Northern tongue. "A nithing; no iron has marked you." The Wends had stripped off Hadding's helmet, byrnie, and weapons, leaving him only his clothes. Underbrush could well have torn them, and the bloodstains were hard to tell from caked mud. "You skulked off and hid, hoping to boast afterward of your heroic deeds. Tell me not that you did us no harm. You were ready to take your share of loot and rape your share of women, eh?" He turned to the keepers. "Hogtie him and throw him among his dead shipmates. Their fellow wolves will soon eat them. Maybe first the ravens will pick out his eyes."

"Well spoken, lord," spat a guardsman. The two in charge of Hadding led him away.

Outdoors, he opened his mouth. "It's a longish walk ahead. Why get wet? Let's wait here till the rain stops."

"You'd hang onto your wretched life that while more?" scoffed one of them.

Hadding shrugged. "The noise yesterday scared the wolves off throughout last night. They'll hardly come from the woods before this eventide, when living folk have stopped picking over the dead. Why soak yourselves as well as me? We can pass the time better."

He had, indeed, already talked with these men after they were given the watch over him. It had not been unfriendly. To them he was a foe who should die, but otherwise a man like themselves. Besides, he brought word from home. Vigleik was a Geat, Ketil a Dane of Scania. As steadily as Hadding bore his lot, they believed him when he told them he was no coward but had merely been lucky during the fight and had stayed in it till everyone else fled. Then he did take to the woods, but in the morning found he was back where he started.

"Why not?" Vigleik said. Ketil nodded. The three of them returned to the hut in which they had waited for the king to send for them. It was even smaller than most; the dwellers had been ordered elsewhere for this while. A peat fire smoldered on the dirt floor, its light barely picking out the stools, box, and cookware that were the few poor furnishings. Smoke mingled with dankness. Rain splashed beyond a narrow, open doorway.

Ketil doffed his cloak, shook what water he could off it, hung it over a beam, coughed and snuffled. "Faugh, what a weather!" he said. "You're right, nothing to be out in needlessly. Bad enough here."

Vigleik grinned. "We've something to keep us warm." He pointed to a cask of mead they had brought in earlier. The king's men helped themselves to whatever they found of suchlike goods. After all, they had saved the owners from the vikings.

"You might share it," Hadding said.

"Why?" asked Vigleik.

"Leave my throat dry and I'll speak no further word."

"Oh, let him have some," Ketil said. "It's cheerless where he's going."

He stood by with drawn sword while his fellow untied the captive's wrists and bound them again in front, to let the hands clasp a horn. He also lashed the ankles together and hitched that cord to a roofpost. Hadding was plainly strong. The guards were sore and weary after yesterday. They wanted no risk.

All sat down. They had one horn between them. Ketil filled it, drank, and passed it on to Vigleik, who in turn put it in Hadding's grasp.

"Tell us about yourself," Ketil bade him. "We'll tell others, so you won't be forgotten right away."

Vigleik yawned. "Make it lively if you can. This has been a dull day."

Hadding lifted the horn, drank, and gave it back. "I can tell you more than you maybe care to hear. You'll take me for a liar."

Ketil tugged his mustache. "A death-doomed man has no need to lie, does he? Nor would it help him afterward, I should think."

"Right you are. Hark, then. I am the last living son of the Dane-king Gram. After he fell, a faithful man of his brought me to some giants he knew, and they raised me."

Vigleik choked. Mead sputtered from his lips. "A tale indeed!"

"True or not, it's something to listen to," Ketil said happily.

Time passed. Rain hammered. The warriors sat enthralled. They lost track of how much they drank. When it came to him, Hadding held the horn tilted as long as they did, but the slightest of sips went past his teeth. The others marked this not.

He told them how he grew up, what the life was like, happenings both everyday and spooky. When it touched Hardgreip, he found he did not wish to say anything. Rather, he went on, quite truthfully, "The jotuns have many sagas of their own. Theirs was the first of the races, you know, and while most of them are no doubt oafish blockheads, some are cunning and some are wise, with lore that goes back to the beginning. They remember things that men never knew and the gods have forgotten, or at least do not choose to tell of. Let me give you one such. A part of it you surely know, but only a part. Of course, I heard this from a giant. It may be that his folk say one thing about it, the gods another. But here is what he told me."

Around and around went the mead as Hadding talked.

"While the war raged between Aesir and Vanir, threatening to bring down all the gods, Odin sought wisdom. At the well of Mimir he bought a draught of it with one eye. Then he saw how much more there was to know, still dark to him. Mimir could not teach him, for Mimir had not yet died. However, he could tell Odin where a rede might be found.

"Therefore the All-Father made ready and set forth. He went alone. Those were wild and wildering ways he must tread. Any fellow farer, without the insights that were now his, would be a hindrance, endangering them both. Even he often lost his path on that long trek. Only slowly and painfully did he find it again.

"Down he went to Midgard, and through the world of men. They too had taken up warfare. Blood feud and robbery were also spreading among them. Passing himself off as a wanderer, he must often fight. For him that was easy, but it slowed him, the more so because he gave help to those who befriended this lonely old man.

"Harder was it when he came to Ironwood. Trolls and monsters haunted it, though never was flesh or fish, fruit or root to be gotten. More than human might and skill did he need to win through that barren land.

"Worse yet was when the way took him on downward into hell. Through the freezing cold and darkness of Niflheim he fared, rushing rivers and swarming vipers, past the dragon Nidhogg that gnaws on the deepest roots of the World Tree, and evil beset every furlong.

"Beyond that he must skirt the fires of Muspellheim, where Surt lairs, who shall one day bear them forth to burn all the worlds. The jotuns themselves know not how Odin came unscathed from this giant, and he never spoke of it.

"In the end, he reached his goal, afar in the highest mountains of Jotunheim. There from ages aforetime had Farbauti dwelt with his wife, Laufey. They alone had the knowledge he needed.

"They guested him in seemly wise in their huge hall, where swart elves served them and wind forever howled around the walls, driving snowdrift and ice-glitter before it. But they did not want to give him his wish, him who had been there at the slaying of Ymir.

"They had two sons, Byleist and Loki." Of a sudden it struck Hadding as odd that Loker's name was so like this. He pushed the thought aside and went on. "Byleist was surly and hateful toward the newcomer. Little else have I heard about him. Loki was otherwise. He himself could have been a god, with the same height and handsomeness, his skin fair though hair and eyes were hell black. Lively and unruly, he had long found life wearisome in this flinty steading, this upland of loneliness and unending winter. Eagerly he listened to the tales and staves wherewith guest repaid host, the words raising before him a sight of Asgard shining at the end of the rainbow bridge.

"After a while Loki pleaded with his father and mother to be more forthcoming. He was fair to behold, ready of tongue, bewitching when he chose to be. Moreover, he whispered to them what it might mean to have one of their own kind among the gods.

"Therefore the elder jotuns, warlock and witch, yielded. They told Odin what they knew, that that which he quested after lay on the far side of death. None had ever dared seek yonder.

"He did. The way would be still more hard and strange

than those he had already trodden. The thursir had some
knowledge of it, gathered through the ages. Loki offered to go
along as guide and helper. This Odin must needs agree to,
with thanks.

"They bade farewell and went down the mountains, over
the glaciers and scree-strewn wastes, across the broad holdings
and past the huge garths of giants, to the sea. There Loki
called a drow from his barrow and made him ferry them in
his half a boat, which sailors see shortly before they drown.
On the farther shore grew a wildwood where no one dwelt and
nothing roamed but the beings of water, earth, and sky. Yet
how manifold and wonderful these are! Nor did anything
speak but the soughing in the leaves.

"Onward the wayfarers went, until they came to the Tree
itself. Mighty beyond men's knowing grows this ash, the
worlds clustered at its roots, about its bole, high in its boughs.
Great ill does it suffer; Nidhogg gnaws below, a hart grazes
above, and rot attacks the wood. Along it races the red squirrel Ratatosk, chattering out ill words between the dragon in
the depths and the eagle that perches aloft overlooking all
things. Yet the Tree lives, for it is life, and it shall abide when
the worlds go under.

"Aloft among the limbs went Odin and Loki, over their
twisting, swaying lengths, through shadowy, whispery caverns
of leaf, until they found the one that they sought.

"There did Odin lay a noose around his neck and leap off
the bough. There did Loki, standing below, wound him with
his own spear. There did Odin die.

"Nine nights he swung in the wind, offered up to himself,
on that tree whose roots go into the unknown. Loki waited.
No loaf or horn was there for them, only night and the wind.

"Then did Odin's staring eye kindle again. He looked
down and saw what none else had ever seen. He shrieked

aloud. The rope, which had creaked to and fro for so long, broke. He fell. Rising, he took in his hands the graven runes and read them.

"They are the runes of the high magic, the deep wisdom, gathered together from the lore of gods, elves, dwarves, giants, and men. With them can one who knows bring help in sorrow and sickness; he can break fetters and blunt a foeman's sword; he can stop arrows, spells, and fire; he can quell hatred among men and storms at sea; he can make witches flee; he can hearten warriors when their hearts are failing them; he can raise the dead and they will foretell for him what shall come to pass; he can win the love of any maiden—and thus did Odin afterward win the mead of skaldcraft; he can know the hidden names of gods, elves, dwarves, and giants; he can know what he will never tell to anyone else.

"So did Odin go beyond death and come back. So did he find the runes. Ever since has the Tree borne the name Yggdrasil, the Horse of the Terrible One, who is Odin. And when men are offered to him it is by hanging, for he is the Lord of the Gallows."

Hadding stopped. Rain rushed loud. Cross-legged at the little fire, their hands held to it unless the mead was going by, Ketil and Vigleik peered blearily at him through the curdling gloom. His tale had been of such uncanniness that they wanted great swigs from the horn while they listened.

"Well, what then?" Ketil mumbled.

Hadding laughed. "The rest is merrier. Mind you, I heard it from a jotun, who may not have felt as worshipful toward the gods as he should.

"Two brothers does Odin have, Vili and Ve. It was with them that he slew Ymir and made Midgard from the body of the father of giants. Afterward he had taken the lead, and they dwelt aside. Less and less did they like this.

"Now, while he was away and none knew if he would return, they went to Asgard. They said—honestly enough, maybe—that theirs was the right of kingship after him, and ill would the Aesir fare unless they yielded it. Indeed, what but lawfulness makes gods different from thursir? Thus Vili and Ve took over the might and riches of their brother, and, yes, his wife Frigg, lady of Fensalir and mother of Baldr the Bright.

"This was what Odin found when at length he had wended the weary road home. With his hard-won new wisdom, he did not want strife in Asgard. The Vanir were still his foemen. Besides, these were his brothers.

"Loki had come along. 'Leave it to me,' he said. 'Bide your time outside.'

"He was the foremost of skinturners. He made himself into a flea and bit the upstart kings, over and over. He made himself into a fly and buzzed around them every dawn. They grew haggard from lack of sleep. When they sat in the high seat before the gods, he was a louse that danced in their beards for all to see, but they could never catch him. He became a worm and burrowed through those apples of Ydun's, the apples of youthfulness, which were to be Vili's and Ve's, making the fruit too disgusting to eat. In all this grief there was nothing of honor. The gods began to laugh. That is worse than hatred.

"When Loki deemed the time ripe, he told Odin to ride into Asgard. 'Welcome back,' said Vili and Ve grimly. 'We have no further wish to dwell in a stead so ill kept and are glad to lay down the burden of it.' Thereupon they left. Odin has heard no more from them. He took back his lordship and his queen. By his wise words he wrought peace with the Vanir.

"But first, after what Loki had done, Odin swore blood brotherhood with him and gave him a seat among the gods. Already he knew something of what a troublebrewer this was. Yet he owed him much. Also, he thought, the gods might well have use for the cunning and deftness of Laufey's son Loki.

"And they did. But ever oftener, the woes he helped them deal with were of his own making; and more and more did he wreak sheer evil—"

Hadding went silent. Tired and drunken, Vigleik had fallen asleep, snoring and sprawled on the floor. Ketil nodded heavily and his eyelids sank. "My throat is dry, wet though the evening be," Hadding said. "Give me another drink."

"Indeed, fellow Dane," slurred from Ketil. He reached the horn over. "Hoo, it's gotten late, no? Vigleik, wake. We've a task, don't we?" He shook the Geat but aroused no answer. "Well, well, a hard day yesterday, we've a right to our rest, no hurry, no hurry. Say on, friend."

There was scant need. Ketil too drowsed off while Hadding told a bit more.

Dusk stole in like the chill. When he was sure both his keepers were deep in slumber, Hadding smashed the horn against the roofpost. It splintered. The shards were sharp. He used them to saw his bonds across.

Groping through gloom, he took a sword and went out the doorway. Nobody else was abroad. A wolf-howl sounded. The hut stood hard against the stockade. He clambered up onto its roof and from there sprang over the uprights. His weight thudded softly on earth. Away he loped to the wood.

It was like his homeland with Hardgreip. Night or no, he knew how to go among trees, through brush, around brambles, over deadwood, across quagmires. Nonetheless he went warily, the sword naked in his hand.

That came which he awaited. Something huge lumbered out of the blackness ahead. Branches broke before it and cracked under its weight. He heard it growl, he breathed the rotten-meat breath of it.

No fear was in him as he braced for its onslaught. In the great dim hall Gangleri had chanted:

> *Leave them behind. Along your way*
> *Soon a monster you meet.*
> *With fang and claw it catches men,*
> *But grip its gristly hide,*
> *Boring your blade into its breast.*
> *Then suck the steaming blood.*
> *Eat of the flesh and all the heart*
> *To straightway gain their strength.*
> *Through your marrow will rush new might,*
> *Enlivening every limb.*
> *I will help you, hovering nigh,*
> *To make those watchers weary.*

If he had fulfilled that promise, he would surely keep the next. Hadding's laughter rang aloud.

When he had slaughtered the troll and feasted as the old one bade, he felt as if reborn. Thenceforward he was as strong as any three other men.

XII

In a boat he stole on the coast, Hadding crossed over to Scania, no small deed of seamanship. From his landfall he went afoot to Bralund. There Lysir's son, Eyjolf, made him welcome. ragged though he was, gave him clothes and other good things, and bade him stay as long as he wished. That was for the father's sake and also because Eyjolf felt awed. He was stocky, sturdy, coppery haired, freckle faced, a year or two younger than Hadding, and had been left behind to look after things here. This was no common man whom he guested.

Hadding abode there through the winter. He lived quietly,

lest word of him reach Svipdag. Bralund was not off in the backwoods like Yvangar. The chieftain's garth was much bigger and finer than Braki's, with more folk there and on the land round about. However, it lay far enough from Uppsala that news did not readily pass between. Furthermore, nobody here wanted to warn a king they loathed.

Thus Hadding was able to ride widely around, speaking with chosen men. Messengers rode farther. They recalled oaths that had been given and they raised fresh hopes. If Lysir had failed and fallen, Hadding would not. He had shown only a little of what he could do, but that was great indeed. He was the rightful Dane-king, the last of the Skjoldungs. Men who stood him true now in his need could look for unstinted reward after he came into his own.

Fewer said yes than had followed Lysir, mostly younger sons and the like. He told them frankly that they might well be gone for longer than one raiding season. He would take none who could not be spared from work at home. That strengthened faith in him as a leader. Those who did come were a picked band, tough and keen. When they met in spring on the shore, they crewed a dozen ships. He offered horses and oxen to the gods. Thereafter his vikings launched forth.

Back across the sea he steered, and again into the Kurland gulf. This time they only landed for a strand-hewing, then rowed on. Where the River Dvina emptied out they bent their backs and pulled the harder. Swiftly up the stream they fared, into those wide lands the Northmen called Gardariki. There was no time to raise a host against them before they lay to under the walls of Dynaborg.

Those walls lifted long and high, of well-dressed timber, with watchtowers at the corners. Above them could be seen the shake roofs of the biggest houses within. This town had waxed rich off trade. Here dwelt King Andvan, who had overthrown the stepfather Hadding never saw.

Ships and boats had fled from the wharfs. The vikings did not give chase. They went ashore and made camp before the closed, iron-bound gates.

Watchmen on the walls jeered at them. How could they storm a stronghold like this? Horsemen were bearing a call to arms across the hinterland. King Andvan had but to wait. In a while his farmer levies would come overrun these upstarts, unless they first got too hungry or sickness broke out among them and they slunk off. He hoped not, said the watchmen. Those were some good-looking ships. He looked forward to owning them.

Hadding gave it no heed. He had asked searchingly of everybody he met who had been here in the past, and knew well what the place was like. "I've laid my plans," he said merrily. "Now they'll hatch."

It was nesting season. Birds that were making their homes in the thatch of homes flew to and fro. Hadding had brought a few skilled fowlers with him. They set out their nets and snares. Soon they had taken scores. They bound wicks to the legs, lighted these, and let the birds go. A number did not scatter but sought back to their nests. Dry reeds and moss blazed up. Shingles caught, then the buildings underneath. Smoke and flame ran high through Dynaborg.

Men fought the fires as best they could, lest they and their families burn together with everything else. Hadding winded his horn. The vikings set ladders against the now unguarded walls and swarmed over. The fighting did not last long.

Hadding had told his men strictly to hurt no one who yielded and to lay no hand on woman or child. He meant to do his business here fast. As his troop reached the king's hall, Andvan came forth, empty-handed, and named himself. He spoke the Northern tongue, having that blood in him like many lords of Gardariki. Through the smoke and reek he squinted into Hadding's eyes; through the crackle of the dying fires he asked, "What would you of me?"

"I could avenge my mother on you," Hadding told him, "but you did not kill her. I will take weregild instead and go away—your weight in gold."

That stripped the wealth of Dynaborg, but the town lived. Some vikings grumbled that they should have been let at the women. Hadding answered that with their shares of the winnings they would soon find plenty of willing wenches. Meanwhile let them be off before an overwhelming host came at them.

They did not go straight home from their raid. Rather, most of them were abroad with Hadding for the next four years, ranging the Eastlands. They rowed along the rivers and over the lakes, sailed by the strands, got horses and rode through green endlessness, saw towns and tents and many different folk strange to them, warred and traded, caroused and hungered, buried fallen friends and took new ones into their ranks, from Ladoga to the White Sea and south to the lands of the Greeks. They huddled together in the gruesome winter of Gardariki and ate the golden apples that grow in the orchards of Krim. They watched a Finnish wizard send his soul in quest out of a smoky turf hut and they heard a poet read aloud from the steps of a white-pillared temple in a Roman city. They talked with kings and merchants, they walked with herdsmen and hunters. They sated their lust wherever they could and sometimes it hurt to say farewell, but always Hadding led them on.

Oftenest they were in service. He had reckoned on this when he spared Dynaborg. Word got around that his was a dreadful band to fight against but sensible in peace and trustworthy. Kings throughout Gardariki needed men like that for their wars with each other and, still more, against the wild tribes that galloped in from the steppes. Traders needed guards for the laden fleets that yearly went down the great rivers and back up again. Hadding's were worth high pay. To this they laid the plunder and ransom that were theirs after a victory: gold, goods, thralls, kine; and they learned shrewdness in selling such of these gains as they themselves did not want to keep. Those who lived brought home the means to buy farms, or whatever else they liked, and settle down well to do. Hadding became rich.

When he deemed he had enough, he began to spend his wealth on ships, weapons, stores, gifts to give, and the hire of men. Many a hard-bitten Northerner who had been knocking about Gardariki sought to him, and many an eager youth sprung from its own soil. He spoke carefully with each one, for his farings had taught him much, and chose the best.

He thought of attacking King Loker in Kurland, to avenge his friend Lysir and seize the hoard that was there. But he heard that Loker was gone. He had taken a few men along into the wilds to hunt, and nobody ever saw them again. Folk said they must have suffered mishap; maybe a pack of wolves had overrun them. Hadding, who knew the ways of wolves, did not believe this. He wondered. This was a kittle thing. It was almost as if Loker had had something to do in the world and then, having done it, went elsewhere. Hadding cast the thought from him. It was too outlandish.

Besides, his real aim lay across the sea. In the fifth year after he went from Denmark, he came back.

This was with a mighty fleet. Hulls in their scores decked the waves. Prowheads reared above gleaming shields and spears. Oars walked spidery, creaking, water aswirl aft of the stroke, now and then casting foam white into sunlight. When hills hove blue on the rim of sight, a whoop went skyward. The startled gulls whirled and mewed in clouds.

So great an undertaking could not be mounted without news of it getting to Uppsala. There King Svipdag had his seat. He sent the war-arrow around and met his foe with a fleet still bigger. Yet when Hadding saw it, he grinned. "Of all men you might pick to fight at sea," he said into the wind, "I am the worst."

They clashed near Gotland. Hadding had spoken long with his skippers, over and over. They raised their masts, though it was not a time to hoist sail. At each masthead flew a banner. Thus every crew could readily tell where their warmates were. The ships kept apart, but not too widely. As often as could be, two closed in on one foe. Arrows, spears, and slingstones hailed from them. They laid alongside and grappled fast. Their men beat a way into the captured hull and cleared it. After that they looked for another. Where a ship of Hadding's found herself alone among craft of Svipdag's, other men of Hadding's could see it and steer over there to give help.

It did not always work so well, but it worked more than it failed, and Svipdag had nothing like it. One by one, his crews saw how they were thinning out, broke loose, and fled off across the reddened waters. As the sun went low, casting a broken bridge of fire from the west, he stood on the foredeck of his own ship and fought his last fight.

Starboard, larboard, forward, aft, the vikings crowded in. Warriors came over the rails in tide after tide. Shield thunked against shield. Iron rattled and rang. Men shouted less than they cursed and panted. Shrieks of pain rose ragged. Feet slipped on blood and spilled guts. Men sank and other feet trampled over them. The ship stank of death. Overhead circled the gulls. The light burned gold on their lean white wings.

Svipdag hewed down at those who pressed against him. Teeth gleamed in his sweat-sodden gray beard, under the helm that shone with sunset, above a shield splintered and cloven. Once the few men left at his side heard him gasp, "We'll take

this up again, Hadding, when you too are dead." His blows fell
ever more slowly. A spear caught him in the throat. He let go
sword and shield, dropped to his knees, fumbled at the shaft,
slumped, and died. The red geyser out of him became a flow,
a trickle, a widespread stain on the planks.

As fitfully as always in a battle, by sight as much as by
word, the knowledge came to Hadding that he was victorious.
Through the light summer night, when stars are dim because
the sun is never far down, he looked across the sea-gleam and
saw only ships of his, besides those manned only by death-
lings.

In the morning he made landing on Gotland and held
Thing with his followers. From there he went on into Denmark.

Everywhere folk hailed him. None said nay. Svipdag's son
had all he could do to hold onto Svithjod and the Norse
homeland. Hadding rode freely through Scania, took ship
across the strait to Zealand, and so the other islands and at last
that shire of northern Jutland which also acknowledged
Skjoldung overlordship. Thus did he come into his own, he
the Dane-king.

XIII

That year the fields throughout Denmark bore overflowingly, kine grew fat, and fishermen filled their
nets. The Danes thought this was because they had a
rightful king again. They flocked about Hadding wherever he
went, wanting him to set everything else to rights for them
also. Nevertheless he must make sure of their chieftains, some

of whom had fared well under Svipdag and might not be overly glad to have a Skjoldung back. He must reward men who had staunchly stood by him, and give to the most trustworthy such power as he believed they could handle. At the same time, he should not do injustice to those of whom he felt wary, if they had not yet done him any harm. In all these matters and more, he strove to learn the skills of kingcraft, from good counsel and from his own watchfulness.

Thus he had no time even to think about taking a wife, but merely bedded whomever was offered him—ofttimes by herself—as he fared around the land. Nor could he give heed to what went on abroad. He knew only that Svipdag's son Asmund was now king in Uppsala and had vowed revenge. It was hardly a surprise. The question was merely how real the threat might be.

The answer to that came toward spring, as Hadding sat in the great hall near Haven that his grandfather had built. Up from the nearby Sound came a band of men on horses they had brought across, into the stronghold, and so to the king's house. It was a gloomy day, skies heavy above croplands still bare and trees still leafless.

But when the newcomers came indoors, warmth, light, and cheer met them. Fires crackled high, hardwood sweetened with herbs. Lamps laid their glow to the leaping brightness and to whatever straggled in through the gutskins stretched across the windows. Shadows made the gods, heroes, and beasts graven on the pillars or woven into the hangings seem to breathe and stir. Well-born women kept filled the drinking horns of the men who sat on the platform benches along either wall. Well-trained hounds lolled at the men's feet. The king's guests and his household warriors were clad in brocaded, fur-trimmed tunics, breeks dyed with woad or weld or madder, belts and footgear of the finest leather and workmanship. Hadding in his high seat was more splendid yet, a silver brooch set with a garnet at his throat, gold rings on his fingers and coiling up his arms. His hair and close-trimmed beard shone the same yellow. His eyes gleamed sea blue in the jutting Skjoldung face.

A skald stood before him, saying forth a stave in his praise. When it ended, the king smiled. "Men will long remember that," he said. "Then let them remember too how much I liked it." He broke off half of an arm-ring and handed it to the man, a generous reward. Folk cheered. The skald said a verse of thanks and took his own seat. Friends thumped him on the back, tendered their best wishes, and bade him wet his throat.

After this it was seemly for the newcomers to tread forth. Hadding spoke first. "Why, Eyjolf!" he cried happily. "Welcome! Why didn't you let us know you were bound here, so we could have a feast worthy of you?"

"There was little time to spare, lord," said Lysir's son. "Nor is there now."

Indrawn breath rustled through the hall. Hadding's lips tightened. Yet he said calmly, "Come sit at my side and drink with me before we touch on anything worse."

The news soon came out. Having fastened his rule on Svithjod, Asmund was quick to make ready for war. They had lately heard tales in Scania of how he was calling up both Swedes and Geats. It seemed clear that he meant to cross the marches between the kingdoms. Such a host could lay much waste before men returned home for the springtime farm work.

Hadding tugged his chin and stared into the dusk that gathered under the roof. "Belike he means to leave as many warriors as he can behind, to hold his winnings and make further trouble," he said low. "Once the crops are in, he'll raise the great levy anew, and this time strike across the Sound. Any-how, thus would I work. So let us forestall him."

An older warrior frowned. "Lord, can we get enough men ourselves, ferry them over, and keep them fed? This is short warning."

The king lifted his head. "I think we can raise as much strength as I'll need," he answered for all to hear. "Asmund shall not be free to waste my lands and harry my folk."

Eyjolf's eyes flashed. "When I helped you, I did well," he said.

Now Hadding became once more roaringly busy. He lacked time for the war-arrow to go around the whole of Denmark, but Zealand and the islands south of it bore many thriving farms, which had bred strong sons. Word went likewise through Scania, bidding warriors meet at set places. Mean-while Hadding gathered ships and stores, with wains and horses to bear the needful stuff along. Hard though he worked, the trees were budding and a mist of green overlay the earth before he could start forth. The leaves were out, small and tender, the grass growing well, and wanderbirds flocking homeward through heaven, when he met his foe.

This was in the north of Scania. The Swedes and Geats had not yet come far. Only a few farmsteads stained the blue with their burning. Otherwise that afternoon was sunny. Breezes went mild, full of birdsong and breaths of soil and growth. Hadding's troops were passing through a broad bottomland flanked by low, wooded hills. On their left flowed and glittered the river. Elsewhere spread open meadow with scattered groves of beech or ash. The yeomen hereabouts had herded their grazing kine away as they fled. The field lay open for battle.

When Hadding saw from afar the host moving toward his, he whistled softly. "That looks like about three to one against us," he said. "I hadn't reckoned on quite so much." His laugh barked. "Each of us'll have to do away with three of them."

No few among his followers swallowed hard. But all walked onward. Lights flared off helmets and spearheads. Banners rippled aloft. Feet made a slow, dull drumbeat. Hadding dismounted. He slung his shield on his back and took a bill off a packhorse. Given the numbers he must meet, he wanted a weapon with a longer reach than a sword, to get at foemen behind the frontmost and thus loosen the sheer weight of them.

Soon, he knew, the fight would break up into knots, where the only way one could hope to stay by his fellows was to keep an eye on the banner of their chieftain. If it went down, strife would go wholly man-to-man, without shape or meaning.

On the Swedish side, riding at the head of his folk, King Asmund laughed louder. "Now have you been as reckless as I hoped, Hadding!" he boomed. He was like his father in looks, big, heavyset, hooknosed, with dark hair and beard that were getting grizzled. To the youth on his right hand he said, "This day your namesake will smile in his howe."

Henrik was slender and fair, barely of an age to take arms. Asmund had given him that Saxon name when he was born, in honor of him whom Gram slew in order to reave away Signy. She thus became the mother of Hadding, but it was to avenge her fallen bridegroom that the Saxons lent strength to Svipdag and so brought about the death of Hadding's father. That young Henrik was here, where they would bring down the son of Gram, seemed wholly right to Asmund.

On either side flew the banners of his two older sons, Uffi and Hunding; but Henrik was his most beloved. Elsewhere went the followers of many Swedish and Geatish chieftains. When the riders among them drew rein and jumped down, a shout rang off the hills. Startled birds flew piping from their nests. Iron flared free. Bowstrings twanged, arrows hissed into flight.

Like two storm waves, a greater and a lesser, the hosts crashed together. Blood-foam spattered into the wind. The tides churned, swirled in among each other, became a seething that howled. Swords hewed, axes smote, spears thrust. Men yelled, gasped, screamed, fell. High on their staffs swayed the raven flag of Hadding and the eagle flag of Asmund. But the Dane-king must needs stand fast amidst his household troopers, while the Swede-king pressed ever forward with his.

"Ha!" bellowed Asmund. "Only wait, Hadding! I'm coming to you!" His blade sundered a shield. Henrik struck from the right and killed that man. The boy was fighting as hard as his slightness was able, as fearlessly as any skilled warrior.

A weapon-clash hit on their left. Nearly berserk with rage, Eyjolf Lysirsson had led his Bralunders straight for the invader overlord. They cut and battered a road through all men in between. They fell on Asmund's bodyguards like wolves on an elk.

But the elk bears great antlers and sharp hoofs. The Norsemen stood shoulder to shoulder. Their blows racketed and clove. Nearby Swedes and Geats saw what was happening. As fast as they could break off their own fights, they came to help.

"Yah!" shrieked Henrik, hawk wild. He rushed out of the shield-wall to smite this foe. Eyjolf's ax smashed down his sword and split his helmet and skull.

Then the press grew too heavy. Attacked on every side, the Scanians went under. Their ranks crumbled. Those that were left hacked ways to freedom and withdrew elsewhere. Eyjolf's banner lay on the reddened ground. He sought to his own king's.

For a span there was quiet around Asmund. He did not hear the groans of the wounded nor the harsh breathing of the hale where they leaned on their spearshafts. He stood looking down on the wreckage that had been his dearest son. It gaped up at him through the spilled blood and brains. He had a gift for skaldcraft. After a while he stared around and spoke flatly.

> *Who will have my weapons?*
> *Helmets are no use now*
> *Nor byrnies worth the bearing.*
> *My boy is riven from me.*
> *Death, that took my darling,*
> *Do for me the selfsame.*
> *Swinging only sword blade,*
> *I seek my end in battle.*

He straightened. His voice rang louder through the uproar.

> *Breast to foeman baring*
> *Where blinks the ice-cold iron,*
> *Fiercely I'll go forward*
> *To fell them in my vengeance.*
> *Men will long remember*
> *This meeting of the war-hosts.*
> *If early come its ending,*
> *Yet I shall not have rested.*

Thereupon he slung shield on back, gripped his sword with the left hand wrapped over the right, and howled for his men to follow. Heedless of life, he made for Hadding. No foes in between could withstand him. He reaped them. His well-drilled guards worked grimly beside him. As the banner thrust onward, more and more of their folk rallied about it.

Standing with his housecarles, the Dane-king had often wielded his bill. Again and again they cast back an onslaught.

But each one cost them. Meanwhile, looking from his height over the heads of most, he saw the rest of his troops driven apart from each other and piecemeal whittled away. As Asmund's human landslide bore down on him, he knew that unless help came swiftly, he was done. None was anywhere in sight. His mind flew back to the wilderness of his boyhood. Little of witchcraft had he learned there. One spell, though, was his to use once.

He turned his eyes northward, braced himself, and loosed it. Men heard his throat give forth unknown words and saw his finger draw runes on the wind. They shivered, thinking he had gone mad.

A smokiness sprang up on the field. It whirled, whistled, thickened. It became the jotun Vagnhöfdi.

In all his hugeness he stood before them. He blocked out the sun; his shadow stretched far over the trampled, blood-muddied earth and the sprawled slain. Shaggy, hide-clad, he gripped a giant ax in his right hand and an iron-shod club in his left. The stone-rough face swung about as he glared to and fro from beneath the shelf of brow. Men stared, frozen.

"Hold!" cried Hadding to his warriors. "That's my foster father! He is with us!"

An earthquake rumble sounded from Vagnhöfdi's breast. He stalked forward. Bones crunched, guts spurted beneath his feet. To the nearest band of Swedes he strode. As they broke and ran, he began killing them.

Fear blazed up and spread, wildfire. Men cast their weapons aside and ran blind, wailing. Danes were among them, the war forgotten. But many more beheld Hadding's banner still aloft. They recalled what they had heard about his beginnings. It was an eldritch tale. Yet they stammered to each other that they must not lose heart, but rally to him.

Asmund also overrode the horror in his nearest followers. By then they were close indeed to the Dane-king. Hadding stuck his bill into the ground and took shield to hand for the attack. Asmund saw. Bitterly he screamed:

> *Why bear you here so boldly*
> *Your bill, as crooked as you are?*
> *A sword or flying spearhead*
> *Shall slay you all the sooner.*
> *Your will is not for weapons*
> *To weight the scales of battle.*
> *You trust yourself to tonguecraft,*
> *To trolls and blackest magic.*
>
> *How dare you act undaunted,*
> *Whose deeds are all unmanly,*
> *The shield against your shoulder*
> *Ashamed of him who holds it?*
> *The name you shall be known by*
> *Is nithing, now and always,*
> *And from your mouth the foulness*
> *That fills it reeks to heaven.*

No man could brook words like that. Wrath stormed up through Hadding. He snatched back the bill and hurled it. Drawing blade, he dashed forward before his amazed guards could stir.

The bill struck Asmund glancingly on the neck. Its sharp hook rent the flesh. Blood leaped forth. Asmund reeled. His men snarled and readied themselves.

Hadding came. Blows flew at him from right and left. As he warded himself, Asmund struck for the last time. His sword caught the Dane-king in the right foot. Through boot and bone the edge went. Hadding staggered. Asmund grinned at him, crumpled, and bled to death.

Hadding's men got there to beat the warriors back from

their lord. For a short while the fight ramped. Then a bulk like
a mountain loomed over it. Vagnhöfdi smashed the Norse that
were left as a man cracks lice between his teeth.

Thereupon he turned to Hadding. White-lipped and
sweating, the king stood on one leg with his sword for a cane.
Vagnhöfdi bent low. "You're hurt, fosterling," he growled.
"Come, let's take you away and see to this."

Hadding shook his head. "I will keep the field," he said
raggedly.

Vagnhöfdi waved a hairy hand. "Look around you. It is
yours."

A few banners were left, all Danish. Men were gathering
around them. Far and wide, their foes fled. Two had somehow caught terrified horses and gotten back into the saddle.
They rode about and must be calling to those in flight
whom they overtook, for some joined them. Nevertheless it
was clear that the folk who had been Asmund's would fight
no more this day.

Hadding nodded. "Yes," he said, "we'd better get me hale
again fast, if we're to make use of our victory."

The jotun took him in the crook of an arm and bore him
off like a babe. Hadding half drowsed through the long strides.
Those of his housecarles as had the boldness and were not too
weary or weakened trailed after them.

Vagnhöfdi went on for some ways. "I think you won't be
ganging off very soon," he said. "You should rest where the
stink, the flies, and the screaming birds can't trouble you." At
a grove beside the river he laid his burden down on soft duff.

Squatting, he touched the wounded foot. It bled less than
before but bone ends stuck out of the gashed leather. "My fingers are too thick to bind this," he sighed like a storm gust. "I
hope somebody with skills gets here before too long."

"Can't your spells make it whole?" asked Hadding.

"No," Vagnhöfdi answered. "That gift lay more in my daughter, Hardgreip."

"I'm sorry she died," Hadding said through his pain to the giant's.

"She went freely to her doom," said Vagnhöfdi. "Now I must begone lest mine come upon me. Already I hear thunder off beyond the hills." Hadding could not, but he believed. Vagnhöfdi's brooding look sought his eyes. "Beware, yourself, of overmuch haughtiness. Your own doom is a strange one. More than that I know not; but I do not think you will always be lucky."

Hadding lifted his head a little. "Whatever befalls, I'll make of it what I can."

"You might do that better if you went at things less rashly." Vagnhöfdi sighed again. "But you are you, and young. Maybe some wisdom will come with the years, if you live. Otherwise, well, that's what your doom is. Haflidi and I will abide the news. We shall meet you no more." A great hand stroked the brow beneath it. "Farewell, fosterling."

He picked up his weapons, rose, and trudged off. A lowering sun threw his shadow across the dale farther than men could see. He himself reared black athwart the sky. They watched in awe until the mighty darkness went from sight over the hills.

Already before then, the swiftest among them had reached their king. One was good with wounds. He undid Hadding's boot, cleansed the foot, hefted and handled it, and told his fellows to bring him what he would need. Hadding set teeth together. He caught his breath only when the work hurt most.

Night fell. Uffi and Hunding had gotten together a number of their men. By the light of stars and waning moon they sought back to the battlefield. There they found the body of their father Asmund. They bore him away.

Days passed. Hadding grew fevered. He never raved with it, and soon cast it off, but it left him weak for a while afterward. During it, his housecarles, chieftains, and other trusty men gathered back those Danes who had fled. They saw to the care of the hurt, handing out of stores, mending of harness and weapons. Those who were unfit to fight more went home, along with those who felt themselves needed on the farms at sowing time: for the term of levy was up, as set forth in olden law.

However, no few stayed camped by the river. Hopes of reward, plunder, revenge, and fame lured them. The wondrous ending of the battle here heartened them. True, Hadding gave out frankly that there could be no more such rescues. Henceforward they would win whatever they won by their own hands. But they thought he must be well worth following.

His right foot splinted and bound, he mounted his horse and led them northward. He would go the whole way to Uppsala and seize the overlordship of Svithjod and Geatland. Thus would he quell the threat, harvest wealth for those who had been faithful to him, strengthen his Skjoldung house beyond overthrow ever again, and for himself win a name that would live till the end of the world.

Meanwhile Hunding brought Asmund's body home. He laid it to rest with kingly grave-goods and great offerings to the gods. He also buried his mother, Gunnhild. She chose not to outlive her husband, but fell on his sword. Their son set her down at his side.

Meanwhile, too, his older brother, Uffi, was at work. He

did not make the rounds of the shire-Things and get himself
hailed king. That could wait until later. He took for given that
he was his father's heir. Nobody cared to say otherwise.

Instead, he fared about raising fresh warriors. Everywhere
he harangued the folk, telling them what grief would be theirs
unless they did what they must at once. In this wise he hammered together a strong troop and led it down to the sea.

Hadding moved north with fire and sword. Seldom did men
stand against him. When they did, he overran them easily. But
then word reached him, borne by riders who had flogged horse
after horse to death. The Swedes were harrying the islands of
Denmark, striking inland before they rowed on to the next
spot, slaying, looting, burning. Hadding was very newly the
Dane-king. If he let this go on, belike his folk would cast him
from them.

He could only take his warriors back. As they came down
through Scania, Uffi heard. He laughed that he had given
enough of a lesson for now, and set course for the Skerrygarth.
The Danish host returned to the same havoc they had been
wreaking and set about rebuilding.

By then Hadding's foot was healed. The leech had been unable to set it altogether aright. Ever afterward the king walked
with a limp. That did not hamper him much. Sometimes it
made him hark back to his foster father's warning. But he
never dwelt long on those words.

XIV

At his hall near Haven, King Skjold had let build a storehouse for his treasures. It stood somewhat apart from the surrounding buildings, close by the stockade. Stoutly timbered, it offered a small but good home in its front half for the hoardkeeper. The treasure room was at the rear, windowless, its only door on the inside, warded by a heavy lock and never opened except at the king's behest.

When Hadding came back from Svithjod, he brought little booty to lay aside. Rather, he would withdraw gold and goods. He must make gifts with a free hand as he fared about the kingdom, so that men would willingly follow him to the war he meant to renew next year.

He went to fetch the wealth on a summer's day. Half a score of his housecarles came along to carry and guard it. Through the open gate of the stronghold they saw young grain ripple in the wind, cows graze red in green paddocks, a fen where storks were stalking frogs. Beyond lifted a wood, bright in its rustling crowns, shadowy below. A hawk hovered far aloft. It hurtled downward at a prey just as Hadding reached the storehouse.

His hoardkeeper met him at the outer door, a man once burly but now swag-bellied, nose thrusting bluish-ruddy from above white whiskers, garb none too clean. "Hail, lord," he greeted a little thickly.

"Hail to you, Glum," answered the king. "How fare you?" The oldster had served Svipdag before him, but Hadding kept him on because he had served Gram before then, and there seemed no grounds for distrusting him.

"Well enough, well enough, since the weather got warmer," said Glum. "Come in, my lord. I've a jug of mead here, not the best in Denmark but the best a poor gaffer can pour for his lord." He hiccoughed.

Hadding frowned. He had heard something about how often Glum was drunk. Hitherto he had lacked time to look into it. "No, I'll only take what I came after," he said curtly and brushed past the other into a front room. For a bit he was nearly blind in its murkiness, after the light outside. Then he saw how dirty and tumbled things were. "Have you no one to keep house here?" he asked. "This is unfitting for the treasures."

"The wench has not come for some while," Glum told him. "I, uh, did not want to trouble my lord about so small a thing."

"I know why," snapped a guard. "Thorid, who had the task, told me; we're kin. She's no thrall, she's a freeman's daughter, and would not have this old guzzler pawing her anymore."

Glum tried to draw himself straight. "Have a care," he said. "I'm a well-born man, I've been a warrior, I keep a post of honor. Have a care how you speak of me."

"He did," Hadding broke in. "Too much care. Why did you not let me know, Einar?"

The chief guardsman bit his lip. "Maybe I should have, lord. But we all had much else on our minds, no? I thought we lesser folk could settle things here quietly, without pestering you and without shaming an old man who used to bear a good name."

Hadding nodded, though the scowl did not leave his brow. "Enough. Let's get the things and begone. Open up, Glum."

The hoardkeeper lurched over to a chest, fumbled among the clothes in it, and took out the big key. Slowly, as if this called for skill, he put it in the lock and turned it. Hadding himself swung the door wide.

Then for a span he stood staring, unstirring. A hush fell upon the troopers. It spread from the few inside to the others outside. The sounds of everyday life seemed thin and far off.

"What is it?" mumbled Glum. He went to the platform where he had set down his wooden drinking cup and glugged from it. "Why are you so stiff?" he cried. "What doesn't anybody say anything?"

Each word of Hadding's fell like a stone. "Thieves have been here."

"What? No, no, can't be, I've been ever faithful, ever watchful—" Glum stumbled across the floor and caught the king's arm. "I have!" he shrilled. "I am no thief!"

Hadding shook the hand loose. "Nevertheless," he said, "much is missing." He went into the storeroom.

Searching about in its gloom, he found much still there, weapons, furs, costly garments, amber necklaces, glassware, and boxes of coins from the Southlands. But his voice rang out, gone iron: "The gold chain that King Skjold wore when the Thing met. The silver goblet set with gems that his Queen Alfhild brought with her from Saxland. The gold-headed mace wherewith King Gram slew Sigtryg. The great silver bowl with bull's-head handles that I brought back from Dynaborg. And I know not how many golden arm-rings. You should be able to tell me, Glum. You have the tally of everything in your head. Come reckon it out, hoardkeeper."

"I know nothing," the elder groaned. "I have not been in there since last you were."

"You should have, from time to time," said Hadding. Then he shouted: "Ha! Einar, Egil, Herjulf, come here and look at this!"

The warriors crowded in with him and peered. A hole in

the floor yawned black amidst dirt piled around it. "Someone dug his way hither," breathed Herjulf.

"Then the thief is indeed not Glum," said Einar.

"Thieves," the king answered. "One man alone cannot have done the work. Who'll crawl down and find where the burrow ends?"

Egil was first, though he was the oldest in the troop. Hadding stepped out into the dwelling room. Glum cowered from him and blubbered, "You see, lord, I did keep faith—"

Looming over the wretch, Hadding said, "I call it not faith that you could never stir yourself to look in on what was entrusted to you, but instead drank yourself deaf to the noise of what was going on. Do you in truth know nothing of this?"

"Nothing, nothing, I swear by the gods and on my honor."

"We may squeeze something else out of him," said a guardsman starkly.

Hadding shook his head. "No, I believe he speaks truth of a sort, and I will not torture a man who once followed my father to battle."

"Thank you, lord, thank you," gasped Glum.

"But speak not of your honor," said Hadding. "That you have thrown away."

Glum sagged down onto the floor and sat with his face sunken between his knees. Hadding went outside. He stood there among his men in the sunlight, waiting. Now and then a warrior cleared his throat or shifted his feet, but nobody spoke.

After a while the searchers came back, muddy and disheveled. "We followed the burrow beneath the stockade and on till it came up near an oak in yonder woods," Egil told. "We found only heaped-up earth."

"You'd hardly find more," Hadding said. "The thieves were at their work a long while—mostly at night, I think, when they could steal out to it with nobody marking them.

The winter nights are the long ones. I'll go later and see. First I have a judgment to call for."

He bade two men stay in the house and others spell them until it could be made more safe than formerly. The rest of his guards went back to the hall with him. Glum walked between two of them, leaning on their arms, head bowed low.

Now Hadding sent word around that on the morrow there would be a meeting to which all men of the neighborhood should come. Thereafter he had those who had passed through the burrow bring him to the end where they crawled forth. "Wait here," he said. "I'll cast about, and don't want any tracks trampled."

They knew what woodcraft as well as seamanship was his, and obeyed. When he returned to them, he sighed, "No, it's too late. Weather has blurred every spoor away. Yet from the look of the mound here, the thieves weren't done digging till a month or two ago. Surely they've hidden their loot somewhere in the woods. Unless they're utter fools, they'll bide their time. Next year, when folk have half forgotten this and the warfaring is the big news, they'll sneak out, pry loose the gems, melt down the metal, and trade for other wares when the merchants gather at Haven. Or they may make off to the Jutes or Angles or Saxons and set themselves up there." His anger flashed, only for an eye blink but so cold that those hardy men quailed the least bit. "That they would dare! With ill shall ill be repaid."

His face became a mask. Speaking no more, he led them back. Likewise was he withdrawn at eventide. His mood spread to his men, and that turned into a bleak meal. When he and his leman sought their shutbed he did not take her in his arms. She knew that he lay long awake beside her in the dark.

At sunrise, though, he got up calmly, if not merrily. At the time set, he walked forth to the meadow where folk met and sat down on the squared-off stone there. Warriors, yeomen, fishermen, craftsmen stood in a ring that he closed, under a sky where tall clouds had risen, sunlit on top but graying underneath. Crows flew about, low overhead. Their caws went harsh through a wind that blew cool and smelled of oncoming rain.

When the lawman had spoken those laws of old that bore on this day's gathering, two guards brought Glum onto the open ground and forward to the king. He shambled along amidst the eyes until he halted and stood hunched. Hadding's words unrolled the tale of what had happened.

"I say that this man has broken faith," he ended. "He swore he would ward the treasures. For that he was well housed, well clad, well fed, and well honored. But he lay sodden and unheeding. Thus we have suffered great loss—not only I, but the Skjoldung house and the whole kingdom. The rings that are gone were merely rings. The rest, though, was hallowed to my forebears, Dane-kings and Dane-queens. Power was in them, and luck. Now we have lost them.

"Glum Styrsson, you shall die. First have you aught to say for yourself?"

The hoardkeeper stiffened his back and met the king's look. Suddenly his voice came steady. "Yes. I was less watchful than I might have been, but I am old and maybe you should have had a younger man there. Leave me what honor is mine. Otherwise do as you will."

Hadding nodded. "It's true, once you fought beside my father. You shall die quickly on the gallows."

Glum ran tongue over lips. "That is well," he said; for by his bearing this day would men remember him.

The folk murmured agreement. A man-offering to Odin should help against the bad luck that was in the loss. And who knew but what the god would take the hanged man home to himself? No one wept except the small grandson he had been raising after the boy's parents died, nor gave any thought to that.

The housecarles led Glum off. Hadding stood up. "Hearken," he said aloud. "Among us are belike the thieves themselves. I speak to them. Think well. What gain is yours? Do you truly want to slink forth again, huddle in the woods at a charcoal fire, make wreck of keepsakes that belonged to great men and famous deeds? Surely no good can come to you from it. In fear and trembling must you trade off what you bring to market. You will not dare ask for the full worth, nor openly enjoy what you buy. Or else you must carry the plunder away and drag out your lives among strangers, forever sick with longing for your motherland. Who will tend your graves, who will recall your names? What have you gained?

"Glum shall suffer death for what he did not do. The thieves need not suffer for what they did. It matters more to get the things back. I promise that whoever brings me the loot unharmed, him will I make welcome. Yes, I will bestow on him honors like to those that were Glum's."

He called on the lawman to set out the oath-ring. Laying his hand on it, he swore to those words, so help him the Vanir and almighty Thor. Wind strengthened, tossing his hair golden around his brows. It whistled. Cloud shadows hastened across the land and thunder began to growl from afar. Men looked at each other, muttered, and left as soon as the king told them the meeting was over.

After the hanging he went for a hunt in the wood with a few friends. They did not hope to stumble on the booty, but it would work some of the anger out of him. He met the onset of a boar that ran up his spear until the tusks nearly gashed him before it died. Then he grew mild, almost cheerful.

They wended their way back. As he strode into the thorp

around the hall, a strong-thewed, sooty man stepped from under a roof and hailed him. "Lord king," he asked, "can we speak alone?"

Hadding knew the blacksmith Bosi. "Yes, of course," he said, and waved his huntsmen aside. Those two went into the smithy. There, by the glow from the coals at the forge, Bosi brought forth, "I've been thinking over your words at the folkmoot, lord. Did you mean them?"

"All heard what I swore to," Hadding answered.

"Then—" Bosi braced himself and went on in a rush: "I am one of those who lifted the treasure. I'll give you back what I have."

Hadding took the news quietly. "That is well," he said. "I'll abide by my oath. But can't you show me the whole of it?"

"No, I fear not. We split it among us, and each took his share off to hide where only he knows. But I will return Skjold's chain and many rings."

"That is worth much," Hadding said. "Better yet will be if you name the others."

Bosi shook his head. "We swore blood brotherhood." He gulped. "You did not say you wanted us to break our own oath."

"No, I did not," Hadding yielded. "Come with me and take your reward. Maybe they too will think twice."

Bosi walked stiffly after him. That eventide in the hall Hadding called him to stand before the high seat. "This man did wrong," he said aloud. "But he is doing his best to set things right. Therefore he shall have a ring off my arm and a place at our feast. Speak well to him, for he shall have more honors hereafter."

However amazed, the men could not but take Bosi in among them and even try to talk with him. As the drink went around and they got mellow, his deed came to seem a daring one, cunningly thought out. There was good stuff in this fellow, they agreed. Henceforward he could put it to good use and win a famous name.

Indeed, Hadding stayed very friendly to him. Although Bosi was not a weaponsmith, the king asked him to make a sword and paid far more than it was worth. Hadding also offered to take Bosi's son into the housecarles when the lad was old enough. He spoke of finding wealthy husbands for Bosi's daughters.

And so after a while another thief came forward, a crofter by name Ro. He brought Queen Alfhild's silver goblet, as well as more of the gold. Him too the king rewarded well, giving him woodland that he could have in freehold after he had cleared it, along with the means to hire help for that work.

Thereon the two thieves who were left gave themselves up and returned their shares of the loot. Hadding bestowed rings on them and made known that there would be a folkmoot again, at which he would put all four of them to rights with the law and give them in full everything he had promised.

Wind boomed and rain showers lashed at that meeting. The king stood before it, facing the thieves, and cried through the weather, "Here are those who would have robbed us of things that are holy. I swore that whoever brought the treasure back should have reward and honors like to those that were faithless Glum's. Now let me fulfill my oath. They too shall hang."

"What?" blared Bosi, and lunged at him. It took three guards to wrestle the smith to a standstill. He struggled in their grasp and raved. The other three were easier.

Hadding smiled at them. "What higher honor can you have than to go to Odin?" he said. His hand chopped downward. "Take them away."

He left their widows and children in peace, nor did he snatch from these any of what he had given the men. Still, he did not think Bosi's son would want to join his housecarles.

Word went around Denmark. Here, men said, was a king shrewd as well as hard. Those who followed him could hope for much.

Throughout that winter and spring he readied for war. He knew he could not go straight at Uppsala as he had wanted to. He must never again leave his kingdom open to such raids as it had suffered. Rather, let most men stay behind to watch over their homes. He would take a well-chosen troop each summer and harry the Swedes. Thus he could wear them down, until when at length the kings met on a battlefield he would overcome once for all.

So it came about. Sometimes his longships prowled around the shores, their crews striking as if out of nowhere, to kill, sack, burn, and bear away captives to thralldom. Sometimes a host ferried across the water and went deeply inland, bearing the same havoc. King Uffi fought back as best he could, and many of those fights were hard, but he never had enough forewarning and the Danes always went up against mere shire-levies. These they could either overwhelm or beat to a draw.

When each warfaring season was past, Hadding returned to Denmark and spent months faring through the land. He gave judgments that folk deemed were wise and often kindly; he gave freely not only to the well-born and the yeomen he met but also to the poor; as a go-between, he brought deadly feuds to an end; he started the clearing of wildernesses, the building of thorps and marts and shipyards; he found openings for lowly youths who wanted to better themselves; by his gifts, words, and smiles he brought a flowering in skaldcraft and handicraft; by his dealings with the Jutish, Anglian, and Saxon kings, he safeguarded and heartened trade. It was often said that he seemed to be two different men, one ruthlessly warlike, one a forethoughtful landfather.

With all this, he found no time for seeking a wife.

Thus it went for five years, until his doom overtook him anew.

XV

Too long have we fought with that wolf where and when and how he chooses,". said King Uffi in Uppsala.

"What else can we do?" asked his younger brother, Hunding. "If we brought together a great host, that would leave helpless the shires from which so many men were drawn. He would go reave unhindered. Ever oftener I wonder if we might not best make peace with him. If he got sureties that Denmark would be safe from us, he might well give up his thin claim to kingship here."

Uffi's fist thudded on the arm of his high seat. "Peace between him and me? Never while we are both alive!" He was a big man like their father, Asmund, with much the same face, though his locks were brown and as yet had no gray in them. Folk reckoned him wilier; he thought ahead. Today he narrowed his eyes and spoke softly. "A wolf leaps into a sheepfold, takes a lamb in its jaws, and is off before the hounds can give chase. If one of them does catch up with him, he slashes it bloody and lopes onward into the wilds where the rest soon lose his spoor. Shall the shepherd therefore yield and let him have the flock? No, a wise man lures the wolf into a trap."

"Hadding is himself wise," Hunding said. "That's why I

think we should ask what he wants for a peace with us. It may be less than what this unending war is costing. Meanwhile, he'll know any trap for what it is, and stay clear."

"Not if it's a kind of which he's never heard." Uffi looked around at his redesmen and headmen. "Here is what I have in mind. During this winter, we'll stack wood everywhere for beacon fires. Come spring, we'll post fast-riding scouts about the kingdom. Thus we will know where he fares. Between the north end of Gotland and the mainland we'll keep more ships at sea than he has ever brought with him. If he wants to fight them, good, he's done for. But likelier he'll sheer southward.

"Now he's already picked those shores bare. If he wants to do more harm and take more booty, he must go well inland. Wherever this is, nobody shall withstand him. Men shall keep away, as if frightened of the very sight. Thus he should be drawn ever deeper inward. When he's come far enough, then the Geats and Swedes shall lay waste the land before him, behind him, and widely around him. Let them fire every barn and grainfield, let them kill whatever livestock they cannot bring with them. No longer shall the Danes live off the land as they're wont to. Meanwhile I will have hastened south with a picked troop and packhorses well laden with food. Along the way I'll gather what more warriors I can, and at the end call the shire-levy there to me. The Danes will be weak from hunger. Then will we fall on them."

"This is unheard of, that a king make war on his own folk!" cried Hunding. The others muttered and growled. But after talking at length they decided it was worth trying, for indeed nothing else had helped.

Summer came again, the sixth of Hadding's strife with the house of Svipdag. He always sent men ahead to find out what might be waiting for him. Now as he sailed past Öland a small ship, swiftly rowed, came back to warn of a Swedish fleet hove to in the north. His craft were much fewer, and mostly broad-beamed knorrs, better fitted for sail than oars, for carrying men and horses than for getting about nimbly. After he had met with their skippers, he turned around and went back south of the island to a Geatish strand he knew. There he left a skeleton crew in each bottom and struck out northwesterly toward the Svithjod marches.

At first his troop moved fast. No foeman met them. No one did at all. They had been here earlier. Fire-blackened snags of farmsteads stood like runestones above scattered bones, among fields gone to grass and brambles. Poppies blazed, finches trilled, deer bolted off into shaws, geese flapped startled from fens, but the land lay eerily still. Nobody spoke loudly around the campfires at night, and looks kept shifting outward into the dark.

The way steepened. These parts were new to the Danes. They came on steadings and thorps that were unscarred, croplands that were ripening. Yet they seldom saw the dwellers. Those had fled. Smoke from hilltops afar showed how word of the raiders got about. "Strange that they don't stand fast and fight," Hadding murmured. "This was always a stouthearted folk. I should think they'd at least try slowing us down. Have they lost heart altogether?" He laughed. "Well, the better for us."

His men had eaten the food they brought from the ships. This many could not live off wild game. The yeomen had taken their herds and flocks with them, but it hampered their flight and soon they let most go. Since Hadding's scouts found no hostile host anywhere near, his warriors could range rather freely in search of strayed kine. It was skimpy fare, but enough to keep them as they pushed on. Behind him smoldered the homesteads and storehouses they had gutted. They would return to the sea by another way.

Suddenly smoke was everywhere in sight. It rose above

trees, it lay like mist over blackened fields, it blued and made bitter the air men breathed. There were no more cows, pigs, or sheep. Hunters came only on carcasses where the maggots and ants were cleaning up what the wheeling, rasping crows had left.

"What is this?" wondered Eyjolf Lysirsson. "Are they offering everything to the gods, in hopes we'll be smitten?"

"I know not," said Hadding, "but neither do I like it." He thought. "We will seek back to our ships."

By then they had trekked onward three more days, for they had not understood how thorough the burning and slaughter were. They were into uplands, thinly settled, thickly wooded, hard going even along the few roads. Hadding took heed of sun and stars. In his head he laid out a course that should swing him wide of these forbidding reaches.

But as the Danes found their way, they found no food. Everywhere the same earth-scorching dogged them. Now and then they spied horsemen in the offing. A few times they caught a dweller or two. These said they knew merely that the king's men had bidden them lay bare the path of his foes, and widely around. Hadding nodded. "That's plain to see," was all he answered, and let the captives go.

When he ordered the killing of packhorses, nobody spoke against it, though it meant leaving loot behind. By then, bellies were growling too loudly. Worse was the loss of strength. With shouts the Danes squatted at their cookfires and drank the smell of roasting meat before they sank their teeth into it.

Yet they had not many horses with them. They could not do without those that bore spears, arrows, and other weaponry. Thus they got only a few bites each day. Some won a little more. Their noisy passage frightened game off, and they could not well stop to fish the streams they crossed.

However, a man might climb a tree if he saw a bird's nest and crunch the fledglings in his mouth. He might grub worms from a rotten log. Better, he might shoot down a forsaken dog. Still, this was a meager meal at best.

One man grew too weak to walk. His friends made a litter and carried him. After a day he died. That was likeliest from illness, for hunger had not brought down anyone else. They buried him when they camped that evening. Afterward a whisper went around that during the night others dug him up and ate of his flesh before putting him under again. Nobody said who they might have been, and Hadding scoffed at the tale, but it was an ugly one and sickened everybody.

Back at last in the lowlands, they stopped at a lakeside. The one sign of man was a farm about a mile off, empty, its fields and buildings charred. The dwellers had even cast their turnips and suchlike pig-truck into the fire before they fled.

The lake itself shone golden with sunset. Reeds rustled on its banks. Frogs leaped. Warriors splashed around for a while, trying to catch them, but little came of that. Nor could they take the waterfowl that flocked and cried yonder, nor hope for the fish they saw glimmer and jump. They were not outfitted for it. Bats were coming forth, darting after the mosquitoes that whined in hordes and nipped blood that men could ill spare. The last light glowed through their wings. Trees beyond stood darkling against an eastern sky where a red star had kindled. Warmth drained from the world.

Without packhorses to carry tents, the warriors must spread whatever they had to sleep in on the grass and dandelions. They did not trouble about fires, but gnawed what scraps of stinking meat were handed out. Hadding, as haggard as any of them, said to Eyjolf, "I've a feeling that here we're at the end of our road."

"It's a ways yet to the sea," answered the viking's son,

"and I mean to plow it again." He grinned beneath eyes gone hollow. "As well as quite a few more women."

"We may wish," Hadding said, "but if it comes to pass, it will not be soon." He turned about through the deepening twilight and sought his bedroll. To Eyjolf it seemed an ill token, hearing such words from the king.

Night fell. A nearly full moon cast a quivering bridge over the lake. Aside from their drowsy outposts, the Danes slept.

A noise yanked them awake. Through the dark, through their ears and marrow, loud as a scream, grinding like a quern, a voice chanted:

> *To woe in warfare you have wandered afar,*
> *Seeking to seize by the sword a prey.*
> *What hasty hope has hooked your wits?*
> *Why blundered you blithely and blindly forth,*
> *Believing the land was lying open?*
> *Unswayed, unswerving, the Swedes have gathered*
> *Stoutly to stand and sternly to fight.*
> *Danes, after daybreak death will be here,*
> *Ruthless and ready to reap your host.*
> *When, beaten in battle, the best among you,*
> *Weakened, give way as the weapons come on,*
> *And frightened flee the field of slaughter,*
> *Your foes will follow your flight like hounds,*
> *Victors vying to avenge their losses,*
> *For easy it is to end a man*
> *When horror has him; helpless he goes.*

Hadding was on his feet, naked but with hilt in hand, glaring about under the moon. His folk were shadows to him, except where the light flowed off iron. They shouted, cursed, moaned, mumbled. "Be still!" he roared. "Hold fast!"

The voice had died away. Alone the night wind spoke, rustling moon-dappled leaves. Dew glittered star-cold. Hadding went among his warriors, bidding them remember that they were men. They knew he had met weirdness before and lived. After a while they quieted down. But nobody slept more.

By the bleak dawn light, Eyjolf asked Hadding, "Shall we be off?"

"No," the king told him. "We've heard what is bound our way. Lacking a height to hold, this is as good a battleground for us as any."

Without steeds or leg-strength, no scouts had ranged in the past few days. Nonetheless Hadding was not astonished when the spearheads of a Swedish troop flashed at midmorning. "We are as many as they," he said to the housecarles within earshot. "If our bellies are less full than theirs, let our hearts be more so. We'll take our stand on the lakeshore. Thus they won't be able to flank us and attack from behind."

"Nor will we find it easy to break and run," drawled old Ax-Egil.

Hadding laughed. "If a man of mine can speak so brashly, there's hope for all of us. But keep this thought to yourselves."

As the Swedes drew near, the Danish bowmen let fly. Arrows whirred aloft in a dark flock and down again. Their barbs thunked into shields, glanced off helmets, rattled against mail. Some struck into flesh. A man lurched and shrieked with a shaft sticking out of his eye, another pawed at one in his neck and sagged to his knees as blood spurted, another swore and ripped one out of his thigh but thereafter went lame—here, there, throughout Uffi's host. The king rapped an order. His headmen shouted it their bands. The Swedes halted while their own bowmen gave answer in kind.

Thus they lost the might that is in an all-out onslaught.
Against this was the losses the Danes suffered.

Yet must the Swedes come to them, across ground
where more arrows hurtled, then slingstones and flung
spears. When they reached Hadding's lines, theirs were ragged.
Working side by side, the Danes sent them surging back in
disarray.

Uffi egged them on. They closed ranks and renewed their
attack. Iron gleamed, banged, made cloven shieldwood groan.
Howls of rage and pain rose raw. The Swede-king hewed tireless, seeking to cut a path to the man he hated. He could see
Hadding's tall shape above the swaying helmets, amidst the
leaping weapons. But always the battle between them was too
thick.

His men had fared hard for a long way. The Danes, though
weakened by hunger, had had a rest before the fight began.
They stood their ground and took their toll. Lichs lay heaped
before them. Less and less eager did the Swedes feel to climb
over those red windrows.

In a lull, where the only sound was the moaning of the
sorely wounded and the hoarse breathing of the hale, Uffi
took thought. "Sound the withdrawal," he bade his headmen.
As the war-horns lowed, his banner went in the lead.

The Danes did not cheer. They were too weary. They knew
their losses had been the heavier. After a while they saw Uffi's
banner stop a mile off and others join it.

"Back to camp," Hadding told his followers. "Maybe we
can get a good night's sleep this time."

That was an unlucky thing to say. Men recalled the voice
in the dark and what it had foretold. Nonetheless they obeyed,
bringing their hurt along. Their dead they must leave behind,
for lack of strength to drag so many burdens along. Nor did
they cut the throats of what Swedes lay helpless on the field.
That likewise was more work than they could well undertake,

and useless. They settled down where they had been before. Most toppled straight into uneasy slumber.

King Uffi mounted his horse, beckoned his warriors to stand close around, and harangued them. They were not beaten, he cried. Already they had given better than they got. He was proud of them. Let them refresh themselves and rest. In the morning they would finish their task.

The hurrahs that lifted were dull. Yet the Swedes did hail their lord. Having pitched camp, they gloated around their cookfires. "May the Danes have joy of smelling our roasts."

Night fell, the light summer night that is well-nigh a dusk. A full moon climbed over eastern treetops to brighten it further. Fires guttered low. Aside from their watchmen, the warriors slept.

The moon drew near the loft of heaven. Earth lay shadowy. The lake shivered with silver. Then, louder than any human voice, cracked and grisly, there ran through the Swedish troop:

> *Why does now Uffi dare me*
> *To dash him to the ground?*
> *Reckless call him rightly,*
> *Rather than bold-hearted.*
> *They he angered thus*
> *For this will make him pay.*
> *I warn that only woe*
> *He wins for all his work.*
> *Sinking under sword-edge,*
> *Soon he loses life.*
> *Strive however strongly*
> *In strife he may, he dies.*
> *A flock of spears aflight*

> *Shall flay him limb from limb.*
> *No cloth will ever close*
> *The clotting wounds upon him,*
> *Nor need is there, for nothing*
> *Can knit dead flesh together.*

Men started awake. They caught hold of weapons, which then shuddered and sank in their hands. They blundered about in the half light and wailed for their friends, any friends, "Ingvar, where are you? Grimulf, oath-brother, come to me!"

Though sweat stood cold on his skin, Uffi knew that if he let horror run free, his troop might well split asunder. Once a few ran away, everybody would. Even if they stayed, brooding on this thing would sap them. He boiled from his tent and shouted for his guards. "Sound the horns! Marshal the men! We go back to war!"

Somehow he rallied them. Iron came forth, icy under the moon. Bands formed up around their banners. Uffi rode in front where all could see him. His folk lumbered forward. He sprang off the horse and took shield in hand himself.

The racket had roused the Danes. Dazed, aching, sandy-eyed, they still heeded their king as he went about bidding them make ready. The best they could do was arm themselves and stumble into three lines. There they waited for the foe to reach them.

Suddenly from somewhere, onto the dewed grass between the troops, came a man striding. Taller he loomed than the tallest warrior, but hideously gaunt. Foul rags flapped around him. In the moonlit gloaming his head shone bare, beardless, eyes too deep-sunken to see, a head like a skull. He gripped a curved sword as though it were a sickle for reaping. Wheeling around, he moved on before the Swedes, toward the Danes.

They gasped for breath. Spearheads flickered above them in their grasp, flames of a dying fire.

Another old man stalked from the other side, as tall, bony, ragged, and bald as the first, armed likewise. He turned to face the Swedes.

"What are they?" The words wavered at Hadding's back. "Trolls, drows, sendings, what are they?"

"I know not," the king answered. "But more powers than human are at strife this night."

The shapes met. Their swords clashed. To and fro they trampled, hewing, fending, faster than eye could follow, ghastly under the moon, in utter stillness.

Men stood staring, numbstruck. Then Uffi bellowed, "We have one friend from beyond, at least! Fail him not! Onward!"

It became easier to fight than to watch. The Swedes screamed like wildcats. They broke into a run. Around the horrible old men they poured, up against the Danes.

"Hold fast!" Hadding cried. Battle burst over him.

A while it went on, blind and witless. But the Swedes now had their backs to the open ground. The Danes glimpsed past them to the grisly sight yonder. It chilled and shook them even as they fought for their lives.

The old man who was on their side gave way. Backward he went, barely warding off the blows that sleeted about him. All at once he was gone from their ken. The other stood there in his rags, skull gray-white in moon-glow, before walking off with sword held high.

At that, the Danes broke. One by one, two by two, in tens and scores, they left their ranks. Most cast aside their weapons to run the faster. Every which way they fled, lost in utter fear. Uffi bayed for glee.

Those of Hadding's housecarles who lived fought stubbornly on, together. A few other Danes kept their wits and joined this small band. Though the numbers against it were overwhelming, the Swedes were also worn out, also daunted by what had happened. When the Danes rebuffed their last rush, they hung back, snarling but with the will beaten out of them.

King Hadding winded his horn. His flagbearer lifted his banner on high. He led his folk off.

Uffi could not make his own follow. Some flopped down and sobbed for breath. Some lay flat by the water and drank and drank. Some began to pick listlessly through the forsaken camp. Some tried to tend their wounded fellows.

· After a while Uffi stopped blustering at them. Later they could chase and kill the foes who had bolted. Let that handful go who had left in fighting array. Already the night had swallowed them.

He had gained enough. His was the victory, in spite of everything that Denmark and hell raised against him. Not soon again would Hadding seek his shores. The Dane-king might well meet death as he struggled homeward. If not, then Uffi would think how to give it. No matter what the tales were that one heard about Hadding's youth, he was hardly a darling of the gods.

XVI

Hadding knew well that he could not make for his ships. Scouts would be searching everywhere between. Soon after one of them saw his little gang, overwhelming might would overtake him. Instead, he headed west. By dawn they had reached wildwood. Wading down a stream, they broke their trail. He spent his skills keeping them from leaving any mark where they scrambled back onto land. "Hardgreip could still have tracked us," he said low. The sadness gave way to half a grin. "But no Swedish farmers."

Now they were staggering with weariness. Where boughs roofed the ground so thickly that no brush grew, they lay down on the leaves of old years and slept. None rested well. Throbbing and burning, wounds made fitful the slumber of some, while nightmares beset that of others. Hadding never told how that day went for him. Though sorely cut and bruised, he bore no deep slashes or broken bones; but the weight upon him was heavy.

Nonetheless, when the men began to rouse toward evening, he stood before them and spoke firmly. His beard and bare locks were the brightest thing they saw amidst the green shadows. His words were a drumbeat under the gurgling of an unseen cuckoo. With a forefinger he counted his dirty, bloody, scrawny, sweat-crusted, tatter-garbed following. "Eighteen of us. But good men, all of you." His smile flickered. "How glad I am to have you alive, Eyjolf, son of my oath-brother. And you, Ax-Egil, you old scoundrel, why, you must be unkillable. Gunnar, you saved my life when those two Swedes felled Thorkel and came at me while I was busy with another of them. I'll remember. Arnulf, it's well you've kept your bow and some arrows; this means we'll eat. Svein, fear not, we'll get you home to your young bride." Thus he went on, with a few words for each; and as he did, bent backs straightened, stooped shoulders squared.

"We've a long way before us," he ended. "We begin by giving up any thought of haste. I'll show you how to make brushwood shelters for tonight. While you do, I'll search for nuts or berries, and if I find any, use them to bait deadfalls. Maybe we'll catch a squirrel or a few lemmings. In the morning, we must first find water, a spring or brook. We'll camp nearby for some days while we rest and start to heal. I can make a fire drill and so a fire, but that's dull work after the first time and I'll be angry if you let it go out. Besides, I, and whoever else has woodcraft, must fetch us real food."

"By Ull the Hunter," swore Eyjolf, "here's a lord with more than gold to give his men!"

Nobody said anything about booty and battle lost or friends left dead. Such things happened. Nor did anyone talk of the wraiths they had seen. No one dared.

Dwelling in the wood, they won their way back toward strength and hope. No hurts of theirs were too grievous to deal with, using what means were to hand. Otherwise the sufferer could not have come this far. But it was not only good in itself, it was a heartening token that none got too badly inflamed. A weir in the stream they found caught fish, while Hadding and others brought in meat. Those who had lacked such skills learned from the king how to carry always a throwing stick and knock down whatever small game they spied. Although his limp slowed him somewhat, he himself was the best of the hunters. Going forth alone, he would stalk a deer, leaving it unawares, until he was close enough to grab hold and slay with a single blow of the knife.

Yet he longed for the sea. As soon as he deemed the warriors ready, he led them on.

That became a hard and ofttimes hungry faring. Surely Uffi had sent word far and wide, offering rich reward for their heads. They must not let themselves be seen where there was any number of folk, and best was if they were not seen at all, even by lonely outliers. Hence they swung clear of settlement as much as they could, groping through woods and over wastes unknown to them, crossing rivers elsewhere than at the fords, struggling through marshes and growth-choked glens, clambering on steep hillsides and in stony ravines. When they had to pass near farm or thorp, they went at night or through a rainstorm. On the move in wildwood, they could not help frightening game. Now the hunters seldom got anything bigger than hares or grouse. Sometimes they felt lucky when their traps took a few voles.

Still, they pushed on. Sheer fellowship helped them mightily. Camped at eventide, if weather let them sit around the fire they would swap memories, tales, verse, jokes, thoughts. Hadding awakened wonder by what he told of life and lore from his strange upbringing. Their homely words taught him more about men and women than he had fully known before.

After uncounted days they came out of a shaw onto open ground rolling gently downward. Tussocks of coarse grass mingled with heather, tossing in a salt breeze that murmured below an overcast where the sun lightened the gray to westward. When they saw the silvery gleam ahead, they whooped, danced, pounded one another on the back. "The sea!" they cried. "The sea!"

Hadding drank deep of that air. "Home to the Mother," he whispered. They did not understand him. Maybe he did not either. But then he smiled and told them, "I think now we are safe."

He reckoned they had reached Helsingland, toward which he had steered them as best he was able to on their twisting way. Dwellers along the eastern shores of the Kattegat across from Denmark, the Helsings were friendly to the Danes. Mostly fishers, neither many nor rich, they paid him a small yearly scot of smoked and brined herring, while his might kept the Geats and Norse off their necks. Moreover, in raiding season he posted ships in the strait to north, which warded off any vikings who might be aprowl in the Skagerrak.

He led his band south. Before dark they found a hamlet. Terrified, the few dwellers snatched what weapons they had. The king bade his men halt and went ahead alone, palms spread, to meet them. They could ill believe his tale. They had heard nothing. It seemed likelier that the newcomers had suffered shipwreck, as gaunt and worn as they were. Yet there had

been no storms of late. And the wayfarers did at least seem
peaceful. Somewhat warily, the households took them in.
Stockfish, flatbread, cheese, and curds were a feast, because
there was a fullness of them.

"You shall have gifts of me after I get home," said the king
in the morning. "But first will you bring us to someplace
where they can more easily guest us?"

The fishers muttered among themselves whether to take
these men in a boat. On the one hand, if this really was King
Hadding, he ought to remember it when he chose what gifts
to send. On the other hand, if he lied, that boat would have
lost two or three days' catches for nothing. At last the
spokesman they picked told him it would be wrong to crowd
such fine warriors into a wretched little hull stinking of fish.
Besides, the spokesman didn't like the look of the weather.
Wisest would be to walk. His grandson would guide them. He
would not affront King Hadding by uttering what any fool
could see, that so deep-minded a lord understood the Helsings
had nothing but his welfare at heart.

"More miles afoot!" groaned Eyjolf. "Has some black warlock turned us into inchworms?"

"Stop grumbling," said old Egil. "You didn't mind tramp-
ing across Svithjod."

"No, but it was full of abodes to sack."

"And maybe there are many such along hell-road, but I'm
in no hurry to find out."

In a way that stretch was indeed the most wearisome. Having the end in sight made men wholly aware of every ache and
lameness, how long they had been gone and how they yearned
for home. They trudged wordless, lost in themselves. Hadding
alone grew eager.

Yet when they reached the steading he sought, he told
them they would stay a while.

Bruni Aslaksson stood great among his folk. Ashore he

held broad acres, where the crofters paid him rent in kind and backed him at the Thing and in trouble. On the water he owned six fisher boats and a ship, which sailed in trade. He offered to the gods on behalf of the whole neighborhood and dealt with chieftains like himself up and down the coast. Though his house was built more of turf than timber, it was of good size, and stood at the middle of its own stockaded thorp. There was no lack of food and drink, furs and stuffs, herds and hirelings, strong sons and shrewdly married daughters.

He had never met Hadding, but had heard enough to know that this was in truth the Dane-king. "Welcome, welcome!" he boomed. He was a burly, snub-nosed man with a ruddy beard, going gray, that curled halfway down his paunch. "What an amazement! What a troll-banging amazement! We've had some news out of Geatland and Svithjod. I feared you were dead. But here you are. Ha, we'll gorge and swill this evening!"

"How fares Denmark?" asked Hadding.

"As far as I know, well. That jarl of Zealand you left to keep care—Eirik Björnsson, that's the name, no?—he seems like a worthy steersman. You'll soon see for yourself. My ship's at sea right now. But I'll have two boats scrubbed clean, and ferry you across the 'Gat with something like swagger. First, though, we'll fire up the bathhouse. You haven't steamed in months, have you? And we'll break out clean clothes for the lot of you. Won't be anything rich, but whole and warm and no bugs in it. And we can't make a rightful feast ready before tomorrow, but we'll be killing the fattest beasts, and meanwhile we've no dearth of pork—or ale and mead, which matters more—and I can tell you we've lively lassies hereabouts."

Hadding smiled on the left side of his mouth. "I think they'll have to wait," he said. "We're not very lively yet. I'd have us abide a while."

"Ha? Not but what you won't be welcome, in this house

and in all. Fresh faces are well-nigh unheard of, you know. Fishers swarm in from everywhere during the herring run, but mostly they're not much fun to meet unless it be in a brawl. Hardly anybody else ever stops by. However, aside from those wenches I spoke of when you feel a bit better, what have we here to lure you with?"

"Peace," Hadding sighed. "The day I set foot again on Danish soil, folk will be at me. Questions, reckonings, tales, begs, grievances, the rounds to make, the folkmoots to head, the judgments to give, the care to take of high-born men's honor—even listening to my own praises and thinking what gift those verses are worth— Let me get back my strength. Until then, it'll be better for the kingdom, too, if Eirik Jarl stays at the helm."

"I see. Never thought how much work it is being a king. I should have. Don't my crofters and skippers and women give me grief enough? Do stay, my lord, do stay."

"A month, at most," Hadding guessed. "Meanwhile, of course, send word to Eirik that I live. Those men of mine who can't wait to get home can ride in that boat, but I think most will decide they too would rather first regain their health. Also, send a boat around Scania to tell my war fleet. If it has not set sail because the Swedes arrived, or because everybody gave up hope of me, one of those ships can come fetch us. Otherwise I will take your offer of passage."

"Good, good. It shall be done. If it happens my knorr is back by then, maybe you'd like to go in her. She's a sweet wave-walloper." Neither said what both understood, that Hadding's gifts from home would more than make up whatever this cost Bruni, as well as the chieftain thereafter having the king's friendship. Anyhow, he was happy to have these guests for their own sakes.

So did Hadding and his warriors come to a snug haven. That their stay ended badly was no doing of their host's.

As the time ran into weeks, some of them won wholly to wellness faster than others, Hadding foremost. These men grew ever more restless. They found the dwellings here rude and poorly furnished, the fare middling tasty at best, and each day the same as the last. They remembered the halls of home, broad and bright, the fat meat and finely milled bread and well-brewed drink, men richly clad and merry, skalds saying forth staves that surged in the blood, ever-changing visitors with new tales to tell from abroad. They remembered fields tawny at harvest, greenwoods, horses and hounds, the graves of their forebears. They remembered women who were not grubby and did not smell of fish but were clean and fair and could speak of more than a narrow everyday. They remembered children.

"I was mistaken, staying when I could have gone in the messenger boat," grumbled Gunnar to Hadding. "How many more years must we sit and yawn?"

"We've friends who still ought to rest. I'll not forsake them," answered the king. "Besides, these folk can ill spare the boats we'd need, even for that short crossing. Nor would it be fitting for me to come in so little and shabby a craft, when I could have better. We'll wait for a ship, either Bruni's or one of ours. It cannot be long now."

"Here sun and stars cross the sky on feet shod with lead."

"Well, I own to feeling penned too. Let those of us who wish make a trip. I hear of good hunting and hook-fishing northward, where a brook runs down to the sea and woods stand along it clear to its mouth."

That thought gave cheer. Half a dozen warriors busked themselves and strode off one morning behind the king. Sunshine poured over them. They followed the shore for two days and came to the spot he had in mind. There they made camp, meaning to stay a short while.

This was half a mile inland, beside a freshwater spring. Tide-brackish, the stream rustled among tall beeches and gnarly oaks. Sunlight speckled the shadows beneath them. Between their trunks flashed a gleam off the sea. The clear weather had gone hot, drawing up a smell of herbs to liven the brooding air.

The night did not cool much. After sunrise the heat waxed worse. Men sat as listless as the drooping leaves. The brook made the only sound except for a thin shrilling of mosquitoes. When a dove began to coo off in the woodland deeps it seemed like mockery.

At length Hadding rose. "I'm stifling," he said. "Who'll come along down to the strand?"

Nobody wanted to do that, or anything else other than sit and bake. Gunnar and young Svein swapped a look. Unspeaking, they hung swords at hip and took their spears. Safe though the place seemed, they were housecarles of their lords. Their eyes told the rest that they awaited some return for this at some later time.

The three walked off still wordless. At the outflow they left the shade for a hard, cloudless heaven. The tide was low but shingle lay dry and gray to the water's edge, nor did the strewn yellow-brown kelp shine wet. The sea barely lapped against the land. Light flew back off it, ruthlessly bright. No birds soared above.

"I'm for a swim," Hadding said. "What of you?"

"I'll wait under the trees yonder," said Gunnar. Svein nodded.

"As you like." Hadding undressed. From the heap of his clothes he took belt and sheath knife. It was merely wont, in this burning emptiness. No man willingly went anywhere unarmed.

The cobbles were hot below unshod feet. He hurried across them to the water. The bottom sloped slowly. He pushed onward, enjoying the work, until he could jump loose and strike out. Amidst the stillness, every splash rang loud.

The thrusting gladdened his thews, the cool sliding thrilled around his skin, salt kissed his lips. Ducking under, he swam through amber. On he frolicked and on.

He was well offshore when something broached a ways off. The whoosh of it caught his heed. Dazzled, he squinted at a big shape. Was it a seal? He had romped with seals before now, in waters where they had not yet learned fear of man. Eager for anything new, he drew closer.

The thing rested quietly. It was a beast. His heart leaped. A beast like nothing he had ever seen or heard of. Seal size it was, with flippers, but a long flat tail trailed it. Long also was the neck, maned like a horse's. The head was long too, and narrow, with great golden eyes. The hide shimmered in soft rainbow hues, as does the inner shell of an oyster. Very fair to behold was the beast, and very strange.

It turned its head toward him but lay afloat, unafraid.

What a catch! Men would wonder at it, and speak of it, and ever afterward remember the hunter who brought it home.

The king drew his knife. Swimming with his legs and left arm, he closed in.

He laid that left hand on the beast's neck, as he had laid it on the necks of deer he had stalked. The mane felt soft, the flesh warm. His nostrils drank a smell like the smell of clover when bees hum through it harvesting.

He stabbed.

The beast did not scream. The sound it made might have come from a harp struck by an angry skald. Though blood sprang red out onto the water, the head swung about and jaws gaped at Hadding's shoulder. The teeth within were sharp.

He fended the bite off with his free arm. He wrapped his legs about the body and clung tight. His knife slashed.

The beast dove. Hadding caught his breath barely in time. Down into green depths they went, while his blade sought the life of his quarry. The sandy bottom rippled in his sight. He scraped across it. Still he struck. Blood streamed like snakes from every wound. Here below it looked black.

The beast threshed back upward. It broke through and sang its anguish to the cloudless, windless sky. Hadding gulped air. Again he cut, and again.

The beast sighed. The maned neck slumped, the tail drooped. Hanging on, Hadding felt its life drain away.

It did not sink, as he had feared it might. He and it rocked together in the stained waters.

Letting go, sheathing his knife, "Ho-ah!" he bawled into silence. "Hai-saa-saa! Victory!"

Shore was well away. This was a heavy freight to tow. But he could rest on it when he needed to. Still full of battle strength, he set forth.

Svein came to him, then Gunnar. They had seen the fight. Straightway they stripped themselves and plunged in. "You worked too fast for us, lord," panted Svein.

"Well, let's see how fast you can work for me," laughed Hadding.

So the warriors brought his catch ashore and, when they were dried and clad, bore it back to camp. The sight pulled men out of their laziness. They cried aloud, they crowded close to touch and pluck. The rainbow sheen was gone from the beast's hide. It lay there dulled, in a heap, mouth open and dry, eyes open and dim. Yet it was a wonder.

Hadding knew better than to boast overmuch. "It gave me a bit of trouble," he said. "But now we'll find out how its flesh tastes, and maybe somebody back in the thorp can tell us what kind of thing this is. Surely it's unknown to me."

"And you have seen more that is eldritch than most men," breathed Arnulf.

The air was even cooling as the sun went low.

After a while, though, Hadding got a wish to be by himself. More and more he felt that his men were jabbering like

magpies, and he wearied of it. More and more did the sight
of the dead beast strike him not as splendid but as sad. He
could not say why. He thought he would think about it. "I'm
going for a stroll," he told them. "No, stay here, all of you.
Make ready the meat. I'm not going far and I'll be back soon."

He walked off under the trees. No brush hampered him.
Light slanted from the west in among boles and boughs. Again
he heard doves, but now it was as if they were sobbing.

He came around a thicket. There stood a woman.

As tall as him she was, slender, a leaf-green gown falling
from her shoulders to silvery shoes. A gold ring around her
brows and rings around her arms bore the shape of snakes that
curl and bite their own tails. Her skin had the blue-shadowy
whiteness of snow, her lips were blood red, the hair that tumbled down her back was like a raven's wing. In a thinly and
finely formed face the eyes glowed huge, yellow hawk eyes. She
lifted a hand. Hadding jarred to a halt.

She spoke. In camp, too, they heard that steely music.

> Sailing the sea or seeking the land,
> Henceforth you have the hate of the elves,
> And wend where you will, the worst shall befall you
> Always on earth and also on shipboard,
> Where foul winds follow your frozen sail.
> Nor shall you find shelter ashore below roofs.
> Weather brings woe, laying waste altogether
> The holdings of him who houses you,
> Till, given no guesting, you gang alone.
> Anger you earned, all ills must you suffer.
> He was a high one, in the hide of a beast
> Decked for this day. To death you brought him,
> The goodly godling. Now go to your ship.
> The winds are wild that wait for you.
> Her hull they will harry, their howls will raise,

> *To crush your craft, the crashing waves,*
> *Till you rue the wrong you wrought on the elves*
> *And give to their god a gild of blood.*

Like a mist in the morning, she was gone from before him. He stood there alone at sunset.

XVII

They did not eat of the slain one. After a sleepless night they buried it as well as they could and made what poor offerings at the grave they were able. Saying little, they started back to the thorp.

Hadding broke the stillness when they camped. "If the land-wights are angry," he said, "it is at me."

"However that may be," growled Arnulf, "I'll stand by my lord."

Gunnar shrugged. "I may as well too," he said. "I helped bring the thing in."

A laugh of sorts went among the men. That night they slept better. But then, they were utterly tired.

In the morning they walked on. Clouds piled higher above the trees to the left. Lightning played in their blue-black hollows. Warmth fled before a rising wind. It skirled ever louder. It tossed the woodland crowns and roared in them. A chop on the sea became whitecaps.

Wrack flew overhead like smoke. The sunlight flickering between was the hue of brass. Clouds thickened and the sun was lost. Lightning whitened the sky. Thunder rolled, unseen wheels.

The rain burst, hurled before the wind, a waterfall that

blinded and lashed. Lightning blazed through its murk. Every fluttering leaf or flattened lingbush stood stark in sight. Then darkness clapped down until the next flash. Thunder crashed unending.

Hail came, great stones that drew blood where they hit a man. They skittered over the ground and lay there to whiten it. The sea ramped, half-hidden by scud blown off billows.

Hadding and his men took what shelter they could find below trees. The storm seemed to go on forever. Yet it ended as quickly as it had begun. Clouds broke. Wind sank. A westering sun threw fires across waves that still rushed and rumbled. Drenched, half-frozen, the men trudged on over sodden earth. Grass and shrubs beaten to death squelped underfoot.

"We still have friends aloft," said Hadding once. "Thor's hammer never struck near us." But nobody smiled.

They reached the thorp shortly before dark. Three ships lay at the wharf. It being small, they had had to be tethered alongside one another, with bumpers between. "Why, those are ours!" Hadding cried. "They must have come while we were gone. You'll soon be home, lads."

As spent and shivering as they were, the warriors said nothing to that either. They plodded on toward the stockade. Its sharpened logs loomed before them, black against the sky, like a jawful of teeth.

Bruni met them in his house. Newly back from riding around his acres, he was himself muddy and weary. "We've lost this year's crops," he said. "Lightning burned three garths, too, with everything they had stored. I don't yet know how much livestock is dead. This will be a lean winter."

"I'll send food from Denmark," Hadding plighted. "Meanwhile, what of my ships?"

"I've housed their crews here and there amongst us," Bruni answered. "I'll send now after the skippers. They told me the rest went home after getting your word from my boat, for

you'd have no more need of them this season. Those that got
to Zealand before the blow, well, they should be safe. Those
whose owners live farther off, who knows?"

Hadding nodded. Every craft had been badly under-
manned.

"And I'm afraid for our fishers," Bruni went on. "None has
yet come back. All of mine were out, and most others from
hereabouts." He shook himself. "Well, storms do scatter
boats. If they aren't wrecked, they straggle home. I'll keep my
hopes while I may. Now let's get bathed and get drunk."

Hadding thought upon what the elven woman had threat-
ened for whomever took him in. He said nothing of it that
eventide, nor did those who had gone with him. But it was not
a merry gathering in Bruni's house.

No fishers had made haven by morning. In all honor,
Hadding must then tell his host the tale. "Mishap," said the
chieftain after a silence. "You couldn't have known. I'd have
done the same. And maybe that was only a troll making fun
with you."

"Maybe," answered Hadding, staring beyond him. "But
you and yours, who gave us hospitality, have had a sudden,
sore loss. I'll be off today, while the weather holds fair."

"That's wise," agreed Bruni. Hadding forgave him his
haste.

Eyjolf, who had stayed in the thorp, drew the king aside.
"I'll make my way overland to Bralund," he said.

"You might fare with better luck that way," said Hadding.

Eyjolf looked him in the eyes. "I'll sail with you if I can
be of any use."

"Which you hardly can. No, do you take the bear's road
while I take the swan's. I'll send guards along to keep you
safe."

"They yearn for their homes, lord."

Hadding smiled bleakly. "I think most of them will be glad to give you this help and go roundabout home."

So the king and the rest of his men split themselves among the three crews, raised masts, undid mooring lines, and left Helsingland. A westerly wind blew loud and strong, but not too foul for poling out sails and tacking. Clouds flew ragged. The sea was a herd of white-maned horses, bucking and trampling. Still, it did not seem dangerous and the passage was merely across the strait, south-southwest to Zealand. They ought to make landfall sometime tomorrow.

Folk stood ashore looking after them until they were gone over the rim of sight—and belike longer, hoping to see a fisher craft.

Clouds smoked up. Soon they had swallowed the sun. The wind stiffened further. The gurly waters ran higher and wilder. Ships rolled, pitched, yawed. Their timbers creaked loud enough to hear through the brawling and whistling around. Waves sheeted over rails and sloshed in hulls. Men bailed hard. The cold numbed their hands.

"I fear we'll get a gale, or worse," shouted Hadding's skipper, as he must to be heard.

"I know we will," answered the king. "Reef sail."

The wind mounted. Spindrift sleeted blinding and bitter. It stung where it struck. The seas were huge and going white. Their rolling began to shock as heavily as thunder.

"Cast out a sea anchor and strike sail," Hadding bade. He took the helm, for whatever good that oar might do. If the ship did not keep bow-on to the waves, she would founder.

Night fell. Maybe it was as well to fumble blind with the bailing buckets. Else crews might see the drow go by in his half a boat and know they were fey.

Sunrise did not lighten the world much. Wind raved, sea ramped. When Hadding squinted through the scud, he spied another of the ships. She reeled as helpless as his. He braced legs the harder and kept his post. Once in a while somebody brought him a draught of ale or a bite to eat.

Slowly through an unknown length of time, a deeper gloom showed forth ahead. Dumb with chill and weariness, they watched it become a shore where breakers burst white. Even through the wind, the rage of that surf reached them.

"Sea room!" Hadding yelled. "We're being driven aground! Claw off!"

The knorr had eight oars, two pair forward, two aft. They were only meant to move her about in narrow spaces or a dead calm. The men who now took them were ready to drop. The skipper ordered shortened sail to help. A flaw of wind caught hold of it as it rose. Sheets tore loose from hands. The yard slewed about, the sail flapped thunderously, the lee rail went under. One of the two men at the windlass had the wit to draw knife and cut the walrus-hide halyard. An end whipped back. It left his face a mask of blood. The yard fell half overboard. The weight of the sail dragged that side deeper. Men scrambled to hew it free. Waves broke over them. Two were swept away.

Now the craft was awash, hopelessly adrift. Hadding left the little afterdeck and waded through the hull toward those of his crew and guard who lived. "The ship is lost," he cried through the wind and crashing waters. "Chop off what wood you can to cling to!"

He caught a glimpse of the second knorr, dismasted, already half broken up. His own mast still stood firm in its partner. Taking an ax, he cut it down. Under his bidding, men used the stays to ease its fall and bring it alongside. "Bind yourselves to that pole," he told them. He stayed aboard, helping them off so that only one was borne away, until everybody had something or other to keep afloat with.

By then they were in the shoals. Breaker after breaker

dashed over them. The ship grounded. The surf got to work pounding her apart. Hadding squirmed free. The mast had gone elsewhere and he had found no piece of timber big enough to uphold him. The water hauled him below. Cast high again, he snatched a breath before the undertow took him back. Husbanding what strength he had, he worked his way inch by inch toward land.

At last he could stand, nose out of water except when it rushed over his head. Sometimes that knocked him off his feet. He recovered and slogged on. After a while he was wading more or less steadily. Soon he could fall down into stiff sea-grass and gasp.

The mast drifted in. It had dashed the brains from one of those tied to it. Another had drowned. The rest cut free and won ashore. A few more arrived, clinging to their bits of flotsam. Three were from the second ship. Nobody ever heard anything of the third. In all, Hadding gathered ten around him.

They slumped together, hungry, thirsty, chilled, drenched, battered, utterly worn out. "This many of us live," said Svein. "It could be worse."

"It will be," said Gunnar.

"You're right, unless we get to shelter," growled Egil. "Up off your lazy butts!"

Hadding's mouth twitched. "All that soaking hasn't softened you, old fellow," he murmured. He dragged himself to his feet. "Come along, then."

They stumbled after him through the wind. Sunset must be nigh, for the streaming skies were growing blacker still. Beyond the grass was a stretch of woodland. Trees tossed and moaned. Some had boughs ripped off. Some lay fallen, splintered. Spume hazed the surf where it boomed.

"Hadn't we better make brushwood huts while light abides?" asked Arnulf.

"I see cattle dung," Hadding told them. "Folk cannot be far off."

A clearing notched the shaw. As they rounded the edge of this, they saw a clump of buildings at the middle. Boats lay moored in a creek. The dwellers must be fishers who did some farming. They might or might not be friendly to strangers. The castways had no weapons left except a few sheath knives and whatever scraps of wood they had taken along for clubs.

Nonetheless Hadding limped ahead of them. Three houses and a shed walled a small yard. Stoutly built of earth and drift-wood, with sod roofs, they might well make vikings think them not worth attacking for whatever meager goods were inside. The king knocked on the first door he came to.

It creaked a little ways open. A man peered out. In the murk behind him stood at least two more, shadowy, spear and ax in hand. "We are wrecked sailors," Hadding said beneath the storm. "The gods think well of hospitable folk."

"Um, you look wretched enough," grunted the house-holder. "Wait a bit. Thormund, rouse the neighbors."

"You're wise to be wary of us," Hadding said, "but you'll see it's not needful. We wish no fight with anybody." He did not add that they would most likely lose it. There was no sense in tempting.

Men came armed, roughly clad, from the other houses. Before long they understood that the newcomers spoke truth. Even so, they split the guests among themselves—though that was also because of crowding. Each family here had children, oldsters, and unwedded kin living with it.

Hadding knew this kind of lodging from aforetime, a single room with beasts stalled at one end. It was full of their warmth and smells. A peat fire guttered on a hearthstone. Rushes decked a clay floor. There he must sleep, for lack of anything better. First the women hung his clothes to dry and lent him a blanket to wrap around himself. They brought him

bread, curds, and sour beer, the best they had when they themselves had already cooked and supped. His friends they treated
likewise.

The newcomers gave their names but said no more about
their sorrows. The dwellers did not guess that this Hadding
might be the king. "You are a good man, Kari," he said to the
householder. "Tomorrow we must talk. You stand to gain by
helping me."

"Tomorrow," answered the fisher. "Now let's sleep."

All stretched out and were quickly lost to awareness. The
banked fire glowed dim. Outside, the wind shrieked.

Louder it blew and louder.

Doors and shutters rattled. Sand and spray flung from the
strand hissed around walls.

Of a sudden, a hinge gave way. The door banged wildly,
tore loose, and whirled off through the night. The storm burst
in. Rafters broke asunder. Half the roof fell down.

Folk had sprung awake. The wind tore cries from lips before ears could catch them. Lightless, men groped at the wreckage. It had buried two of Hadding's warriors, with three of
Kari's children, his old father, and his kine.

This was not reckoned up till morning, when folk crept
from the unharmed houses in which they had found lee but
slept no further. The weather had raged itself out. Though seas
still ran high, sunlight speared past clouds onto a land lying
wet and death-quiet.

"I think we had best begone," said Hadding flatly. "Give
us some food to take along, and in a while you'll hear from
me again."

Kari looked elsewhere. "I know not if we want to," he
mumbled. "This stay of yours was less lucky for us than you
foretold."

However, the dwellers did hand something over from their
stores. They could have killed these worn-out wanderers, and

maybe they would have if they had heard the full tale. But it was easier to get rid of them.

Hadding led his handful off. They had learned that here was the northwestern end of Zealand. If he kept the water on his left he would come to the Sound and thus to the island where Haven was and his hall nearby. But they were in no shape to go fast. Nor could they withstand any foe. It was well that he had scoured robbers from the land—not that he now bore much worth robbing.

The day warmed. Where a streamlet trickled through a heath, they lay down and slumbered.

Afterward they plodded onward. Toward evening they came into cropland and found a hamlet. A yeoman there knew King Hadding by sight. Folk shouted when they heard that he lived. They made the best meal they could. Meanwhile they offered ale, a bathhouse, fresh clothes, weapons, horses, housing.

That night fire broke loose. Nobody afterward knew how. One seldom did. A lamp knocked over, an ember unwittingly kicked, even a stray spark could touch it off. Great homes had cookhouses standing apart from them to lessen the likelihood. Few smallholders could afford that. This blaze took hold of a thatch roof. A stiff breeze had arisen to fan and spread it. Everybody got out alive, but the hamlet burned to the ground.

"It seems we bring bad luck wherever we go," said Egil as the flames crackled. Shadows deepened the furrows in his face.

"No," answered Hadding. "I do. But follow me yet a while."

They walked on. Thenceforward they begged their bread along the way, without naming themselves, and spent their nights in the open.

When the high gables of his hall rose in sight, Hadding ordered, "Go you in. Bring me a tent and whatever else I need. I will house in this field."

The men obeyed. Eirik Jarl was quick to rally around. Before long Hadding was on the road with a goodly troop.

Never did he enter a home. Always battling wild weather, he fared about Denmark, among the islands, over them, across northern Jutland, wherever he had holdings. From these he chose the finest coal-black cattle that grazed them. Over land and water were they brought, and herded up through Scania, while still he gathered more.

In Bralund was a grove hallowed to Freyr. Within it stood the image of the god, carved man-sized, painted and gilded. Astride a golden boar, he brandished his yard, as long as his arm, for begetting, growth, and ongoing life.

"What will you here?" asked Eyjolf.

"What I must," said Hadding.

"How do you know what that is?"

"Maybe from a forgotten dream. I only know that I know."

Word went around. From all over the shire, and farther, men came. They set up their booths as if for a Thing; but when the time fell, they stood hushed.

Fires burned before the god. Men led the black kine forth, one by one. Some grew frightened and struggled, bawling, but those were strong hands on the ropes. As each drew nigh, Eyjolf stunned it with a hammer and Hadding cut its throat. Blood gushed into bowls. Wisemen dipped switches carved with runes and sprinkled the onlookers. Yeomen standing by hauled the carcasses off, hacked meat from bones, and threw it into the seething kettles. Deep voices chanted olden staves.

Then at last other men rolled casks of ale and mead forward. The feast began. It was mighty and mirthful. Hadding smiled through the blood that reddened him. He had lifted the evil spell. That night he slept under Eyjolf's roof. Later he made his friend the jarl of all Scania.

He had sent gold and silver to those who suffered because
of him, the lawful amends for every loss and death with a gift
laid thereto. More could a king not do. The Danes spoke well
of him again.

Each year after this he gave black cattle to Freyr. The wont
spread beyond Denmark and long outlived him.

XVIII

After so much ill hap, Hadding could not soon renew
his war in Svithjod. He stayed home the following
year. There was enough to do, faring about on the
king's work and seeing to his own holdings. Yet he grew ever
more restless.

Thus he was twice glad to greet Ivar Bardsson in the springtime after that. He always made wayfarers welcome and listened closely to what they told of their homelands and travels.

Ivar was a Norseman of the Nidering kingdom, some five
hundred miles by sea from the Skagerrak, whence it was a
good two hundred more to Haven. Ships from there seldom
called in Denmark. It was a tricky way to go, past countless
fjords and holms where vikings often lurked. Norway had no
one strong king to put them down. Svipdag had brought together a few small lands in the south but then had gone into
Svithjod. There his sons and grandsons had been ever since.
Their Norse shires still paid them scot, but had otherwise
fallen away from them in all but name. Now thinking of themselves as Swedes, they cared little about yonder poor acres.

Hence goods from farther north mostly went hand to
hand, which made them costly in the Danish marts. Nonetheless, from time to time a bold seaman dared the voyage. His

cargo of walrus hides and ivory, narwhal tusks, furs, and the like would bring him a rich haul of amber, gold, thralls, Southland glass and wine and silk, and other wares that flowed to the Baltic trader towns. Ivar's knorr, uncommonly big, bore enough of a well-armed crew that few rovers would care to attack. Besides, they were unlikely to spy her. A skilled reader of sun, moon, stars, and waters, he kept well out to sea. Only weather had given him trouble.

This time he brought news of something worse than robbers.

Coming down through the Sound, he stopped off at Haven. He was bound for Gotland but thought to rest here a short while and maybe do a little business. When he heard the king was at the hall nearby, he took a few of his men and ferried across from the island to pay a call. Hadding gave him the guest-seat of honor and bade the whole band stay the night, or as much longer as they wished. Those two had met before and hit it off well.

Only one hearth fire flamed and smoked, for doors and windows stood open to mild air. Afternoon sunlight streamed in, bright on hangings and metal, soft on graven pillars and wainscots. The noise of household and thorp came low, voices, feet, hoofs, wheel-creak, a hammer ringing on an anvil. Well-born women brought beakers of mead to the warriors and sailors on the benches. Beside Hadding sat Gyda, his leman when he was hereabouts, a handsome young woman. Her braids fell fair over red apron panels and pleated white gown; rings on her arms, brooches at her shoulders were of heavy silver. The king was likewise richly clad, in brocaded tunic, blue linen breeks, kidskin cross-garters, and buckskin shoes. A headband with gripping beasts woven into the wool circled his own yellow locks. Others sat quietly and listened while he talked with the skipper.

"Well," he asked after a while, "how go things in Niderland?"

Ivar frowned. He was a lean, sharp-faced man with brown hair and beard turning gray. His sea-worn wadmal and leather were offset by a gold chain about his neck, from which hung a small silver hammer. "Not well, lord," he answered. "Woe is upon us. The shame to come will be worse."

Hadding straightened. "Say on!"

Ivar had foreseen he must, and readied his words beforehand. "You may know that a jotun hight Jarnskegg has long dwelt in the wild uplands of the Dofra Fell. That's three or more days' stiff trek from the great fjord. Hardly anyone lives around there, and they lowly folk with naught worth reaving. So we formerly had little or no trouble with him. He was hardly ever even seen, striding along a ridge against the sky or in the pine gloom of some deep dale."

Hadding nodded. "Yes, I've heard tell of such a one." He did not add that that had been at his fosterers'. Vagnhöfdi had never met Jarnskegg, only gotten word of him. Those few giants who abode in Midgard wanted aloneness.

"But I don't suppose you know about King Haakon's daughter, Ragnhild," Ivar said. "She's a young woman now, very fair to behold, but on the reckless and stubborn side. Always she loved the mountains and sought to them. Her father let her. She's his only living girl-child and he cannot easily say her nay. Of course, he sent guardsmen along, as well as her serving maids.

"Last year, up in those wilds, it befell that Jarnskegg came upon her. She stiffened with horror at the sight of him, but he was smitten with her, it seems, unless this was a whim of his. I should think he might well go a bit mad after so many human lifetimes by himself. Be that as it may, he bawled at her to come with him. Her following drew close around her, weapons aloft. Maybe they were too many for him, maybe not.

He's not in any way a warlock, as I've heard some giants are. What he growled was that he didn't want a fight in which she might be hurt, but that she would be hearing more from him. Then he stalked wrathfully off toward the heights.

"A while after this he found a cowherd grazing his kine. He told the man to bear word to the king for him. If not, he would kill the beasts and burn the little homestead. Of course the man obeyed. For token he brought a wisent's skull, roughly set with quartz rocks in the eye sockets, which Jarnskegg gave him to give Haakon. The word was that the giant wanted Ragnhild. If he got her, he would fight for the king whenever need arose."

"That in itself shows he's not quite right in the head," murmured Hadding, remembering Vagnhöfdi.

"If he was refused, he would lay the kingdom waste," Ivar went on. "As you'd guess, lord, no father would willingly give a daughter to so foul a being. Haakon sent the cowherd back with that answer, and guards to keep him from suffering what bearers of bad tidings ofttimes suffer. Jarnskegg heard him out and said King Haakon might change his mind later. Then he returned to the wilderness.

"Soon he began striking out at men. The cowherd was the first to die, his head crushed with one blow after the guards went home. Jarnskegg then raided throughout the uplands. The few men in a lonely steading cannot hold him off. He's murdered them and their families. Those who ran off and hid, he's searched out to kill.

"Moreover, he's come into the foothills and at last the lowlands. Again and again has he burst from the night to batter down gates and doors, slay folk and herds, set houses afire. Sometimes more strength has been mustered against him than he could readily deal with. Then he's needed only to withdraw, faster than they could give chase. But he's bound to smite again soon, elsewhere. Everybody lives in dread of him,

whether he's come near them or not. Now and then he'll shout
at them that whenever King Haakon wishes for an end to this,
he has but to send Ragnhild alone to the Troll's Hood for him
to claim.

"Of course the king's ordered troops out to do away with
him. Each time they've blundered uselessly around in the
mountains. Clear it is, Jarnskegg's known where they were, and
kens that wilderness better than any man. He can easily keep
from them till they quit. He might well slip off while they're
searching and find yet another helpless home to smash."

"Has not the king called on the gods?" asked Hadding.

"Indeed he has, again and again, with mighty offerings,"
Ivar said. "Nothing has come of it. No wizard, no spaewife,
no dream has been able to tell anybody why Thor won't make
an end of this monster."

Hadding's look went far away. Men barely heard his voice:
"I'm no soothsayer myself, but what I've seen in my life whis-
pers to me that sometimes the gods themselves must go by
strange roads toward ends that are unknown to men."

Ivar scowled. "However that may be, lord," he said, "folk
mutter that somehow the king has angered the high ones. They
say more loudly that he has no right to squander them for the
sake of one willful girl. When I left, things were looking hopeless. Everywhere I was hearing that the king ought to yield her
up and be done. Else they'd overthrow him and send her off
to the giant. Thus far that was only talk. But let their grief grow
much greater, and I think we will have an uprising."

Hadding stroked his beard. "Hm," he answered after a silence in which the fire crackled loud. "What has the woman
said to all this?"

"I've heard different things about that as time went by,"
Ivar told him. "It's understandable. There must be a storm in
her, blowing now this way, now that. At first she was as
haughty as her father. Never would they crawl before a stink-

ing huge hog. Later, when the landwasting had run for months, she swore she'd kill herself rather than lie with him. But—I know not from my own ears, but they say that lately she thinks if she went to hell instead of to him, Jarnskegg's rage would be the worse. I wonder if she hasn't begun to hope she can find a way to kill him in his sleep, once they are together."

"I doubt she could," said Hadding grimly. "I know his breed."

"But why would he lust after her?" blurted the housecarle Svein. "A giant and she—" He broke off, flushing. He was young.

"He may split her in twain the first time, do you mean?" said Gunnar. "Maybe he hasn't thought of that, or maybe he doesn't care after hundreds of years with nothing better than elk cows, or maybe he'd enjoy it."

Arnulf snickered. "Or maybe he's not so well hung for his size."

"Or he might make her please him in other ways," said old Egil. He spat. "Yes, she's better off dead."

Hadding lifted a hand. "Be still," he bade them. "This is a grave matter. More than kingly honor is at stake. Kingship itself may be. We cannot let the harm done to a goodly folk like the Niderings go unavenged. Otherwise lawlessness will spread like wildfire, along with trollery and everything else unhuman. Could this be why the gods hold back their help?"

He leaned forward. "Ivar," he asked, "how much longer do you think Haakon will hold out?"

"I know not, lord," said the Norseman. "He's a brave and proud one, him. And then there's his love for the daughter. She's very fair and winsome. But I fear I've seen her for the last time."

"Maybe not," said Hadding low. "Maybe not. Stay a few days while we speak further."

"We need to reach Gotland in time for the mart, lord."

"Ha, if I keep you from that, I'll make it up to you. Bide here. It will be good guesting."

Eagerness flickered in Ivar's eyes. He had not stopped at Haven without unspoken hopes of his own. Being a trader, he kept his face blank and said merely, "As the king wills."

Hadding lifted his beaker. "Come, let's drink, let's be merry," he cried. "Hard thinking can wait till tomorrow."

"All at once you're ashiver," his leman, Gyda, whispered to him.

He laughed. "Well, at last I've something to be impatient about."

However, mirthful though he was for the rest of that day and evening, he beckoned men one by one to the high seat and talked softly, earnestly with them—men of weight and wisdom. In the morning he sent messengers off, bidding some more who had not been there to come at once. These messengers went no farther than two days' hard ride. Meanwhile he was much alone with Ivar and with the redegivers he had called upon earlier.

On the third night, as they lay in their shutbed, Gyda said to him, "You are going to Norway, are you not?"

"What makes you think that?" he asked.

"I have come to know you as well as anybody does, though that is not very much," she sighed in the darkness. "You will be leaving soon, too. If you felt no need of haste, you'd have sent for chieftains from more widely around, to get everything battened down here at home."

He chuckled and laid an arm around the warmth of her. "You're shrewd, my love."

She stiffened. "Why are you bound off? What is this to you?"

"Well," he answered slowly, "as I said before, it's wrong that a high-born maiden fall into the grasp of a filthy unbeast that wins her by running wild through her father's land. If such a tale got around, it'd hearten too many outlaws. Best the thing never happen."

"You've more in mind than that."

"True. The Niderings are the strongest folk in Norway. It would be helpful to have bonds with them, loosely though Uffi holds the southern shires. He'd think twice about attacking us."

"Bonds of wedlock? The Norsemen call Ragnhild comely." Hadding laughed. "I've never seen her myself."

"But she is a king's daughter. After you are dead, the Danes would more likely hail a son of yours by her than any of the by-blow you've got scattered around among them."

"I ought to look beyond my own lifetime, yes. A fight between sons of mine could wreck everything I've wrought." Hadding laughed again. "But you stray from what we know or can foresee. All I know tonight is that you are shapely and you are here." He drew her to him. The straw mattress rustled beneath them. Her unbound hair smelled summery. "Give me a glad send-off."

"Oh, I will that." She swallowed hard. "And a glad welcome home, if you come back. If you want it." Her mouth found his, there in the narrow and lightless shutbed.

A few days later, Hadding was on his way.

He had indeed not taken time to put matters fully in order. After hasty talks with the Zealand chieftains, he left Eirik Jarl to steer the kingdom. He had bought Ivar Bardsson's cargo for more than the traders could have gotten on Gotland. They sailed with him, to be his guides and helpers. The freight they now bore was horses.

Otherwise he had but one ship. He could not have raised

a war-host fast, if at all. Anyhow, the giant would have kept clear of it, to wreak havoc elsewhere. Hadding alone, with his knowledge of wilderness and of jotun ways, had any hope of dealing with Jarnskegg.

The craft was his darling, the *Firedrake*, a longship of thirty oars. A crew of housecarles hung their shields from the bulwarks. She danced on the Sound, red and black and golden-trimmed. Mast up, the brightly striped sail caught wind. Not until he was well at sea would Hadding break out the dragon head and set it on the stempost. He had no wish to anger the land-wights of home. But already the ship leaped forward like a wolf at prey. He must keep on a longer tack than needful, not to outrun the knorr. His warriors shouted. They also had been too idle for their liking.

Gyda stood on the wharf, in front of everybody else gathered there, and watched until the hulls were lost to sight.

XIX

When he had passed through the narrows into the great fjord, Hadding did not make for King Haakon's seat at Nidaros. Sailing through the light night, he followed Ivar to a spot on the Bight of Buvik where the skipper dwelt. Trees walled the steading off, and a boat shed meant for the knorr hid *Firedrake*. Ivar told his family and household folk to stay on the grounds. These were guests whose coming should not be noised about. He himself saddled a horse and set forth to Nidaros.

The town was not far. He came back the same day. "I thought the king would lodge you overnight and want to know how you are home again so soon," Hadding said.

"I had no need to visit him, nor would he have had heed to give me," answered Ivar. "Tomorrow Ragnhild goes to the giant. Nidaros seethes with the news. It'll shortly be over the whole kingdom."

Hadding nodded. "They've had some foreboding of it here at your home," he said tautly, for he had talked with them.

"Yes, that happened what I told you could happen, though not quite as ill as it might have been. Chieftains throughout the land called a Thing a short while ago, and yeomen flocked to it. They decided that unless the king gave her up, they would overthrow him and take her there themselves. Anything to make an end of their woe. Some said this would be not only a lawless deed but a luckless one, for the woman would kill herself first, or ask her father to slay her. But others cried that then at least they two would die, whose selfishness had brought on so much death and ruin. They were on hand, though they kept aside and silent.

"Yesterday the meeting passed its award. Then Ragnhild trod before it. No man should call her coward, she told them. She would go, but only if they swore a renewed troth to King Haakon. They shouted it forth. I hear that some wept."

"She has a bold soul," said Hadding. "I feared we'd be too late to do more than avenge her. Now I see she's worth avenging, or, better, saving."

"What if the matter had still been moot?" Ivar asked.

"Why, we've spoken about that, you and I. I'd have tracked the giant down. But it could have been a wearisome task. Instead, he'll come to me."

Ivar gave Hadding a long look. "I wonder if this is altogether happenstance," he murmured. "From all I've heard, your weird is unlike other men's."

The Dane-king shrugged. "I know not what it is, any more than you know yours. Let's get to work. I must start off betimes."

They had in truth talked when their crews camped ashore along the way. Best would be for Hadding to arrive unbeknownst. His undertaking was wildly risky even without Jarnskegg being somehow forewarned. His men would take the longship to the lonely little Tarva islands and bide, except for a few who would go with him. They had come close to blows over who those should be. When he picked them he must take utmost care not to make the rest think that in his eyes they were less doughty. One man of Ivar's who was willing would guide them, Thorfinn Thorgeirsson. He hailed from Dofra Fell and knew the Troll's Hood.

Jarnskegg had long since blared his terms of peace. On that bare height, from which he could scan far and wide, he had heaped wood for a huge and smoky fire. Let a man set it alight. Let Ragnhild wait there by herself, or at most with a serving maid or two. Belike he would see the beacon. If he was off waging his war, he would get the news otherwise and hasten to her.

There was no hope of sending a host to kill him as he drew nigh. Nowhere for miles around could it lie hidden. Jarnskegg was a hunter, with all a hunter's wariness.

Hadding too was a hunter.

He left with his small following as soon as they had packed food and gear. The horses were rather stiff after their time in the knorr, but quickly grew limber. They were the best from his stable at the Soundside hall. He rode them the hardest they could bear, changing gait or halting no oftener than was unforgoable. In the short, wan summer night his band would stop to eat, roll up in their saddle blankets, and sleep. Sunrise found them already again on the road.

At first the way was easy and quick, south down the broad green dale, among ripening grainfields and meadows full of grazing livestock, past farmsteads and hamlets where folk dropped their work to stare at these warriors hurrying by.

Then the land began to climb, steeper and steeper. Woods became mostly birch, with settlement sparse. The riders passed clearings where stood only charred wreckage and bones lay strewn in the grass.

Thorfinn led them onto a narrow track that twisted off westward and upward. The woods thinned out until they fared amidst tussocks, bearberry, moss, and lichen. Streamlets clinked through wastes of scree. Wind whittered chill. Bluegray bulks, streaked with snow, shouldered into heaven. Soon there was no more trail. Thorfinn took his bearings from the peaks he saw.

At the end of four days and nights, he raised an arm and drew rein. "I think this is as far as the others had better go," he told Hadding. "If they stay in yonder cleft, fireless, they should be unseen. You and I have about half a day ahead of us on foot."

"I like this not," growled Gunnar, "cowering like a marmot while my lord fares to battle."

"You knew beforehand you must wait," Hadding answered, "and I know that can be the hardest of tasks."

"If you fall, no housecarle of yours will rest till we've avenged you."

"Well, some should go home to help the next king of Denmark. They'll find fighting aplenty. But settle that among yourselves. Now let me rest."

Hadding lay down and slept. His men kept wakeful, holding a stockade of spears around him.

At dawn he and Thorfinn left them. The Norseman was a good waymate, big, a full ruddy beard reaching nearly to his broad chest, withal long-legged and nimble as a goat.

The faring was harder yet, but they reached the Troll's Hood a little before noon. The peak reared stark, overlooking crags, cliffs, ridges, rock-strewn slopes, stretches of ice, and snow, all lifeless but for mottling lichen, moss in clumps where

stones gave shelter, starveling grass tufts here and there.
Nowhere was it flat, though the top was broad enough to hold
a few great boulders. Today it also held a mound of split
wood, higher than a man's head. Wind went bleak through an
empty heaven. The men felt short of breath.

"I see why the thurs chose this for the tryst," Hadding said.
"Not only could no troop catch him unawares, they'd lack
footing and room to fight."

"How then shall one man?" wondered Thorfinn.

"We've been over that. Let's make my lair."

They had thought about this, using Thorfinn's memories
of the two or three times he had come here. That was years
ago, he a boy, his father a hunter and trapper. The search for
wild reindeer, wolverine, fox, and birds often took them from
one ground to another across these heights. Then it was a mettlesome thing for him to scamper off and scramble onto the
Troll's Hood. It showed him fearless of the beings said to
haunt it. Something like that stayed in one's head.

Two outsize boulders leaned against one another at the rim
of a downslope. Only a crack was between them where they
faced the peak, while behind lay a kind of three-cornered
room some four feet long, with a three-foot opening onto
the mountainside. A man could sit there hidden, unless his
foe climbed up from straight beneath, and scree would
hinder that.

Hadding and Thorfinn set about making it a little better.
The king might have to lurk a while. They took lengths of
wood from the heap and wedged them overhead where they
wouldn't show. To this they tied a leather cloak for a roof of
sorts. A second such cloak covered the damp stones below.
The men chinked the inward opening with pebbles and bits of
turf, taking care that it was nothing anybody would likely
mark, lest a straight-on glance or a stray sun-flash off iron give

Hadding away. They brought in a skin of water, dry food, and blankets they had carried hither.

As they worked, they spied a stirring and a gleam afar, winding over the high waste from the north. Soon Hadding's keen eyes told him it was half a dozen folk. "We're none too early," he said. Thorfinn had taken a roundabout way through the mountains, not to leave spoor for others to see. "Make haste, and keep clear of the skyline." His hopes hung on utter surprise.

They ended their task in time. "Begone," Hadding bade. "Thank you. You shall have the honors you've earned."

"More honor would be for me to fight beside you," the Norseman said.

Hadding sighed. "This too we've been over and over. No more than one man can crouch here, nor does any man but me know what to do. Get well away. You can find a cranny for yourself within earshot, if not sight." He grinned. "Earshot will be a goodly walk! Afterward I'll want your help. Or, if I fall, your service will be to tell that I fought the fight I said I would."

Softly Thorfinn voiced the words of old.

> *Kine die, kinfolk die,*
> *And so at last oneself.*
> *This I know that never dies:*
> *How dead men's deeds are deemed.*

"True," said Hadding. "You'll see to that, good friend. Now farewell for a time."

Thorfinn gulped. "Fare you ever well, lord." He turned and went downhill fast, on the slope away from the oncoming band.

Hadding had already donned his byrnie and whatever else belonged with it, except for the helmet. He crept around the

boulders into the room, wrapped blankets about himself
against the cold, and squatted in shadow. It was almost like one
of those stone chambers said to have been built by giants in
the morning of the world. Folk shunned them. Nothing
haunted this one but his thudding heart.

After a while the newcomers climbed into his sight. They
seemed to be all men, most of them heavily laden. Then as
Hadding peered he saw among them, dressed like them, surely
Ragnhild Haakonsdottir. Skirts were ill suited for this last
part of the upland trek, where even the hardy little Northland
horses could not go. Her long, coppery-red hair was braided
and coiled on a head borne high. Wind flapped her cloak back
to show, in spite of the thick garments beneath, that she was
tall and shapely.

Hadding could not make out their words. He watched a
graybeard warrior speak what must be a last plea, and her
naysay it. Slowly, as if the burden were still on their shoulders,
the men set up a leather tent. They stocked it with food, drink,
blankets, clothes, a stool, and a spear. "No use to her as a
weapon," Hadding muttered, "but maybe of help to her soul."

The woman's hand chopped downward. A man dragged a
fire drill, with block and tinder, from his pack. Hunkered before the balewood, he got it kindled. She walked off and stood
looking northward over the mountains.

Flames hatched. They fledged. Great wings of fire beat red
and yellow. Sparks streamed. Air roared. Smoke stormed upward and upward. The westering sun touched it with gold.

The men gathered before Ragnhild. The oldest drew sword
and raised it. The others did likewise with whatever arms they
bore. The noise of the fire drowned out any speech, but it
looked to Hadding as though they said nothing, their throats
being too full. They lowered their iron, turned about, and left
her standing there.

Hadding waited.

The fire whirled higher and hotter. Ragnhild began to walk around and around it. This brought her close to him as she passed by. He saw that she was fair of hue, with gray eyes, curved nose, firmly held lips, strong chin. Though now and then her fists clenched, she strode unfaltering.

The sun went below the heights. Shadow swept over vastness and pooled in the deeps. The fire guttered low, but must still gleam like a red star across many miles. Wind died away. Air grew swiftly colder. Ragnhild went into her tent. Hadding waited. He kept tautening and loosening his thews, shifting from ham to ham, making any movement he could where he was. Ill would it be if his body stiffened.

A few stars blinked forth, but the sky was blue gray and only the lightest of twilights dwelt below. One could see nearly as far as by day, though clefts and gorges were darkened, cliffs and peaks dim above them. The dying fire growled, spat, hissed.

Ragnhild came back out of the tent. She had not undressed. She stood again with fists knotted, tight and aquiver as a struck harpstring, to stare eastward.

Hadding amidst his boulders heard the noise shortly afterward. Rocks rattled. They slipped aside and downward. Small landslides made a racket like dry waterfalls.

Footsteps sounded, stone-heavy, ever nearer. Breath went stormwind-loud.

Jarnskegg climbed onto the Troll's Hood.

Taller than three men he loomed, broader and thicker than that, a hill murky against heaven. Skins wrapped bearlike hairiness, with a sharp stench. His mane and beard bristled stiff, rusty black, around shelving brows, pocked lump of a nose, mouthful of greenish snags. In his right hand he bore a club, and tucked under his thong-belt was a sax, both made to his bigness.

He stopped and stood agape. Ragnhild held fast, looking up toward eyes hidden in their bony caves.

"Ha!" Jarnskegg's voice grated thunderous. "It is you, then, come to your lover."

Only the embers answered, sparks snapping from their white heart.

The jotun's left hand reached downward. It shook. Nor were his words altogether steady. "We will be happy, you and I. We both belong in the uplands. I will show you wonderful things. I will stamp on your foes. You shall be queen with me, Ragnhild."

Hadding slipped a coif onto his head. Above it he set and fastened his helmet. It was of the closed kind, hiding his face behind an iron plate graven with a wolf's mask. He would need every warding he could have. Shield in hand, he writhed out of the room and around it to the open. Drawing sword, he ran at the giant.

"Faithlessness!" Jarnskegg screamed, as the earth itself might scream.

"No doing of hers!" Hadding shouted. "Get aside, woman!"

The thurs swung his club on high and back down. Hadding slacked the tightness in his left leg. The right pushed him barely fast enough. The club crashed on stones. Flinders flew. Hadding hewed at the arm behind. The iron bit. Blood welled from a gash, more black than red in this dusk.

Jarnskegg howled and swung anew. Again Hadding slipped free, though by inches. He had long since taught himself how to make the lesser use of his lame right foot, but was not as swift as once he had been.

He sprang close in against a calf whose knee was not much below his eyes. He slashed. Jarnskegg stooped. His left hand snatched. Hadding bounced back from it. His sword sliced across the fingers.

He knew of giants that their sheer weight made them slower than men. Most humans knew it not. They had naught to do with such beings. They had heard, or seen, how fast a giant walked. They seldom stopped to think that that was because the stride was long, not quick.

Back and forth the battle went. Ragnhild stood offside as far as she could get without fleeing. Her eyes were wide, her fists held above a bosom that rose and fell.

Hadding ducked and wove, shifted and leaped. When he saw an opening he sprang in and cut. At once he bolted clear. If that club smote, he would die.

Bellowing his wrath, again and again Jarnskegg swung. The fight surged near the low-burnt fire. Hadding skittered along its edge. The heat from the coals laved him.

Suddenly he yelled in the Old Tongue that he had heard when he was a boy, "Maggot from Ymir's rotten flesh, Hel herself shall spurn you!"

Never had the jotun thought to hear from a man words out of Jotunheim. Astounded as much as enraged, he blundered forward, brought down his weapon, and shrieked. Sparks and a last few reborn flames sheeted high. He had stepped in the coalbed. His boot smoked. The bare calf above it seared. The club fell from his grasp. As he lurched back, Hadding lunged after him and struck once more at the other ankle.

Half witless with pain, Jarnskegg nonetheless drew his sax. The crooked blade whistled. It caught Hadding's shield and clove half through. Numbed, the king's fingers lost the handgrip. What was left of the shield thudded to earth.

Jarnskegg came after him. The sax was harder to dodge than the club. Iron met iron. Clumsy though the giant now was, he knocked Hadding's blade aside and nearly tore it loose from the man's hand. Jarnskegg's blow kept going. It laid Hadding's own right calf open to the bone.

Before he could lose much blood, the man darted forward. He slipped under Jarnskegg's wobbly guard and hewed yet again at the blistering right ankle. Already he had cut through boot and flesh. Now the tendon gave way. Jarnskegg tottered and toppled. As he did, he struck out with his fist. It caught Hadding on his shieldless left side. The warrior soared before it and landed on the stones. Ragnhild wailed, less for fear than wrath.

Jarnskegg had dropped his sword. Earth shook when his weight came down. Snarling, he rolled over, laid hands on ground, pushed himself up. On his knees he rocked to make an end of Hadding.

The man rose too. Blood flowed freely from the hurt leg. It made dark spots on torn cloth where the fall had sanded skin off him. He limped straight at the thurs. A hand reached for him. His blade sang. It ripped a gash in the arm from wrist halfway to elbow. Blood poured out. Jarnskegg stared at the flow. That gave time for Hadding to draw nearer. He stepped onto a hairy thigh. Sword hewed at throat. He fell off. The blood of his foe gushed over him.

He had not reached ground when Jarnskegg's hale arm batted. Again Hadding pitched through the air, to crash yards away. There he lay still.

Jarnskegg crumpled. He gasped, horrible hollow wheezes, while the life ran out of him.

Over the wet stones sped Ragnhild. The jotun's eyes tracked her until they rolled back and dimmed. The whole great body went slack. The death-stench rolled forth, chokingly strong.

Ragnhild heeded it not. She knelt by her champion. He breathed. She bent to peer closely through the twilight at the wound in his leg. It was grave but should not be deadly if the bleeding could soon be stopped. For a flicker of time she gazed at the mask of his helmet. Then she threw off her cloak and tunic. She unlaced the shirt beneath and pulled it over her head. With her sheath knife she slashed strips of the fine linen. She hauled the breeks leg up to his knee and began to bind the calf.

Gravel scrunched. She lifted her face. A stranger had come. Big and shaggy, he stared at her. She scrambled back. Her arms crossed over her bare breasts. "Who are you?" she breathed.

"I followed here," said Thorfinn, pointing at Hadding. "He sent me off to wait, but when I heard the fight I could not stay. I see he did what he came to do." He squatted down. "And he lives. You're doing well by him, my lady. Finish the task."

Ragnhild gave herself again to it. Thorfinn watched for a little, then went over to squint at the fallen giant. "Yes, lord, your name will be undying," he said.

"Who is he?" asked Ragnhild. "Who are you?"

Thorfinn scowled. "Maybe best I not tell that here. This is kittle ground, the Troll's Hood, and he newly slain was not human. Who knows what vengeful ghosts are aprowl?"

Ragnhild shuddered but kept at her work. Hadding stirred and groaned. Suddenly she slipped a ring off her right middle finger, a plain gold band, laid it in the wound, and poked it deep. At once she went on binding.

Thorfinn returned. Hadding struggled, as if to sit up. Thorfinn lowered himself and took the helmeted head on his knees. "Are you well, lord?" he asked. "This is me, your guide. The thurs is dead."

"I, yes, I—maybe—" mumbled Hadding. He moved his arms, caught his breath. "Broken ribs, I think."

"And a slashed leg, bruises and scrapes, a knock on the noggin. But you're a tough one. Lie still. When you're more awake we'll begone."

Thorfinn took off his cloak, rolled it up, and very gently laid it beneath Hadding's head. Rising, he met Ragnhild's eyes. She had donned her tunic and stood steadily. "You're the king's daughter, eh?" he said. "Well, tell your father how the best of men saved you from the worst of dooms."

"I will," she answered, "but who is he?"

"I told you, we'd better not say that till we're well away from here. His following is camped half a day's trek hence. It'll take longer than that, of course, the shape he's in, but we'll get there and bring you home."

Ragnhild shook her head. "Thank you, but best I seek my own folk. They were to bide a while, maybe a little nearer than yours. I know the way they've taken. We can bring the hero to them."

"What of his men? If neither he nor I come back, they'll be wild. They'll recklessly seek hither. They're not uplanders. Belike they'll get lost and grope around till they die. He'd never forgive me that."

Ragnhild smiled with tight lips. "It seems you and I must part."

He nodded. "I understand. You don't know what kind of men we are or what we'll do—the more so if our lord dies, as he might. We could be foes of your father, Vikings, or outlaws, nearly as bad as him over there."

"I meant no scorn or fear of you."

Thorfinn chuckled. "I wonder if you have any fear in you to give. And as for scorn, no, I do understand. You have to keep on the safe side. Honor binds us both. I only dislike the thought of you waiting alone till morning, amidst this filth and stink and black witchiness."

"I need not. There's light enough for one who's wont to mountains. If I can be of no more use, I'll set off." Ragnhild took both his big hands in hers. "I leave you with my highest thanks." She knelt, bent low above the helmet, and said, "You have those too, warrior, and all else I can ever offer you."

Before Thorfinn could help her up, she jumped to her feet. He whistled softly. "What a wife you'll make," he murmured. "I hope that'll be for him. Few others are worthy," and he grinned, "or could cope with you."

She smiled again, now fully and gladly, before she sought the tent for clean clothes and a long draught of water. "How fares he now?" she asked when she came out.

"I'll stay till he's more fit," said Thorfinn. "But if you're leaving, best you start, my lady."

"May we meet anew," said Ragnhild.

He watched her go down from the peak and on over the heights until the sight of her faded into the light night.

XX

It was a struggle for Thorfinn to get Hadding down from the peak. What strength the king had regained quickly drained from him. Ragnhild's bindings were soon drenched with blood that oozed out whenever he put weight on that foot. It squelped in the shoe. Though he clenched his jaws, the pain in his ribs at every movement ofttimes made him so faint that he must lie flat for a while. Or maybe that was the aftermath of the blow his head had taken; when Thorfinn took off the helmet, he saw it was dented.

Once past the steepest, trickiest downgate, the Norseman rigged a harness and took Hadding on his back. But no man could go long at this height under such a load. At last he left the other by a streamlet, with some food, and hastened alone to the camp. There he had the housecarles lash spearshafts and saddle clothes together to make a litter. With it they sought back to the king. They found him fevered, witlessly muttering. Two ravens that had been perched on rocks nearby flew off.

So they bore him away, tending him as best they knew how. On the edge of lands where men dwelt, they found a crofter's hut and laid him in that poor shelter. They thought it would be only for the night, but the woman there said she had healing skills. "I know this breed," Thorfinn told the warriors. "I'll believe her. At least she won't likely make him worse."

The woman called herself Gro and said her husband was elsewhere. Those who remembered King Gram's first wife were taken aback. However, the name was a common one, and this bearer of it clearly had nothing to do with the long-dead queen. Sparely clad and housed though she was, something about her made them ask no more. Rather, they went around the neighborhood buying their food, cooked it themselves, and did the work of the little farm.

Meanwhile she brewed herbs for the burning in Hadding's wounds and body. The men heard her sing to him after dark, words they could not follow. After a night, a day, and a night, the fever broke and his mind steadied. He was so weak, though, that he stayed for days more.

It grew harder and harder for his friends to keep him abed. When at length Gro deemed him fit for the road, she warned him to fare easily.

"You shall have rich reward for this," he said.

She smiled. "Send no messengers, for they'd not find me here," she answered. "I need no pay. Once I had a greater reward than any you could give me, for a less lucky outcome to my leeching. Sometimes the token of it shines before dawn. Spoil not my work by heedlessness, and I'll be content."

Indeed the trek onward was slow. However much Hadding chafed, he could not sit a horse or walk for any long span, but must lie again on the litter. Still, each day he was stronger.

Thus they reached Ivar's home. He ferried them out to the isles and their ship. "Say naught of this for now," Hadding bade him. "If the news got out that I am sick in a strange land,

Uffi and others would be swift to make trouble."

"Surely King Haakon would take you in," Ivar said.

"I want to come to him as a fellow king, not a sapless wayfarer."

"You would come as a hero, lord."

"Still, it isn't fitting. Worse, the truth about me would be bound to go abroad, and Denmark would suffer. If nothing else, Uffi could go reaving through Scania. It's not worth that risk."

Hadding sat thoughtful until he went on, "Ivar, you have been a friend to me. If you would be a brother, now help me more. See to it that any word of us that may have gotten out is hushed. See to it, also, that what we need in the way of food and other goods is quietly brought us here. Then sail again south. I'll give you tokens so Eirik Jarl will know I sent you. Bring back treasure such as I will tell you of."

The Norseman agreed, and they fell into close talk. Some days later his knorr stood out to sea. Hadding abode with the housecarles, working to build back his health. That went ever faster.

Meanwhile Ragnhild and her following had returned to Nidaros. Great was the joy and wonder. Folk thought her unknown rescuer could have been an elf, or even a high god. However that might be, surely one who had flown from the bottom of hopelessness back to freedom was born to luck. Also, of course, her father was rich and mighty.

Men had sought Ragnhild's hand before the grief came upon her. She had not wanted any of them, and King Haakon had found mild ways to turn them down. She was, after all, quite young. Now she was fully grown and famous. Sons of chieftains and neighbor kings, and some of those leaders themselves, arrived to woo her.

"It tore my heart when I must yield you up to the thurs," he said to her as they walked alone. "I know not if I would have, had you not told me you chose to go for the sake of our house. Nevermore shall you be betrothed against your will. But we are getting well-born guests, who bring many more with them. They stay on in hopes of you. Quarrels are rising among them. I fear uproar, killing, and all the aftermath, if you do not pick one soon."

"Or none," she said.

"If you take one, the rest will not go away angry. They'll see it's merely that you like him best. But if you tell the whole lot of them nay, then everybody will be wroth. They'll think you feel that not a one is worth having."

"I'll wait a while yet."

"You will take a man soon, won't you? You'd not go barren to your grave."

She nodded. "Him who saved me."

"But you never saw his face. You met only a fellow of his, likewise unknown to you. He has not come forth. How do you know he ever will?"

"I will know him if he does." She looked beyond the fields and the fjord. "No, when he does."

A few days later Hadding entered the harbor.

Folk cried out when they saw his ship draw nigh. Ragnhild was among those who sought higher ground from which to watch. It was a splendid sight. The weather had gone bright and warm. White clouds stood tall to north, over the land that rose green across the water, but the sun rode free and light spilled down to sheen and glitter on wavelets. Hadding had waited until the breeze blew such that from Nidaros his colored sail with the woven raven showed broadside on. The warlike figurehead was lowered, the white shield of peace hung at the masthead, but the shields along the sides flashed in their many hues above the red and black and gold of the hull. Himself at the helm, as he came near he winded a horn. Men struck and smartly furled the sail, others took up oars, and *Firedrake* walked on thirty legs to a berth.

Richly clad, as were his crew, Hadding stepped ashore. One ran ahead toward Haakon's hall, to say that the king of the Danes was bound thither. He led his troop at a staid pace. The crowd gave way, closing in again behind. Voices buzzed. From her hillock Ragnhild saw his height and the slight limp in his gait. She caught her breath.

King Haakon met King Hadding outside the hall and made him welcome in seemly wise. Hadding kenned the graybeard who had bidden Ragnhild farewell on the Troll's Hood, but said nothing of it. "I hear great men are gathered in your house," he told Haakon. "I thought this might be a good time to speak with you and them of things that touch all our kingdoms."

"They are more the sons of great men," answered the Norseman. "They seek the hand of my daughter, for everybody thinks she will be a lucky as well as gainful match."

"Yes, I've heard something of this too," said Hadding. "I've been hereabouts a while." More than that he did not tell. His men were as close-mouthed as he.

He did not want to blurt forth that it was he who had saved the woman. Rather would he first feel out how things stood. These were haughty, hot-tempered men that wooed her. If any of them called him a liar, for his own honor he might well have to fight; and if he killed, that meant a blood feud on his hands, not easily settled. Of course, Ivar, lately back from Denmark, Thorfinn, and others were witnesses to the truth. Nonetheless he felt it beneath him to call straightway on them, as if he were a worker whining to be paid.

Moreover, there could be reasons why wedding Ragnhild

was unwise for him. He only knew the Niderings by word of mouth and what little he had seen. They might not be the best of allies. She herself might be a bad sort. He doubted that, but he had no sure knowledge. All in all, he reckoned it best to wait and watch. His years of kingship had taught him carefulness.

Haakon's queen met him at the threshold of the hall. She was young, for Ragnhild's mother had died, but she knew well how to speak to so high a guest, lead him to the seat of honor, and with her own hands bring him a beaker of mead. The man who sat there before, a king from the Uplands, glowered, though Haakon was quick to give him a fine sword. These could indeed be gurly waters.

The light of the long, late afternoon filled the hall. Housefolk were busy laying the fires and otherwise readying for eventide. Some of the guests were there. They talked with Hadding's men, trying to learn more about his aim but getting short answers. The rest were elsewhere, riding, hunting, boating, wenching, playing ball games, or egging two stallions on to fight.

Ragnhild bore his second beaker to Hadding. She had put on a shift of Southland silk under embroidered apron panels held by silver brooches set with gems. Her coppery hair flowed free from beneath a headband of gold. An amber necklace draped over her bosom. "I too make you welcome, king," she said slowly.

They looked one another in the eyes. Red and white fled through her face, but she held herself and her voice steady. "Thank you," he said with a smile. "It's twice a welcome from so fair a maiden."

"You have come a long way. I hope the voyage has been worth your while."

"Yes, I've gotten a thing or two done."

"Have you more in mind?"

"We'll see. Today I'm taking my ease and getting to know folk. May they become my friends."

"I think you will always have friends here."

Hadding laughed. "For a beginning, would you like to sit with me?"

She hung back for a heartbeat or two, then nodded and joined him in the seat. Like most such, it was big enough for two. They could talk together beneath the hubbub, softly if they wished. Though both might be men, a woman did a guest honor if she gave him this kind of fellowship.

Wooers glared. Hadding heeded them not at all. Benched among them, his battle-hardened warriors were enough to keep anyone from saying anything untoward. Haakon and his wife were clearly pleased, while striving to show everybody due respect.

Hadding and Ragnhild sat eagerly talking. He spoke less about himself than he asked about her, but she learned how witchy a life his had been. Hitherto only snatches of the tale had reached this far north. He saw that it did not frighten her, and found that her doings with the jotun had given her few nightmares afterward. When she tried to find out what he had been about in Norway, he said again that it had been a thing or two, then shifted to another ground. She could not well ask him outright. More than once he saw her fleetingly frown and bite her lip. Yet she was glad of his nearness, and often they laughed at something funny.

The sun lowered. More and more men arrived, cleansed and well clad for the evening. Ragnhild told Hadding she must go help her stepmother. But it was her father to whom she went and spoke low.

Fires sprang down the length of the hall. What smoke did not escape through the roofholes drifted, sweetened by juniper boughs. Though summer daylight lingered, shadows deepened, as if to bring weightiness; but the fire-flicker made them unrestful.

A hush fell when the queen led the other high-born women in to give out filled drinking horns. To King Haakon she handed the horn of a great aurochs, banded with gold and graven with runes. He lifted and said, "We drink the cup of Freyr."

This was olden wont here, with which a feast began. Whoever wanted to make a vow would then get up and cry it aloud. None did, so now the servants brought in the trestle tables and heaped them with food. Men ate and drank and made merry. Guesting this many every day heightened the king's renown, but he would not be sorry to see an end of the outlay.

Dusk had fallen when the tables were cleared away. Then Ragnhild trod forth to stand before the high seat and raise a horn of her own. Firelight went like sea waves over her. She seemed to glow against the gloom behind. Breath and a mumble flew around the hall. This was unheard of for a woman. Yet they knew that she was not like other women and that the Norns had sung no lowly weird over her cradle.

"Freyr and Freyja hear me, and all high gods," she called. "It is not right that when men come asking for my hand we keep them waiting long. You know my father lets me choose among them. Hard is that to do, when each is mighty and well thought of. Yet I must plight myself to one and one only. This eventide I will do so."

A surf of voices rumbled along the benches. She let it die down before she went on: "How I do this will strike you as odd. But on the Troll's Hood I learned what sign it is I am to seek. You are wise men, who will understand that what is at work here is more than human.

"Sit where you are. I will go among you and feel of your legs." A few startled laughs sounded. "Your legs upbear you on earth and bring you wherever you fare. Even on horseback, even in wain or ship, your legs are your strength. I tell you, this is knowledge I have from beyond the world of men."

Some shivered at that, and everyone grew quiet. King Haakon spoke soothing words. The wooers sat tight strung.

From each to each did Ragnhild pass. Bending low, she felt a man's calves up and down. He might well quiver as that touch pressed breeks against skin. But he held his mouth. Her face she kept unstirring.

To Hadding she came last. A sigh went through the hall when she stopped and stooped before him. He had said nothing about seeking her. Yet they two had been much together this day. He waited stiffly, not altogether sure what she meant.

Ragnhild's fingers searched over his calves. They found a spot, a small lump beneath a scar over the hard flesh. They roved and thrust.

She straightened. Her hands clasped his. Her voice rang. "Here is my man, he who slew the jotun! I laid a ring in his wound, that I might know him again, and now it has come back to me. Hadding, Dane-king, I will be yours."

After that he could not do otherwise than say how glad he was, laugh at how she had outfoxed him, and promise gifts to those who drank his betrothal ale. In truth he was happy, though things had moved faster than he looked for. In his life they often did.

XXI

Overawed, the wooers spoke no word against him, but sought instead for his goodwill. King Haakon sent far and wide, bidding more come to the wedding feast. It took place as soon as might be, lasted for days, and was remembered for lifetimes. Foremost among the torchbearers who lighted the bridal pair to bed on the first night were Ivar and Thorfinn.

Hadding and Ragnhild bided through that winter in Nidaros. He wanted to talk at length with King Haakon and other high-standing men. They made plans, swore oaths, and bound themselves strongly to each other against any common foe. Thus after his losses in war he regained much.

Near the turning of the year, a thing happened stranger than aught that men had ever heard of.

The evening meal in the great hall had been early, as short as the days at this season were. Darkness had fallen outside. Fires, lamps, and rushlights cast a ruddy glow, but shadows were everywhere, uneasy, black above the crossbeams, misshapen upon the walls. Servants went to and fro with drink. Along the seats, rings, pins, brooches, and necklaces gleamed athwart the richness of furs and brocade on the wellborn men, their ladies, and the warriors. Talk and laughter rolled like surf. The very hounds lolling on the floor were as cheerful.

Hadding and Ragnhild sat in the honor seat, across from her father and his wife in the high seat. Between these pairs a fire burned on its hearthstone. Though the newlyweds kept the bearing that behooved their rank, now and then they glanced at one another and smiled.

Then without warning or sound, before them near the hearth a head came out of the floor. It rose until half a woman's body was there. They could not see whether she had the uncovered hair of a maiden or wore the kerchief of a wife, for a hooded blue cloak darkened sight of her face. But she seemed to be tall and gaunt. What showed of her dress sheened ghostly. Her arms held up her front apron panel. In it lay a sheaf of hemlocks with green leaves and white flower heads.

A roar went up. Men sprang to their feet. None moved farther. They stared, stiff and daunted. As cries died away, hard breathing rasped through the fire-crackle. Hounds that had hunted wild boar cringed back. One howled.

Hadding stood lynx-taut. The woman's head turned. Her eyes found his. For a span they two were thus frozen, and stillness deepened throughout the hall. She showed the hemlocks forth to him as if she asked where in the world such fresh herbs might grow at the dead of winter.

He made a step toward her. "She beckons me," he mumbled. Ragnhild gripped his arm. He shook her off and moved on over the strewn rushes. Afterward he said he felt himself adream, bound off with no thought of doing otherwise. Yet he knew by every red glimmer of firelight, whiff of smoke, rustle underfoot, that this was real.

"Yes," he said aloud, his look never leaving the woman's, "I would like to know."

Helpless, Ragnhild saw him reach her. She rose up fully, her height matching his, and cast her cloak about them both. They sank from sight. The floor there bore no mark of having been touched.

He came to rest in thick gloom. Fog swirled cold. Unseen, the woman nudged his elbow. At that slight urging, he walked forward beside her. She strode as if they were not blinded. He thrust aside fear of stumbling and kept beside her. Their footfalls sounded hollow.

It seemed to him that they went a long way, slowly downward, before the mist thinned out. When they were clear of it, he found himself under a gray overcast. Dull light seeped across a waste of rocks. Air lay windless, without heat or cold. The path they were on was dry but deeply worn. He thought that many feet must have trodden it before him.

Still she walked unspeaking. He thought he had better not

say anything either. Stealing a look at her, he saw a bony face, unsmiling, ivory white, as if she had never been out beneath the sun. She herself always gazed straight ahead.

He knew not how much longer they had gone, for he had lost feeling for time or span, when he came in sight of some men standing near the wayside. They were very big, handsome, magnificently clad in red and purple. Golden shone the rings on their arms and the brooches at the breasts, even in this dreary light; and the head of the spear that one held gleamed steely blue. Another gripped a heavy, short-handled hammer. A sword hung at the hip of a third, who was missing his right hand. A fourth held a sickle. A fifth had a bow and quiver on his back. A sixth clasped a harp. Slung from the shoulder of the seventh was a horn like the horn of a huge ram; his skin was the whitest, his hair the fairest, and his cloak was banded like the rainbow.

They did not watch the wayfarers, but Hadding felt they must be aware of him. Nor did the woman halt. Still she led him onward.

Boulders and rubble yielded to grassy soil. The gray overhead went blue, though no sun was in it. Warmth breathed forth. The smell it awakened became harsh, for the way passed through a meadow full of hemlock like that which the woman bore. She tossed hers aside. Hadding thought it had served the end of bringing him underground. He remembered that hemlock is deadly. It came to him that somebody wanted him to see what no living man ever had seen. He could not think why. Dreamlike, his way took him on.

After another long while a noise of rushing water waxed ahead. A ringing and clatter went through it. Ever louder it grew, until the woman and Hadding reached the bank of a mighty river. Leaden-hued, it flowed as swiftly as if it were plunging straight down to the bottom of the world. Weapons floated crowdingly upon it, swords, spears, axes, whirling, tumbling, banging together as the stream bore them away. The water roared deafening. The spray that flew up made a mist wherein the daylike light was lost. Where it struck skin, the cold of it stung like an adder's bite.

A bridge crossed it. The woman beckoned and trod onto that narrow span. Hadding could not but follow. It swayed and shuddered beneath him. Often he nearly fell. Only the quickness he had learned in woods and war saved him.

Beyond the bridge of dread stretched a plain of sallow grass and a few crooked trees. As the sound of the river fell behind him, Hadding's ears caught another racket rising frontward. The hair stirred all over his body. He knew that din.

Onward walking, he saw the wellspring of it come over the dim edge of sight and grow clear. Two hosts fought in battle. Weapons clashed, blood reddened byrnies and earth, the wounded sank down under swaying banners and the feet of the hale crushed them, the slain sprawled gaping.

Hadding jarred to a halt. Words tore from him. "What fray is this?"

The woman stopped too. For the first time on their trek she looked again into his eyes. Her voice was low, a sigh like the wind at night. "These are the men who died by the sword, who here wage ever a shadow strife and fell each other, so that their deeds are a glimmer of what they wrought when they lived."

She turned and went on. The fight was slow to fall away behind them. Meanwhile Hadding gave scant heed to the land around. It was a heath, utterly empty. Light waned until they fared in dusk, chill, and stillness.

At last he began to make out something else. Drawing near, he saw it was a high stone wall. From end to end of sight it stretched across the rutted road. He spied no gateway, nor could he see over the top. On a boulder nearby perched a red cock. Otherwise there were only the whins and ling of the waste.

"We must try to get over this," said the woman.

Hadding felt of the stones. They were smoothed and closely fitted, with neither handhold nor foothold. "I know not how," he said.

"Some few have overleaped it," said the woman.

She withdrew, crouched, and broke into a run. Arrow-swift she sped, and at the end gave a mighty spring. Her cloak and skirts flapped with the speed. Nonetheless she did not reach the top, but fell back, landing catlike on her feet.

Again she walked off. Her shape went misty. Renewed, she was small and light. Now she bounded higher still, but once more failed.

She made herself tall again. "No," she said grimly, "this is not in your weird. Yet shall you ken something of what lies beyond."

She went over to the cock and laid hold of him, wings and legs caught in her left hand. Her right closed on his neck. With one twist, she tore his head off.

Blood spattered, none of it on her. She swung the body around. Plumes streamed. She let it go and it soared over the wall. After it she cast the head.

From the other side, Hadding heard the cock crow.

All at once the woman seemed weary. "Enough," she said, and started back the way they had come.

So did Hadding return to the world of the living. He passed up through the floor of Haakon's hall and stood there before Ragnhild. She fell into his arms. Folk told him he had been gone for only a few breaths.

XXII

Had the thing happened to anyone else, he might thereafter have been shunned. Enough eeriness was already bound to the name of Hadding that this raised no fear of him. However, it was seldom talked about. One would rather keep on thinking of him as a hero who was also a likeable human, and get back to everyday matters—which was his own heartiest wish.

By spring Ragnhild was great with child. Nevertheless she went eagerly aboard *Firedrake* when her husband left for home. First he rigged a small tent that could be raised when she and her one tirewoman needed freedom from men's eyes. Other times she was in the open with him.

Heads thumped somewhat after the farewell feast King Haakon gave. Sea breezes cleared them, and Hadding's warriors brought their lord south toward Denmark.

Wind blew strongly, waves rushed high and green under flights of ragged clouds, on a day when they were passing the steep cliffs of Sogn. Out from a fjord glided three longships. Iron flashed aboard them. Today was no weather for rowing on open waters. Their crews drew oars in and bent sail to masts already raised. Swiftly they plunged to cut off Hadding's lone craft.

"I hardly think they're friendly," growled Gunnar as he peered against the sea-blink. "They've lain in wait for prey to come by."

Hadding shook his head. "It's early in the season," he said. "No traders are yet out along these shores. Nor would vikings likely go after a ship of war like ours. I wonder if King Uffi has not sent them to lurk for me."

"Well, we'd better busk ourselves. We'll win. None of their hulls is like to ours for size, and they'll find that none of them are like to us for battle."

Again Hadding shook his head. "I'll not risk my wife and unborn child unless I must." He called on the most skilled seamen to stand by at the sheets and sail-pole. The strongest he told to man oars if need be. The rest were to take weapons and mail but then keep out of the way. Himself he went aft to the helm.

From beneath Ragnhild's kerchief, stray locks fluttered in the wind like flame. She gripped a bow and had slung a quiverful of arrows on her back. "Let them draw nigh and they'll learn what the upland deer learned!" she cried.

Hadding laughed. "Let's see if we can spare them," he said.

Thereafter he steered. Gauging wind and seas, shouting orders, working the tiller with the strength of a wisent and the cunning of a wolf, he became the soul of the ship.

Rigging thrummed, timbers creaked, wind shrilled, billows crashed. Again and again *Firedrake* lay nearly on her beam ends. Again and again spray burst white and bitter at the prow. Her hull swayed, swung, bounded, athrob with the surges she rode and clove. The yard rattled, the sail slatted each time she came about. Yet never a wave did she take. Hadding used the sea as he used the wind.

No steersman among the foe could point that close. Twice, those who tried almost swamped their vessels, which then rolled sluggishly till the crews got them bailed out. Once the Danes were past the spot where the strangers had aimed to meet them, they drew ever farther away. They whooped for glee.

Hadding sailed thus until well after the foe had dropped

from sight. He said he wanted to make sure of not being over-taken, should the wind fail. Ragnhild smiled. "I think you're having too much fun to stop," she told him. Something flickered across her face. She looked elsewhere. "Yes," she whispered, "there's more joy for you in this than I can give you, or any woman."

Still, she went gladly with him into his home and set about making it hers.

A while afterward she was brought to bed. As wont was, nobody stayed with her in the women's bower but the midwife. Hadding feasted in the hall with his housecarles and guests. Noise, fire, and merriment helped frighten evil beings off.

The midwife came in at last. "It went hard, lord," she told him. "The queen is slim in the hips. But she rests now. Behold your son."

She stooped down, unrolled the blanket in which she had swaddled the bairn, and laid him on it at the king's feet. Hadding waved other men back and looked close. Small, red, the newborn kicked and cried lustily. The father took him up onto his knees. So did he acknowledge that the child was sound and would be kept alive. Cheers thundered.

The midwife returned the bairn to his mother. Hadding followed. Ragnhild lay white and haggard, but she cast him a fighter's grin. "You did well," he said.

Back in the hall, he told them there that the queen was wearied and had lost much blood, but ought to regain strength in time. Now let them be as happy as he was.

"I will," murmured Gyda. "For this little time I have you."

Great was the naming feast a few days later. Hadding poured water on the babe's head and dubbed him Frodi. That surprised some. He had already honored his forebears by naming his offspring by other women for them, but men had not thought he would call his queen-born son "wise." When Eirik

Jarl asked why, the father smiled. "I'm doing what I can to help him grow up wise," he said. "The warlikeness he can make for himself."

He waited until Ragnhild was healed before he made his rounds of the kingdom. She kept the hall at Haven for him, nursed Frodi, and ran things with a stern hand. When his faring was done, she greeted him lovingly, but her womb was slow to open again. So did that year pass in Denmark.

It was otherwise in Svithjod. Word drifted in from Norway of how Hadding had slain the giant, wedded King Haakon's daughter, and sworn fellowship with the Nidering and neighboring lords. Later came hearsay less clear, about one who had sought him out from beyond the world of men. All this made ever more folk think there must be something wonderful about him. The offering to Freyr that he had founded spread north from Scania to the holy shaw at Uppsala itself. Yeomen muttered that it would be madness to fight him. Their chieftains began to say it aloud.

"Best we make terms," urged King Uffi's younger brother, Hunding. "Denmark is rich and mighty. We ought to gain as much from friendship as we give, or more."

"Never while I live and that hound befouls the earth," snarled Uffi. "Our father would groan in his howe."

"I think not. It's no shame to make peace with a worthy foe. Surely it's better than for him to overrun us. He may well seek to do that, once he's rebuilt what he lost. Yet I have a feeling that if we give him no grounds to strike at us, he would rather not."

"What thrall-blood sneaked into ours, that you speak well of such a one?" rasped Uffi, and stormed from the room where they were.

But he understood that outright war would be rash and

might be wreckful. Through the long nights of winter he brooded. His hatred stewed in him like the brew in a witch's kettle. Slowly he thought out what could be done.

He had a daughter, Arnborg, a maiden of fourteen years, already very fair. Toward spring Uffi made known that whoever slew Hadding should get her to wife, along with great gifts, broad acres, and high standing in the kingdom.

Word buzzed about. Some bold seamen took ship for Norway to waylay the Dane-king, but he outsailed them. Later on, Uffi heard that Hadding had been told of his offer, and had laughed. Uffi took an ax, went to his stables, killed a horse with one blow, and hacked it to shreds.

Next year Thuning the Finnfarer came to him. This was a Norseman from the Westfjord, up beyond the land of the Niderings. Though a chieftain with holdings in the Lofoten Islands and the nearby mainland, in those bleak parts he had few folk under him, mostly fishers. He had taken to trade, sailing north around the end of Finnmark and onward. From there he freighted walrus leather, ivory, furs, and thralls to marts in southerly shires. When he must fight, he handily won. Otherwise he worked shrewdly and learned deeply.

To Uffi he said, "I can take King Hadding out of his days if you will lend me what I need."

"What is that?" asked Uffi.

"A fleet of ships for hundreds of men, with crews and outfits for a long voyage. If any Swedish warriors would like to come along, they'll be welcome, but mainly I'll raise my own host. I'll bring you Hadding's head, or at least news of his downfall. I'll bring plunder as well, reaved in Denmark when he is no more. And you will give me your Arnborg."

Uffi looked at him. Thuning was a sturdy man, but fat and not overly clean. Lice could be seen hopping in the thin strands of his hair. His beard fell matted from his jowls down his chest. A sour smell hung around him. The girl would not be glad if he won her. However, he promised an end to Hadding.

"Where will your men come from?" Uffi asked.

"From among the Bjarmians, who dwell along the White Sea," Thuning said. "Their tribes are poor and wild, but fearless. I've gotten to know them well, and can tell you that they'll flock to me. Iron tools and weapons are worth more to them than gold, so you and I will take our share of my loot in costlier things."

Uffi frowned. "We've long laid toll on Finns like those, because we have better arms and more skill in their use."

"True. Yet I can bring more fighters against Hadding than he'll reckon on, if you'll lend me the ships to carry them."

Uffi nodded. "Yes, he won't likely hear other than that some kind of fleet is bound his way, and think he can drive it off with his housecarles and neighborhood levies." His frown became a scowl. "However many your followers, he may well be right, too. Man for man, his warriors will be better. And uncanny powers seem to hover about him."

"I know," said Thuning. "But you must have heard, lord, that the Bjarmians breed warlocks more cunning than even among other Finns. Often have I bought a bag of favoring winds from one. And I have seen greater works done yonder, fruitful or frightful. Help me as I wish, and I will set black witchcraft against his luck. It will overwhelm him."

XXIII

The next spring a flock of ships passed through the Sound and out into the Kattegat. No man aboard answered any Dane who rowed close enough to give hail, but it was clear that the crews were Swedes. However, they did nothing hostile, not even camping ashore at night. Nor had they more than a few warcraft. Most of their vessels were knorrs and other kinds of freighters, lightly manned. Eirik Jarl dogged them from afar till he saw them head in for King Uffi's Norse lands. Later Hadding got word that after resting for a while the sailors had set forth again, south around Agder and north along the coast.

He sent a swift ship to warn King Haakon. She brought back the news that the fleet had gone by the Niderings. Haakon had not learned what its errand might be, yonder where folk were first few and poor, then wild Finns. He would send out spies and scouts for whatever they could turn up.

Late in summer a messenger craft, ruthlessly rowed, came from him to Denmark. His searchers had found that a Norse chieftain by the name of Thuning, somewhat known to him, had gathered a host of Bjarmians and was bringing them back down from the White Sea. Since only a king was able to get together so many keels, belike they meant to fall on Denmark.

By the time Haakon's men got to where the Dane-king was, little remained for marshalling warriors. Moreover, he could not lawfully call a levy now at harvest. He could only have the war-arrow carried from house to house as widely as might be, at horse-killing speed, asking for freely given help. Meanwhile he brought ships to Haven and stocked them for sea.

Even so, it was a goodly troop that fared north astern of *Firedrake*. Two score hulls were filled with fighters. All were well outfitted and hardened to battle. "I could almost feel sorry for the foe," bragged Gunnar.

"They'll outnumber us," Hadding said.

"What of it? Woodsrunners and spearfishers. Maybe we'll each have to cut down two."

"Thuning is no fool, from what I've heard of him. He

knows those folk. There go dark tales about them." Hadding shook his head as if to throw off the thoughts perched on it. "Enough. We've sailing to do."

Helped by fair weather and a full moon, the ships made a fast crossing to Norway. Thereafter Hadding took a day on an island at Boknafjord and another day off Hordaland, that men might stretch cramped limbs and have a sound sleep. In between, they rowed as hard as thews could drive oars, turn by turn by turn.

The shore rose, cliffs sheering cloudward, cleft with inlets, above a maze of islets and skerries. Here he kept the sea and gave his crews no more ease than they must have if they were to carry on. He hoped to join his wife's father at Nidaros before Thuning got that far.

A west wind sprang up, shrill and raw. Green-backed waves rushed to break in foam and thunder on the rocks. Ships rolled and pitched. Rowers braced feet against rib timbers as they heaved to keep clear. However chill the air, sweat ran down their skins till its salt mingled with the spindrift on their lips.

Hadding squinted landward. Behind him the sun struck through a gray wrack. Brightness flared off the surf. Beyond it a narrow strip of strand ran below heights where a few dwarfed pines clung. A man stood there. Hadding saw him take off his cloak and hold it high. It beat in the wind like a great blue wing.

"Is he wrecked?" wondered Svein. "He seems to want us come take him aboard."

Einar barked a laugh. "If so, his woes have driven him mad."

Hadding stiffened. He gripped the rail and leaned far over. The rolling brought him breast-on to the water, then aloft into the weather. Still he peered. All at once he shivered, turned about, and said, "We'll go after him."

"What?" shouted Einar. "Lord, you can't be mad too!"

"Tell the crew," Hadding said. "I'll take the helm myself." He made his way aft through crowded, crouching men.

"Do as he bids," Ax-Egil said. "He kens more about some things than you or I would like to."

As folk watched aghast from the other ships, *Firedrake* came around. Stern to onshore wind and seas, she bounded at the deadliness ahead. Breakers sheeted white above reefs. Water swirled and chopped between. The roar drowned the groaning of strakes. Grimly, for none would show fear, the rowers bent to their oars, the riders hunched down and gripped what handholds they could find.

Hadding wove his way. The ship was not broached, she did not strike. The bottom here must slope slowly, for the surf that elsewhere pounded the land broke well offshore and was low. As Hadding steered through the smother of it he took no worse than a drenching. Nor was this a stony ground. Only sand grated when he drew to a stop.

The man waded out. Hadding came forward to give him a hand up. "That was well done," the man said. His voice was as deep as the sea's.

Hadding looked into his one eye. "We have met before," he answered. "I knew you at once."

"You shall not be sorry," said the man.

The crew stared silent. Shaken and bewildered though they were, every warrior rose to his feet. The newcomer was very tall. Somehow, in this wind, he kept a broad hat on his gray locks. It overshadowed a lean face from which a long gray beard fell over the cloak he had donned again. He seemed to have no weapon except a spear.

"This is Gangleri," Hadding told them. "I owe him much from aforetime."

"Best you rejoin your fleet," Gangleri said.

"Indeed." Hadding gave orders. Men snapped to them,

sprang overboard and shoved the ship off, climbed back when
she was afloat, and set to the oars. It was harder work than
coming in, but they were happier doing it.

Already the wind was lower. When Hadding reached his
folk he found the seas running easier. The wind shifted. Soon
he could cry, "It's fair for our course. Up masts and sails, in
oars, and out ale casks!"

"Does he bring luck, him Gangleri?" muttered Gunnar.

"When he chooses to, I think," said Ax-Egil as softly.

"How did he happen to be on yon strand right when we
passed by?"

"It didn't merely happen, I'm sure. But let's speak no more
of this."

Still, the mood aboard *Firedrake* became, if not altogether
merry, hopeful. It spread to the rest of the crews. Hadding
bore speedily north.

As the voyage went on, men saw Gangleri eat and drink,
sitting on a bench, as a king might eat and drink in his high
seat. They never saw him drop his breeks, nor did they see him
sleep. They wondered, but not aloud. Few got more than a
word or two with him, aside from Hadding. The pair of them
were most of the time alone in the forepeak.

Now and then others overheard them. Though strange, the
words were heartening rather than daunting. Gangleri was giving Hadding redes about war.

"You are bound against a bigger host than your own," he
said. "Most are poorly armed, but a stone-headed ax or spear,
a bone harpoon, or a wooden club deals the same death as
iron. Moreover, their bowmen are as good as any Dane, and
their slingers are better. Hardly any of them have byrnies, but
few of your yeomen do either. Although Bjarmians have seldom fought in great numbers, these have had Swedes to teach
them something of it, who will lead and stiffen them. They
are hunters of bear and whale. They have their blood feuds

and clashes between tribes. Far from home with nowhere to flee to, they will fight like trapped wildcats. Their warlocks will egg them on and cast spells to strike fear in your men. You have no light task. Well can you leave your bones in the high north."

"Your wish may be otherwise," answered Hadding slowly.

"I do have things to tell you. Hitherto hosts like yours have had no true shape. Men try to stay near the banners of their chieftains and shoulder to shoulder with their friends. If set on from all sides, they make a shield wall and stand in a ring as best they can. Once that is broken, the foe reaps them piecemeal. Otherwise both troops go forward with no better plan than to come to grips. A battle is hardly more than a huge brawl. Nobody knows what is happening beyond his arm's length. Anything may spark fear, it will spread like wildfire, men will cast their weapons from them and run as blindly as chickens, the foe will come after them like weasels, and so the battle is lost."

Hadding nodded. His face went bleak. He knew this all too well.

"Now I will tell you what is better," said the old one, "and if you think about it you will see that it is."

"I know already that it is—coming from you," whispered the king.

They spoke much together as the ships sailed on.

With the wind holding fair, Hadding reached the fjord of the Niderings as soon as he had hoped. But he could not go in, greet Haakon, and raise more warriors to help. Even as the remembered landmarks hove in sight, over the northern sea-rim came a fleet outnumbering his. Those who had spied it earlier now told their fellows, who howled. Here were the Swedes and Bjarmians.

"How have they moved so fast?" wondered Svein. "The winds that bore us along were against them."

"That need not be," said Egil starkly. "I've heard tell of how Finn-wizards hold sway over the weather."

Svein cast a glance at the graybeard with hat and cloak who stood silent astern. "I think we have one such ourselves." He shivered.

"This, then, is where we'll meet them," called Hadding, the length of the hull and across the water. "Make ready!"

He steered for the island of Hitra, which lay with others near the mouth of the fjord. Long, low, and green, it offered safe strands for landing and meadows for fighting. The only dwellers he saw were a pair of cowherd children, who made haste to drive their kine into the background woods.

One by one the Danish ships touched shore. Anchors went out. Men jumped over the sides and splashed to land. Soon it was a roiling of warriors. Iron blinked under the midday sun, banners tossed in the wind, gulls wheeled and piped overhead.

Standing in the prow of *Firedrake*, Hadding blew his horn. The sound brought men packed close around. He harangued them a short while about how well it was to stave off the foe this far from their homes, the fame to be won, the booty to gather afterward—if nothing else, ships that would fetch good prices. Their cheers rang.

Then they quieted, for he spoke sternly of what he wanted them to do. Gangleri, who stood beside him, spearhead shining above, had taught him a new array of battle. He put it forth in a few words. There was no time to say more, he told them, nor to quarrel over who should stand where. All posts were alike honorable. Gangleri would go among them and lead every banner-band to its place. Let none question or hinder him. Anyone who did would rue it.

The Danes were quick to obey. Although most had not seen the old one before, the beholding awed them.

He spread them on the field as a great wedge. Hadding and

Gunnar made the first row—not because Hadding was king, for it would have been wisest to have him farther back were it not that they two were the mightiest of the fleet. Four men behind them made the second row, eight behind these the third, and thus until the last, who were promised that there would be enough fighting for everybody. On the wings Gangleri set the bowmen and slingers.

So did the Danes take their stand. They had not long to wait.

Thuning had known who they must be. If he tried to sail on past, they would be after him, harassing all the way. His men could not even land for a night's rest without being attacked before they could busk themselves. Best was to have it out this day. He led his fleet to a strand a few miles off, grounded, and brought his host ashore.

As they came near, they were a grim sight. Widely over the grass they spilled, a swarm of hornets angrily buzzing, stings out and agleam. Swedish warriors in helm and ringmail went at every uplifted banner. They were well-nigh lost among the tribesmen. The Bjarmians were stocky, sturdy, high in the cheekbones, and narrow in the eyes. Most were clad in leather and felt; some coats bore sewn-on iron rings gotten from traders. Few owned helmets. Their hair showed greasy but often as fair as any Norseman's. Their rude weapons had felled beasts stronger than men. Many had bound tokens of magic onto themselves, aurochs horns or reindeer antlers at the brows, necklaces of bear teeth or ferret skulls, ruffs of eagle feathers. Toward the rear a few elders were squatting down. They carried staffs topped with the same kittle things, and small drums. They began to beat on these with the flats of their hands. From their wrinkled lips a keening wove into the thutter.

Hadding drew sword. "Hey-saa-saa!" he cried.

The Danes bayed and followed him. Thuning bawled answer. His own banner led a rush to meet them.

Battle burst loose. Weapons clashed and thudded, men yelled, grunted, panted, bowstrings twanged, gulls mewed and ravens croaked on high where they wheeled watchful, and through all the racket went the drumbeat and chant of the warlocks.

The Danes were new to their array. It held together less well than it might have. Yet it clove into the disordered foe, scattering those it did not straightway overrun. Bowmen and slingers were more free than erstwhile to spy targets and pick them off. Thuning's banner reeled aside. Others stood forlornly fast, cut off from help.

And now Gangleri threw back his cloak, to show that a bag hung around his neck. From it he took a bow. It seemed a toy, then suddenly it was the longest that men in these lands had ever beheld. Standing on the right flank, he strung it and took arrows from the quivers of the nearby Danes. They forgot their own fighting as they saw the old one draw that bow to his ear. When he loosed the shaft, string and wood sang like a stormwind. A Swede crumpled, spitted through byrnie and body. Again Gangleri shot, again, again, again. It was as if he sent ten arrows at once. Each killed.

The warlocks drummed and wailed. Wind strengthened outworldishly fast. Its boom and shriek drowned the noise below. The carrion birds fled. Salt spume flew off the sea, over the field. Clouds boiled up black in the north and across heaven. They blotted out the sun. Rain lashed from them, slantwise over the Danish ranks. Hailstones hit like fists.

A wavering went through Hadding's troop. This was something more than a squall. Who could stand against witchcraft? The Bjarmians yelped in glee, rallied their broken gangs, and pressed inward. Stone axes, bone harpoons struck down man after man.

Gangleri laid his bow aside and raised his arms. His cloak and beard blew wildly, but still the hat clung to his gray head and half hid the gaunt one-eyed face. He called to the sky.

From over the eastward mainland lifted a new cloud. In the blue-black depths of its nether half lightning leaped blinding. The heights shone snow white. Onward the cloud thrust. The wind that drove it warred with the wind behind the rain. Wrack whirled, thunder crashed, while woodland trees tossed their boughs and moaned.

The rain withdrew, a grayness bound south. The heavens opened and the sun stood forth. Wet·grass sparkled many-hued. Blood on the slain lay shoutingly red.

"Hey-aa!" roared Hadding. "On!" His warriors rebounded from fear. They fell on a foe whom it had seized. What followed was slaughter.

Afterward a vast stillness fell. Men went about doing what they could for wounded friends, or sat a few together quietly talking, or sat alone and stared across the water. The westering sun cast a long light over gaping things asprawl on trampled earth. Soon the Danes would shift elsewhere for the night. Tomorrow they would bury their dead, leave their fallen foemen to the birds, and take over the empty Swedish ships. Later they would row to Nidaros and feast before setting homeward. But now they were weary deep into their marrow.

Hadding and Gangleri stood near the hacked, reeking lichs of the warlocks. Thuning's was among them. "You saved us, lord," said the king. "How can I ever repay you?"

The old one leaned on his spear. "There is no need," he answered. "This was my will."

"But we must at least give you your honor at Haakon's hall and afterward at mine."

"That shall not be. I am bound elsewhere."

"What? How can you get off this island, unless in a ship of ours?"

"I have my ways." Gangleri was silent a while. Two ravens swung low, croaked, and flew off. "You shall see me no more in this life," he then told Hadding. "Remember what I have taught you."

"I shall." And indeed the wedge of men lived on throughout Northern lands. It came to be known as the swine array, for it ripped through an unready host like the tusks of a wild boar.

"But—this life?" Hadding dared ask.

"Yours will not end at anyone's hand but your own," Gangleri said.

After another span in which only wind, sea, and hovering fowl spoke, he went on: "This do I rede you. Squander not your years on small quarrels, but seek such wars as are worth fighting. Wage them abroad rather than close to home. The work of a king is to ward his folk.

"Farewell."

He turned and strode off toward the wood. His tallness was quickly gone into its shadows.

XXIV

That midwinter Queen Ragnhild was again brought to bed with child. Her fight was still harder than before. Sometimes a moan slipped out between her teeth. The blankets were so bloodied they must be burned afterward. It took months for her to get back her strength. Yet the bairn, a girl, was healthy. She came into the world shrieking as though in wrath, and at the breast she bit painfully hard. It seemed right to her father that they name her Ulfhild, Wolf Battle.

In spring a ship arrived from Svithjod bearing high-born

men who sought out King Hadding. They brought word from King Uffi. He was sick of a war that gained him naught. Surely it cost the Danes, too, more than it was worth. Let them make peace.

Hadding sent back a stiff answer. His folk had much to avenge. However, he was willing to think about taking a weregild, and meanwhile would stay his hand if the Swedes behaved themselves.

Messengers went to and fro during the summer. Uffi did not want to pay, as much because that would be knuckling under as because of the gold. Nor had Hadding awaited it. He merely did not wish to seem overly eager. He lowered the award but said that oaths must be sworn that Danish traders would have entry to Geatish and Swedish marts, free of hindrance and scot. And thus the dickering went between those two.

Toward fall they seemed near agreement. Uffi's last sending was almost friendly. Let Hadding come to Uppsala, where they could speak man to man. If they reached understanding, they would plight fellowship in the grove of offerings, the holiest spot in all the Northern lands. Did the meeting fail, the Danes would go home unharmed, loaded with gifts. But Uffi felt sure it would not. He had said that whoever got Hadding slain should have his lovely daughter Arnborg. Now he took that back. Once peace was made, Hadding himself should have her, to bind their houses together for aye.

"There's a bid that beckons!" laughed the Dane-king.

Ragnhild bit her lip but said nothing until that night in their shutbed. Then she spoke harshly. "No other woman shall be queen in Denmark while I am here. If you give her such honors, I will go back to my mountains."

"It's only kingcraft," he told her.

She stiffened at his side. "Do you reckon her blood better than mine?"

He thought for a while before he said, "No, surely not. Nor would I throw your father's friendship away for the sake of a girl. It's stood me in good stead. But there needs to be some kind of tie between Skjoldungs and Ynglings, or war can too easily break out again, as bootless as ever. She can dwell in Scania, you in these islands, if you feel so strongly about it."

"I do. Your lemans at least do not have the name of queen. Nonetheless I worry that some by-blow of yours will someday seek to snatch the kingship from my son."

"From our son."

"If you will not think ahead, I must."

"You don't think much of him who saved you from the giant, do you?" he snapped.

"I will think as well of him as he does of me."

His mood softened. "That is well indeed." He laid his arm around her and drew her toward him. She was warm in the dark. Her hair smelled of summer days, the summer that was waning.

"Then do not go." Her voice shivered. "Only ill can come of it. How can a man set aside a hatred as deep as Uffi's for you?"

His anger woke afresh. "Am I to show myself afraid of him?"

"No, but neither should you show yourself heedless."

"I'll be the deemer of that," he growled. "Enough, wife."

Again she stiffened. He took her. She suffered it silently.

In the time that followed she stayed cold to him. He gave it scant thought, being busied with making ready.

Yet on the eve of his leavetaking, Ragnhild got him aside, the two of them alone, and said low, holding both his hands and looking up into his eyes, "Whatever you do yonder, come back. The days and nights here will be hollow until then."

His heart glowed. He smiled at her. But she was having her courses. He spent the night with Gyda.

In the morning Ragnhild watched him go, along with the
household and most of the neighborhood. A hundred warriors fared off in two ships. More would have seemed threatening. Besides, this was harvest season. They rowed lustily, a
brave sight athwart the Scanian shore that lay low and hazy
across the Sound. Soon they were small in her eyes, soon they
were lost.

The run went easily, with overnight stops along the way, up
the Baltic to the Skerrygarth and in among its many islets. A
troop of Swedes were camped at a landing that the messengers had told of. Uffi's brother, Hunding, led them. He stood
on the wharf to greet the Dane-king with a handclasp.

"We have been waiting here for you, that we may bring you
to Uppsala with your rightful honor," he said. "Thank you for
that you came. Glad will all our folk be of peace with you, but
none more glad than me." He gulped, fumbled at the brooch
that held his cloak, and pulled the garment off. It was of scar-
let wool lined with silk and trimmed with ermine. The words
burst from him: "In token of welcome, take this, and, and may
goodwill always cover our houses."

Hadding looked closely at him while saying thanks. Hunding was young and slim, though well knit. Hair so fair that it
was nearly white fluttered about sharp features, as yet only
thinly bearded, with big eyes. "My hopes are high," said
Hadding.

The troops ate together that evening in the nearby hamlet.
After ale had flowed freely, wariness became merriment.

In the morning they set forth. Hunding had brought horses
for all. They rode briskly through a rolling land, broad and
rich. Fields rippled tawny, kine cropped meadows, hayricks
stood shaggy for winter, smoke lifted from farmsteads and
thorps, laden oxcarts creaked on the roads, harvesters lowered

their sickles and children shouted as the warriors passed by with iron aflash and ringing. Wind soughed in woodlots, but no big stands of trees were left. "Yours is a mighty kingdom," Hadding said once.

Hunding flushed and looked away. "We can't guest you as well as behooves us. I hope you won't take it amiss."

"Why, what's wrong?"

"The kingly hall is not fit for men such as you and yours. Uffi did not fare about this year, but stayed the whole while at Uppsala. He said he must, to look after some things hereabouts that were getting troublesome—I'm not sure what they were—and so he could send quick answers to any word from you. The upshot is that there's been no time when the privies could be mucked out, nor to scrub the buildings and let them sweeten unused. They're all dirty and they stink. I tried to warn him, but he wouldn't listen."

Hadding choked back a laugh.

"Of course he won't mock you with that," Hunding went on in haste. "He's had a new guesthouse built. There you will stay and there will he feast you."

"Well, I know how a king and his household must needs shift around during the year," said Hadding, "and if Uffi was unable to, he has my fellow feeling." He turned his grin away from the young man.

"You are kind," blurted Hunding. "It bodes well for friendship."

They reached Uppsala in the later afternoon. The sun behind it, the town loomed on the high western bank of the river with its walls and watchtowers a block of darkness. Above that stockade gleamed the roofs upon roofs of the halidom, where stood the gold-bedecked idols of the great gods. Beyond the walls reared the oak and ash trees of the holy shaw. Although leaves were still green, somehow that grove too seemed murky,

as if it brooded over the bones of beasts and men offered
there.

The riders stopped a little short of the bridge over the
stream. A house lay hard by a bigger patch of woods. Shadows under the boughs and in thick brush made brighter the
newly trimmed timbers. Though rather narrow, the building
was long, fully big enough for Hadding's troop and as many
more. Not only the cookhouse but the stables and other outbuildings stood well to the rear of it, which was seldom done;
they wontedly enclosed, thus making the whole easier to defend. "Does Uffi think no foe will ever get this near him?"
wondered Hadding.

"We have the town for a stronghold," Hunding said. "Here
is the house of peace." Thralls and hirelings were hastening
out. "Now I bid you farewell for a little. We all need to wash,
rest, change clothes. I'll see you again this eventide after you've
eaten. Tomorrow we'll hold a feast worthy of you. Later I
hope you'll let me guest you in my home."

"Yes, I hope so too," answered Hadding, less warmly.

"King Uffi should have been on hand to bid you welcome," said Hunding. "I'm not happy about that either. Maybe
something suddenly called him away. But he should surely
come like me to drink with you tonight before we sleep." He
pulled hard on the reins, wheeled his horse around, and trotted off, followed by his men.

The servants were few, no women among them. Their
headmen said there would be plenty in the morning, to work
with food and drink and everything else. Meanwhile these
would attend the Danes. As grooms took their steeds away, he
led them into the house.

The room beyond the entry was rather gloomy, for the windows were small and high. Fires were being laid and kindled
against a chill that affronted the mildness outside. The outfit-

ting was meager. "I should think King Uffi would show off his wealth to us," Hadding said.

Gunnar shrugged. "Well, I've heard he's a stingy one."

Ax-Egil scowled. "He wasn't unwilling to lay out for war on us, or in seeking our lord's life."

"I care not," said Svein, "as long as his ale doesn't run out. It's been a thirsty day."

Drink was forthcoming. The Danes drained the horns fast, then more slowly while they took off their mail. No bathhouse could take so many, but kettles of water had been heated in the cookhouse and were brought in with washcloths. Having cleaned themselves, the warriors broke out fresh clothes. The servants carried in food, roast pork and other good dishes, which they ate rather hastily, for by then the sun was down and twilight thickening.

"Well, let's begin on the ale in earnest," said Hadding after things had been cleared away. "Our kingly hosts ought to join us soon."

That time lengthened. An awkward silence fell over the troop. The fires guttered low, the night seeped inward.

Hadding was about to call for more wood and for lamps, when Svein cocked his head. "I hear something outside," he said. "Like men afoot. Does anybody else?"

"So, the Ynglings—at last," grumbled Einar.

"No," said Svein. "Listen. They're not coming straight to the front door. Some are going around. And they're many."

After a bit, others nodded. Hadding glared at the servants The stares he got back were bewildered, frightened. "Yes," he muttered, "they'd not have been told. Not even young Hunding, I think." The hair stood up on his arms.

"I'll go see," said Gunnar. He strode to the entry, out of their sight.

They heard a roar and a rattle. "Take your weapons!" Hadding shouted. He leaped for his own sword and shield.

Two more guardsmen ran after Gunnar. They saw him on the ground at the open door. He clutched at the spear driven through his belly, struggled to rise, and sank back. His blood throbbed forth to drench the rushes. Above him, the mail and helmet of a warrior caught the dim firelight from within. A sword hewed. It struck Einar's bare head and clove the skull. Men behind pressed into the entry.

"Hold the doors!" cried Hadding. Danes snatched their arms. They went to stand at either end of the house. Battle crashed and snarled. Their fellows scrambled to get iron back on bodies.

"Help me up," Hadding bade Egil. The old housecarle went to one knee. The king stood on the other thigh. From there he was tall enough to peer out a window, by starlight.

He stepped down. "A host is around us," he said. "Uffi must have had most of them lurking in the woods. That means he readied them well beforehand, and had scouts posted to spy us coming and let him know. We've walked into a trap."

"Best we break out of it, then, before he sets it afire," Egil growled.

"This is new timber, not easily kindled," Hadding answered. "But they much outnumber us. Never will we cut a way free through them. We can only hold fast where we are. Maybe something will happen before we've all fallen."

He went among his men, arraying them. Those who had kept the doors, without byrnies, were dead or dying. However, they had bought time for the rest, who now drove the foe back from those narrow spans. "Fight till you grow weary," Hadding bade them. "Then step aside and let a fresh man take your place while you catch your breath."

Himself he warded the front door longer at a time than any other. Two guards died beside him, two more at once bestrode their bodies. Still his sword crashed, still it bit.

Yet the Danes were inside. The fires died down. Whatever

wood the cowering servants might have fetched was elsewhere. Men groped more and more blind. At length they could not tell how their oath-brothers fared at the doorways. They fell over each other's feet, trying to get to where they could do some good.

The onslaught broke through.

Warriors churned about in the murk, chopped and stabbed at shadows, shouting war-cries for their fellows to know them. "Dane-Hadding!" yelled Svein as a black blur rose before him. "Dane-Hadding," panted the unknown one. Svein lowered his sword. An ax struck him.

It was no longer a battle where men stood side by side. It was a maelstrom, everybody sightless and alone. Surely friend often smote friend and let a foe go by. Uffi had more men to spend than did Hadding.

He, though, fosterling of jotuns in wilderness, kenned every sound and knew whence it came. He snuffed the air and felt it stir to every movement around him. He prowled the gloom like a lynx, killing and killing.

He could not save his followers. Slowly the fight ebbed away. Men stumbled about croaking their calls, fewer and fewer, until no more calls were Danish. The wounded gasped underfoot. The stench of death lay heavy. Hadding stole over blood-wet rushes and clay, across bodies writhing or still, toward the rear door. Two men kept watch at it. Starlight barely touched their helmets. Hadding pounced from the inner night. Right, left his sword whined. They fell, half-beheaded. An outcry arose at the noise, but by then he was gone.

The sky stood black, the land stretched dim. He crouched and wove a snake's way off to the woods. They would never track him there.

But it was far to Scania. When they did not find him dead in the morning, the hunt would go forth across the kingdom.

He would need all his craft, hiding by day, faring by night, living off roots, herbs, frogs, lemmings, maggots, and whatever else he could take. That too was something he meant to avenge on Uffi. First and foremost, though, were his housecarles, slain in the dark.

XXV

awn broke as white as Hunding's face, where he stood atremble before Uffi. Hurt king's men lay or sat on the dew-heavy sward around the guesthouse. Women had come from Uppsala to help tend them. Soon they would be brought back into the town. Early bird calls seemed louder than their few weary words. Thumps and rattles sounded dully from within, where warriors went about cutting the throats of wounded Danes and ransacking the dead. A breeze blew chill.

For half the night, since he got the news, Hunding had raged and ranged around. Only now had he found his brother. "This was the, the foulest unfaith," he stammered. "You've cast our honor on—the dungheap."

Uffi scowled. "Naught did we ever owe that wolf but revenge for our grandfather, our father, and all the harm he did our folk."

"He felled Svipdag and Asmund man against man, in open war, after Svipdag killed his own father. He wrought no worse in Svithjod than we in Denmark. We won fame for what we did, fighting such a hero. Then he came here willing to make the peace that you, you, offered. And all along it was false. You were plotting his murder from the first."

"Be still!" rasped Uffi. "I'll hear no more of that yammer."

"You shall hear nothing further from me," Hunding told him. "I disown you. Never more will I stand at your side, nor will any man who is true to me."

He turned and stalked off, shuddering. Uffi glowered after him. Suddenly the king's shoulders slumped a little. He made himself very busy giving orders about the care of men and booty.

Day brightened. Guardsmen who had known Hadding by sight came one after another to tell him they had not found the Dane-king among the fallen, neither his own nor servants who had gotten in the way of a blow. At last Uffi howled, went in, and threw the lichs aside like a dog burrowing after a badger. None of the gaping gray faces was the one he hated.

He straightened. For a while his throat was too tight for him to speak. "The wolf has sneaked free," he thereupon croaked. "We must set the hounds after him."

For days riders went everywhere in the shire, searching, asking, uttering threats and offering rewards. They caught a few Danes who had also gotten out, and sent their heads back to Uffi. But nowhere did even the most skilled trackers find spoor of Hadding. Uffi slaughtered kine and thralls in the shaw, calling on the gods to make his foe be dead. More could he not do.

As leaves turned yellow and geese trekked through windy heaven, word reached him. Hadding had won back to Denmark and taken up kingship again. Uffi sat dumb, alone in his high seat, until he mumbled, "Can it be me whom the gods are against?" He raised his head. "Nor will I yield to them," he said into the flickering firelight.

Throughout the winter and spring Hadding made ready. There was no dearth of strong men, mostly younger sons, eager to become his new housecarles. He picked them shrewdly, outfitted them fully, fed them overflowingly, gifted them freely, and at the hands of older warriors drilled them ruthlessly. He sent word around the kingtime that after sowing there would be a great levy for war abroad. Likewise did he send to King Haakon, who promised twenty ships full of armed Niderings. Meanwhile he gathered food and drink to keep his host for two or three weeks—meat smoked and salted, stockfish, hardtack, cheese, casks of ale—along with wains, horses, and whatever else would be needed.

At the set time, then, his fighters swarmed to Haven and ferried across the Sound. As they went north overland they met the men of Scania under Jarl Eyjolf. All fared onward.

Theirs was a mighty troop. At the head rode King Hadding with his highest chieftains, the housecarles behind them. Cloaks rippled from their shoulders as bright hued as the banners overhead. Here and there, rearward, were others mounted. Most went afoot, a dun throng ablink with iron, in loose little bands. They thronged to right and left, talking, singing, laughing, shouting. The earth drummed to their tread. Fields lay trampled flat behind them. In their midst dust smoked white off whatever road wound between. There bumped and creaked the laden wagons. Often men must lend their strength to the draught horses, shoving wheels out of ruts too deep, dragging them through tall grass or over stones where a road gave out altogether, pushing them uphill, braking them downhill, splashing them across fords, hauling them from mudholes when rain had been heavy. Sweat sheened on skin and darkened shirts, breath went hoarse and oathful in mouths.

Still, the host moved fast. Hadding led it first east, then north, skirting the hills. The lowlands along the Baltic were much easier going, mostly plowland and meadow. They passed many a farmstead and thorp, but stopped only to camp for the night. When they were out of Scanian land and pushing on through the Geats, dwellers fled, but Hadding forbade plunder and even burning. After he had a few men beheaded who disobeyed, the rest believed what he told them, that this wasted time and added burdens. Only to such near friends as Eyjolf did he add that he would rather not leave more ill will than he must.

Through traders and seamen as well as spies, Uffi knew well beforehand of their coming. He sent the war-arrow throughout Svithjod, called on those Geats who were plighted to him, and so raised his own troop. It was less than it might have been. Hunding hung back, with those who looked to him instead of to the king or who thought that following a killer of guests would be unlucky. However, the host was bigger than Hadding's, and many in it felt that they fought for their homes.

The two met near the shore. Land sloped green with young grass, black and torn where they had passed, studded with trees, range for herds whose owners had driven them off. A narrow strait winked and chuckled. Beyond it, low and linggrown, stretched the long island called Öland. Over this, thunderhead clouds were rising ever higher and thicker. A wind blew off the sea, loud, cold, and salt. Already ravens from inland and gulls from the water were gathering in it. They had learned.

Hadding laughed as a wolf might laugh. "He's picked a fine ground for fighting, good King Uffi has," he said. "How kind of him."

His chieftains scurried to and fro, barking orders, getting the men into a wedge. Across the span between, the foe formed their straight ranks. A horseman galloped from them. He bore a white shield. The housecarle who rode out to meet him brought him to Hadding as he asked.

"I bear you word from King Uffi," he said boldly. "He dares you to meet him man to man."

"Whatever the outcome, it would not quiet our followers," Hadding answered slowly.

"No. Let them clash. But the way to him shall stay as open for you as he can keep it."

"Then I will take it," Hadding said. "Tell King Uffi that I look forward."

The messenger nodded and rode back. Hadding gazed after him. "Uffi is a worthier foe than I thought," he murmured. "Whoever fells him will win a great name. He shall have thanks for that."

The ranks were taking shape. Riders went aside, dismounted, tethered their steeds, and came back. For a little, only the rising chop on the water stirred, only the wind and the nearing thunder spoke. Wrack hid the sun. Lightning flared in the clouds.

Horns sounded. The hosts roared and broke into a trot. They shocked together.

The two big men at the Danish forefront smashed with axes. One knocked a sword aside and bit through the bone of the leg beneath. The other clove a shield and sent the bearer staggering backward, to tangle with those behind him. The four Danes in the second row smote rightward, leftward, and ahead. The weight of those at their backs helped press them forward. In and in the swine array drove.

The Swedish ranks buckled and split. No longer did man stand side by side with man. Warriors milled about, striking where they could, each for himself. From the Danish wings arrows sleeted, slingstones hailed.

Hadding had taken the right end of his fourth row. That kept his unshielded side open to attack; but the men behind were ready to cut down or cast a spear into anyone who came at him. All those closest to him were from the pick of his housecarles. The man on his left upheld his banner. Its raven flew wildly in the wind.

Before the onslaught he had marked King Uffi's. As he hewed he kept an eye on it, where it swayed and flapped above the helmets. The Swede-king did likewise. By jags and jerks they drew nearer one another.

Lightning sheeted. For that blink of time the strait shone molten. Thunder crashed down the heights of heaven. Rain fell in a flood whipped by the storm. Men fought half-blinded. Soon streams ran around the fallen, washing away their blood.

The tide of battle swept clear the ground between Hadding and Uffi. The Dane-king caught the arm of his banner bearer, pointed, and loped from the wedge. After him dashed those men he had told to go always with him. By then it mattered little. The swine array was breaking up into bands, for only thus could most of the warriors now get at foemen hopelessly scattered.

The last of Uffi's guards had made a shield wall around their lord. A score or so, they outnumbered by a few Hadding's oncoming gang. Rain runneled down them. Their iron shimmered with it. Whenever lightning glared, each sword or spearhead stood forth stark in sight. Thunder hammered the world.

The wall parted. Out from its midst trod Uffi. Bearlike he hunched, waiting. The top of his shield was in splinters and the rain coursed red from a gash on his right cheek, for he had fought hardily himself. But it was no weakening wound, and the sword that he gripped was heavier than most.

"Strike at the others," Hadding called over his shoulder to his men. "That one is mine."

He stopped a yard or two short. Through seven lightning flashes they stood and stared, feet braced in the mire. "I think you ken me," said the Dane-king across the wind-howl. "I am Hadding Gramsson, whom you have sought for so long."

The Swede-king nodded. "And I am Uffi Asmundsson," he answered. "Hadding the Halt, this day you shall go down hell-road with the limp my father gave you."

"I think you will go first," said Hadding, "but we shall see."

He took a step forward. His blade whirred. Uffi caught it in his shield. He cut at a leg while he tried to twist the sword from Hadding's hand. Hadding had already slacked the thews in his other leg. He swung aside and the blow missed. Nor had he driven his own edge too deeply into the wood. He had hewn slantwise, to strike across the grain, and merely nicked it. With nothing to drag at, Uffi's twist swept his shield aside, baring the arm behind it. Before he could bring it back, Hadding had slashed from elbow to wrist.

Uffi lowered his head and bored in. Iron banged and rang. Hadding's sword found only helmet or byrnie. Uffi struck Hadding on the left thigh. There likewise ringmail turned the edge, but it was a mighty blow. With no padding beneath, that low down, it bruised like a slingstone on bare flesh. Hadding faltered. Barely did he get his shield between Uffi's blade and his own neck. Uffi chopped at his calf. Hadding sidestepped, but his lame foot betrayed him. He slipped on the mud and went over.

Uffi yelped and moved in to hack him from above. Hadding rolled onto his back. His two-legged kick got Uffi in the belly. The Yngling fell too. He was up on his knees as fast as the other man. For a while, kneeling, the two flailed.

Hadding worked his way backward. When he knocked Uffi's swordpoint to the ground, he could leap up. The Swede swung at his shin. Awaiting that, he blocked with his blade. His right boot dug into the mire. It flung a spattering gob into his foeman's eyes.

Uffi screamed. Before he could see again, Hadding caught him once more on the left forearm. This time the sword hit better. Blood spurted. The shield fell free.

Rain flooded Uffi's face clean. His blade winged to and fro. Hadding could not come near. Uffi rose.

Dauntlessly he lumbered to attack. Swords met. Hadding's was well-nigh torn loose. He sprang back. Blow after blow gnawed his shield. Never could he trap the edge. Suddenly, though, he rammed it ahead to meet the next cut. The iron glanced off. He had an opening. His blade struck like an adder. Into Uffi's left leg it went, above the knee that thrust out from the byrnie, to the bone and onward.

Uffi sank to earth. On his right knee, the left leg useless and blood rivering from it, he snarled up at Hadding through the rain. "Come and get me," he grated, "if you dare." Thunder rolled around his words.

"I could stand here and watch you die," said Hadding, "but you are worthy of better. Yet I wonder if you would have given me this much."

He trod close. Sword clanged on sword. It was hard and dangerous work until Uffi sagged. He lay in the mire while the last of his blood drained off into the gurgling brown streamlets. Rain beat over him. Lightninglight flamed on his mail.

Hadding looked about. The Swedish guards had fought stoutly, slain four Danes and wounded all the rest. But they took worse losses, and when they saw their king go down, they broke and ran. Their foes were too worn out to give chase.

Everywhere over the field, their fellows were likewise in flight. None stayed behind but the crippled and the dead. Hadding set about getting his troop back together.

The storm passed. The night was calm. Morning shone lovely. Mists steamed low above the battleground, where birds flocked and cried. Hadding gave his men a day of ease, except for those who buried fallen friends. Himself he ordered that

King Uffi's body be undressed, washed, and shrouded in three good cloaks.

Next morning he sent most of his followers home under their shire-leaders. With three hundred long-seasoned warriors he bore northward. Taking remounts and pack horses for food and gear, they rode speedily. One horse bore King Uffi.

As Hadding had foreseen, they met no trouble along the way. Beaten men were straggling back to their dwellings by ones or two or threes. Nothing was left that could stand against even so small a troop as his. Nevertheless he kept them from doing any harm except, maybe, now and then stealing a chicken or a pig. He had a higher end in mind.

And thus after a few days they came to Uppsala. That was on another rainy day, but a mild one. Only a drizzle grayed the land, cool and still. It was as if the earth mourned. The town across the river stood dim, almost dreamlike.

Fast though the Danes went, word of them was bound to have gone ahead. Some scores of warriors waited before the bridge. Hunding sat mounted in front. He rode forward, sword in sheath, alone. Hadding rode to meet him. They halted.

"Be welcome, if that is your wish," said Hunding low. Raindrops glistened in the hair of his bare head and trickled down his face.

"It is," answered Hadding as quietly.

"You are bold to come into our lair with no more strength than this."

"I thought it would be strength enough to break through anything we might find."

"Yet you did not await more fighting."

"No. I have heard how it is with you."

Hunding nodded. He pointed offside. "See yonder," he said. Charred snags stuck out of an ash heap. "I've had the house of shame burned."

Hadding's voice warmed. "That was good of you. For my part, I've brought your brother, Uffi, home." Hunding stared. "He was a fearless man, who did mighty deeds," Hadding said. "I would give him his honor."

He could not tell whether it was raindrops or tears that caught in Hunding's lashes. "Now I know you are great-hearted as well as great," the Yngling whispered.

Fully cleansed, the kingly hall took the Dane-king in. He and his men abode for many days. Since they hurt nobody but were, instead, kindly behaved, the town and neighborhood soon felt friendly toward them. No few wenches wandered offside with these dashing newcomers, while men were often glad to share a stoup and a gab.

Hadding was busier. First he, with Hunding, saw to the burial of Uffi. They got the lich into a box before rot had gone too far, then put workmen to digging and bringing in big stones. When the grave chamber was ready, they laid Uffi in it with a hoard of gold, silver, glass, and amber. Hadding laid thereto weapons he had brought along from the battlefield. The workers heaped earth high above to make a howe, and set the stones around it in the outline of a ship. Folk came from widely around for the death feast. With their own hands Hunding and Hadding slaughtered oxen and horses in the holy shaw. In kettles hung over the fires in the halidom, that meat seethed before the gods until men partook of it. Afterward there were three days of eating, drinking, games, and roistering, that Uffi have a good farewell.

With these honors did Hadding end the feud between Ynglings and Skjoldungs.

Meanwhile he and Hunding were much together, talking. "You shall have my niece Arnborg as was promised you," the Swede said.

"I thank you, but no," Hadding answered. "I've thought on it, and indeed the maiden is very fair. But best not have two queens in Denmark. Strife between their sons could well split the kingdom asunder, and maybe this one too. Find her a strong man you want beholden to you."

Hunding smiled. "I'd liefest that were you yourself," he said. "But I yield to your wisdom."

Hadding sighed. "Maybe it's not so deep. I've all I can do keeping Denmark together. With you for king here in Svithjod, I'll be free to deal with lesser foes."

They had touched on this before. "Then you will help me to that?" Hunding cried. "Never while I live shall you lack for a friend—no, an oath-brother."

Hadding nodded. "That will be well. Bare is the back of the brotherless."

As word went out that he stood behind Hunding, the Swedes became the more willing to take the young man for their new king. Hadding rode with him from Thing to Thing around the land and heard them hail him. Summer was far along when the Danes set homeward. They went laden with gifts, and as the years flowed by, the friendship between the two kings grew ever closer.

XXVI

For season after season, their lands lay at peace. Spring came with a shout of wind and rush of rain, sunlight smote through and was victorious, wet earth went everywhere suddenly green, frogs whooped in the marshes, the wanderbirds returned. Summer brooded huge over grain fields tawny or whitening and leaves more manifold than the stars; clouds loomed on worldrim halfway up the sky, swan-hued but shadowy blue in their depths; the sea shimmered and blinked. Fall turned the world red, yellow, bronze, until wind stripped the bits of color off and whirled them away on its song. Winter stretched snow about bare trees and empty meadows, under leaden skies; nights lengthened, days shrank to glimpses of a sun low and wan in the south; but when weather cleared, frost glittered under the moon and the wheeling Wain.

Folk followed their lives. The yeoman plowed, sowed, reaped, slaughtered, filled crib and pen and stable with the wealth of his acres. The craftsman hammered, cut, fitted together, saw his work grow beneath his hands and found it good. The fisher cast his nets, the trader fared with his cargoes, bold men sought farther abroad than ever before and brought home tales of wonders. Their wives cooked, spun, wove, sewed, and raised strong children. At fairs and offerings, weddings and grave-ales, voices rose from the crowds as merrily as the smoke from their fires.

In Denmark King Hadding warded and tended it all. From shire to shire he rode. Wherever there were dwellings, though they stand on the least of the islands, he set foot now and then. The greater burghs and thorps saw him often. He sat in the Things, and he gave ear to anyone who bespoke him as he passed. None were too lowly. His judgments were strict but fair, with no more heed paid to rank than the law called for. If someone needed help and was worthy of it, that help was forthcoming. Withal, under his eye the chieftains, sheriffs, and their warriors went ruthlessly after illdoers. They hunted down robbers, they scoured out nests of vikings, they did not let a man who had been outlawed go freely about still bullying his neighbors. At last a maiden could walk alone, mile after mile, without fear.

Thus freed from strife and danger, folk did whatever they

did best, and Denmark waxed rich. Trouble came yet, sickness, murrain, blight, wounds by mishap, the weakness of age, all the olden griefs. Men quarreled as always, and sometimes the quarrels became murderous. But such was the human lot. On the whole, they called this the happiest time ever known in the kingdom.

So did fourteen years go by.

During them, Queen Ragnhild bore no more children. Nonetheless, at first she and Hadding lived blithely enough together. He did not even keep a leman at his side, only bedded other women on his wayfarings around the kingdom and then only if he found them comely and they were willing. He and his wife watched their offspring grow. Both were being raised in other households, as was the wont among the highborn, but the parents visited these whenever they could, or had the families as their own guests.

In Frodi they, like his foster father Eirik Jarl, had gladness. The boy was handsome, stalwart, quick-witted. When he chose, he could delight anybody. However, a fierce heart beat in his breast. Early on he was eager at weapon-play and in the hunt. He talked much of the wars he would wage after he reached manhood. Hadding smiled. "Yes, you will have your fights," he said. "You may start by coming along with me on mine. I'll surely get some more, wherever they may arise."

Ragnhild bit her lip.

They saw less of Ulfhild, for she lived afar in Scania with Eyjolf. When they did, she was apt to stir up unease in them. Thin, keen-faced, hair fox-red, she seemed to have little womanliness. She hated the tasks she was set to learn, did them badly, and screamed at those who taught her. Likewise could she fly into rages at anyone else who overrode her will. That will was for ordering others about, for running off recklessly by herself over the hills and into the woods, for climbing trees and throwing stones and handling sharp things. Sometimes

somebody coming on her unawares spied her torturing a bird
or small beast she had caught. With Eyjolf's hounds she got
on well, and when she grew able to ride she was always pestering him to let her take off on a wild gallop.

"I wonder whence a soul like that came into her," Ragnhild said low.

"Oh, she's only mettlesome," Hadding answered. "And
bright. She'll soon find out that misbehavior gets her nowhere.
It's no wonder if a youngster like her waxes restless." He did
not sound as if he altogether believed it.

Ragnhild gave him a long look. "You do yourself, don't
you?"

"Well, the days and years are becoming much the same,
over and over. My housecarles begin to chafe. They have their
lands to oversee, their gains to garner, but where can they win
fame?"

"Must they make their names by killing, looting, and dying
young? Are there no better ways?"

Now Hadding looked at her. "I think you also feel somewhat caged."

"So you have seen that at last," she sighed.

He frowned. "I've other things to deal with than moods
and whims."

Ragnhild bridled, and they spoke no further that day.

Afterward, though, she told him more. This was bit by bit.
She herself did not clearly know what was wrong, why she so
often felt sad and thwarted. Nor would she whine about it. But
in the end, they both saw.

"I am homesick," she owned. "Denmark is a sweet land—
but how flat, how tame! I live in high honor—but once I roved
the mountains, wielded a bow, sped on ski, beheld bound-
lessness around me, almost as freely as a man. Yes, now I understand a little of what is in Ulfhild."

Hadding gave thought. More was at stake here than her

wishes. Her father King Haakon was aged, would surely die before long. Hadding wanted to keep whole his ties to the Niderings. To that end, he might well be wise to spend more time among them than hitherto.

"Things are in hand in this kingdom," he said at length. "Should aught go awry, it's not too many days by sea for me to come back. We could lodge yonder for months at a time." He laughed. "I'd like some newness myself!"

She gasped. Fire leaped in her eyes, behind tears. She flung her arms about his neck. They being alone in a loft room, he could kiss her, and one thing led to another.

So did it come about that in the ninth year of the great peace they took ship for Norway. They had sent word ahead the year before, asking that a house be built for them in the wild uplands, though at a spot readily reachable. In Nidaros they got a welcome that went on for days. Already gladness shone from Ragnhild. Yet she yearned elsewhere, and for her sake Hadding left with her sooner than he really wanted to. He had been sounding out the men of weight, above all the sons of Haakon. One of them would be hailed king after the old man's death. Hadding hoped to learn who among them would be best, and begin quietly lending that one what help he could. A kingdom torn by warfare between brothers would be of small use to him. Still, he went off with his wife and their housefolk.

The dwelling stood broad and tall, high on a ridge overlooking peaks, dales, hasty streams, and silver streaks of waterfall. Slopes strewn with boulders, their grass starred with gentian, tumbled down to where, not far below, birch and pine stood thickly mingled. An eagle hovered aloft, sunlight golden on his wings; lesser fowl sped to and fro, hares scuttered, marmots whistled; now and then a bear stumped by, and most nights wolves gave tongue across the wind. That wind blew cool, clean, the farthest mountain as clear to see through it as if one soared there oneself alongside the eagle.

"I am home again," Ragnhild whispered. "Thank you."

At first Hadding roamed happily about with her, hunting, fishing, or climbing cliffs that belike no human had ever dared before. It took him back to his boyhood. He wondered how Vagnhöfdi and Haflidi fared. He remembered Hardgreip, and uncouth though she had been, the thought of her stung more than he had awaited. He shied back from it, into the sport he shared with Ragnhild.

But as the days dragged into weeks, pleasure dwindled out of him. She blossomed; his answers to her mirth and her singing grew ever shorter. Here he sat, the lord of a few servants, doing nothing more heroic than chasing deer, his mind taken up with nothing more meaningful than next day's outing, while beyond these hemming heights the world roared. He began to hate them. They held him back from his greatness, they barred him from the sea. In the end he wanted only to break loose from them.

Like most well brought up men, he had some skill in skaldcraft. On a day when rain held everybody indoors, hunched in chill and gloom at stinking fires, the bitterness crashed forth as a stave. He prowled the length of the room, a shadow in which eyeballs and teeth caught flickers of what light there was, his footfalls heavy, and spoke what was in him.

> *Why must I dawdle, huddled in darkness,*
> *Caught in a cleft of the barren mountains?*
> *The freedom of faring on waves have I lost.*
> *High through the night goes the howling of wolves;*
> *Never their noise lets me shut an eye.*
> *Wildly they wail as they prowl the clouds;*
> *Grimly the bears growl at their prey;*
> *Lurking lynxes yell when they pounce.*

> *Empty reaches and rocky wastes*
> *Hold for heroes only horror.*
> *Foul to them seem the rearing fells.*
> *Ill it is to live in this land.*
> *They long for the sea that lures them hence,*
> *To plow the waves with the prows of ships,*
> *Winning in war a deathless name,*
> *Starkly striking from off the waters,*
> *Bearing homeward an outland booty—*
> *That is a handicraft fit for heroes,*
> *Rather than squat by the scaur of a berg*
> *Or build and bide in useless woods.*

"Are you that weary of my homeland?" asked Ragnhild sharply through the twilight.

"Well, the time is overpast for me to get back where I belong," he mumbled.

"Yes, doubtless we must," she sighed. "Next year we'll return."

He said nothing to that, but busied himself making ready to go. They did not speak much on the way to Nidaros, nor afterward when sailing to Denmark.

Sight of its low greenness, nestled in the sea like a woman in the arms of a lover, woke his mirth from its long and sullen drowse. He shouted, he slapped the backs of crewmen, swapped coarse japes with them, and laughed so that a flight of gulls sheered off. At Haven he gave a feast that filled hall and town to overflowing and went on for days and nights, while oxcart after oxcart groaned up laden with fresh casks, until the last guest lurched home clutching his head. Afterward there was much to do, things that had waited for the king's word. He gave himself gleefully to them.

But as soon as might be, he moved away. The Sound, softly lapping on weed-strewn shingle, its tides mild as the breathing

of a slumbrous bairn, was not the sea for which he had
yearned. Instead he took his men and servants to another
kingly hall, on the Skaw. Here, at this northern tip of Jutland,
heath rolled down to great dunes and heaped driftwood, below
them the broad sands running from end to end of sight. Trees
were few and dwarfed, gnarled and sideward-leaning, from the
winds that blew ever out of the west. Surf tumbled and
brawled, thundering inward, hissing back again to meet the onslaught that followed. Beyond ramped the waves, green and
gray, foam-swirled, ragged-maned, sunlight a steely flare along
their flanks when weather was clear, lashed to black anger
when storms swept in. Seals tumbled among them or basked
darkly agleam on the skerries around which breakers spouted.
Northward across the Skagerrak, westward across the North
Sea, the eye found no spoor of land, only this wet wilderness.
The air was damp, mostly chill, always laden with taste of
salt, smells of kelp and fish, never really at rest. Gulls wheeled
and mewed in their hundreds.

This hall was built for a stronghold, keeping watch over the
sea lanes and the fisher hamlets along these shores. Some ways
away, on the east side, was a town of craftsmen and traders,
where ships went in and out. Across the Kattegat from it stood
a bigger town of the Geats. In these easy times, hulls plied
steadily between them. From the hall, in season, were seen
many others going by bound on greater farings, up to Norway
or over to Friesland and England, returning home battered but
laden. It was no more than a sight, like the passing of birds.
Ragnhild seldom got to the town. She stayed at the stronghold,
running its everyday life, while Hadding rode around his Jutish
shire.

He would come home glad, tales crackling from his lips,
eager for the night and their shutbed. But now, as winter set
in, it was she who slowly became curt and withdrawn. He offered her what he could—sailing, horseback riding, hunting,

days-long trips through the hinterland—such things as he himself liked. Less and less did she take them.

"It's too low hereabouts," she said once. "You can never see farther than from your own height. Nor is there much that's worth beholding."

He pointed to a hill, steep against the lowering sky, ling-decked to the crest, where sheered a menhir raised of old by a folk unknown. "I've always thought that a tall sight," he told her.

Her laughter scoffed. "In Norway we'd call it a hole in the ground."

She brightened whenever they had guests with something to say that she cared to hear. This was less often than when they had lived deeper within the kingdom. Still, chieftains, traders, outlanders, and others not of the ruck were bound to have dealings with the king; skalds brought their verses, wanderers their gifts of strange things from afar, in hopes of reward; the hall would ring and seethe with their gathering, gold would gleam and ale gurgle forth, and on the high seat Ragnhild would be a queen in truth. Yet when the guests had gone she sank back into moodiness.

"Do you feel left out of the world here?" Hadding asked her bitterly when she had been two days well-nigh unspeaking after the Yule feast ended. "Maybe this is not Haven, but more happens than ever did in Nidaros. And—you dwelt months in the uplands, where we saw hardly anyone for weeks on end, without yawning or sulking."

She stared away from him. "I had been so long gone from my mountains. Oh, I would have come back down again to be among men. But in Nidaros the mountains are always near."

He growled deep in his throat and stalked off.

The year died in sleet and spindrift. Slowly the sun climbed up toward the new year, higher every day. Snow lay in dingy clumps, melting to mud, puddles, and clucking streamlets.

Snowdrops scattered white across earth, and from darksome, leafless woods the thin piping of lapwings sounded through the creaking of the gulls.

Hadding found Ragnhild by herself on the strand. She gazed across a gray sea that tossed and crashed below a gray sky. A ways out yonder, seals thronged a reef. Their calls went hoarse through the wind that skirled above the booming surf. That wind was too bleak to carry much smell. It fluttered her cloak and a stray lock of red hair, the only real color inside this worldrim.

He stopped beside her. "I've been looking for you," he said.

Her glance kept northward. "What do you want?" she asked dully.

"Nothing."

"Then why did you seek me?"

"I thought if I came on you alone, we could talk freely."

"About what?"

He struck fist in palm. "About what's wrong with you, hell take it! Are you sick? Bewitched? You go through the days like a walking stone. Your face is haggard, your eyes are ringed with darknesses like bruises, at night you lie stiff whatever I do and then afterward toss about till dawn so I too get scant sleep. What ails you?"

"It is where we are." Not yet did she look his way nor have any hue in her voice.

He stood for a while starkly thinking. Wind whistled, withdrawing breakers seethed. "Why?" he asked at last.

She drew breath. "Once you made a stave for me," she said. "I have been making one for you. Will you hear it?"

His nod jerked. "Say on."

Now her look went straight at him. She spoke with more life than he had heard from her for a while.

> *No home can I have upon the strand.*
> *The barking seals break my sleep.*
> *Billows burst across the rocks.*
> *And rob me of rest in my fog-wet bed.*
> *Too soon does the scream of the gull arouse me,*
> *Filling my ears with its ugliness.*
> *Never it lets me lie in peace,*
> *But always I hear it harshly mewing.*
> *Better by far to be on the fells.*
> *Here are no heights, no lordly quiet,*
> *But shattering waves and shrieking fowl.*

He stood wordless, arms folded, head bent down toward the sand.

"Well," said Ragnhild, "I will outlive it. In summer we go back to Norway." She stopped. "No?"

Hadding straightened. "No. I cannot be gone so long."

"You could last year. It seems me a fair trade."

"To swap wretchedness for wretchedness?" Hadding gusted a sigh. "Ragnhild, in the uplands the wolves kept me awake, though never had they done so before when I lay out in the woods on a hunt. Nor do I think the gulls at Nidaros ever troubled you. It's when a place grows hateful in itself that the little things begin to gnaw."

"That may be. I told you, on the fjord in Norway I knew I could be quickly back in my mountains."

"I think there's more to it than that," he murmured. "But we'll never understand what. Well, we need not live here any longer. We can hold ourselves mostly to the towns—and, yes, now and then call at Nidaros."

"And even make a meager short visit to the uplands?" she cried. "No! You have your man's freedom to ride around wherever you will and then sail off overseas. I will take whatever freedom a woman may have."

He swallowed hard, but had the wisdom to say no more that day.

After all, he thought later, her brothers, younger than her, looked up to her. Their goodwill was important to him. Shrewd and bold, she could very well speak to her landsmen on his behalf, softly as behooved a woman but with steel underneath, and send news to him of how things were going. She might even help nudge more kings in the high North to swearing fellowship with him. Though Hunding of Svithjod was his friend, who knew what ill hap might suddenly take Hunding off, or what foes might raven in from elsewhere?

The upshot was that in spring they sailed to Nidaros, and he came back without her. They gave out what was true as far as it went, that she would spend a while being his eyes and ears in these parts. If she did some of that while off in the wilderness, who dared question the Dane-queen? Otherwise let tongues wag as they would.

Their last night together had not the lustfulness they once knew, but it left them feeling closer in their hearts.

Hadding bade farewell and hoisted sail for Denmark. There he would have no dearth of women. Mainly, though, he found himself among men, from jarls to crofters, wrights to warriors.

It was the warriors who most thrust their wishes upon him, his housecarles, youths everywhere, even graybeards who had been keeping their battle axes whetted. Too long had they lain idle or plodded the rounds of farm and burgh. Where now were masts aslant and rig athrum, new shores upheaving from the waves, shield-gleam and weapon-clash, great deeds, fearless dyings forever remembered, booty and brags brought home for the wonderment of maidens, the bond between man and man that goes deeper than love? How could a hero forever sit still?

"I remember how we slogged through mud and shivered beneath rain, how the flux came on us in camp, how the newly dead stink and stare, how ready one is to kill one's comrade if he belches just once more in the selfsame way," Hadding had said once to Ragnhild. "And yet—"

Besides, he could not well keep strength in being if he never used it.

In the following summer he led a fleet across the Baltic. They harried widely among the Wends, they rowed up the rivers of Gardariki, they came back loaded with gold, amber, furs, and thralls. Thus for a while afterward there could again be peacefulness in Denmark.

On the way home, Hadding sent most of the ships on ahead while he, with a few, grounded on Scanian shores. There he and some guards got horses. They rode to Bralund that he might call on his friend and jarl, Eyjolf.

One day during this visit, he went for a walk with his daughter, Ulfhild. Her foster father had told him that though she curbed herself better than erstwhile, beneath it she stayed as willful and flighty as ever. Hadding thought he might try getting to know her a little. She was Ragnhild's daughter too.

The trail they took wound by a stubblefield. On its other side rose trees kept for a woodlot. The birches had already lost most of their leaves, which lay yellow and scrittled drily aside from feet. Elsewhere greenness lingered, but fading. Sunlight spilled through silent air that smelled of earth. Geese trekked overhead. Their honking drifted faintly downward. Crows cawed, hopping bits of night, where they picked the cropland over for grain the gleaners had overlooked. Let wanderbirds go off into the unknown; the crows would abide.

"So now you will soon round out your twelfth winter," Hadding said. "Good for you. Before long you'll be a woman."

The girl clenched her fists. "It's too long for me." Her voice was small and cold.

He laughed. "That's because you are young. I draw nigh my fiftieth, and yet it feels like only yesterday I was a boy among the giants."

She cast him a look. He did not seem old. The gold of hair and beard was going fallow; furrows trenched his cheeks and when he squinted the crinkles stood forth around his eyes; a skin once fair had gone to dry leather; he limped a bit more than formerly; but still he had most of his teeth, still he stood straight and broad-shouldered, still the sword at his hip hung ready.

"We must start to think about your morrows," he said. "I'll be asking around about a husband for you. He'll be a man whose strength we want at our side—but also a good man, dear, one you can be happy with."

She tautened. "How happy has my mother been with you?" she screamed. "I've heard!" She turned from him and ran.

He did not follow, but stood watching her slight form speed away. That evening in Eyjolf's hall he did not talk much. Next day he rode back to his ships.

Winter fell.

Its endless nights came to an end.

In spring Hadding sailed north. Old King Haakon had now died, but his son Knut had been hailed without any naysaying. Hadding gathered that Ragnhild had had something to do with that. Knut made the Dane-king unstintedly welcome, and from the first night Ragnhild shared his bed it was as if nothing had ever pushed in between them.

"I've missed you, oh, I've missed you," she stammered in the warm blindness.

"And I you," he said. "Come back with me."

She was slow to answer. "We were too stubborn, both of us. I think we always will be. Our souls are not the same. But surely we can meet halfway—often enough."

In the days thereafter they went aside from others and spoke of how this might be done. His ship bore her home with him to Denmark. As for what else they agreed to, later he never fully recalled it.

In the summer she grew great with child. A while past Yule, on a night when wind wailed and sleet hissed around the hall, she was brought to bed of it.

Through the long darkness and the glimmer of day and the darkness again she fought. Lamps guttered, torches smoked, shadows wavered thick. The bower stank of their smoke and of the sweat, cold and slick, that drenched every gown the women gave her. Straw ticks, gone sodden with blood, were taken off to be burnt. The midwife hovered helpless. In the corners, three witch-wives whom she had sent for hunched on their three-legged stools, singing their spells.

Ragnhild gasped. The midwife brought water and held up her head that she might suck of it. She fell back onto the bed. Another wave passed through her belly.

Again and again.

Hadding sat in the hall among his housecarles. They drank. By daylight they ate something, without giving it heed, and then drank more. Sleep overwhelmed one after another, until at last they all slumped on the benches or sprawled on rushes, snoring. Hadding sat alone in the high seat. His gaze smoldered ember-red.

Dawn grayed. The midwife came in to him. "Lord, I bring you sorrow," she said. "The queen has died, and the birth was cold."

Hadding looked at her as a blind man might look. "Was it a boy or a girl?" he croaked.

"A girl."

"I think she would have liked that."

He rose and stiffly followed her to the bower. The flames of a few lamps were fading into the dimness that leaked from the sky outside. He was used to blood and reek, he need give them no heed. Instead he walked across the floor, between the awed witches, to the birthbed. A while he stood, looking down. Ragnhild stared back at him. Her face was gray and hollowed out, nothing like the face that once he kissed.

He bent over to close her eyes. "You were a warrior," he said. "I could never have fought the fight you did. Wherever you are bound, let them honor you."

His hand stroked the wet ruddy hair. He straightened and went out.

XXVII

A man hight Tosti. He it was who broke the long peace. In those days the Danes lived mainly on their islands and in Scania. Only the northern fourth of Jutland paid scot to their king. However, more and more of them were moving in, as younger sons overflowed from olden farmsteads. For the most part this happened quietly. The Jutes thereabouts were not many and much land lay open for the taking. The newcomers cleared, built, plowed, and married daughters of the earlier dwellers. Thorps grew, some until they were towns; ships sailed in and out; overland trade waxed; households did well.

Otherwise the Dane-king held only a pale, some two miles

long and wide, on the eastern shore across from Funen. Hadding's father Gram had taken it with the sword, that he might have a sheriff there to keep watch on the Little Belt that sundered island and mainland.

Elsewhere the Jutes were in the hands of kings who were hardly more than quarrelsome chieftains. They did not have all the rest of the peninsula. The Anglians owned much of its western half and lands reaching on toward Frisia. The Saxons filled the eastern side of its lower neck, though most of their country swept from the valley of the Elbe through the valley of the Ysel. Some of their kingdoms were strong.

Though Dane, Jute, Anglian, and Saxon thought of themselves as unlike each other, they were closely akin in blood, tongue, and lifeways. Many of them were going west overseas to harry the Franks and carve new homes out of England.

Tosti hailed from the backbone of mid-Jutland, the son of a poor yeoman who barely grubbed a living from a few gaunt acres. The father died while the boy was small, and Tosti did not get on with the man who took his mother in. Nor was he ever willing for such a lowly life. Early on he ran about with other youths of his bent. Their wildness fed on itself. As they got their growth, they started to waylay men, whom they robbed and left beaten half to death.

Word went around and charges were brought at the Thing. The fathers could not pay weregild. The gang would not even come speak for themselves. Instead, they broke into lonely garths while the owners and carles were at the meeting. They raped, killed, and robbed. Thereafter they were named wolves in the halidom, whom any man could slay without having to answer to the law.

They took to the heath. First Tosti split the skull of his stepfather.

A few fights made him their unquestioned leader, while he never owned any man his lord. In the course of the next ten years or so, he gathered more ruffians to him. By their raids they gained skill and weapons, as well as plunder which they could trade for whatever else they wanted. When king's men came after them, sometimes they threw back the attack on a camp of theirs, sometimes they withdrew to another. Deep woods, misty fens, trackless moors were full of lairs for them.

Bit by bit Tosti began selling his strength too. Outlaw he was at home. No king anywhere wanted beasts like this in his guard. Yet when the war-arrow went around, the robbers could be useful hirelings—or better than useful, raging ahead to rip the throat out of the foe.

Afterward they would go back to the stronghold they now had. It stood alone on a high heath, looking widely over ling, gorse, tussocks, scattered thickets, and murky meres. The frame of its stockade was a ring of standing stones left by the giants of old. Tosti gibed at their ghosts. Thralls died hauling the timbers, digging the turf, breaking the rocks that went to build it. When they were done it crouched as a thorp, bulky, filthy, unruly, but his. Kine lowed around it, grazing in summer, fed in winter on hay cut wherever grass grew. This and all other work fell to the thralls, some reaved from their homes, some bought in marts where nobody kenned the buyers. More than half of them were women, who trudged about their tasks, spread their legs when a warrior bade, and seldom lived long. Nor did any children they bore.

Other needs, such as grain, cloth, and iron, came from outside. Tosti's gang had won the means to pay for it when paying was easier than snatching. He had, in truth, become a kind of chieftain in his own right. Any one or two of the little Jutish kings could have raised a host too big for him, and taken the time to hound him down. But he shrewdly furthered wariness among them. Thus he said once to Orm of Donlund, "If ever you go up against me, that will leave your own land open to Svengir of Hrossmark. You know well what grudges he nurses.

Would you not both do better to stay on the good side of me? Make me a yearly payment and we brothers will leave you alone. Well, maybe once in a while there'll be some small raid, but nothing much. Besides, all Jutes should remember that the Anglians are always watchful. Tempt them not."

So it was that Tosti waxed in might. Maybe he could have grown greater than he did, were it not that his faithlessness and cruelty shocked too many hardened men. They came to call him Tosti the Wicked. That delighted him.

He was not tall, but very broad and thick, bandy-legged, strong as a bear. His face was ill to behold, with eyes sunken deep under a narrow forehead, snoutlike nose, buck teeth in a gash of a mouth, unkempt black hair and beard. His garb was greasy, he seldom bathed, and more fleas hopped on him than did on most folk. He liked using his fists and boots on the women he took.

Withal, he had the somewhat fearful worship of his men. It was not only that they had nowhere else to go. Without him to lead them, they would soon be scattered and slain, and they knew it. He had brought them to what they thought was a better life than a poor yeoman's or a homeless landlouper's. He could be merry when he chose, in his rough way, livening drinking bouts that would otherwise have been cheerless. He held dreams up before them.

The day would come, he said, when they were no longer outlaws hunting meager prey. No, they would be at the front of a wave that swept over all Jutland, drowned every foe, brought down haughty Hadding, and raised a mighty kingdom.

It was not all boasting. After years Tosti felt ready to move.

Besides his own henchmen, he gathered Jutes from the Saxon marches. Warface back and forth had left abiding hatreds, and there was moreover the hope of loot. The host was not very big, but its men were bold and war-wonted. They gave no warning as they went swiftly south. Soon the red cock crowed on roofs as far as eye could see.

The king's reeve in those parts, Syfrid, mustered what strength he quickly could and met them. That was a bloody affray. The Saxons held their ground, but barely, and behind windrows of their dead. Near sunset, the Jutes drew back and sat down to rest. Tosti sent a man with a white shield to ask if the Saxon leader would like to talk.

Syfrid would, however bad it tasted. The two of them stalked toward one another across the ling between their men. Ravens flapped heavily up and sought their food farther off. Their croaking was almost the only sound. The west went red.

"Will you have peace?" Tosti greeted.

Syfrid folded his arms and glowered. "You should be he who begs for it," he answered.

"Why? We drubbed you today. Tomorrow we'll wipe out the last of you."

"That will be as the Father of Victories chooses. But surely your pack will never get home alive. Already the king must be calling up a levy to stamp you flat underfoot."

"We can be gone faster than you think, laying waste along our way. Why should your landsmen suffer needlessly? You can have great gain instead, that may in time bring you higher than your king."

Syfrid stood long silent before he asked, "How can that be?"

"You must join us in making war on Denmark. Hold!" Tosti lifted a hand. "What I mean is to lure King Hadding to his death. Without him, his lands will lie open to those who go in at once, before his jarls or his young son can rally the Danes anew. There'll be no dearth of chieftains who'll join us, eager to share the spoils. But first we must be rid of Hadding."

"No, you're mad!"

Tosti fleered. "If I am, you needn't share the madness. Only tell me no, and die tomorrow. But if you have any wisdom, you'll at least hear me out first."

They talked long into the night. Stars wheeled, owls hooted, wolf-song wailed. Tosti wheedled, browbeat, uttered terrible threats, made vast promises, and wore the Saxon down. The upshot was that at dawn they swore oaths.

Folk at Haven knew nothing of this. They were holding a feast that would be long remembered, when Hadding's son Frodi wedded Viborg, daughter of King Hunding in Svithjod. Whole herds had plodded across Zealand to feed the guests, whole wagon trains brought ale, mead, and outland wine to slake them. Houses bulged with sleepers, tents and booths crowded acres. Fires brawled, racket rang to the sky, skalds chanted their verses, mummers played their pranks, everybody talked, sang, told tales, dickered, seldom quarreled and never too badly, spoke of what was to come, sported, japed, and after dark begot no few children.

When the torchbearers had led the young man and woman to their bridal bower, while raw good wishes were shouted forth to frighten off evil beings and help bring fruitfulness, the fathers withdrew for a while. They strolled out through the fields under stars and a sickle moon. The air rested cool. The noise of merrymaking grew faint behind them.

"Well," said Hadding low, "now it's done. May they find gladness."

Hunding chuckled. "From what I've heard of Frodi and know of you, my Viborg will never feel slighted."

"It's not easy, being man and wife, and more may hang on this wedlock than on most."

"You're thoughtful. Why now?"

Hadding smiled wryly. "A man grows older."

"But we can only make the best of our lives, no? What our offspring may do with theirs lies beyond us."

"Still, I watch them as they grow up, and wonder."

"Keeping track of that many must keep you busy." Suddenly Hunding caught hold of the Dane's arm. "Fear not, good friend. You'll stay above ground a long while yet. You may outlive me, and I'm not worrying."

Hadding looked at him. "You're younger."

"No man may flee his weird. But while you're alive, I'll be happy, and peace will abide between our kingdoms." Hunding shrugged. "Come, this is getting too grave. Let's go back and drain some more beakers."

As they walked, he saw how Hadding limped more heavily than erstwhile.

The feast ended, the guests trekked home, quietness fell over the trampled earth. Then out of a rainy day came horsemen galloping.

Ships had grounded on Lolland, they cried. The crews seemed to be mingled Jutes and Saxons. They were harrying about as no vikings had dared in Denmark for many years. Though they numbered only two or three hundred, they were too much for the neighborhood's men. From things overheard it was known that one Tosti was at their head.

"We have heard of him before," said Hadding between set teeth. "Soon the world will hear no more." He sent for his housecarles and by dawn they were riding south.

Down Zealand they sped, gave themselves and their horses a short sleep in the light night, then ferried across to the island Falster. This they laid behind them in hours, reached another strait, and ferried again. Above the green fields and daisy-studded meadows of Lolland, smoke stained heaven. It pointed the way more surely than did the folk who stumbled past, fleeing with whatever they had been able to take.

High woodland walled in the last part of the path to that strand. Hoofbeats broke its stillness. The light of late afternoon streamed through leaves and struck spearheads, helmets, byrnies so that it was as if a flickering fire raced through the shadows. With a shout, the Danes beheld seawater at the end.

They burst into a trap.

From right and left, warriors swarmed out of the woods. Swords, axes, spears sank into flesh, first of all horseflesh. Before Hadding's troopers could dismount to fight, they were in a maelstrom of screaming, rearing beasts and hewing men. Horses threw their riders, or fell with broken legs or splitted bellies down upon them. Arrows whined from boughs overhead. No Dane could stand by a shieldmate, even if he got safely to the ground. Each for himself, they hacked about them blindly in the ruck and died.

Some broke free and got off into the brush. Hadding, at the forefront, leaped from his saddle and cut his way to the strand. As it opened to his sight, he spied ships up and down the length of it. They were many more than he had been told of.

One sturdy young guardsman had won through beside him. For this scrap of time, nobody was coming at them. The crash and uproar was all from beneath the trees. "Come," groaned Hadding, and bore off easterly. "Before they find us."

The man could not help asking, "Why?" in a harsh breath.

"My guess is that the firstcomers landed yonder. Now, fast!"

They hastened on alongside waters shining with eventide. Blood dripped into their footprints, but neither was badly hurt. It was sweat that soaked their underpadding and filled their nostrils with rankness. Their mouths went kiln-dry. After

a while Hadding began to drag his bad foot. The other man
gave him an arm and they pushed onward.

The sun trudged lower. A breeze awoke. A flight of rooks
passed by.

The two climbed a ridge that sloped down across the
strand. Standing on top, they saw a cove where half a dozen
ships lay drawn up. "Yes," panted Hadding, "these must be the
ones we heard about."

"What of that?" asked the housecarle.

Hadding grinned without mirth. "Why, see you, that Tosti
fooled us neatly. He came first with no more than some viking
skippers might get together. And so they behaved, like plun-
derers who'd skip off as soon as any real strength showed itself. My main hope was that we could catch them before they
got away. But meanwhile his full fleet crossed from Saxland.
They set about burning to draw us straight to them, before we
could learn the truth. Oh, he's wilier than I knew, him Tosti."

"Then his head will look well on a pole," growled the
warrior.

"For that, we must first save ourselves." Hadding limped
down the ridge.

The foe had left merely three men to watch over these
craft, against weather and thieves. Weary though they were, the
newcomers cut them down in a few strokes. "We can't go on
overland," sighed Hadding. "By now we'd be too slow. We'll
take to the water."

Some of the ships had towed boats, which lay on the strand
beside them. Hadding chose the smallest, most easily rowed.
"We'll not be too handy at the oars, the way we are, if they
chase us," said the guardsman.

Hadding nodded. "No boat can outrace a ship. But we can
see to these."

Tools were always aboard a vessel. Hadding and his housecarle took up the planks laid in the bottoms, drilled holes, and

put the planks back again. "That should slow them," laughed the king.

Taking also a water cask and some dried food they found, they launched the boat and set forth. Once well offshore, they doffed their mail, shipped their oars, and drifted. They ached to their bones.

Slumped in the stern, Hadding looked at his follower. He saw a big man, fair-haired, blunt-nosed, too young for sorrow to have marked him much. "Forgive me," said Hadding. "After this day, my head feels blurred. You are Gudorm Thorleifsson, are you not?"

The warrior nodded. "I joined your housecarles only a month or two, ago, lord, while your thoughts were mostly on the wedding. You don't know me well yet."

"I think I do now, Gudorm. That was the name of my brother. A good sign for us two? Tell me again as you did before—sleep is coming on me—whence you hail."

"From Keldorgard west of the Isefjord, lord. It's among the greatest holdings on Zealand."

Hadding nodded. "Yes, I should have remembered. I will remember. But let us rest."

He drowsed off. Gudorm sat a while gazing at him through the sunset light. It gave back a little gold to the king's gray head.

When the battle was done, Tosti howled, "Who will ken Hadding?" Some of his troop had seen him in the past, and most had heard something about what so famous a man looked like. They grubbed through the fallen. As the search went by without gain, Tosti joined it, tossing bodies aside, grunting and snarling. He too found naught.

He straightened and glared. "Did he then get away?"

"I think not into the woods," said Syfrid. "He led his men and was well-nigh out onto the strand when we attacked. Then he sprang from his horse and back to the fight. But the press was hard. Nobody could have hewed from there into the thick of it. The Danes who happened to be to the rear, they were the ones who had some opening for escape when they saw they were beaten."

"Yet Hadding's not here," Tosti grated. "Unless he made off down the strand itself. Hr-r-r, if he slips from us, this day will not have seen our victory."

He asked about and cast about. A man or two recalled marking a pair who fled east along the water. Tosti bent low and scuttled around like a hound after spoor. "Ha!" he cried. "Footprints and bloodstains! After them!"

Men whooped. They pounded along for a few miles, topped the ridge, and saw their other ships, with three dead warriors lying under the prows. Tosti shaded his eyes and peered outward. The sun was nearly set, the dazzle off the water half blinded him, but it seemed that something yonder might be a boat. "Launch! There's our whale! A pouchful of gold to the first who harpoons him!"

Hands gripped, backs bent, a ship rumbled down to the shallows and onward till she lay afloat. Men waded out and hauled themselves aboard. Oars rattled forth. The ship surged forward.

The sea welled up from below. It gurgled around the deck-boards, raised them, set them sloshing to and fro. The crew broke out buckets. They could not bail fast enough. Soon the craft wallowed awash.

Tosti shrieked his rage. There was nothing to do but creep back to shore. They found that all the hulls had been holed.

"We've more ships waiting!" Tosti shouted. "Be off!"

"If we run back all that way," mumbled a Jute, "we'll be dead tired."

Tosti pulled out his knife. "You'll be dead now if you don't come along," he said. They trotted at his back as best they could.

Night fell. It was the light night of midsummer, dream blue, giving wide range to sight. A warm wind lulled.

Most of Tosti's band had stayed behind, resting. He filled a ship from among these. Oars creaked, a bow wave purled, wake sheened, the vessel drove forward.

Gudorm saw it afar, a darkness in the dusk, and wakened Hadding. The king peered with a sailor's eye. "Yes, they're after us sooner than I'd hoped," he said calmly.

Gudorm's fist thudded on the rail. "We should have gone ashore and struck inland ere now."

"I thought of that, but we'd have been close to where we set out, and too weary to cover our tracks. That takes time and care, I can tell you. Now, at least, we have some strength and wit again."

"They'll be on us before we can make shore."

"Not unless they see us. As yet, to them we're very low in the water, a blob, if they've spied us at all. Nor will they likely spy two swimmers, if we're not noisy."

Gudorm stared. "Do you mean, lord, we should go overboard?"

"Yes, before they're sure what we are and what we do."

The guardsman's broad shoulders slumped. "I can't swim," he said. The boat rocked a little. Wavelets lapped and glimmered under the dim sky.

Hadding tugged his chin. "Hm. That's a bother."

Gudorm straightened. "Save yourself, my king," he said, not altogether steadily. "I'll put my mail back on, and when they find me, maybe I'll take a few of them with me to the deeps."

Hadding half smiled. "So must a housecarle speak," he answered. "But it's wrong. You would not die at my feet as you should, you'd die while I ran off."

Gudorm stared at him. "What else could happen?"

Hadding laughed. "I've a trick or two left in me yet. If this one saves us, the tale will live long after us. If not, maybe the gods will tell it in their halls. But quickly, before they get closer and see clearly."

Gudorm shivered to hear. This man, he remembered, had been raised beyond the world of men.

Hadding knotted a short length of mooring line about the waist of his guard and hitched it to a thwart. Springing to and fro, they capsized the boat. Hadding slipped underneath and laid hold of the thwart himself. There was an air space under the planks. In darkness, in sea, the two hung waiting.

Tosti's ship drew nigh. "Overturned," he snarled.

"How might that be, in this calm?" wondered a sailor.

"Who knows?" said another. "A riptide, a skerry, a whale—a kraken, a drow— Let's away."

"Someday," said Tosti, "I may catch a fish that ate Hadding, and eat it. How I wish I could know. Well, we can take this boat back with us."

"That'd be troublesome," warned a crewman, "and the thing might be unlucky by now."

The crew muttered agreement. "As you like," snapped Tosti.

Under the boat, king and guardsman listened to the oars stride off.

When he deemed it safe, Hadding helped Gudorm squirm forth and clamber onto the upended bottom. They could not right the craft again, but Hadding fetched the oars. He had tied them down inboard so that it would look as though the capsizing had happened hours ago. Sitting astride, he and Gudorm paddled to land. Stumbling into the shelter of a thicket, they slept.

Thereafter it was to find a house the raiders had not reached, where they got food, drink, and more rest. The owner's son ran off to the sheriff with word about them. Though the sheriff was sorely beset as Tosti's band scoured around, he brought horses. And thus Hadding won home.

There he sent forth the war-arrow. With a full levy he sought out the foe and went to work. Few were the Jutes and Saxons who did not leave their bones on that field. Having recovered what loot he could, he went on vengefully into their homelands. Not soon did those folk think again about faring against Denmark.

But Tosti had gotten away.

XXVIII

In the next summer, on his yearly ride through Scania, King Hadding stopped as always in Bralund. Eyjolf welcomed him with the same friendliness as ever. Yet it seemed to Hadding that a shadow lay over the household.

On the third day Eyjolf asked if they could speak under four eyes. They saddled horses and went forth. The steading dropped from sight behind them; only a thin twist of smoke lifted over a grove, and other homes lay dwindled by farness. Fields ripened, cows grazed in paddocks, wildflowers nodded blue and pink along the roadside, the miles round about faded hazily into sky. Bees buzzed in clover. Dust puffed up from hoofs, into windlessness, and fell slowly down.

"This warmth does an old man good," said Hadding at length.

Eyjolf glanced at him. "You're not yet old."

"I've seen more winters than most men do. It's time for me to think of those who'll come after me."

Eyjolf drew breath. "That's what I wanted to talk about."

"Ulfhild, not so?" asked Hadding softly.

"Yes."

"She seems well enough behaved."

"That's because you're here. Lord, she's often a she-wolf. At best she does her tasks surlily. If crossed in any way, or for no reason we can guess, she screams, smashes things, lays about her with a switch or even a whip. The housefolk dare not say so, but plain it is how they hate and fear her. She gallops off by herself, without a by-your-leave, and won't say where she's gone. Nonetheless she can bewitch when she chooses, with her beauty, quick wit, and sharp mirth. In that mood she flirts more than is seemly, not only with youths but with married men, yes, and lowly crofters."

Eyjolf stopped. For a while only plop of hoofs and creak of leather sounded. "That was a hard thing to say," he added. "I must, though, for I know not how much longer I can keep this trust you gave me."

"Wildness runs in our blood," Hadding sighed. "My daughter Svanhvit, by my leman Gyda, has no liking for women's work either, and talks of becoming a shield maiden."

"We hear tell of such, but how many have there ever really been? Well, at least Svanhvit's no threat to anyone but herself, is she?"

"Not yet. Ulfhild, though, stems from kings on both spear and distaff side. I'd thought of wedding her to a king, but now I wonder. She might stir up hungers in him. I don't want Denmark torn by war, Frodi fighting for his rights, after I'm gone."

"Well, she's of an age for a husband—sixteen winters, if I've reckoned aright."

"I'll take her home with me," said Hadding, "and we shall see."

Eyjolf's head lifted, as if a burden had been taken off his shoulders.

At first the young woman was blissful. She skipped over the grounds, she hugged her horse almost as if it were her man to be, she chattered like a brook in between fits of laughter. "I'm going away, I'm going away, I'm going away!" she sang. "Away from sour sameness, away from this pen, back to the world!"

"You might thank your fosterers for their kindness," growled Hadding.

She gave him a narrow look and said no more. When they left she did indeed speak well to Eyjolf and his wife. "I know you had much to bear with," she told them, "but I'll never forget what I learned from you."

Afterward Hadding thought that that could have two meanings. But on the trek to Zealand she was the best of waymates, blithe and lively.

When he settled her in the hall at Haven, she was likewise delighted and delightful. The roominess, the wealth, the comings and goings, strange goods and stranger tales from abroad, the skalds and their lays, everything was new and bright to her eyes. "So should a queen live!" she cried more than once. Hadding held back from saying that she was not a queen.

Then as the months slipped by, bit by bit it changed between them. Her wrath blazed high or sank into slow fire. Again she took to lashing out at housefolk, riding about alone, affronting guests and making eyes at men.

Hadding had not found a second wife who would give him a good tie to a strong house. Nor had he sought hard. Since Ragnhild's death, he slept with whatever sightly woman was on hand and willing when he felt like it, which was not as often as formerly. However, he was still fond of Gyda. She dwelt in Haven in a house he had given her, but he would go there or she visit him while he was staying hereabouts.

When Ulfhild quarreled with her, shrieked that she was a nasty old slut, and scratched her cheek bloody, the news brought Hadding to a wintry anger. He sought his daughter out in the bower, gripped her arm bruisingly tight, and said, "Come along." She pulled against him, spitting like a cat. "If you will not walk, I'll drag you," he said. She walked.

They went along a path beside a meadow. The year was waning. Below an overcast, rags of cloud flew smoky on a chill wind. The grass had gone sallow. Leaves blew off a stand of beeches nearby. Crows winged low, hoarsely calling.

"There will be no more of this trollishness," he said.

"Over and over has that woman belittled me," answered Ulfhild. "She sits by you in the high seat. She gives no thought to my wants, mine, the king's daughter. When I offer a rede, she cares no more about it than if I were a bairn. Today I told the thrall Kark to groom my horse Gullfaxi. Gyda heard. She wanted him to fetch a box of stuff from her house. She had already bidden him, but— It was too much. I've had too much from her."

Hadding grasped both her arms, swung her around to face him, and said, "Didn't you hear me? There will be no more trollishness. I too will brook only so much."

She stared into his eyes. Giants had reared him. Another giant had he slain, and many mighty warriors. He had won in battle against warlocks and had passed through a land of the dead. Never had she seen anything more bleak than his eyes.

Her thews slackened. She bowed her head. "I'm sorry, father," she whispered.

He let her go. "See that you stay sorry." After a while he

went on, half to himself, "I've been thinking about this. The time is overpast that we get some worth out of your life."

He turned and strode back to the hall. She stood long alone in the wind.

From then on she behaved better. Sometimes she whitened and snatched after breath; but she would unclench her fists without letting a word fly free. Other times she would be withdrawn and sullen. But more and more she went among folk as mannerly as befitted a highborn lady. More and more often she called up the merriment that could be hers, or listened to what somebody was saying as though she cared, or sang in her lovely voice.

Meanwhile Hadding took men of weight aside and spoke quietly with them. Thus he found his way forward to what seemed him best.

Nights grew long. Rains made mire of the earth; later, pines and firs gloomed above thin snow. Folk huddled over their fires and yearned for the renewing of the sun.

Ulfhild still liked young men. She got to talking and laughing most with Gudorm Thorleifsson, the guardsman who escaped with Hadding from a stricken strand and dangled with him beneath an overturned boat. The king took heed, and began seeking this man out.

Yuletide neared. The household brawled with readymaking for the feast and for the offerings to the gods. One day Hadding bade Ulfhild, "Come."

They crossed through the murky day over to the women's bower. Maids were weaving and chatting by lamplight, though they must strain their eyes. Hadding told them to set the work aside and go. When he and his daughter were by themselves, he waved at a stool. "Sit if you wish," he said. "I have tidings for you."

Because he kept his feet, she did too. A vein fluttered in her throat. "What is it?" she asked low.

He smiled, more sternly than happily. "At midwinter we'll drink your betrothal ale."

Only midsummer would have been a time more high. Ulfhild's hands lifted to her breasts. "Who is the man?" she breathed.

"I've seen how you and Gudorm like each other, and I've let him know he would not get a cold answer. Now he's asked for your hand. He'll be a good man to you and a stout friend to all of us."

She gasped. "A yeoman!"

"He's no smallholder. You remember that his father has lately died. He, as the oldest living son, is the head at Keldorgard. It's among the richest on Denmark. And the family has land elsewhere, as well as a ship in trade. Nor is he low-born. His grandfather Bjarni was a leman-child of my great-grandfather King Skjold."

"But still a yeoman."

"I'll raise him to sheriff. If he does well at that, and I think he will, in time I'll make him a jarl. His name shall be great in the land, and so will the sons you bear him."

"This is your will?"

"It is," he said.

She spoke no more that evening.

XXIX

It seemed as though Tosti the Wicked was done for. Hadding had broken his following on the battlefield, killed most, scattered the rest, and brought home a good booty. Thereafter the Dane-king went around quelling the lands from which his foes had dared come. He rode through Jutland to the cromlech stronghold, slew what fighting men were there on watch, and razed it. Naught should have been left for Tosti but to skulk with every hand against him, living like a wolf on what he could steal until he found himself with nowhere to flee and died like a wolf.

Yet he kept a ship, a crew, his cunning, and his hatred. For a year they laired in deep fjords of Norway, rowing forth to fall on lonely hamlets or fisher boats, slipping off before avengers could track them down. During this while he lost some men, and others quit; but at the end he still had enough to seek Jutland again.

Lying offshore, he went word inland to lurking places he knew. No few outlaws heeded the call, and likewise men who were wretchedly poor or homeless. They had little to lose, and Tosti had in his way been powerful. He might win back to that and more. No one could foreknow what the Norns had laid down for him.

Not all in his gang were poor. Some who got away from Hadding had been well off at home. The Dane-king had burned those houses and made the Jutes and Saxons outlaw the owners. But they had brought along golden arm-rings, purses full of outland coins, costly weapons and clothes.

"We'll get friends overseas," Tosti told them in the second year. "We'll come back ready to strip the shores of Denmark, till Hadding pays us ransom for his kingdom. After that we'll build our strength further. You'll end your days on broad acres, sleeping under down quilts with whatever maidens you want."

So they set forth for England.

The ship was crowded. Cheek by jowl, men easily grew angry at each other. Hard words crackled. When a fist thudded, Tosti was there before the one struck could draw his knife. "Easy," he bade. "Easy. I'll have no bloodshed here. We'll settle these things on land." But he did not try to make anything but a patchwork peace.

England seethed with newcomers. Vikings denned on the islands and in the bays. Land-hungry tribes from overseas hammered the Britons back and back. War-bands roved and ravened. Smoke smeared heaven, women wept hopelessly beside the ashes of dwellings, birds picked out the eyes of the unburied dead. Withal, where Anglians, Saxons, Jutes, or Danes were clustered there rang the noise of axes, hammers, adzes, laughter, and heroic verse, as they built a new world for themselves.

Tosti made camp along the outflow of the Humber. Nobody lived there now, though charred timbers nearby showed where a small town had been. "We'll catch our breath here before we look around," he said.

"That'll soon grow dull," grumbled a warrior.

"Why, you can play games all day," laughed Tosti. "Let me show you some."

They could pitch balls, they could run foot races and wrestle, they could shoot arrows, and they did. But Tosti had brought along a small bagful of dice. Soon men were wildly tossing and wagering.

They were still overwrought after their voyage. They recalled words and blows. When a man lost too many throws, he was apt to say another man was a cheat. Now Tosti did not go between them. Instead, he slily egged them on. Fights broke out. Weapons flashed. Men died.

"Ill is this," Tosti would say. "But he fell on his own deeds. He'd have robbed me of a sworn brother. The weregild is mine." And he took everything the fallen man had owned. Since none of them had kinfolk on hand, and none of the living cared to speak against Tosti when his gaze prowled across them, he gathered to himself most of what wealth had been on the ship. Also, by this means he thinned out his crew to a more fitting size, the toughest of the lot.

At length they upped anchor. Through the rest of that summer they searched the eastern side of England. When they could plunder, they did, but mainly their chief was looking for war-fellows.

When he met leaders like himself, they would come together warily, sit down and drink while their men stood taut, sometimes grow mellow and swap gifts. Yet it was not until the end of summer that Tosti found one he thought he might want.

This was at the Wash, where the Norse viking Koll lay with three ships. Tosti's drew slowly toward them, white shield at masthead but hands not far from hafts. Hails sounded across the water. After a while the newcomers felt safe in coming ashore and mingling.

Koll had heard of Tosti, both from his earlier doings and his raids this year. A man who had almost gotten King Hadding killed was worth knowing. With all the lawlessness in eastern England, pickings were becoming lean. Moreover, the settlers were no soft prey. As their burghs grew, so did the numbers they could quickly raise to meet unwelcome callers. Koll had thought of seeking to Scotland, thence south along the western shores and maybe over to Ireland. However, those parts were little known to Northmen, and likewise full of hardy warriors.

"Aside from what I wrought in Lolland, the Danes have been at peace for many years," Tosti said. "They've waxed rich, and they've gotten slack. We can strike and be off, again and again. Hadding grows old. His fire burns low. When we've reaved enough, he should be willing to buy us off. With such wealth we can go on to make ourselves lords."

"No, your wits are aflight," Koll answered. "Four viking crews, to hold at bay the mightiest king in the North?"

Tosti calmed him. "I did not say we should strike tomorrow, or soon at all. Let's see how well we can do together."

The upshot was that these bands wintered at that spot. In spring they set forth and harried widely. Having then based themselves on a holm they could defend, they spent the next winter building up their strength. Their gains, along with what Tosti had gotten from the killings among his own men, bought them two more ships and crews. The year after that they sought north and west as Koll had wanted to. There they won more than they lost.

Thus it went for five years altogether, while Denmark dwelt under Hadding's peace. By then they led a dozen craft. "If we don't now go after greatness, we never will," Tosti said. "The old king yonder dodders toward his grave. His son will be a worse one to deal with. We'll need time to make ourselves a match for Frodi."

He had won Koll over. "Yes, I'm wearied of this rootless roving," his partner said. "I'm ready for a home, where I can watch the sons I beget grow up and know they'll remember me when I'm gone."

Tosti bared his teeth. "And I'm overready for my revenge."

Thus, early that summer, they took their fleet back across the North Sea.

They raised the hills of southern Norway and knew they were in the Skagerrak. Having rested a day ashore, they bore south of east for Denmark. The wind was fair, which seemed a hopeful sign, and they sailed steadily through a moon-bright night. In the morning they saw to starboard the heather and sands of the Skaw.

Then they saw what they liked less well, a score of longships with oars at work. Shields hung bright along rails, helmets and spearheads flashed aboard. Tosti uttered foul words. Koll yelled to him over the waves, "You told me there'd be no warders here!"

"Who could have known?" Tosti howled. "Strike sails and come about!" For the others were to leeward of them. Someone had been watching from land and laying his plans.

Hard though the vikings pulled, the Danes, fresher and in longer hulls with more rowers, slowly overhauled them. As the sun passed noon, they drew within shouting range. A tall man stood up in the bows of the foremost. His voice boomed across the rush and glitter of waves, the whittering of wind: "Ahoy! Who goes there?"

"No foes to you," Tosti cried. "Not today," he added for his crews to hear, lest they think he was afraid.

"We'll board you and make sure of that," the tall man told them.

"No!" blared Koll. "Not unless you cut your way! Who dares give us orders?"

"Hadding the Dane-king," answered the tall man.

Tosti shrieked in wrath run wild.

Hadding shaded his eyes and peered. "Is that you, Tosti? I thought it might be. Welcome to the end of your wanderings."

"Make ready to fight," ran along the lengths of the viking craft.

"Lie to and we'll talk," called Hadding.

"What?" barked Koll.

"Maybe you can outlive this day. But if you want to, first you must hear me."

The rover skippers hallooed among each other. Rowers rested their oars. Hadding's brought him within yards. "A bowshot, a bowshot," Tosti rasped.

As if he had heard, Hadding warned, "One spear or arrow, and you're all dead. Hark well.

"If we do battle on the water, it'll be harder for us to get at you than on land, and whoever falls overboard, his mail will sink him. We'd clear your decks, but it would cost more than I want to spend. Better for us if we go ashore. You know that, so you won't.

"Now what I offer, Tosti, is that you and I seek the strand and meet man to man. We'll each take a boat, while our ships draw too far apart for any sudden onslaught. Then if I fall, you can get back to yours in time to flee. If I win, I'll have scrubbed the world clean of you without squandering good lives. Have you that much manhood?"

"Yes, and more!" Tosti choked out of a throat gone thick. With every eye upon him, where every ear heard him mocked, he could say nothing else. Besides, he quaked with blood lust.

"I've brought two skiffs that a single man can row," Hadding made known. "We'll set one adrift for you. I'll meet you on the strand below that bluff where three pines grow."

Thus it came to be. The Danes laid two miles between themselves and the vikings. They left behind the boat Hadding had promised. Tosti's ship went to it, a hook pulled it alongside, he scrambled down. "Kill him, kill him," hooted his followers.

"I will, the old lame hound," he cried back, and rowed.

For all his farings these past years, he was an awkward seaman. His oars caught crabs, the boat wallowed, water dashed over the side and sloshed about his feet, he grunted and puffed. Though Hadding had farther to go, the king got there first. He rode the surf neatly into the shoals, sprang out, hauled his craft up, and made it fast by its anchor. The breakers capsized Tosti's. He was within his depth, but staggered as billow after billow brawled over his head. Hadding waded out, caught his arm, and helped him to land.

Tosti stood gasping and snorting. Brine rivered through the rings of his byrnie. Nonetheless he had been quick to draw sword and unsling the shield on his shoulders. Hadding kept aside. The sea drummed and foamed. Sunshine baked tang from kelp. The sand sheened dark here and glittered higher up where it rose into dunes. Gulls soared, dipped, mewed.

Tosti glowered. "Did you mean for me to drown?"

Hadding shrugged. "I'd not have been too sorry. But I've looked forward to feeding you, myself, to my seafowl."

"How did you know of me?"

"Did you think I'd forget about a troll like you? I rewarded whoever brought me news of your whereabouts and misdeeds. When I learned you'd gone to England, I sent trusty men there to find out what they could. When word came that you were linked with that Koll, it seemed likely you'd be back to irk us anew, and I sent still more spies out. When you bragged that this year you'd be going, word got around, and a swift ship sought home to me. True, I couldn't foresee where you'd come, but I lay here at the Skaw later than I otherwise would have, in hopes." Hadding grinned. "Hopes fulfilled. The Father of Victories shall have a big thank-offering when you and I are through."

"Yes, I'll give him you."

"He'll pick which of us he wants, though I should think he'd kick you down to Helheim. Are you ready?"

Tosti yowled, stepped forward, and struck. Hadding's blade met his in midflight. Iron clanged, sparks flew.

Hadding kept his shield high, squinting over it, shifting it the least bit to and fro as he saw a blow coming. Some hit his mail or helmet, but did not cut the metal. Tosti hewed like a woodman. He was younger, he did not limp, he would wear his foe down. Hadding tried for neck, arms, legs, but drew scant blood. Mostly he saved his strength while he fell slowly back, up the slope of the strand.

Tosti bellowed and banged.

They reached the high-water mark. All at once Hadding spun on his heel and took a long sidewise step. He smote again at Tosti's knee. The outlaw swung around barely fast enough. Now it was he who faced the sea. And now Hadding bore in on him with storm fierceness. His sword whirred, rang, pounded, bit. Tosti pulled farther back. Surely the old man would soon wear himself out.

Tosti betrod the dry sand. It crunched, slithered, gave beneath his feet, not much but he lurched a little. His shield, half splintered away, wavered in his grasp. Snake-swift, Hadding struck at his neck. Blood geysered.

For a while, then, the king stood over the deathling and struggled for breath. The ships lay lean on the sea, too far off for anyone to see what had happened. As he rowed out to his, belike the vikings would turn tail. He would not give chase. Without Tosti's baneful will to bind them, they would soon scatter, some maybe again to England, some maybe slinking forlornly about till the warders of the Danish waters caught and killed them.

"Yes," he murmured, "I am old."

He looked aloft. Clouds scudded from the west, their white going gray, rain on their heels. "I wanted one last victory that was wholly mine, as a man among men," he said into the loudening wind. "But what has this been? I knew how it would go. He who called himself Gangleri told me I can die only by my own hand. I did not understand what he meant, and I do not, but now it comes back to haunt me. Do you hear me, you up yonder? What is it that you want of me?"

XXX

Uproariously though his men cheered him, ringingly though the skalds chanted his praises, the king's mood stayed dark. "Better would it be were Frodi with us," he said once.

A guardsman who heard blurted in astonishment, "But, lord, none could know when Tosti would come or by what sea lane. Watchmen had to lie in wait from here to Haven, and all down the Great Belt."

"Frodi would not take a share in that," Hadding answered.

His foremost son had snapped, "Should I sit the whole summer yawning till my jaw falls off, with an ant-small likelihood of getting anything to do? No, I've already told my friends I'll lead them where fame and riches can be had."

"You should have spoken with me first," said Hadding. His voice fell dull.

Frodi tossed his handsome head. "Younger were you when you fared forth than I was when I first did on my own. Nor were you ever much for letting anybody's wish rein you in."

"In those days I knew nobody with the wisdom to show me what was best. What wisdom I now have was dearly bought. I hoped it would not die with me." Hadding sighed. "Well, if you've given a promise, honor binds you. Go. We'll talk after you come home."

He did not say the unlucky word "if." And indeed Frodi had thus far won all his battles, which were not few.

From the beginning he had loved weapons and weapon-play above all else. He became a horseman, hunter, and sailor, but no more skillful than behooved a well-born man. With sword, spear, ax, bow he grew deadly. Even as a little boy, fighting others with sticks, he bloodied their heads so often that at last none would agree to the game. But by then he was learning the use of iron, forged for his size. Those things must be made bigger each year.

At the age of twelve, he could lawfully go in viking, though skippers hardly ever did take striplings. Frodi asked if he could join a crew busking for a raid on Friesland. Belike they would have let him, he being the king's son. However, the king said flatly no. When Frodi raged at him, Hadding gave the lad a backhanded cuff that sprawled him on the ground. Frodi stormed off. Nobody saw him for days. He came back ragged, dirty, scratched, and starving. He would not tell where he had been, but folk guessed at the woods. Nor did Hadding dwell on the matter.

When his father left his mother behind in Norway, Frodi took it hard. He did not ask about it, nobody did, but he brooded. His scowls and curtness helped stir unrest in the housecarles and other warlike men. To quiet them, Hadding took a small fleet across the Baltic and harried about in Wendland and Gardariki. On that faring Frodi went along, now fifteen, tall as most men and daily getting stronger. He and his father fought side by side, sat together at their campfires, stood watch and watch at the steering oar when a gale nearly sank them, grew closer than ever before or afterward.

The next year Ragnhild returned to Denmark and died giving birth to a dead child. Her son Frodi was not there. He and a band of youths, off overseas to fight and plunder, were win-tering in Frankland. From that he gained less than the outfitting had cost.

His wedding cheered him. The bride was comely, and she brought lands and riches with her. It happened Frodi was not on hand when Hadding rode into Tosti's trap, but later he went in the forefront of the avenging host and reaped a red harvest.

No wolf's heart beat in Frodi's breast. To his wife, children, and household he was kindly, at such times as they saw him. Among his warriors he was mirthful whenever they were, steadfast when thing went ill for them, unstinting of gifts, fearless in battle, then afterward ready to help bind up wounds or sit by a dying man and tell him he had done well. They would have followed him to Jotunheim if he bade them.

But year by year his warfaring drained his wealth.

When he came back from Finland after Tosti's fall, Hadding rode to his home and told him, "Now we must talk."

"Alone?" asked Frodi.

"Yes." Hadding spoke too softly for others to hear. "You know what it will be about, but neither of us knows what may fly out of his lips."

Frodi scowled. "I'll not gladly sit while you try to upbraid me," he muttered.

His eyes widened a little when the king did not stiffen at his frowardness but said merely, "We can be doing something else as well. I've often found that helpful."

"Hm. I've been meaning to hunt waterfowl sometime soon. It can be the two of us."

In the morning they walked forth, carrying bows and nets. Not far from the hall a stretch of woodland wedged into fields and meadows. The men passed beneath leaves whose green had begun to fade with the year. The weather was cool and quiet. Frodi took a deer trail he knew.

After a while Hadding said at his back, "You go rather noisily, my son."

"What have we to fear?" Frodi rapped.

"Naught. I was thinking of skill. To go soundlessly through brush is like sailing as close to the wind as your ship is able."

"What has either to do with warfare?"

"There's more than that to being a man, and to being a king."

Frodi made no answer.

The ground went boggy, the air damp. Mist stole through the shadows. When at length the twain reached the fen they sought, fog eddied dank around them. There was no more sun, no more sky. Sight of reeds and dark water was lost after a few yards. The one sound was a dripping off willow boughs into the mere.

"Death and dungheaps!" snarled Frodi. "We've come all this way for nothing."

"Maybe not," said his father. "It's the kind of place for the kind of thing I have in mind. I wonder what made it thus."

Frodi shivered. "Best not name land-wights or elves or other uncanny beings here. Not even gods."

"No. You are not used to them."

"And you— Let's go back."

Hadding laid a hand on Frodi's arm. "Abide. Talk with me. Unless you're afraid."

The younger man gripped his bow so that his knuckles stood white. "Speak, then."

"You know what it will be," Hadding said. "We've touched on it and shied back, again and again. This day I'll have it out with you."

He looked off into the fog. Droplets of it glistened in his gray hair. "I too once lusted for war, victory, fame, greatness.

Over and above that, though, I had my father to avenge, my kingdom to win, less for myself than for the house of Skjold. Then came the long feud with the Ynglings. Oh, yes, I also roved and fought for my own gain, as men do, but I see now that that was not really what my life was for.

"And along the way, I learned other things." He chuckled. "Or else the gods rubbed my nose in the knowledge. From Hardgreip I learned something about love, from your mother far more." He gave his son a hard stare. "That is not an oldster's mawkishness. Remember who it was that lately slew Tosti, hand to hand.

"Frodi, my peace with Hunding has not weakened us. It strengthens, as well you should know who wedded his daughter. Still more does the work of our folk, yeomen, craftsmen, traders, all the Danes over whom my warriors and I stand guard. And I have striven to uphold the law at home, for men should turn to it before they turn to the sword. There lies the rightful work of the king.

"From time to time we must needs take up arms. And I'd be foolish to tell men they cannot fight abroad when they stand to gain thereby. But, Frodi, the king's care should always first and foremost be for the kingdom."

The young man stood wordless. The fog swirled and dripped.

"Do you think I am merely another viking?" he asked at last.

"I do not call you unworthy. You are my son by Ragnhild and he who shall be lord after I am gone. I must hold by that, or Denmark will tear itself apart and outlanders again make prey of the Danes. But you spend gold and lives as if they could never be emptied out. Take thought. Already you have sons of your own. What will you leave to them, to your grandsons, to the house of Skjold? How will they remember you?"

"With honor," said Frodi.

Hadding turned about. "We may as well go back."

The next day he bade goodbye and rode off with his guards. He reached the hall by Haven in the evening.

That night, lying by himself in his shutbed, he had a dream.

Once more he stood in skyless, blinding mists. They streamed by him on a wind he could not feel or hear. Never had he been so alone.

Out of the gray into his sight came Ragnhild striding. The wind fluttered her grave-clothes and tossed her unbound locks about her. Their red was the only hue in all the world.

Her eyes gazed through him, a dead woman's eyes, and he heard her as if from endlessly far away.

> *Wild is the one you begot,*
> *Who bends to his will the beasts.*
> *Grim and hard his glance,*
> *Which well can tame a wolf.*

He could not cry out. He reached but could not lay his arms around her.

She said:

> *Watch that you ward your life.*
> *Foul is the bird you fathered,*
> *Ill as an owl her soul,*
> *Sweet as a swan her speech.*

He sat up in darkness and slept no longer that night.

In the morning he sent for a soothsayer. The housefolk

could hear how he forced himself. When the wizard came, the king took him into a loft room and closed the door. Afterward, as he gave him a coil of gold, Hadding said low, "Yes, I had my forebodings."

XXXI

The home of Gudorm Thorleifsson lay in northwestern Zealand, a day's ride from Haven. Broad and rich were his grainfields, grasslands, woods, ponds; herds and flocks, fish, and game abounded. Well over a score of free folk lived and worked there, carles, women, children. Even the dozen thralls were well fed and well treated.

The house was long, stoutly timbered, turf-roofed. It and its outbuildings made three sides of a flagged yard. On the fourth side two barns flanked an opening with a gate for defense. Nearby clustered the lesser dwellings of hirelings, and farther off the huts of the thralls.

Northward rose the wood closest by, a thick shaw of mingled oak, beech, elm, and hazel. At its edge, which axes had long since sharply marked off, stood the high barrow of Keldor, founder of steading and family. The household made him an offering at the time of each full moon, a sheaf, a fowl, a piglet, on the holy days a lamb or calf. Otherwise it was looked on as an eerie place and mostly shunned.

Always the garth throbbed and shouted with life. From the milking at dawn to the stabling at dusk, they were busy cleaning, cooking, brewing, chopping, shearing, slaughtering, spinning, dyeing, weaving, nailing, forging, on and on, the tasks of every year and the tasks nobody had foreseen. Footfalls clattered, hoofs thudded, wheels creaked, hammers crashed, voices of human and beast went through smells of smoke, sweat, meat, hides, hay, dung, earth.

The dwellers had their pleasures too. In between the bouts of heavy toil, and in snatches throughout those whiles, free time was not scant. Seldom did it go in dumb idleness. Tales, riddles, verses, songs, ring dances, races, wrestling and other matches, ball games, draught games, or getting drunk filled it well. A man might carve twining vines on a clothes chest, or he might go fishing. Lads and lasses wandered off by twos, to come back flushed and bright-eyed. When Gudorm's fellows called on him, or he on them, trenchers were heaped, ale flowed, and the merriment could last for days. When merchants pitched their booths at the fjord some miles off, men were wont to bring their women along to the fair. And then there were all the small, quiet joys that one took for given. Denmark under Hadding was happy.

Ulfhild was not.

She had borne herself well at the wedding. As mistress of Keldorgard she was stern with underlings but did not shout or strike at them. However, they learned to beg forgiveness and jump to her bidding when her voice turned cold. Among the neighbors she was ladylike, often winsome. They told Gudorm she was as fair to behold as she was highborn. She quickly found how to gladden him in bed. At first he reckoned himself a lucky man.

Thus it hurt him sorely when, month by month, she withdrew. Less and less did she talk to him about anything but the business of the household. More and more seldom did she give him back his kisses. When they had their first child, a healthy boy, she stood by at the namegiving, but never did she smile.

He let his pain come forth at last, in the close darkness of the shutbed, as she lay unstirring at his side. "Has the blood frozen in you? Are you sick?"

"Sick in my heart," she answered.

"Why? What's wrong?"

"That a king's daughter is bound to a farmer."

"What? You knew what I was, you know what I am—a great landholder, formerly a guardsman of the king and now his reeve in this shire."

"Bathe as often as you will, I always smell what you are."

She gave him a few more bitter words and ended, "So shall our son be, and every child I bear you."

He shuddered. "I could hit you for that," he said raggedly.

"Do, and I leave you. You know the law. Nor will my father any longer be your friend. I'll see to that."

Gudorm's anger broke. "We, we were blithe together in his hall," he stammered. "We sat in the same seat, we drank from the same beaker, you were with me more than with any other young man. How have you come to hate me?"

She let his heart beat a while before she said, "Oh, I do not hate you. I only hate this lowliness. I want you to rise above it, to make yourself worthy of yourself."

"The king says he'll raise me to jarl."

"When? He has as many now as he needs. They'd not take kindly to another, nor would you be of any use. In these dreary times of peace, none is likely to die soon and get out of the way. The king, though, he is old. And Frodi, who is to come after him, has slight liking for you and none for me."

"What, then?" rasped Gudorm. "Shall I go in viking? I might maybe find enough gold to glut your greed."

"No." She rolled over to lie close against him. Her arms went across his breast. "I said I don't want to lose you. I want the best for you, for us both and for our children. Think about it."

Soon, though, she had him setting thought aside for that night.

She did not stop there. It was not that she nagged him.

Rather, she worked slowly, a little at a time, month by month, year by year. She planted one seed in his mind, gave it sunshine and warmth by kindnesses toward him, watered it with thunderstorms of wrath, fended off the worms and crows of his doubts, let him harvest the fruit himself, and sowed two new seeds where it had been.

"Even as Eyjolf's fosterling, I wore silk on the high days," she recalled. "Here it's linen at best." She made light of her furs and fine-spun wool.

"We will plod through the same flat rounds till they bring us to our graves," she said. "That's if we are lucky. Come a blight, a murrain, an untimely hailstorm, and we'll hunger. I'd bleed to hear our children cry for food we could not give them."

"We call ourselves strong," she said. "But what do we rule over? A few thralls and hirelings, some head of livestock. We call ourselves free. But we are bound as fast as any of them."

"A great man sees beyond the rim of eyesight," she said. "He makes of his life and his world what he will. In the minds of his men he stands higher, more beloved than their own fathers. Wealth flows into his hand, and he bestows it freely, so that all know his heart is as mighty as his arm. They flock to him from afar, with their gifts and tales and ventures. Skalds chant his praise. His name will live undying after him and his sons be thankful to him for what he wrought. You have the makings of a great man in you, Gudorm. I felt it when first I saw you. Let it not wither away!"

Such things did she say to him, not once but again and again, in many different ways and words. In the beginning he told her she was wrong, overweening, a woman who could not understand the doings of men. She gave him answers soft or hard, mild or icy, as she deemed best, and never pressed him too long. She merely came back to it, and back, year by year.

"I fear for us if Frodi becomes king," she said when she

was ready to. "He's wild and wasteful. His heed is for nothing but himself. Ill will it go with Denmark. You and I may not yet be in the earth when the red cock crows here."

"He's your brother!" cried Gudorm.

Ulfhild smiled grimly. "Yes. Though we were raised apart, I know him well. The same blood runs in us both. But I am only a woman. I cannot do the harm he can."

"The king has chosen him. Hadding's other sons have goodly holdings, high standings, naught to chafe at. And I hear he's made them swear oaths not to rise against Frodi."

"Those men are not the only boughs on the tree of the Skjoldungs," Ulfhild murmured.

He gaped at her. She sighed, turned her head, and said no more about that for a span.

But step by step she won him over to believing that he, even he, would be a far better king than Frodi. He was a young man, mettlesome, who often longed back to his days as a housecarle. Then he fared, feasted, and fought. They had been too few, those days. He felt as if his life were narrowing, dull little tasks among dull little folk. Ulfhild stoked the restlessness in him. Now and then they were guests at the king's hall. Early on Gudorm brought home cheerful memories of those visits. Later he bore dreams that would not leave him in peace.

"But it would be madness to try overthrowing Frodi," he groaned one day.

Ulfhild nodded. "Yes. However, what of forestalling him? Say he was abroad when Hadding dies. He is half the time anyway. A well-liked man with blood of Skjold in him, who won some fame as a warrior against the Jutes and Saxons, with Hadding's own daughter to wife—if he trod boldly forward, he could make them hail him at enough Things that the rest would go along. Frodi would strike at him, but now Frodi would be the foe of the Danes, the outsider reaving our shores. Reckless as he is, he should soon fall in battle."

"The, the new king—he who'd be the new king—he'd have to have strong backing."

"Yes. It's none too soon to start laying groundwork. Hadding is old. Who knows when something will take him off? A fall from his horse, a boar or bear he's been hunting, a sudden storm as he crosses the Sound or sails among the islands, a sickness, an elfshot—who knows? For the sake of Denmark as well as ourselves and our sons, we should be taking forethought and quietly talking with men of weight."

"They'd look on such thoughts as faithlessness."

"I can tell you which of them will not, if you pick your words carefully. I've always kept my eyes and ears open."

Another year passed before she said to him, "It's not as if Hadding himself were a good king."

They were walking alone at the end of a winter's day. Thin snow crunched beneath their feet. A streak of cloud smoldered sullen where the sun had newly gone down, otherwise dusk deepened fast. Trees stood bare and black; the garth was a huddle of murk in the offing; closer loomed the gravemound. Breath smoked white. A belated flight of crows cawed afar.

"What do you mean?" burst from Gudorm. "He leads us, he wards us!"

"Yes, as you lead and ward your kine. But I am thinking beyond that. Remember his life. He grew up among jotuns. He was the lover of his own foster mother. He dealt with witches, wizards, monsters, and who can say what other beings? Who can say he does not yet, to this very night? He slew a godling and fell under a curse for it. Has that ever really been lifted, or does it bide its time? He went down among the dead. He sails closer to the wind than any rightful skipper can. How much of him is human, how much is something else? Woe falls on a land whose king is wicked. Worse must befall a land whose king is a warlock or a troll."

"He's your father," Gudorm whispered.

"I hate him." Ulfhild's voice shook. She stared straight before her into the gathering dark. "When he limps off on hell-road, I will laugh aloud."

"What wrong has he done you?"

"That I will never tell." Nor did she ever. She left the words in his head like an adder's egg.

Meanwhile she fed his fears as she fed his dreams. In the fourth year he began riding widely around the kingdom. He needed no more than two or three followers, mainly for helpers. There were no robbers left. He gave out that he wanted to talk with men elsewhere about some undertakings he had in mind. Those he called on were those Ulfhild had named to him, and he spoke to them according to her redes.

"Yes, as nearly as I can tell, if Hadding dies while Frodi is abroad, they'll stand by me," he said to her upon coming home from the last of these farings.

"Then we should see to it that that is what happens," she answered.

"How?"

"Think. We'll take this up later."

They did at the barrow. Their fifth year together was waning. A wrack of clouds flew low above bare fields and sere grass, before a skirling, biting wind. The woods behind the howe roared with it. Dead leaves broke loose, whirled and rattled, fell on an earth that had gone cold.

Ulfhild drew her cloak close around her. "Here we can be truthful," she said from below her hood. "Your forebear the land-wight watches over us."

Gudorm knotted his fists. "Say on."

"It's as if the gods do too. You know that, late though the season is, Frodi and his men have left for England and will winter there. I've asked some visitors from his neighborhood about it—they came by while you were away—and learned that it was shortly after his father had been to see him. Knowing them, I think Hadding tried to curb Frodi, and only made him ireful. He'll hardly return till the end of next summer, if then, as ravenous as he is. We'll have time to make ready for him."

"How do we know Hadding won't still be alive?"

"We will make sure."

He had fought in his head with the horror. Now that she uttered it, he could only say, leadenly, "No. He is my king."

"Too long has he been. Whatever usefulness he ever had is gone from him. He squats in his seat like a toad while our hopes wither. If he wished to do well by his Danes, he'd at least lay down the kingship. But no, he'll outlast us all, that barren troll, draining dry the land that should be yours and your sons', unless we take from him what is ours."

"You're berserk. Who but you would want to lift a spear against him? Who would dare?"

"Yes, he is well guarded. But you recall that I got him to say he'll come here when we ask, if he can. At the time, my thought was mostly to lull any doubts he might have gotten about us. Now— He'll be by himself, unaware. One slash of a blade can set us free."

Gudorm staggered where he stood. "Murder? Under my own roof?" The wind howled with him.

"No, not at your hand," said Ulfhild swiftly. "Folk would indeed take that amiss. He has other foes."

Her eyes burned at him. "Hear me. I've been delving into the past, finding things out, holding my own secret meetings. Some forty years ago, thieves broke into the king's treasure house. Its warden, one Glum, had been slack about keeping watch. Hadding hanged him for that, old and honorable though he was. A son of Glum's had died a while earlier, soon after his wife, but left a son of his own, hight Styr, whom Glum was raising. Because of what the king did to his grandfather,

Styr grew up poor, a worker for others wherever he could find work, never able to wed, his name besmirched, nothing left to him but hatred. The thought that he might avenge himself has kindled him as lightning kindles a parched woodland. Little he cares what becomes of him afterward.

"I think his stroke will be more deft if he knows he can bolt out the door, and afterward meet somebody who'll give him some silver and lead him to someplace where he's not known." She grinned. "That somebody may, instead, kill him. Or he may be cut down straightway after the deed. We can think about that. What matters is that Hadding will be dead."

"No," croaked Gudorm. "No." But already he knew she would win.

XXXII

That spring, on his way to the Skaw to lie in wait for Tosti, King Hadding had stopped at Keldorgard. "No, we'll not need a levy for this," he told Gudorm. "You'll be of more use here, working your land and keeping my peace."

In the morning, before he left, Ulfhild drew him aside and asked if they could talk alone. They walked along the rail fence of a paddock where mists steamed off the dew that glistened on the young grass and cows stood rust-red above it, the sound of their cropping loud in the quietness. "Father," she asked, "when will you come here again and abide a while?"

Hadding shrugged. "How can I tell? If none of our outposts catches the illdoer, I mean to hunt for him as long as need be. And even if we take him soon, I've my rounds of the kingdom to make. There's much for me to see to."

"But how seldom you see your kindred."

Her head drooped. He heard the sadness in her voice. "Do you want for something? Everything here looks well-off to me."

"I feel myself sundered from you, father."

He stopped in midstride. "Now that's a surprise. Ever were you willful, Ulfhild. I thought you'd be happy to move to a home of your own." After a bit he frowned and added slowly, "And of late Gudorm has somehow grown cold toward me. I know not why. But when we meet, his words are curt. I hear how he's been riding around sounding men out about some or other undertaking he has in mind. I'd be glad to give him counsel and help. Yet he, who brushed death at my side, tells me nothing."

"He feels restless, unfulfilled. And I—harking back, I begin to ken how much you've cared for me and how little thankful I was. Oh, father, we've many things to talk about. Say you'll come! Not with a troop of warriors and lords. We'd never have freedom from their nearness. Nor could we house and feed them. Come so we can sit together at the hearth, be together, as kinfolk should."

Hadding smiled. "Well, now, that's sweet to hear. But I told you, I know not when it can be."

"Before Yule, surely? You'll be at Haven. You almost always make your midwinter offering there. And first you take your ease, after the year's trekkings and strivings. Say you'll come when we ask you. Promise me, father!"

She stood there before him in the morning light, his daughter who looked so much like his Ragnhild, and held out her arms to him. "It's a good thought," he said. "Yes, if nothing holds me that I can't break loose from, I'll come. And thank you, Ulfhild."

"It's we who must thank you," she breathed.

He rode off, followed by his household. Once more, after

the losses on Lolland, they were so many that their camp had overflowed a meadow. For a while he was merrier than they had seen him be in a long time. But lying idle until Tosti came by, he began again to brood. His slaying of the outlaw seemed only to lay a deeper darkness over him.

Afterward he went around in the kingdom as of yore, meetings his folk at their Things and in their homes, giving redes and judgments, calming those who were at odds, telling them it was better to build and trade than burn and rob. Men spoke among each other, sometimes with grins, of how the wild young rover had become the mild old grandfather. But some said, "It's as though he's bidding us farewell."

In Scania he stayed a few days with Eyjolf. "I'd like to go on north to Uppsala and greet King Hunding," he said on their last evening. "The road between friends should be trodden oftener than ours has been, these past years. But the season wears on. I'd best turn homeward."

"You'll surely meet again, you two," the jarl answered, "and I've a feeling that that's not far off."

Hadding sighed. "One can hope."

Back in Haven, he went to see Frodi and they had speech at the fen. He returned to his hall and the dream came to him.

A week later he heard that his son had left Denmark.

—Soon after, Gudorm's men arrived.

They were four, sturdy carles whose legs dangled down close to the fetlocks of their shaggy little horses. Hadding knew them by name. They stood awkwardly before him in his high seat. "What brings you here?" he asked.

"Well, lord," said the leader, "they at the garth sent us to ask if you'd come visit for a bit, if you'll do them the honor. They told me you'd told them you would if you could, nowabouts. That's the word we was to bring you, by your leave."

"Did they say why they want this?"

"Well, I understand it's for family's sake, like. They'd rather you come with only us, if that's not beneath you. But it's not for me to know, lord."

Hadding gazed at the honest red face and murmured, "No, Olaf, you and your fellows can hardly know. Maybe I myself don't. But I did promise. Yes, I'll go. No man may flee his weird."

The men shivered. Housecarles who overheard looked askance at the king. He smiled a tight-lipped smile. "I've a few things to take care of first," he said. "We should be able to set forth the day after tomorrow. Then we'll get there the day after that, as short as the days have become. Meanwhile rest yourselves here, goodfolk."

"May one of us head straight back and tell them, lord? The lady Ulfhild said as how she wanted to have everything ready, fit for you."

"He may as well," said Hadding.

A youth rode off at once. The others saw little more of the king until they left with him. They thought that was best, as lost in thought as he seemed. They could drink, gab, and be cheerful with the workers around the hall and with such guardsmen as cared to join in.

The next day Hadding drew the new chief of his housecarles aside outdoors. They spoke long and earnestly. Afterward the chief sent off a score of men. He gave out that he had heard there might be a robber denning in the midisland woods, and wanted to learn whether the tale was true and, if so, track the man down.

As for Hadding, he went into his treasure hoard. From it he took a splendid battle horn, made from the horn of an aurochs, banded with silver in which the smith had hammered Valkyries bearing fallen heroes to the gods.

At sunrise he rode from his hall. None followed him but

the three men from the garth to which he was bound. They fared silent, for so the king did.

As night drew nigh, they halted at a house he owned on the Isefjord, where he kept a yacht. The caretakers put a meal together. That also went glumly. However, at the end the king got up and said, "Bring these men as much more ale as they want." To them he added, "Refresh yourselves. I'm going for a stroll."

"Not overly gladsome at seeing daughter and grandkids again, is he?" muttered one of them when the tall shape had limped out the door.

"Hold your jaw," said Olaf. "Kings, they got much on their minds, they do. I'd not willingly be a king, I wouldn't. Hoy, this is a mighty tasty brew here. Let's swill while we can."

—Dusk closed in. Hadding stood on the shore, looking north over the water. It lay still, a steely glimmer broken by the black hulk of an island, out to the worldrim and beyond. Once he said into the hush and chill, "I think you are the home I have ever been seeking." A few stars trembled forth, small and far. "But how can a man have his home in the sea?"

He turned and went back to the house. The men were already snoring on the benches. By the light of the dying fire he found his own place. In the morning he did not look as though he had slept much.

They reached Keldorgard before midday. The sky hung low, a sunless gray. A mile or so northward the shaw stood like a stronghold wall for jotuns, the barrow a hill before it. Lesser dwellings stood nearer, and neighbor farms afar, their smoke more clear to sight than the dwindled buildings. Otherwise the land stretched flat, shadowless, bare fields, withered grass, tangled briars. The air was not very cold, but it gnawed.

The garth bustled. Hoofs rang in the flagged yard. Smells of roasting meat rolled around it. Folk milled about the newcomers, shouting. Even their most faded woad-dyed wadmal was colorful today, and Ulfhild's red cloak blazed like her hair as she hastened forth to greet her father. Gudorm lagged behind, well enough clad but his face locked.

Hadding swung down from the saddle. Ulfhild caught both his hands. "Welcome, welcome!" she cried. "Thank you for that you've come. Did you have a good journey? You shall surely have a good stay with us. Now, into the house with you, a stoup of mead, a bite of food if you like, then the bathhouse."

"Yes, welcome," said Gudorm roughly. "We have much to talk about."

Hadding's eyes met his. "We have much to remember, you and I," he answered.

"We're happy to see you, lord."

"I keep my promises."

In the entry Hadding unslung his sword and racked it, as was the usage with weapons. He carried a bundle he had along to the shutbed set aside for him, and unrolled fresh clothes from it. "Yes," he said, "I'm more than ready for cleanness."

A thrall in the bath poured water on red-hot stones. Hadding basked and breathed. As the hut cooled, the man dashed a bucketful over him while another brought in more heated rocks. After the third time, they toweled him dry and he came forth aglow. In a room alongside he dressed himself in green woolen breeks with kidskin cross-garters, calfhide shoes, tunic brocaded and marten-trimmed above linen shirt, silver-buckled belt and silver brooch at throat, gold coils on his arms, gold headband circling his well-combed locks. He entered the house smiling and sought Ulfhild out among her busy women.

"Well," he said, "now I'm fit to meet with the children and

see how they've grown since last. I've brought a few little
things for them."

"I'm sorry, father," she told him. "I thought they shouldn't
be underfoot, and sent them off to stay with a crofter of
ours."

"Oh."

"We'll fetch them back before you go, of course. But first
there's this feast, and then tomorrow we'll have everything to
talk about, the three of us."

"Yes."

Hadding went over to where Gudorm sat, moodily whit-
tling on a stick with his eating knife. "I gather you've more to
take up with me than you've let on," he said.

Gudorm's gaze did not leave his hands. "We've met too seldom," he mumbled.

"Maybe. I would like to hear about whatever hopes they
are that have had you going up and down the kingdom."

"You shall. Later."

"As you wish. I've not forgotten that night under the boat."

"Nor I." Gudorm rose. "Forgive me, lord. I'd better see to
things. They'll soon bring out the tables."

The winter day was well into its afternoon. Already the
house was gloomy, high though the hearth fire crackled. One
could not eat in seemly wise by flamelight, though drinking
might well go on till sunrise.

Servants bore in the trestles and laid the boards across
them. There was no high seat, but Hadding took his place
at the middle of the platform bench along the south wall.
Across the rush-strewn floor from him were Gudorm and
Ulfhild. To right and left on both sides sat three or four men,
clad in their rough best. They were the foremost of Gudorm's
carles, skilled smallholders in their own right, together with
the most well off of his neighbors. He would have affronted

those had he not asked them to come the first evening and meet the king.

Women went about pouring ale for them. Hadding whispered to one. She brought him something from his shutbed, wrapped in a cloth.

Gudorm stood up, lifting his beaker. "Drink we to the gods," he said into the smoky, flickering twilight, "Njord, Freyr, and almighty Thor," the gods of fishery, harvest, and weather.

"Skaal," rumbled through the room, and men drained their draughts. The women refilled for them.

"Now drink we to our guest King Hadding," said Gudorm. Suddenly his voice was harsh. "Health and long life be his."

"Skaal, skaal."

The king rose. Firelight glinted off the cup of costly outland glass he had once given this household. "Drink we to Gudorm, our host and my reeve in the shire, and to his lady, Ulfhild, my daughter," he called. "May their honor be ever as high as their worth."

Gudorm caught his breath. Ulfhild sat unstirring.

As the ale went down, Hadding unwrapped the battle horn. The long curve of it sheened in his hands. "Gudorm," he said, "I know you for a warrior, a man born to do great deeds and win great fame. Take this of me, and may it soon call up the men that we want."

A woman carried it between them. Gudorm held it aloft for all to see and wonder at while he spoke slurred thanks. He had already been drinking hard. The house boomed with cheers. Ulfhild hung the horn by its sling from a peg in the wainscot above her.

Now trenchers and trays came laden from the cookshed. The men fell to. Talk growled and buzzed, often breaking into guffaws. Gudorm was mostly silent; Ulfhild answered mildly whenever someone spoke to her. Hadding stayed grave, as befitted a king and an old man, though willing enough to swap words.

Yet his eyes were always watchful, the eyes of a hunter or a sailor. The day waned. Servants kept wood on the fires and brought in lamps, but still the light dimmed. Hadding saw a man come in by the rear door and sit down at that end. Though the room was warm, he hunched in a shabby hooded cloak, another shadow.

Hadding pointed. "Who's that?" he asked Olaf on his left hand.

The carle peered. "Um, hard to see from here, but I ken him. A poor wretch hight Styr, lately shifted to this neighborhood from somewhere else. Gudorm lets him sleep in a barn, help the thralls, and share their food. I take it Gudorm's told him he can have a bite and listen to somebody besides the cows. He's a kindly fellow, him Gudorm."

Eating came to an end. The housefolk took the tables away. Two of them rolled in a cask of ale, set it upright near the hearth, and knocked the end off. Men whooped. As they went to fill their cups and horns for themselves, the free women of the garth, no longer needed for serving, and having had their own food beforehand, returned to drink and mingle likewise.

Gudorm and Ulfhild joined them on the floor. Even the lowly Styr crept from his corner. Hadding kept his seat, as a king should, and let those who wished speech with him seek him out. They took his cup to and fro for him as he emptied it.

Blithely chatting, Ulfhild drifted toward the far end of the room. Not only women but men wandered that way, for in the shifty dusk she was brighter than the flames and lovelier to behold. At length they were all gathered laughing around her. Styr, whom nobody cared to talk to, stood alone.

He glanced at Hadding, squared his narrow shoulders, and

shuffled toward the king. "Well?" Hadding asked. "What would you of me?"

Styr halted before him. Within a nest of hair and beard, the hollow face twitched. "This," he said hoarsely. He flung back his cloak. Beneath it hung a sax. "This, murderer!"

He whipped out the curved blade. Flamelight followed its whirring leap.

Had his dream not made him wary, Hadding would have died then and there. As was, he sprang aside. The edge bit into the platform where he had been. Styr bounded after him. Hadding withdrew across the floor. His eating knife was in his hand, but no match for the sword.

Men shouted, women shrieked. They did not at once understand what was happening, as murky as the room was. It stunned them. Styr bore in on Hadding. The king reached the north wall. He snatched the horn he had given Gudorm and set it to his lips. All the while he was dodging his attacker. The war call blasted forth.

Men dashed to help. They got in each other's way. None was any better armed than Hadding. Styr barred the floor between them and the weapons they had left in the entry. The first of the yeomen reeled, clutching an arm slashed open. Blood hit the hearth fire and hissed. He stumbled back to the others.

"Get together!" bellowed Gudorm. "Stand close!" Bewildered, knowing him for a warrior, the men clumped clumsily in front of the women.

Twice and thrice did Hadding wind the horn amidst Styr's onslaught. Then he smote with it as though it were a sword. It stopped the next blow but shattered in his hand. He cast the stump. It hit Styr on the brow. The man tottered. Hadding made for the entry. He was too slow on his lame foot. Styr recovered, headed him off, drove him back.

"We'll go around the house," Gudorm called. "We'll get our weapons and stop this."

Blindly, the men followed him out the rear door and into the night. Under its cloud deck they must fumble their way along the wall. Inside, before the eyes of the women, Styr worked Hadding into a corner.

Gasping for breath, the old king tautened. He would not finish his jump, but his knife might find his foe.

With a roar of wrath and a rattle of iron, his housecarles burst in from the entry. Styr barely saw them before a flung spear pinned him. As he fell, the warriors stormed thither. They hewed him to shreds and splinters.

Their headman laid hold of the king by both arms. "Are you hale?" he cried.

Hadding slumped. The knife dropped from his grasp. "Yes," he answered. "Thanks to you." They helped him to a bench. He sat down and stared into the shadows at nothing they could see. "Thanks to you, Ragnhild," he whispered.

Ulfhild ran from among the women. "Oh, father, father, you live!" Her arms were spread wide to enfold him. But the housecarles in their byrnies had thrown a shield-wall around their lord.

One by one, dumb, shaking, the yeomen and carles crept in. Under the stern gaze of the guards they sought to the women in the rear. Only Ulfhild stood at the middle of the floor, alone, straight, her face become a mask. Her kerchief had fallen off. Firelight played over the coils of her hair as if they too were burning.

"Bring me a stoup," said the king. A warrior hurried to do so. When he had drained it he straightened and spoke firmly. "Open ranks. I must find out about this."

The guards moved right and left, though they kept spears

in hand, axes on shoulders, swords drawn. Hadding looked through the smoke and hush. "Where's Gudorm?" he asked.

"I know not," answered Ulfhild as steadily.

"Strange," said Hadding. "Strange how he did not think to lead a rush or have men throw things, and was so slow to take them around the house. I'd have been dead by the time they got back, and Styr begone out the rear. Strange, too, how skillfully that wretch wielded his blade. Who gave it to him and taught him its use?"

"I know not," said Ulfhild. "I only hope this is a nightmare, and I soon wake from it."

"Well, I had a dream of my own," Hadding told them all. "It made me wonder. I'd not speak ill of anyone here without more grounds than that. But I had these men of men come over byways and yesterday night slip into the shaw behind the howe. That was a cold camp they made, and they might have had to stay there till I went home. But they kept faith. When they heard my horn call, they sped to my side.

"Now, where is Gudorm?"

"I'll go look," said the leader of the housecarles. He and four others kindled torches at the hearth and trod out into the night.

They soon returned. "He lies a little beyond the gate," the leader said. "He must have taken his sword away with him. He's fallen on it."

The ice of Ulfhild broke. She lifted claw-crooked hands. "Witchcraft, black witchcraft!" she shrilled. "Ever has trollery clung to you, Hadding Jotun's-foster!"

"That's as may be," said the king. He sat for another while. The fire and the lamps guttered low.

He rose. His words clanged. "Hark. This could have been Gudorm's work and nobody else's. I do think you goodfolk are honest. But it could be part of something deeper and wider. Everybody will stay here for the next few days. We'll give out that I'm dead, and see what happens."

His voice sank. "Now I am weary. Can someone who dwells nearby lend me a bed? I'll not sleep under this roof again."

XXXIII

Over the Sound, up through Scania and Geatland, on into Svithjod flew the word. Hadding the Dane-king was gone, fallen at the hand of a madman. They who bore and believed the news were housecarles from Haven. Their chief, who sent them off, with others to go elsewhere around Denmark, believed it too. Each time their horses stopped, the tale raced across the neighborhood. It warned jarls, sheriffs, chieftains, and yeomen to busk themselves for trouble.

None came. There was no uprising, no onset from abroad. When he knew that was so, the king rode back to his hall. Thence he sent messengers after the first ones, carrying the truth.

But a huge storm had sprung up. It lashed the waters for days and nights. Until it ended, neither boat nor ship could cross over to Scania.

Thus the tale came to King Hunding in Uppsala, from the lips of men he knew to be trustworthy. Hadding, his oath-brother, the man who had made him what he was, lay dead.

The lord of the Swedes sat dumb when he heard. Then he said slowly, "That was a life longer than most, and it went more high than any other. But it was not long enough, and hence-

forward we must walk warily, now that the might which upheld our peace is no more."

Later he said, "To him who gave me all, I will give back all
I can, a grave-ale worthy of him."

The year stood within two months of midwinter, when
folk would flock here from far and wide for the offerings. He
knew that most could not make the journey twice in so short
a span. But he sent to every great man who dwelt nearby, bidding him come. With their families and followings, these
guests would number two or three hundred. The kingly hall
at Uppsala was the biggest and finest in the North. For a week
it boiled with readymaking.

The king was seldom on hand. Most often he was riding
about the hinterland, ruthlessly spurring his steeds, through
wind and rain and early gloom, trying to wear down his grief.

The guests gathered. Hunding greeted them well, each by
each. As they went to the benches, he and his wife took the
place kept for those most honored. Across from it, his high
seat stood empty.

Fires blazed the length of the hall, beating back the chill
outside. Dried herbs sweetened their smoke. On the trestle
boards shone drinking vessels from the treasury, gold, silver,
glass; even the horns were banded with costly metals. At the
far end, workers had brought in a tub twice as wide as a man
is tall and half his height, which they filled with ale. But first
the women went pouring Southland wine from pitchers. The
carven gods and heroes on the pillars, the woven heroes and
beasts on the hangings, seemed to stir amidst the shadows, in
the wavering light.

Hunding stood up, his beaker aloft. "Drink we to Freyr,
son of Njord, the god whose feast King Hadding did found,"
he called.

"Skaal," rumbled through the sputtering of the fires.

Hunding looked across the hall. "Drink we now to King

Hadding, for whom I have kept my high seat open," he said.

The answer had an undertone of unease. Some of the folk shuddered.

But no ghost came in. And now the servers brought the food, heap after heap of beef, pork, mutton, deer, duck, goose, grouse, swan, salmon, leeks stewed with chicken, wheaten bread, butter, cheese, honey, more and more and more. The drink became mead, until heads buzzed with the summers that bred it. Talk and laughter went like surf, except when skalds stepped before the king to say forth the praises of him and his friend. He rewarded them freely.

By the time the tables were cleared away, night had fallen outside and everybody was awash. The guests shifted around the floor like the waters in a tide-race, still gripping cup or horn. They gossipped, bantered, boasted, recalled days long ago, wondered about the morrow, forgot what they had been saying, and drifted to something else. Yet if anger flared, someone would quickly step between. For they were in the house of their king, mourning him whom that king had held to be above all others; and they too had been in awe of him.

Hunding got up from his seat. "I will honor him," he said thickly. "I will myself serve those who're here to honor him."

His queen caught at his sleeve. "Stop," she begged. "You're being foolish."

"I am not," Hunding answered. "I am honoring him."

He lurched to the tub. Though men and women were dipping from it as they liked, he filled his golden beaker and went about slopping ale into other vessels. Most of it splashed on the floor or onto clothes. Nobody said anything, but they looked. After a while he felt it.

"Whatever you wish," he said. "Be your own servers if you want. But I, I will bring a drink over to my oath-brother there in the high seat."

He pushed through the crowd back to the tub. Sticks had

burned thin under a log in a fire-trench. They gave beneath it and it crunched downward. Sparks showered. Shadows flooded and ebbed.

Startled, his eyesight bewildered, the king stumbled. He fell forward, over the tub and into it. His brow struck the rim. In a splash like a wave that breaks on a reef, he went down under his ale.

Drunk, the guests were slow to understand what had happened and pull him out. Nor knew they what to do when he lay sprawled on the floor, breath and heartbeat still, unwinking eyes turned toward the high seat.

XXXIV

That year the weather around Yule was cold and calm. Folk swarmed to the offerings at Haven. The tents and booths of those who did not find housing ringed the holy shaw. By day the fires outside them sent smoke higher than the trees, by night the embers glowed redly up at the stars.

From farthest off, Bralund in Scania, came Eyjolf Lysirsson, which he had never done before at this season. He guessed what sorrow must be in his old friend and king, and wanted to stand by as best he was able.

The noise and stir became uproar on midwinter day. Low in the south, the sun shone heatlessly on the gathered beasts. Horses stamped and neighed, kine rolled their eyes and lowed, swine grunted and squealed and churned about in their pens. They knew something ill for them was toward, and the smell of their fear grew rank. But ropes snugged about their necks, strong hands took hold, and one by one they went bucking into the grove. Under its bare trees, before the halidom that stood at its heart, the altar stones waited. A hammer stunned, a knife slashed, blood spurted into bowls, the beast died and was dragged off, the next came up, while the crowding watchers shouted to the gods.

Thereupon they pressed into the building. It loomed long and lean, darkly timbered, three tiers of shingled roofs above rafter ends carved into dragon heads. With brushes newly made from willow switches, the offerers sprinkled its walls with blood, both outside and inside. The same hot red spattered the folk as they passed the door. A great fire burned within. Kettles hung above it, in which seethed the flesh of the slain. At the far end reared the figures of Odin with his spear, Thor with his hammer, Freyr with his upstanding yard. On the pillars were graven doings of the gods, how Fenris was bound, the Midgard worm drawn from the bottom of the sea, the riding of the golden boar. Deep ale casks stood near the fire, and a heap of drinking horns. There too was King Hadding. No women or hirelings, but housecarles of his, sweating in helmet and mail, filled those horns and handed them to him. He made the sign of blessing over each and passed it above the fire to a worshipper. The men took long to go around. They packed the floor. More casks had been set about for their use.

The king led them in draining the first draught to Odin, for victory and might, and the second to Thor, for freedom from evil beings. Thirdly they called on the Vanir for peace and good harvests. Thereafter they drank as they wished. Mostly they did so in remembrance of dear ones who were gone; but some of the younger raised the Bragi beaker and made loud vows to do this or that deed.

When the food was ready, the king blessed it too. The cooks ladled it out into bowls the worshipers had brought, soup with chunks of meat, fat, and leeks, for the otherworldly power which is in that herb. So did the Danes feast, guesting their gods.

Sunset was upon them when they left the halidom. In racketing gangs they sought their shelters and stoked their fires. Merriment would go on for two more days and nights before they wended home, and many a woman who had come along with her man, to partake in the rites that women held, would give birth nine months later.

Those who had housing had farther to go. No few followed the king as he rode to his hall. The moon was nearly full. A crisp layer of snow glittered with its light. Hoofbeats rang loud.

Eirik Björnsson was in front beside his lord. They spoke quietly together. "You seem wearied," said the jarl.

"I am," Hadding owned. "More weary than you know."

Eirik nodded. "I've marked it on you since we learned of King Hunding's death, if not earlier. You should not let that burden you, lord. It was a mishap."

Hadding shook his head. "It was more. He, my oathbrother, died untimely because of a lie that I spread."

"Still, I say, a mishap."

"No. I feel it in my marrow. Hel was angered by a grave-ale drunk for a living man. I fear ill luck unless a rightful weregild allays the affront; and the king's luck is the kingdom's."

Eirik drew his cloak about him against the chill. "You've ever been closer to such things than other men. What are you thinking of?"

Hadding lifted his head beneath the stars. "If naught else, I will honor my oath-brother as he honored me."

"With as great a feast—and a better outcome? Well, this is the time of year for it."

"No." Hadding laid a hand on the jarl's arm. "I have no heart for giving hospitality. Stand by me now, as you have often done before. Be the host in my stead. See to the well-being and good cheer of my guests. Tell what is true, that a sign has come to me and I have business with the gods that cannot wait."

"Yes, I can do that much," said Eirik unwillingly.

"You can do more. In the past, when I was abroad, you steered the kingdom for me, and steered it well. Should anything happen to me, you can again. Keep the peace that I built. Send a ship off in search of Frodi as soon as weather allows. He won't be hard to find. Bid him come straightway. See him hailed king. That is all."

Eirik frowned. "It does not seem small to me. Troublous days lie ahead. If I may speak frankly, lord, your daughter Ulfhild—"

Hadding sighed. "I have my thoughts about her, but I will not utter them. She is still my daughter, and Ragnhild's. Let her be, to wed whom she will. Whatever shall come of that lies with the Norns. And well do I know that the soul of Frodi is as wild as hers. But so mine once was. I have done what I could. All things end."

Eirik gazed at him a long while before murmuring, "Memory dies not, the memory of what a man did in his life."

They rode on to the hall without further talk. Though the bathhouse was too dark to use, servants had set forth tubs of hot water. Men stripped, washed off the clotted blood, donned clean clothes, and laid themselves to rest, in beds, on benches, around the floor.

Hadding rose at dawn. Stealing among the sleepers, he opened the shutbed given Eyjolf and shook the Scanian awake. "Come," he whispered. "We ride today, do you remember? No need to stir up a fuss."

"I'm with you, lord," said the man as softly, and swung his feet out onto the rushes.

"You always have been," answered Hadding.

They had spoken of this before the offering, by themselves. The king had said merely that he must leave right af-

terward for a few days and would like fellowship. Otherwise
he had told only two housecarles, men whom he knew could
hold their tongues.

They had horses and travel gear waiting. A few yawning
thralls saw the four ride off. Sunrise found them on the road
north along the strand.

Nobody else was upon it, nor did they spy many during
the day. To the left were snow-decked fields, murky groves,
scattered farmsteads, now and then a hamlet where boats lay
drawn ashore and dwellers mostly sat inside at their peat fires.
To the right the waters of the Sound lapped on stones and kelp
and shimmered below the hills of Scania. Gulls mewed, crows
cawed. The air was clear, cold, and still.

"You look rested, lord," said Eyjolf.

Hadding nodded. "I slept well. The weight that lay on me
is slipping off." His back was straight, his head high.

"I don't understand."

"You need not. I've something to see to, then you can return." Hadding clapped Eyjolf's shoulder. "Thank you for
coming along. Friends make faring gladsome."

Seeing the king in a good mood, Eyjolf gave him a rueful
grin and said, "Well, I was looking forward to the drinking and
swiving back there. But maybe we can make it up later."

"You will, if I know you," laughed Hadding.

He went on to speak of bygone times, and roused such
talk that the other man lost any forebodings and well-nigh
forgot that their errand was unknown to him. They had all
their years to call forth, strife, joy, threat, gain, grief, deeds,
fun, wonders, tumbling around the North from Denmark to
Gardariki, from haunted wilderness to wealthy town, and for
Hadding always the seafaring, throb of waves in hull and
thrum of wind in rigging, spindrift salt on the mouth, foam
and surge before the eyes. They hardly felt the short day
pass.

But when the sun went from them, they fell silent. It was as if they had emptied the horn of memory. A full moon rose out of Scania to throw a shivery bridge across the water and strew sparks over the snow. Elsewhere the Winterway frosted heaven; the Wain wheeled upward around the Lodestar; Freyja's Spindle gleamed amidst glittering throngs. Here at the northern end of Zealand were no dwellings, only heath hoar under the moon, thickets, and a few lonely trees standing black upon it. Off in the west gloomed an edge of wildwood.

The road had become a track, but there was not much farther to go. Where the trail gave out, a hut of wattle and daub stood by itself, behind it a bubbling spring. Hadding drew rein. "I keep this for when I wish to hunt hereabouts, or be by myself for a span," he said. "Wayfarers may use it, but they seldom come. It will do for the night. If you open the door, you'll have moonlight enough within. You'll find split wood and kindling, should you want to start a fire and warm your food."

"What, you'll not stay with us?" asked Eyjolf.

Hadding shook his gray head. The moon whitened it. "No. I told you I've business with the gods. If I'm not back by morning, seek me at the strand." He pointed northward, onward.

The two housecarles glanced at each other. Under cover of shadow, one drew with his finger the sign of the fylfot, the sun.

Eyjolf's look was on the king. "Is this your will?"

Hadding smiled. "You should know me well enough by now to know that it is. Goodnight, old friend." He reached forth to clasp Eyjolf's hand. "Fare ever well."

He spurred his horse and rode off over the heath. Their gaze followed him until he was lost to sight.

The land had been rising a little the last part of the way. Where it met the sea it dropped in a steep bluff down to a strip of cobbles. An oak tree stood on the height, gnarled and twisted by untold human lifetimes of wind. Its boughs reached like arms, its bare twigs like fingers, athwart the stars.

Here the Sound opened out into the Kattegat. Scania was no more than a darkness in the east. Otherwise the eye found only sea. It murmured to the land, moonlight shattered where small waves broke, but beyond went the long, easy breathing of the deeps, as mighty in their sleep as ever in their wrath, and the light ran over them like a fire as cold as the air.

Hadding dismounted. He tethered his horse to a bush. It whuffed and drooped its head. Hadding rumpled the rough mane. "You've done your work," he said. "Take your ease."

Untying the bundle behind the saddle, he spread it on the ground. The moonlight showed bread, cheese, smoked meat; other gear for the road; and a rope, which no one had seen him put in. He uncoiled an end of it, ran fingers over the noose there, and nodded. "Yes," he said, "I have my skill yet."

Hanging it over his shoulder, he walked to the brink of the bluff. For a while he watched the sea that was his. Stars came out of it eastward and sank into it westward, as do ships faring by.

Then, "Here I make my last offering," he said aloud, "for my honor, my blood, and my folk. Wherever I am bound, know, know well, you yonder, he who comes was a king."

He turned and strode to the oak tree. There he unslung his sword, drew it, dropped sheath and belt, and drove the blade upright into the earth. Moonlight sheened on iron.

He tossed off his cloak and bared his feet. Reaching, he caught hold of the lowest branch and began to climb.

Aloft and aloft he went. So had he climbed when he was a boy, laughterful, afar in wilderness and all unaware of any strangeness in his life. As he rose, he saw ever more widely across the waters he had sailed, toward lands where he had warred, won, lost, and gone back to win anew. Scania became a moon-misty ridge. Beyond it, northwesterly, lay Ragnhild's Norway. Ever had she yearned for its mountains. South and west reached Denmark, low in the arms of the sea. Overhead were the stars.

The tree was not big. Too long had the sea winds grieved it. The topmost limbs would not bear his weight. But he had risen far enough. With a boy's nimbleness, he walked out until his footing bent beneath him. With a sailor's deftness he hitched his rope to the branch above. The noose he laid around his neck. A while more he stood looking at the moonlit sea.

He sprang.

Eyjolf and the housecarles found him in the morning. A wind had awakened. Whitecaps chopped. The rope creaked as Hadding swung to and fro. On each of his shoulders perched a raven. They had not taken his eyes. As the men drew near, they spread black wings and flew off eastward.

XXXV

Leaves rustled, alive with sunlight. He stood beside an ash tree whose trunk was mightier than a mountain and whose crown reached higher than heaven. Those boughs spread as wide as all the worlds, and he knew that three roots ran down to three of them, the worlds of the gods, the giants, and the dead.

Wind tossed his hair. He glimpsed a lock. Its hue was golden. His clothes were the blue, green, and white of summer seas. When he walked forward over ground hidden by low-eddying mists, the lameness was gone from his step.

One stood awaiting him, tall, gray beard falling over bluegray cloak. Only the right eye shone below a shadowing hat. Its look struck as keenly as would the spear he held.

His voice rolled thunder-deep. "Greeting and welcome."

The newcomer halted before him. "So we meet again," he said slowly. "You told me we never would."

"Never on earth, while you were what you then were. But that is now ended."

The newcomer passed a hand across his brow. "I do not understand."

"No. You have made the longest trek of all and are still bewildered. But you shall soon remember that which you laid aside for a span. Come."

They set forth across the clouds. "It was needful," said the Wanderer. "Great was the wrong you suffered, and great was your wrath. When you foreswore our friendship, you were wholly within your rights. Yet the sundering would have led to another war among the gods, a war that would have brought them down in untimely wreck. How could we cleanse ourselves of what had happened and make whole again your honor?

"The word of the Norns cannot be gainsaid. That which is done is done forever. But seeking through time, with the knowledge I won on the far side of death, I found that deeds may be done over again in the morrow, and thus may a wrong be set right. They must be true deeds, however, done without foresight of their meaning, a life lived in and for itself."

"I begin to see," whispered he who had returned.

Also he saw with his eyes. Somehow he and the other had already walked down from above the sky. It reached half-clear, half-cloudy over the high hillside on which they now were. Rain had lately fallen. The wet grass flashed with its drops. Nonetheless sight swept far and far, across woodlands, meadows, homes of men, and the sea roaring along a broad strand. A rainbow glimmered.

"But this is earth!" he cried.

The Wanderer nodded. "You ken it again—better, I think, than ever aforetime."

They strode onward with the same unwearying swiftness. "I was Hadding," knew he who had returned.

"Thus were you born to the house of the Skjoldungs," said the Wanderer. "Thus did you live, a man of flesh, bone, and blood, hero, father of kings, but still a man. You shared the gladness and grief, wounds and weal, victory and vanquishment, love and loss that are the lot of humans, and at last you died as they do.

"Yet the soul in Hadding was yours. He had the freedom to choose that is every man's, but being you, he took what you would have taken. And I launched his life on Midgard into such waters that it would likely in some wise follow the course that you follow among the gods. I helped him steer clear of the worst that had befallen you, and helped him again when black wizardry would have overwhelmed him before he had won what was his. Otherwise he who was you wrought his own fulfillment, which was likewise yours. He won a name that will live as long as the world stands, and that honor is also yours."

"You sent him on strange ways."

"Yes, for I wanted him to know fully who and what the one was who befriended him in his need. He had seen too much of trollcraft, too early and too closely."

"Not all of them who wielded it were his foes."

"True. Such was the way he must go, like to the way that you and your kinfolk had gone. In the beginning, the untamed earth, ruthless, reckless, and shameless. Then war and wild farings, the way of the Aesir. Then the flowering of the soul that is yours, which shall grow beyond ours.

"For you alone among us will live without blame; and the spaewife who made known to me what shall be has foretold that at the downfall of the gods, you will go home to your

Vanir; and when the new world rises from the sea and Baldr comes back from the dead, you will be there to help build its peace."

They stopped, for they had reached the foot of the rainbow. Its trembling bridge soared to the walls of Asgard.

Before they betrod it, Odin laid a hand on his fellow's shoulder. "But first," he said, "here and now, will you renew the oaths we swore? At the end of his life, Hadding gave himself to me. Thereby you took what I offered you, and we are in brotherhood again."

"Yes," answered Njord, god of the sea, "from this day to the last, we are brothers."

Afterword

D ark and violent even by saga standards, the story of Hadding is also one of the most enigmatic that has come down to us from the old North. Looked at closely, it reveals itself as more than a series of adventures and exploits. They have a unity, a deeper meaning; but what? For a century and a half, mythologists and folklorists have wondered.

Aside from a few incidental mentions elsewhere, our only source for it is the *Gesta Danorum* of Saxo. That we know so little about this writer adds to the irony.

He was a Dane. He states that his father and grandfather fought for King Valdemar I, who reigned from 1157 to 1182. Thus he himself must have been born about 1150. His favorable references to the people of Zealand, compared to others both in the kingdom and abroad, indicate that he hailed from that island and probably spent most of his days there. He says that he undertook his work at the behest of the great Archbishop Absalon. The latter died before it was completed, and so it is dedicated to his successor Archbishop Andreas and to King Valdemar II. This was about 1208, which seems to be more or less the year of Saxo's death.

His clerical connections, the fact that he wrote in Latin, and his (somewhat limited) classical education have caused most scholars to take for granted that he was a monk. However, we have no direct evidence. His chauvinism, delight in scenes of derring-do, and occasional eroticism imply that he could have been a layman. The appellation "Grammaticus," meaning "master of words," only came to him in the fifteenth century, when interest in him revived.

As for his chronicle, he meant to write the history of Denmark from the days of King Svein Estridsson (d. 1076), but Absalon persuaded him also to seek out and set down traditions from earliest times. Although they had been Christian for some two hundred years, the Scandinavians remained fascinated by the deeds and beliefs of their ancestors. In this, the Icelanders became pre-eminent, and Saxo gives them due credit. A person or persons on that island recorded those poems we call the *Elder Edda*. A generation after Saxo, Snorri Sturluson wrote the *Younger Edda*, the *Heimskringla*, and very likely the saga of Egil Skallagrimsson. Others were similarly engaged.

We do not know how long or how widely Saxo delved, whom he questioned, what notes he took, how much he simply recalled of what he heard in childhood or at hearthsides, how much he patched together from scraps or his own imagination. It is clear that he was acquainted with ancient poems still on the tongues of skalds and common folk. He either made prose of them or translated them into his Latin. Sometimes we have Norse versions to compare. Mostly, though, we can only attempt to reconstruct the originals from the materials he has left us.

His narration is usually bald, his style usually florid and often preachy. He has misunderstood a great deal of what he was handling and garbled a great deal more. Nevertheless he saved this treasure hoard for us, damaged though it may be. It includes the oldest extant account of Hamlet. All honor to Saxo Grammaticus.

The story of Hadding comes near the end of the first book. There is no point in searching for a historical kernel of it. Saxo places Hadding three generations before Hrolf Kraki. Some truth undoubtedly lies behind that saga, which can be dated to the middle sixth century. But a fuller, though later Icelandic rendition does not square with the *Gesta Danorum*. For instance, Hadding's son Frodi cannot be identical with Hrolf's great-uncle of that name. Saxo was probably fitting together what pieces he had in a rather arbitrary fashion.

Besides, the tale of Hadding is not properly even a legend. It is a myth. Saxo may have had some intimation of this, but if so, it was dim. Into his chapter he inserts an awkward description of Odin as a mortal sorcerer, then completely fails to recognize Odin when the god appears to Hadding in person.

Just the same, here is a grand yarn, full of action, color, and glimpses of a world altogether strange to us. I have long wanted to share it with modern readers. Georges Dumézil's brilliant study *Du mythe au roman: La Saga de Hadingus et autres essais* shows that Hadding was actually the god Njord. This first suggested to me how the tale might be made into something more than another sword-and-sorcery swashbuckler. I owe considerable as well to the *Eddas*, the *Heimskringla*, and the work of archeologists and literary scholars.

On the whole, the earthly part of this retelling follows Saxo's text. Mainly I have tried to flesh it out, find causes and motivations for events he leaves obscure, and limn their back-

ground. That background is frankly anachronistic—not the
Germanic Iron Age, in which the story ostensibly takes place,
but the viking era. Societies, technologies, horizons, and doings belong, in an ahistoric fashion, to the ninth or tenth century, as they do in Saxo. However, though avoiding Latinisms
as much as possible, I have not sought to imitate the austere
style of the Icelanders. What was familiar to them is alien to
us and needs explaining. I hope I have evoked a little of it.

Some things may strike you as unfortunate. For example,
various names are easily confused, notably Hadding, Hunding, and Haakon. I did not presume to change them, or any
other important part of my source, but I made an effort to
write for clarity. Nor did I pussyfoot very much about the bru-
tality, the ethnic prejudices—especially against Finns—or the
status of women—although that was rather higher than it got
to be later. These were of the milieu. Most persisted through
subsequent centuries. Our own has seen massive resurgences
of them. As for people's feelings about wolves, animals that I
too like and admire, that was also the way it was; and there is
some reason to think that in fact they were more dangerous
to humans before the appearance of firearms than they have
been since.

Now and then I must resort to sheer guesswork, most con-
spicuously in the case of the Niderings. Saxo tells us nothing
about them except that they were somewhere in Norway. The
ancient name of Trondheim, Nidaros, gave me the idea that
they might have lived in that area. Perhaps they were absorbed
afterward by the historical Thronds, or perhaps they merely
sprang from a linguistic confusion in Saxo's mind. Apart from
this fantasy requiring some real-world geography, it doesn't
matter.

With the cosmic framework I have taken a still freer hand.
After all, we have lost much. Lines here and there hint fleet-

ingly at what must once have loomed high, and more heroes than Hadding seem to be gods in disguise. Snorri too euhemerizes myths, leaving us to guess what they formerly said—not that the mythology of preliterate peoples was ever very coherent or consistent. We know almost nothing about the war between the Aesir and the Vanir, except that it happened. I found that with a bit of rearrangement and a few minor additions I could unify a number of fragments. To some extent I have drawn on Viktor Rydberg's nineteenth-century conjecture about the captivity of Njord, Freyr, and Freyja under Hymir. It is written that Odin and Loki once swore blood brotherhood, which helps explain how Loki got away with what he did for as long as he did; but we do not know why. That incident is my own invention. So, of course, is the whole concept of Hadding not as a redaction but as an actual avatar of Njord.

Here names are generally in their current English forms. Among other things, this means that *d* frequently represents *edh*, i.e., *th* as in "that," especially when following a vowel or at the end of a word. As for other pronunciations, *j* is sounded like *y* in "yet," *ag* is approximately *ow* as in "how," and *ei* as in "rein." The rest should be fairly obvious.

Terms get their nearest English equivalents, e.g., "chieftain" rather than *hersir*, "housecarles" rather than *hird*, "sheriff" rather than *lendrmadr*, etc. In some cases this was not practical. Thus, *jarl*, though cognate, does not really correspond to "earl."

Nor does *Svithjod* to "Sweden." The southern end of what is now that country, Scania, was then Danish. North of it seem to have been the people known in *Beowulf* and elsewhere as Geats; this is not certain, but I have assumed it. North of them in turn lay Svithjod, the realm of the Swedes proper. Borders were rather vague and changeable, and there were complications, including still other tribes, which I have ignored. Similarly for such areas as *Wendland* (roughly, maritime Prussia, Poland, Lithuania, and Latvia) and *Gardariki* (roughly, northwestern Russia).

But these details are of no importance to any but enthusiasts, who already know about them. All that this book does is tell a story. May you enjoy it.